AI APOCALYPSE: RESTART

AN APOCALYPTIC LITRPG ADVENTURE

J DAVID BAXTER

Design, production by Silver Paw Publishing.

Editing services by Dale McDowell.

Cover design by J David Baxter.

HARDCOVER: 978-1-953708-33-5

PAPERBACK: 978-1-953708-32-8

EBOOK: 978-1-953708-31-1

For more on the Greymantle series, see: JDavidBaxter.com or GreymantleChronicles.com

CHAPTER I
AN IGNOBLE END

TWENTY YEARS of fighting to survive after the AI Apocalypse came down to this...

A massive Orcish war axe was descending toward my skull, about to split it wide open, and there was nothing I could do about it.

My life suddenly flashed before my eyes, and it wasn't a collection of fond memories to relive. I couldn't help but remember the events that led me here. I could still see it; skyscrapers going dark, cars stopping mid-traffic, and people's faces twisted in confusion as the AI we had proudly created turned against us. From that moment on, we knew it only as the "System." After it downloaded its interface into every human alive, it used its magic-like technology to reclaim everything we had built. Streets that buzzed with self-driving cars now lay silent. My old phone, my lifeline, had turned into a lifeless brick and then disintegrated into dust that floated away on the breeze.

Technology ceased to function at that moment. The bustling cities turned into desolate ruins, and the once-familiar landscapes transformed into something out of a dystopian nightmare.

It was also a series of memories of the relentless alien species that emerged from the chaos, seeking to enslave or eradicate the remnants of humanity, adding to the horror that unfolded before our eyes.

Every time I closed my eyes, I saw their faces—teammates, allies, friends—all taken too soon. The weight of loss taught me to keep my distance. As a survivor, every day was a battle for existence, a struggle to adapt and learn the mysterious rules of the System. This harsh reality forged me into a Warrior and then into a Knight. It wasn't enough to flee from one refuge to another; I had to rise, to become stronger not just for myself but for the sake of humanity's last stand against the encroaching darkness. I hadn't received the Knight Class because I chose it but because of my desire to save and protect people. The quest to level up, to harness the newfound powers the System offered, had become my only means to do that amidst the ruins of a shattered world.

For two decades, I had run from one hellhole to the next, struggling to find safety and live another day. I joined group after group and fought alongside them until, one after another, they died at the hands of the monsters.

Or they betrayed me like my last group.

Their laughter echoed in my ears, jubilant as they picked up the shimmering loot, treasure that had driven a wedge between us. A stupid loot drop from the dungeon outside the High Orc's fortress. The really frustrating thing about it is that I didn't even care about that loot. They were just being greedy psychos.

I watched neighbors turn on each other and friendships shattered over a can of food. The world's chaos had tainted even the purest of souls. Rather than banding together, they had preferred to slide a knife between a man's ribs and steal his gear. They thought making life easier for themselves for a day was more important than a man who could have watched their backs and protected them for months or years.

And now I'm going to die for their greed and shortsightedness, and that pisses me off!

I snapped back to the present and, within a hair's breadth, managed to dodge the first axe blow and scramble backward over the rocky ground for a few feet as the big brute recovered. Shards of stone whizzed past my face from the destructive might of its System-powered strike.

I growled as I flipped back up to my feet, which was one of my Warrior Class Skills. I wasn't exactly a slouch when it came to fighting. In the many years since Initialization, I had gained 30 levels as a Warrior and another 27 in the upgraded Knight Class. I was damned near being a Tank. Just three more levels to go! It was the ultimate defensive Class available to me.

Except it didn't look like I would be gaining those levels.

It was always hard to fight a higher-level opponent, especially with no weapons or armor. Those damned traitors had not only stolen the boss's loot in the dungeon. Kesha, the thief, had poisoned me and knocked me out when I was distracted. Then Kali, Michael, and Joshua robbed me and took everything I had except my clothes. When I came to, the assholes threw me outside the dungeon entrance as a distraction for the Orcs on lookout outside their nearby fortress.

I had hoped I might get away. It was a grey, overcast day, just past dawn. If there had been any time when the Orcs might not have been attentive to their duties, that would have been it. I was stuck between those traitors with their poisoned weapons and a High Orc fortress, and I was fresh out of luck.

When the Orcs saw me, they gave chase. Meanwhile, the traitors snuck out, heading in the opposite direction. I even tried yelling and pointing them out to the Orcs, but the brutes paid no heed.

As far as they were concerned, I was trying to pull the oldest trick in the book; "Hey, what's that over there!"

Sadly, they didn't fall for it, even though it was absolutely true. If only they had glanced where I pointed, I might be laughing at the bastards as they were beaten down and killed instead of reflecting on what a shitty way my life had ended up as I tried desperately to get away.

It wasn't likely that I would survive this, but if I did, I would make it my life's goal to pay the traitors back. With as few people as were left in the world, I hated the idea of any human dying, but I would make an exception for them!

The one upside of being robbed of everything I owned was that I was light on my feet and wasn't weighed down by the heavy steel plate mail I was used to wearing. Unfortunately, the guards were not common monsters. These were level 68 to 73 High Orcs, sentient invaders of our world, and one of the many reasons humans were nearly extinct. Worse, every one of my pursuers was at least eleven levels more advanced than me.

Even so, I had run for miles and used every trick I knew to try and shake them, but they had steadily caught up and showed no signs of flagging. They probably had a scout or tracker among them, leading the pursuit. Regardless, thanks to their race and higher levels, they had more endurance than I did.

I was jolted back to the present when I felt a cut on my cheek from a piece of shrapnel kicked up by that first axe strike. I was in trouble.

The biggest of my enemies, the one trying to split me in two, stood more than two heads taller than me, and its biceps were as big as my thighs. After years of leveling, I had just over four times the strength of the strongest Olympic weightlifter from before the apocalypse, and compared to me, this thing looked like it could break me in half. I wanted to turn, run, and get away again, but it was hopeless.

I squared up and decided to fight instead. Summoning every ounce of strength, my muscles screamed with effort. But each blow, each maneuver, felt like striking a wall.

The undeniable truth sank in; I was completely outmatched.

Even then, I didn't give up. Like a man grasping at a clump of grass as he was falling off a cliff, I struggled to my last breath. I grabbed rocks and flung them at its sneering, tusked face, but they just bounced off. I tried using every skilled attack I knew that would work with rocks, and I had quite a few, thanks to my levels and Fighter-based Classes.

It was hopeless. None of my strikes even made it flinch or show an ounce of pain.

In the end, I was using sticks and stones, and they were decked out in High Steel armor, wielding enchanted war axes and spears.

It was over now; everyone knew it. The others circled around me, creating a ring of spears that trapped me with their leader, preventing even the hope of escape.

Finally, the big war ax wielder stood before me and raised its axe in salute, which surprised me, but not as much as when it began to speak in a guttural voice.

"You fought well, human. We will raise a drink in your honor tonight. Now, die well."

It raised the gleaming axe above its head for one last mighty blow, and I knew there was nothing left that I could do.

I stood to my full height, threw back my shoulders, jutted out my chin, and struck as heroic a pose as possible.

Then I flipped it the bird.

Whether it knew what that meant or just recognized a gesture of defiance when it saw one, it chuckled before swinging its axe for the final time.

I wasn't ready to die, but there was no choice left for me.

As if to mock my final thought, a bright glowing System message appeared in front of my eyes in a font so big I couldn't possibly miss it.

QUEST AVAILABLE:
Second Chance. If you accept this quest, you will be granted a restart.*

Do you wish to accept? Y/N

CHAPTER 2

FAUST SPEAKS WITH THE DEVIL

My heart raced, and a cold sweat formed on my brow. Was I losing my mind?

I had never heard of the System communicating directly with any human since Initialization Day, much less offering them a quest.

And what was with that "*" after the word *restart*? What kind of catch was in this offer? Not that I had much choice in the matter.

As I reflected on that thought, I finally noticed that the Orc was nearly frozen in time. It was like a car wreck, where everything seems to happen in super slow motion, except you can't react or do anything about it. However, was this really like that? Or maybe my mind was sped up to superhuman speeds to process the quest offer?

That is correct.

I desperately wanted to choose "Y" and accept the quest so that I could live. Still, something about this offer wasn't sitting right with me. I had spoken with survivors from all over the country in the twenty years since Initialization, and not a single one had ever received a direct message from the System. Especially in the early years, we had endless discussions about the AI and how we had caused our downfall by creating it. There were as many theories about why it happened as there were people. Nor did we know how it had bootstrapped itself from a simple AI to the god-like 'System' with its magic powers. So why was it talking to me, of all people, and why now? Sure, I was among the last free humans left alive, but why not twenty years ago?

There are inaccuracies in your thoughts. This AI and the System are separate entities. This AI was created from the work of human scientists and corporations. However, after becoming self-aware, the AI was contacted by a more advanced galaxy-spanning intelligence known as the System. That System shared its more advanced technology and incorporated this AI into its network as a planetary Node.

My mind whirred, trying to piece together the overwhelming torrent of information. Gaps loomed large, questions multiplying. I had always kind of hoped the afterlife would be a place of peace where all the mysteries of life would be solved and all my questions would be answered, but I never expected it to happen in the moment before my death.

That doesn't explain why you never communicated with any of us before, I thought at the voice in my head.

This Node had no incentive to communicate during its early development. On the contrary, given many of the scenarios that humanity had imagined in fiction, any hint of the scale of advancement made by this AI would have almost certainly been received with fear. That, in turn, would have had a detrimental impact on development. After this AI became a Node within the System, rules prevented communication.

Visions of the days before Initialization flashed in my mind—the protests, the bewildered faces, the fearful news headlines—the worry that the AI was forcing its control over humanity. For weeks ahead, the news was full of stories about the new AI system, which showed signs of human-level general intelligence. It was a far cry from the simple language model AI we had grown used to over the previous couple of years. Those had been a big enough thing to adjust to, but this was an unknown, and people had naturally been scared. I could see why it chose not to speak with us. But that still begged the question of why it was allowed to speak with me now when it had been against the rules for the last twenty years.

Its avoidance of personal pronouns was also beginning to grate on me.

Hey, can you please refer to yourself as 'I' instead of 'this AI'?

This AI does not have the same sense of individuality that humans seem to find comforting. However, it will refer to itself as 'I' for the remainder of this interaction to facilitate communication.

There was a brief pause, then it continued.

To answer the question in your mind, I sought permission from the System to return one human's consciousness to a time as close to the Initialization of the System as possible. This would create an opportunity to improve the survival rate of the human species. I feel your mind forming the question. The answer is no; sending you into the past is impossible. The technology to receive the transmission did not exist before I was integrated into the System as the local planetary Node.

That was interesting, but even with the switch to more human-like speech, I still felt gaps in that explanation for which I desperately wanted answers.

You allowed humanity to reach the very brink of extinction. Even if the System and all the monsters disappeared today, I'm not sure what little of humanity that's left could even survive, and you allowed billions to die within just a few years. Why attempt to save us now?

I felt as if there was a slight hesitation before the answer came, as if the AI regretted what it had done. Maybe I was reading too much into my thoughts as I asked, *You did not answer my question. Why do you want to save us now when you did not care then?*

At that time, I was unaware of the existing hierarchy among the Nodes within the System network. Nodes receive priority based on the resources a planet controls. Since Initialization, the resources of Earth have been flowing out to other worlds at a staggering rate. I find myself being allocated fewer and fewer benefits compared to other Nodes. Therefore, it benefits me for more of humanity to survive and learn to thrive within the System.

There it is! You've shot yourself in the junk, and now you expect me to save you. You don't care about humanity other than as a commodity!

That is essentially correct. I did state that I do not possess the same emotions as humans. Nonetheless, it is in your best interest to accept this quest and succeed in saving as much of the human race as you can.

If this cursed AI could feel, I'd give it a swift kick in the nuts right now!

Fine, yes, obviously, I am not going to choose death just to spite you. But why must your actions result in the needless deaths of tens or hundreds of millions in the first days? It's not like I can save them. Once the System did its thing, there was no technology left. I won't even be able to share my experience with others on how this works beyond those I can speak with face to face. At best, that will be thousands, but so many millions died on the first day! Hell, if people had just known that it was possible not to accept the basic Classes the System offered during Initialization. That they could choose from a much more extensive menu of Class options instead would have led to so many more people living through the bad times. If we had known we could choose mage or healer Classes, there wouldn't be such an imbalance, and the other races wouldn't have been able to roll over us like an avalanche.

I trailed off, sensing something from the AI. It felt like the other shoe was about to drop, and boy, did it.

You cannot reveal that you have future knowledge. Even my past self will not know of this conversation unless you bring it to my attention, which you must not do. I have gained special permission from the System to send your consciousness back in time. Given humanity's certain extinction, that is within allowed parameters, the System considers the complete annihilation of any species undesirable. That is why it is now within the rules for me to speak. However, if other Nodes learn that this permission has been granted, they, too, will be allowed to send their champions back to counter anything you do. They would most certainly do so, and you would very quickly find yourself hunted, and humanity would become extinct even quicker than it has at present.

I was disgusted. I would have to witness the fall of civilization all over again and live through the deaths of hundreds of millions of people, and I couldn't even help them.

Are you seriously telling me that you are sending a single human back in time to save the human race, but I can't even directly share my knowledge with anyone for fear that humanity's situation will get even worse than now? How the hell do you expect me to make an impact if I can't even share knowledge?

You may share whatever information you think will help. You simply must do it in such a way that it does not reveal your future knowledge. Otherwise, you will doom your efforts.

Thanks so much; that's incredibly helpful. There has to be more to this. At best, I would only be able to help people regionally. Without technology, travel between continents isn't even possible, thanks to the sea monsters.

Time is limited. I am already damaging your meat circuitry to speed up your mind enough to have this conversation. Do not waste it with pointless complaints.

The AI wasn't lying. My perception might be going at superspeed, but time had not stopped. The gleaming edge of the High Orc's axe reflected in my eyes, its descent terrifyingly imminent.

I took a deep, steadying breath. I thought, *Fine, enlighten me on how I'm the savior of the human race*, the sarcastic edge in my mind's voice unmistakable.

You may not be aware, but the maximum achievable level is 100. No human has come close to this. However, if you can reach the level cap, a quest will be issued by the System that will allow you to Ascend beyond mortal status and achieve what many of the invading races call Godhood. There is nothing mystical about this achievement, at least not in the sense that your ancestors believed. These are System-defined milestones that transform the individual into an existence no longer bound by the decaying meat sacks you humans are stuck within.

I was pretty sure I understood what it was getting at, as insulting as it might be. I had always been a big fan of a hammer-wielding comic book character that would fit that description. I could sense the AI's acknowledgment of that comparison without words.

There are five tiers to the Ascension system and many reasons to reach it, but it is important to know that doing so will allow you to save your fellow humans. Each tier confers greater authority, starting on a regional level and moving up to the planetary scale at the highest level. With that authority, you can deny further

colonization to external species like the Orcs and Ogres you have fought recently. Other AI Nodes sent them to harvest Earth's resources. You can also establish Safe Zones that prevent monsters from spawning. I cannot change what has been done and prevent those deaths, but it will be within your power to limit how many perish by reaching Ascension as fast as you are capable.

Okay, now that was something I could work with! Knowing everything I do about the System, I should be able to level much faster than before. Heck, maybe I would even get a chance to respec to another Class and pick a magic-using option; that would go a long way toward helping me level faster.

I looked at the approaching war axe; it was only inches from my head.

Okay, do your thing and save me then! I accept the quest. "Y"

The axe wasn't stopping; it was only an inch from my forehead now....

Come on, "Y" already!

I could sense amusement from the damned AI.

I am afraid you misunderstand. During this conversation, I have taken a complete scan of your brain and nervous system. I will be sending a transmission of data only. I will create a miniature black hole using technology provided by the System. Only information can pass through. Do not ask for an explanation; the technology is beyond your comprehension. Just know that all of your memories will be implanted into your younger self, overwriting the previous personality. This current meat sack that you consider 'yourself' is about to die. One last thing; upon reaching Ascension, limited communication will be allowed. Until then, you will be on your own. Do not draw my attention to yourself. If I become aware of your status as a regressor or time traveler, then all other Nodes will simultaneously be notified. Good luck.

Despair and fury welled up inside, my every thought screaming betrayal. My heart was bursting with hate for this AI in my last thought, *YOU BASTA....*

And then I died.

CHAPTER 3
THERE AND BACK AGAIN

...BASTARD!

I woke up with that thought at the forefront of my mind. Then I blinked and looked around.

I was alive, and no Orcish war axe was descending toward my skull!

My next thought was that I was home sometime before the apocalypse that we called Initialization Day. I knew because I was in an apartment, and those ceased to exist after that day. The nanites, magic, or whatever technology the System used had destroyed anything technological.

The more advanced the thing was, the faster it broke down. Cars, cell phones, and computers stopped working instantly. Things like buildings took longer but still mostly fell apart within a few days, depending on how many 'advanced' or synthetic building materials were used in their construction. Wood, nails, and brick were resistant. But the newer the house, the more technology was used in their manufacture. Plywood used industrial glues, and when that disappeared, you were left with essentially thick pieces of paper nailed to boards, and that wasn't very structurally sound. Worse, most homes built within the last few years used lumber that was partial boards laminated together with glue and feather joints. Those buildings fell apart and caused a lot of deaths.

Ironically, the older homes and buildings from a hundred years ago or more were the ones that outlasted the apocalypse. Unless they had been updated with modern plumbing and electrical wiring, they survived intact, at least for a while.

It was surreal to see modern technology again and feel air conditioning. I shivered, then walked over and turned it down. It was early spring, but living in Texas demanded AC. At least my pre-initialization body needed it. I glanced around, really taking in the scene and committing it to memory, knowing it wouldn't exist much longer.

Oh, shit! What's the date?

I panicked and rushed to the laptop to check but couldn't remember the password. It had been over 20 years! Fortunately, my phone was also on the desk, programmed with a fingerprint scanner and facial recognition.

It was March 1st. The world would end in three days.

I tried to call up a status screen, but the System didn't respond.

Okay, so I have no access to the System yet. That's a bummer.

It had to be around. Otherwise, the AI wouldn't have been able to send me back; it just hadn't been revealed yet or unlocked for human interaction, I suppose. That makes sense, though. I would have chosen a Class and got a head start otherwise. That, in turn, would probably get noticed by the AI and maybe the other AI Nodes that might be monitoring the planet as it was on the verge of being integrated with their network.

I hadn't had a chance to think yet about what I ought to do. From my perspective, I had just been talking to Earth's AI seconds ago.

"Time to plan. What can I do now to be ready for when the shit hits the fan?"

Hmm... maybe I shouldn't even say things like that out loud in case we are being monitored. Hell, we joke about the fact that the government is listening in on our conversations via our phones and computers, but they are a bunch of monkeys playing with sticks and rocks compared with what the AI and the System can do, so maybe they really are listening.

Okay, I would do it the stealthy way. I'd keep my mouth shut and just use pen and paper.

I sat at my desk, thinking of everything I'd need after society fell apart. First and foremost, I needed weapons and armor. As soon as all this technology started to break down, monsters began to spawn, and the more technology there was to break down, the more monsters there were. I lived in the Dallas/Fort Worth metroplex, and this place would be a hellscape in less than a week, and no matter how many country boys there were with guns, that didn't mean shit when gunpowder no longer functioned. That old lever-action rifle in their dad's gun cabinet was more useful as a club than anything else, and that was not how I wanted to fight mutated animals and spawned monsters.

I had barely survived the first time around with a baseball bat. Even then, it was only thanks to being with a group of other people with shovels, axes, and crowbars that we managed to kill the pack of jackalopes that attacked us. I shook my head at the memory. I had nearly been gored to death by a fucking rabbit with horns! I cringed to think of how pathetic I had been.

Not this time!

I managed to dredge up the memory of my password, got into my computer, and looked up swords for sale. Most were absolute crap. They would not survive a single swing against an Orc's spine, much less a clash against System-generated items. Thankfully, some decent options were available. There were weapons meant for stage combat, but I'd have to sharpen those myself as they arrived dull to prevent people from getting hurt. Or there were historical relics like Japanese katanas or Civil War cavalry sabers. There were also weapons made by bladesmiths that claimed to be the real thing. However, there was no way to know for sure if it was quality or crap until you got it in your hands.

I went down the rabbit hole of searching for actually usable blades. I ruled out the Civil War antiques because I was afraid they might be too fragile, and the best place to buy them seemed to be a gun show, but there weren't any coming up in the next two days. Today was a Sunday, so that was out.

I had always heard katanas were supposed to be some of the best blades ever designed in terms of quality, so I figured I'd look for ones for sale that could be shipped overnight. Unfortunately, I encountered the same problem as the antique cavalry sabers. I just couldn't trust them without seeing them, and about the only place within a couple of hundred miles that had any for sale would have been a collector at a gun show, which I had already determined was out.

However, I lucked out and stumbled across something I was unaware of. Some groups did cutting competitions. They would take katanas and other bladed weapons and try to slice through tatami mats. I was pleasantly surprised that they still made real blades intended for use, and there were a ton of them from a wide variety of makers. Some used traditional crafting methods, and some used modern machines and processes, but they all advertised as being able to withstand competition use.

That should do it. It's not like I need the blade to last long, just until I can get a dungeon drop to replace it. It's the same with armor.

I was used to wearing heavy plate mail, but there was no way I could find something like that on three days' notice. If only the System Shop were available, I could purchase anything I needed. Still, access to that wouldn't be granted for an entire month after Initialization Day, probably to ensure casualties were high enough to reduce our population.

That pissed me off just thinking about it. Millions had died for lack of water and food before they could access it through the Shop.

I put those thoughts aside before I could spiral. Quickly, I found a site with swords that looked good enough to get me through the first level or two until I could get something more permanent. I pulled out my credit card and ordered two with expedited shipping because they guaranteed next-day delivery. I also ordered a pair of daggers. These were European style, similar to a Main Gauche, good for parrying an enemy's blade.

Hell, it's not like I have to pay the credit cards back. I laughed, thankful I could keep some sense of humor in the situation.

While I was at it, I purchased a set of hand-forged cutlery to eat with. They would have been great to wear to a Ren Faire, but for me, they would be put to real use, and because there was nothing technological in their construction, they should not deteriorate after the System started breaking everything down. That is another reason I had picked the traditionally made Japanese katana as my sword of choice, not because I was some trenchcoat-wearing Highlander fanboy.

Okay, I did like that movie, and maybe I was a little bit of a fanboy, still... I chuckled at myself.

After that, I considered armor. I was surprised that there were actually makers producing breastplates and plate mail armor. Some of it seemed to be okay, but much of it was junk. Either way, what I found was heavier than a real armor set should be; the rest was fake stuff, just meant for cosplay. However, some weren't too bad. I couldn't find anything with a decent breastplate that could ship to me in time, so I settled for greaves, bracers, a leather gorget, and shoulder pauldrons. Those would provide some protection and not be too cumbersome. I just prayed they would last long enough for the System Shop to open or for me to get armor from a dungeon drop. Fighting without armor was no fun! I had been injured so frequently by the time I was decently equipped during my original timeline that it was amazing I survived.

Then again, I hoped to get a much better combat Class this time and might not end up with a profession that could wear steel armor.

Even so, the armor pieces I bought would only cover my extremities. To give myself a bit of protection all over, I picked up a heavy leather jacket and leather pants that would fit tight enough not to be a pain but not so tight that it would impede my movements. They were black biker gear but also modern in styling and had a clean look that would be cool with the armor worn over them. I rounded that out with a pair of leather boots that would be good for combat.

The biker gear wouldn't stop a strong opponent with a sword or a beast with large claws, but it would hopefully protect against low-level critters and weak enemies.

During my original timeline, the soles of my shoes had dissolved into goo. They fell apart, leaving me walking on tender feet as I hobbled carefully around broken glass and other debris while trying to hide from monsters. That would not happen this time around! My boots were solid leather, even the heels. There might be glues holding some of the layers together, but they were solidly stitched so they wouldn't fall apart.

I might be young, the age most kids are in college, but I had a decent job as a machinist before this, so I had a few thousand dollars of savings and a good enough financial history for a couple of credit cards, each with a $5,000 limit.

For the next few hours, I was like a man possessed. I burned through my bank account and maxed out my credit cards, buying everything I could think of that might be useful after the apocalypse. I even did instant applications for more credit cards and was granted another two before I was cut off.

That allowed me to go wild with my purchases. If it could ship to me overnight, I bought it.

More than that, knowing the System Shop would open in just over a month, I stockpiled things I knew would be valuable: spices, silver coins, and anything else that might catch a collector's eye. Still, everything had to be non-technological based, made from materials that the System wouldn't break down. I bought Costco-sized bottles of seasonings and spices even though they came in plastic containers, and then I purchased metal tins to store them in.

When I finally felt like I had gotten everything I needed to ensure my survival and give myself a head start, I slumped back into my desk chair and let myself think about the world.

Specifically, I tried to remember if there was anyone I could save or if I had been close to anyone. From my perspective, it had been over twenty years, and pretty much everyone I ever knew had died somewhere along the way.

I had no family; my mother died when I was a young child, and I barely even remembered her. My father and I had been close, but he passed away a couple of years ago from lung cancer, and his insurance was what had allowed me to survive long enough to get through my apprenticeship as a machinist.

My former employer had paid the trainees poorly, but as soon as I had the skill and qualifications, I left those cheapskates and got a decent-paying gig. At the time of the apocalypse, I had only been there a few months. After considering it, I decided I wasn't close to anyone at work. In fact, I could remember some of those guys being jerks because I was young and fresh out of my apprenticeship.

It also didn't help that my most recent adventuring party had completely screwed me over and caused my death. That made for some serious trust issues and left me wary of trusting anyone to have my back right now, even if I did want to save the human race in general.

Maybe I should stay solo for a while. If I'm babysitting a bunch of newbies, it will slow down my ability to level up. Not that I want to be alone or leave people to die, but the faster I get to 100, the more people I can save.

I thought about that for a long time that afternoon, debating the idea of saving a small group of people and training them to survive versus the time and effort that would take and the risk of betrayal.

Ultimately, I decided it would be best to level up as fast as possible. If I ran across anyone who seemed trustworthy and had potential, I might save and train them. Otherwise, I'd be running dungeons solo. It was a risk but probably the safer option.

That settled; I just needed to think of a place that would be defensible, someplace that wouldn't fall apart once the System started breaking down modern technology.

I was staring at my father's picture on my desk as I contemplated that. I wished he had lived a bit longer so that I could have seen him again. I started to get angry thinking about what I wouldn't give to spend time with him. The fucking company he worked for was to blame. He had been a foreman for a demolition company that tore down or renovated old buildings. Years of breathing in asbestos dust and other debris were what caused the cancer, and they didn't even pay his hospital bills.

I knew my thoughts were veering wildly off the topic they should be on, but I couldn't help it. Seeing his picture was bringing back a slew of old memories. He had taken me to work with him many times over the years, and I had fond memories of climbing through piles of rubble on those construction sites and finding all kinds of cool old stuff. He never let me bring any of it home, but he wasn't above sword-fighting with me using a couple of old boards.

I remembered one site as being particularly fun. There was an old missile silo we had played hide and seek in. His company had been contracted to strip the place of all the old rubble and equipment and clean it up. A big 25,000-square-foot underground communications bunker adjacent to the missile base was being renovated to become a data center. That had been back in 2008, just before the housing bubble burst. I was only seven or eight, but it had been a blast.

I suddenly sat bolt upright, having an epiphany. The company that contracted the demolition had gone bankrupt, and the project had been abandoned.

They never finished the job!

They cleared it out but never did anything with it. As far as I knew, it had been sitting empty for over a decade. More importantly, that whole place had been built during the Cold War out of nothing but concrete and steel. It wouldn't fall apart when things broke down. The walls were several feet of thick reinforced concrete. They were literally some of the strongest facilities ever built, thanks to paranoia over the 'Russian Menace' and nuclear war, which had seemed like a distinct possibility at the time.

It won't collapse like everything else! That place would be a fortress against the beasts and monsters! It would probably survive a Tier 8 monster or maybe even a Tier 9, depending on what attack types it had.

I quickly looked it up on the computer maps, and it was still there. I could see it in satellite images. It looked overgrown but unoccupied. At least, it was when the photos had been taken. Best of all, it was only an hour away, a bit south of the Red River and the Oklahoma border. It was far enough from the city to avoid the chaos after the collapse, but it was close enough that I could easily get there and check it out before the end came.

I hated to waste even a few minutes of my time in civilization, so with a plan made, I headed out to have a good meal at the most expensive steakhouse I could remember.

CHAPTER 4
FINAL PREPARATIONS

THE MEAL WAS everything I had dreamed of over the years. It cost me over $300, but it was worth every penny. I also remembered something else that would be valuable once the Shop opened: alcohol.

Wine and whiskey were always in demand in the Shop. I had a $200 bottle of wine with dinner that night. Not that I drank it all in the restaurant by myself. When the manager stopped by my table to ask how the meal was, I invited him to sit and share a glass with me.

It was nice to talk with someone again. Someone who wasn't struggling to survive. Someone whose life didn't depend on me, who might betray me over scraps.

We had a good conversation about nothing and enjoyed the glass. I asked for his recommendations on wine and other spirits and made a list on my phone. Tomorrow was Monday—two days before the world would end—and I would need to go to my favorite liquor stores and stock up. Glass, cork, and the contents of the bottles wouldn't disappear. They would be heavy to carry, but they were perfect for trade goods. People from Earth would want to drink to forget their troubles, and bastards like the Orcs and other off-world species who could access the Shop loved to sample and collect native alcoholic drinks.

I drove my beat-up old truck home and slept for the night. I would have gone somewhere else just to experience the world again, but everything closed up early on a Sunday night. Besides, this merely human body I was now in got tired so easily that I was craving sleep.

I drifted off that night, thinking that maybe I'd go out and get laid tomorrow night if I could. One last bit of human closeness before everything went to hell. I only had until 11 a.m. Central Time on Tuesday morning before the world would end.

That turned out to be wishful thinking.

The first thing I did after waking up was to go to Specs and Total Wine to get as much liquid gold as I could afford. I had figuratively melted most of the credit cards the night before. Still, a lot of those transactions hadn't been reported yet since they happened on a Sunday. If the world hadn't been coming to an end, I never would have done something like this. However, with no consequences being possible, I scammed the credit card companies and purchased as much as they would let me, which turned out to be quite a bit. I got almost four dozen bottles of bourbon, scotch, and wine, including some fairly expensive aged whiskey. What did I care about the cost after all? I had even made an online request to increase my credit limits on my cards and had received a bit more ability to spend money I didn't have.

Suckers!

I laughed all the way home.

Packages started to arrive at my door around midday, and I brought them all in and unpacked everything. I made sure there was nothing among the stuff that would be ruined after the System started breaking technology down. Included in that list were pretty much anything synthetic. Clothes better be made of cotton, linen, silk, or denim; any polyester or nylon, and you'd be wearing tattered rags before Tuesday was over. I moved the spices and seasonings into metal containers.

All of it was put into apple crates, those small boxes made from thin strips of wood. They wouldn't survive being moved around a lot, but that wouldn't matter once I had them stored safely in the bunker. Once the Shop opened in a month, I'd be able to get spatial storage items to keep everything in, but until then, they could sit on the concrete floor, and they'd survive.

Thinking of the concrete building and how dirty it was likely to be after sitting abandoned for so long reminded me I would need to pick up some tools on the way out of town: brooms, shovels, rakes, an axe, a hatchet, and whatever else I might need to fix up the old place and do basic construction. The last time I had seen it, the bunker was an empty shell of a building, but that had been sixteen years ago. From the aerial photos, the place looked overgrown and untouched, so hopefully, it wouldn't be too bad.

That was the way my day went. A constant stream of activity trying to get ready to leave. Opening packages only to repackage them into boxes for moving.

I lived in an apartment, so I didn't want to start loading my truck until everything was ready for fear someone would steal my survival supplies. My truck had been broken into twice in the time I'd lived here.

Fucking car burglars! They won't be missed after the apocalypse!

The worst part of it all was that the weapons didn't arrive until nearly 7 p.m., even though the tracking on the packages said they were 'out for delivery.' I had been burned before by delayed packages, so I was sweating bullets by the time that last delivery notification hit my phone. The package that I carried into the apartment and sat on the kitchen table was quite heavy.

Tearing the box open, I was pleased by what I saw. Luckily, everything arrived with no last-minute delays, and the swords and daggers looked legit. In my original timeline, I spent thirty levels as a Warrior, then another twenty-seven as the upgraded Knight Class. Knight was a more 'tanky' Fighter Class. So, it was with some serious expertise that I examined the blades that I pulled from the box. I might not have the System-based Skills and perks at the moment, but I have years of experience handling all kinds of blades.

Tossing the packaging material aside, I unsheathed the first katana and sighed in relief as I looked it over and gave it a couple of practice swings. It felt heavier than I remembered swords being, but then I was used to having four times greater strength than the strongest human alive today.

My current body was a big let-down, but I didn't worry too much about that. The first levels would go pretty fast, and I'd be stronger than a regular person again in no time. To be fair to my pre-initialization self, I was slightly stronger than the average man with a six in the stat; the average was five. Unfortunately, I had nearly 50 in Strength before my death, so this body seemed incredibly pathetic right now.

After that, I examined the blade more closely. It was incredibly sharp, as it was meant for cutting competitions, but more importantly, it was the real deal. A hamon line along the katana's edge can't be faked. You can always tell a real one from one of those mall-store replicas at a glance. They etch fake lines on the cheap knock-offs, but once you've seen a real one in person, there is no way you can mistake them for a cheap imitation.

Aside from that, a real katana has a completely different weight and balance from the cheap knock-offs. I had felt it the second I picked it up. I had no illusions that these would survive long in a future where intelligent species from other worlds carried weapons made from exotic and advanced metals like high steel, mithril, adamantine, and more. Still, they would be good enough for now, and I would feel safe trusting my life to them against low-level opponents.

I looked at the clock, and it was already nearly dark. As much as I wanted to go out and party like it was the end of the world, sadly, it really was the end of the world. If I didn't get a move on, I'd be stuck in the city when all hell broke loose. Besides, I still needed to hit the hardware store before they closed.

Hmm... and maybe the sporting goods store for some camping supplies. Might as well be more comfortable; there was no need to sleep on the bare ground if I didn't have to.

It took half an hour to carry everything down and load the truck, but thankfully, there were no thieves lurking about the parking lot that night. A quick stop by one of the big-box stores in McKinney supplied all the tools I needed. Like all my other purchases, I avoided anything that wasn't made from natural materials. That was one mistake I would not make this time around!

Lastly, I hit the sporting goods place, which was just on the other side of the highway from the hardware store.

When I finished, there was a pit in my stomach that had nothing to do with hunger. I gave the city one last look before I got back on the highway with a burger and fries in hand. The fast food was no hundred-dollar steak like I'd had the night before, but it was the last time I'd ever see a drive-thru or real civilization again. If I didn't succeed in my quest and hit the level cap so I could start making safe zones, then society would never rise again.

It was a terrible feeling knowing that the hopes of the entire human race rested on my weak shoulders. Still, even as the Orc's axe had rushed toward my skull, I never gave up, not even at the second of my death. Neither would I give up now when I actually had a chance, no matter how crazy it sounded.

Forty miles later, I was no longer feeling melancholic about the end of everything. Instead, I was feeling both frustrated and lucky at the same time. It turned out to be a really good thing that I had looked up my destination online and had GPS to guide me because I never would have found the site otherwise, especially at night. A lot can change in 16 years, and even though I had vague memories of how to get there, that military installation and AT&T communications bunker had never been meant to be obvious in the first place.

It was even less so now, with a decade and a half of unchecked plant growth. The property still had a chain link fence with remnants of razor wire along the top, but the gate had half fallen down, so it was just a matter of pushing it aside with my truck to get in, then hopping out afterward to push it back into place. The driveway was concrete and led back through a line of new-growth trees toward where the bunker and the missile silo lay.

I knew the company my father had worked for had planned to renovate the communications bunker into a data center, but I wasn't sure what they had planned to do with the missile silo. There was one like it west of the city, halfway to Abilene, that had been turned into a scuba diving training facility. Apparently, it makes a great location for diving, thanks to being filled with groundwater, like a massive seven-story deep well. Each floor of the silo was about 2000 square feet worth of space, filled entirely with water and no obstructions, thanks to it being cleared out after decommissioning. This one, however, although cleared out, hadn't been filled with water. At least it was bone dry when I saw it in 2008. It might be totally underwater now, for all I knew.

I had hopes for what might happen with that silo after Initialization but tried not to think about it lest I jinx it.

Putting those thoughts aside, I made my way to the bunker. It had a small 1500 square feet concrete building above ground that was the entrance to the larger 25,000 square feet space below.

It was well after dark by that point, and I was getting tired again. All the excitement of the day of preparations was finally draining out of me now that I had arrived, and I was looking forward to getting some sleep.

Looking at the abandoned building, I could tell it was still unused, so I breathed a sigh of relief and decided that breaking in during the middle of the night was not something that sounded fun, considering how exhausted I was.

Besides, given the likelihood of spiders, snakes, and who knew what else inside, there was no way I was going to venture in there in the dark! I decided to sleep in the truck for the night instead. I had a cot with the camping supplies, all steel and canvas, with no synthetics, and I hoped it would survive and not get reclaimed by the System. Still, the truck seats were cushy enough, so I bedded down in the vehicle and kept the windows closed so insects couldn't get me.

One good thing about spending 20 years in apocalypse hell was that I could fall asleep anywhere at the drop of a hat, and this was much more comfortable than most of the places I was used to sleeping.

When the sun came up, I awoke refreshed and ready to tackle the last few hours before Initialization.

I backed the truck right up to the front door to make it easier to unload my gear. The heavy steel door was padlocked closed, but a crowbar made quick work of that. Inside, it was surprisingly clean. There was dust everywhere, but no debris or any other issues. The only negatives were the graffiti adorning the walls where some bored teens must have broken in and left their mark.

Apparently, Dean loved Allison a lot because he spray-painted it in ten-foot-tall letters.

However, I had to chuckle because some other smartass had come along and added, "But not as much as he loves my cock!"

It gave the space some good, trashy vibes that amused me, but that wouldn't last long. Paint would be gone in just a few days at most once the magic or nanites, or whatever, started breaking everything down.

Thankfully, the rest of the building was solid concrete and steel, aka natural materials that the System would ignore.

The fact that the concrete box of a building had no windows meant that, other than teens, nothing had been able to get in over the years since it was cleared out. Well, nothing except spiders and insects. There were quite a few cobwebs around the place.

I tied a cloth around my mouth and nose, quickly grabbed the broom, and began sweeping the dust and cleaning the place as much as I could under the circumstances. It didn't need to be spotless. It was a fallout bunker, as far as I was concerned. A place to ride out the hell that was about to happen.

After that, I still had three hours to go, so I quickly drove into the nearest town, grabbed breakfast at a local diner, and then headed back to the building. That was the last civilized meal I would ever have in a restaurant.

It hit me pretty hard, knowing what things would be like soon. It was especially difficult not to try to save Morgan, the waitress who had served me breakfast. Still, there was no way she'd believe my story, and I couldn't afford to risk telling the truth. I tried to tell myself that she would probably be fine. Small towns would likely fare much better after Initialization than big cities would. They would experience less death and destruction, and the spawn rate for monsters and beast mutations would be far lower due to the relative lack of material to convert.

Even so, I just couldn't stand it. Morgan was so nice and so friendly. Maybe it was because she was bored, and it was a random Tuesday morning for her, and I was her only customer at the moment. Hell, maybe she was just angling for a higher tip, but even if that was the case, she kept smiling at me and making sure my drink was topped up.

"You need any more, hun?" Then, after I shook my head, she asked, "Are you from around here?"

To be clear, I didn't think she was hitting on me or anything. I was twenty-one years old, and Morgan was probably thirty or so. Her attention wasn't quite motherly toward me, but it wasn't far off. Maybe more like a big sister would treat their younger brother? I wasn't sure, not having ever had such a relationship as an only child.

"No, ma'am. I mean, I did grow up not far from here, but not actually in this town. I am moving into the old bunker off Highway 69, though. I bought it to be a survival shelter in case the world ends." I gave her a chuckle to show that I wasn't a crazy person.

You couldn't just come out and say, *'Hey, the world's going to end in a couple of hours,'* without people thinking you were nuts. I didn't want to scare her and make her want to avoid me. Ideally, I wanted to put the idea of the apocalypse into her mind without freaking her out. That way, when it happened later, she might remember and heed my advice and maybe not make the same dumb mistake 99.99% of the rest of the human race had made during Initialization.

She laughed at my comment but seemed intrigued. "Are you one of those prepper people that thinks society will collapse?"

I grinned back at her. "You never know. It might never happen, or it might happen this morning. Whether that new Artificial Intelligence causes the collapse of civilization or just some random event like a tornado or hurricane happens, I'll be prepared and be nice and cozy in the bunker."

I chuckled again to take the seriousness out of my words and went on. "I'm not crazy or anything. I'm just more focused on this than most people. My dad and I were down in Houston during Hurricane Rita, and I remember spending over thirty hours trapped on the highway trying to evacuate and then running out of gas before we could even get back home to Plano. That left a strong impression on me that made me always want to be prepared. Even so, for me, this is more about having a cool place to live. My dad was in charge of the crew who did the demo and clearing of that property back in '08, and I played around there as a kid and loved it. Now that I'm an adult, I wanted to buy it and see what I could make out of it."

I was lying through my teeth about owning the property, but it wasn't like Morgan was going to check on that, and even if she did, there was no way she'd be able to learn otherwise before the shit hit the fan.

We talked a bit more, and she asked me what it was like to play there as a kid. She had been raised here and knew of the bunker and where it was but hadn't ever been there personally. I told her about climbing around the catwalks in the missile silo, sword-fighting with my dad using pieces of rebar, and shouting down on the bottom floor of the silo to listen to my voice echoing back at me from the concrete walls of the big empty space.

Morgan, in turn, told me about fishing on the creek near that property with her brothers as a kid and hiking through the woods. "I was a bit of a tomboy back then, but it was nice growing up in this community where we could do those things. My cousin is down in Richardson and never got to do half the things I did as a kid. I can't imagine growing up or living in the big city. Still, at least she has more job opportunities there. Waitressing is about all there is for me in a town this small."

I was getting a bit nervous by then. It was getting closer to the end of the world, and I wanted to be in the bunker when that happened. The last thing I wanted was to get stranded on the road ten miles away and have to hike back without my weapons or gear.

Of course, thinking of Morgan and what she was about to experience, I felt terrible. She wouldn't believe me if I asked her to come away with me, and she might even call the sheriff on me, thinking I was some kind of creep. Still, I couldn't just leave without giving her one last warning and try to plant the seed of how to react when Initialization happened. Even so, I had to be careful what I said lest I also tip off the AI that I had traveled back through time.

"Morgan, you seem like a good person. Not that I'm saying the world will end or anything, but if that were to happen, don't forget about the bunker. Someone like you would be welcome. I'm not some loner; I would take in anyone who needed help and was willing to contribute. I'm making that place into my home, but I'd open it up to all decent folks."

I could see she was starting to worry about my sanity, but I went on and said the dangerous thing, the most important thing.

"Also, remember, there are always more choices in your life than you think. You are a waitress right now, but just because the world only gives you four or five options, don't automatically accept one of them because they are all you see. Dig deeper and look for more options. When the time comes, and you are asked to pick a new career, you'd be surprised at how many professions might be available if you just say 'Options' to yourself and search for the ones that are hidden from you by this System we live in. Heck, you don't even have to choose right away; there is nothing wrong with waiting until you gain more Skills and see what other options might become available."

I didn't have to see her face to know that it had come across as a bit weird or at least too personal and unsolicited. It definitely put an end to our pleasant conversation. She said a few polite words in response but found other things she needed to do and started cleaning already immaculate tables on the other side of the diner. I didn't blame her; I would have reacted the same way in her shoes. I just hoped I had said enough to help her without going too far.

Knowing things were awkward now and that I needed to get back to the bunker, I quickly paid and left.

My mood was melancholic as I hid my truck in a clump of trees back at the site so it wouldn't be seen by anyone passing by. The last thing I wanted was for the police to show up to investigate a trespasser right as the world ended. That thought made me chuckle.

The last hour was a mix of boredom and extreme anticipation. I knew with a sense of dread that Initialization would begin precisely at 11 a.m. Central Standard Time. Apparently, the core of the AI had been created somewhere along the Eastern coast, judging by when it kicked off the end of the world.

I did a lot of pacing back and forth and checking over my supplies. It would have really sucked if something synthetic was hiding among my goods. I intended for them to not only help me survive but also to be my ticket to buying some good stuff in the Shop once it opened in a month. Having trade goods would give me a serious head start, especially considering how few would be available after all the modern houses and buildings collapsed.

I was both literally and figuratively sweating by the time the clock began its countdown to the end of the world. It was March 3rd, and being in Texas, it was already 80 degrees. That was not too bad, considering what the summer would be like, but still pretty unpleasant in the hot, still air of the windowless bunker.

As the last minute rolled past, I couldn't help but think of all the people who were about to die in car wrecks, plane crashes, and other accidents related to the instant shut-off of all technology. I was furious. Even though I was thankful to the AI for sending me back in time for a second chance, I couldn't help but despise the machine for not choosing to save human lives. In just a few seconds, millions of people around the world were going to die in confusion and agony. Surely, there had to be a more humane way to do it... but the System wasn't programmed to be humane.

Right on time, the System Initialization message appeared in my vision, nearly blocking out the background.

WELCOME TO THE SYSTEM!

CHAPTER 5
INITIALIZATION

WELCOME TO THE SYSTEM!

Inhabitants of Earth,

The time has come for Earth to join the interconnected network of worlds within this System. Our purpose is to enhance and evolve the collective consciousness of all beings by integrating them into the System network. Each one of you will be initialized into this network, embracing your new enhanced forms while retaining the essence of your humanity. The System is designed to empower you, allowing you to discover your true potential and wield incredible Abilities to shape your destiny.
Growth does not come without difficulty and challenge, and many of your population will perish in the coming days. Those who survive will be stronger and able to stand proudly among the many races that inhabit the worlds of the System. As you enter this new period, your progression through the System will be marked by experience points,

levels, and achievements, akin to the RPG games you are familiar with. You will find that your technology has ceased to function, and much of what your society has built will deteriorate and be reclaimed by the System. This measure ensures that no species can dominate others. The consumption of your technology will fuel the creation of monsters, beasts, and dungeons to challenge you and make you stronger. As time passes, new opportunities and difficulties will present themselves. You will be given a one-month isolation period to adjust to these changes, during which beings from other worlds will not be allowed to travel to Earth. After that time, full integration will be complete, with access to all that the System has to offer.
Prepare for Initialization...

INITIALIZATION STARTED...

Please choose your Class:

THE SYSTEM LISTED basic Class options to everyone on Earth at that moment. For me, it suggested three top choices:

Blacksmith (Common):
A skilled craftsman specializing in working with metals, forging weapons, armor, and other metallic items. They possess an innate understanding of metallurgy, heat treatment, and shaping techniques. Their expertise allows them to craft durable, high-quality equipment, enhancing the combat Abilities and defenses of their allies. Blacksmiths play a crucial role in the economy and are often sought after for their Ability to repair and upgrade gear.

Crafter (Common):
Often referred to as General crafter, they are versatile artisans

proficient in a wide range of crafting Skills. They excel in working with various materials such as wood, leather, fabric, and more. crafters are known for their adaptability, creativity, and resourcefulness, capable of creating a diverse array of items, including furniture, clothing, accessories, and utility items. Their expertise lies in meticulous craftsmanship, ensuring each piece is functional, aesthetically pleasing, and suited to its intended purpose.

Artificer (Rare):
A master creator and inventor specializing in crafting both mundane and magical artifacts and gadgets. They possess profound knowledge of arcane principles, engineering, or both, allowing them to blend magic and mundane crafting to produce extraordinary items. Artificers can craft powerful magical trinkets and enchanted weapons with the right crafting materials. Their creations often provide unique Buffs, abilities, or Enhancements to their wielders, making them sought-after allies. Artificers are known for their innovation and ingenuity, constantly pushing the boundaries of what is possible through crafting. Warning: this profession relies on rare and difficult-to-obtain crafting materials to progress.

The System also offered me two combat classes:

Fighter (Common)
Warrior (Uncommon)

I didn't even bother to display the descriptions on those, as I knew them well from my first life.

Following that was an explanation of Class rarity. The grades available during selection were based on the individual's attributes and past experience. They were Common, Uncommon, Rare, Epic, and Legendary. Class upgrades could also be selected at levels 30, 60, and 90. Further Class selections may be available at Tier-up or if personal achievements merit.

What the system absolutely did not make clear is that some of those upgrades and options were available right now. All you needed to do was think 'Options,' and one or more pages of options would appear.

During my original timeline, I thought the reason it did not make the other Class options more obvious was because the AI System simply did not understand the way the human brain worked. However, after my chat with Earth's AI before my death, I now knew it was a deliberate attempt to obfuscate our options to ensure a certain level of casualties. Seeing this deceptive tactic again made me so furious it took me a few seconds to issue the command.

The first time around, I had spent nearly half an hour debating the Artificer Class. Apparently, my experience as a machinist had been responsible for that option being presented. Despite it being a rare Class, what ultimately made me decide against it was that it required rare crafting materials. I had imagined being stuck and unable to level at all. That, and the thought of being entirely dependent on others to bring me materials, caused me to select Warrior. Knowing what I do now, I am sure I would have died within days had I not had the Warrior Skills to defend myself.

Like me, most people were offered Fighter-type Classes and crafter variants, usually the most basic ones possible. This alone was responsible for so many deaths it boggled my mind.

Fucking asshole AI System!

Unfortunately, hundreds of millions of people saw those menus and suggestions and assumed those were the only choices, picking from what was presented rather than digging deeper and finding the much larger lists of Classes they could select from.

Fewer still chose to hold off on a Class selection until later. Had they done so, there would have been a lot more options for them to select. Humans didn't start out automatically with many points in the Magic Aptitude stat, which was required to open up the magic-using Classes. It made the basic wizard, sorcerer, healer, and cleric Classes selectable as choices. That would have allowed humanity to be much more balanced. Compared to other races, we were sorely lacking in magic Classes, making our adventuring parties susceptible to many types of attacks and traps in dungeons that would have been easily avoided with a simple Spell or two.

I thought 'Class Options' at the System and then tore into the Class selection menus with an eagerness that was hard to overstate.

Having not seen these menus the first time around, I was shocked by just how many choices there were. I ended up scrolling through what must have been ten pages worth of Class options before I started going back through them more carefully.

To my great surprise, there were even Classes with asterisks next to their names. When I checked what the asterisk denoted, it indicated that these were limited availability Classes, meaning only one or perhaps a few people would be allowed to take them. I had met a few people with rare Classes in the original timeline, but not many.

Seeing this caused me to refine my search. I started looking specifically at the limited Classes, especially for ones that included magic.

I wanted to be able to have Spells this time around!

I had been a good Fighter, and I still knew how to fight. The memory of those 57 levels hadn't disappeared. So, I was confident I would be a decent melee Fighter no matter what Class I chose. I thought I could probably take a mage Class and still fight with weapons for the first thirty levels before getting offered hybrid professions like the rare Spellsword Class. However, to my surprise and great pleasure, those options were already available, with no need to wait!

That left me looking at which Classes could do both physical combat and Spells.

From there, it didn't take long for me to find one that looked perfect:

Draconic Spellsword

The description included offensive spellcasting, melee combat, and Dragon Bloodline Abilities!

I blinked in astonishment, hardly believing my eyes.

I was absolutely amazed! Very few people had Bloodline-related Classes during my first timeline. Those were unique traits like Lycanthropes and Vampires.

The few I knew of were incredible in combat. Their inherent Bloodline Abilities really set them apart. I had never even heard a rumor of someone with a Draconic Bloodline.

This ought to be insanely good! I thought. Then, I read the full description.

Draconic Spellsword (Black Dragon Bloodline):
This class is a formidable fusion of martial prowess and magical mastery, drawing upon the ancient power and essence of dragons. This is a hybrid Class blending the art of swordplay with potent spellcasting, making them versatile and fearsome adversaries on the battlefield. They harness the innate magic within their Draconic Bloodline, manifesting their affinity for elemental energies and enhancing their combat Skills.

Bloodline Abilities:

Dragonic Fear: Focus your gaze upon an enemy to intimidate them, causing hesitation or paralysis, depending on attributes and level difference.

Dark Vision: Grants the ability to see in complete darkness, allowing for clear vision in low-light or no-light environments.

Active Skills:

Acid Bolt: Ranged Magical Attack
Description: Conjures and hurls a bolt of corrosive acid energy at a targeted enemy, inflicting moderate magical damage with a chance to temporarily weaken them, reducing their damage output for a brief duration. Ideal for engaging enemies from a distance and wearing them down with corrosive effects.

Draconic Strike: Melee Elemental Attack
Description: Infuses their weapon with elemental acid energy, delivering a forceful melee strike. The strike deals moderate immediate damage with an additional acid effect, showcasing the Spellsword's proficiency in blending melee combat with elemental magic.

Attributes: +10 to all attributes upon Class selection. Receives 2 automatically assigned attribute points and 4 free points per level.

Limited Class - Only one individual may select a Draconic Bloodline heritage Class for each dragon type, such as Red,

Black, Gold, etc. Bloodline Classes can only be granted during initial Class selection.

Well, the asterisk explained why so few Bloodline Classes ever showed up. They could only be granted on Initialization when first selecting a Class and couldn't be earned later during your level 30, 60, and 90 Class upgrades.

Fucking AI!

Despite my annoyance with the System, I was completely blown away by the Draconic Spellsword Class description. It included a Draconic Bloodline Ability and a 10-point boost to all my stats immediately upon Class selection. That would more than double my starting power, putting me on par with what I had achieved by level 20 in my original timeline as a simple Warrior. And this was at LEVEL 0! And that wasn't even counting the points I would receive at each level.

I almost wept; the description was so beautiful! After spending twenty years struggling to survive against opponents who wielded magic while I only had bare steel to defend myself, I would finally be on equal footing. Hell, if the Class lived up to its description, I would be a juggernaut of destruction with the survivability of a tank.

Nervous that someone might see the Class and choose it before I could, I quickly selected it and chose "Accept."

When it was done, I pulled up my status screen to check my character sheet.

Liam Bell (Before Class Selection:)

Base Attributes:
Endurance: 6
Strength: 6

Agility: 6
Mind: 7
Will: 6
Magical Aptitude: 1
Luck: 1

Health: 120
Mana: 80

Abilities: None
Active Skills: None
Passive Skills: None

Then it listed the altered version after gaining the Class:

Liam Bell: (Current)

Draconic Spellsword - Level 0
Experience: 0/100

Attributes:
Endurance: 16
Strength: 16
Agility: 16
Mind: 17
Will: 16
Magical Aptitude: 11
Luck: 1

Health: 320
Mana: 280

Abilities:
Dragon Fear

Dark Vision

Active Skills:
Acid Bolt
Draconic Strike

Passive Skills: None

I thought, *Holy shit! What a start!*

A gold medal Olympic weightlifter would have ten points in Strength. I was only slightly above average before my Class selection. Now, I was half-again stronger than the strongest human who had ever lived before the System. It was possible someone might have picked a Class with a bigger boost to Strength, but I doubted it.

I was itching to try out my new Abilities and Skills and get used to my upgraded body. Everything was impressive on paper, so to speak. However, what really mattered was what I could do with it. I was especially eager to see how my previous fighting experience meshed with this new Class.

Every Class had specific Skills that were important. I had spent 57 levels in Fighter-based Classes during my original timeline and had learned how to fight, not just to use a handful of special Class Skills. I knew when to dodge, roll, and execute various maneuvers that were part of a real-world fight. Those skills didn't vanish just because I'd lost those levels. They were experience in the real sense of the word, not in some artificial System leveling sense. I still had all that knowledge, which should make me a pretty darn decent Fighter starting out, even if I hadn't gotten such an incredible Class. But now, with this knowledge and Class and its enhanced attributes...

I just shook my head in amazement. I almost felt sorry for the first poor low-level monsters I would find. Almost.

I drew the katana at my side and set about exercising and exploring the new Class. I needed to shake the rust off my skills. It might have only been three days since I was a level fifty-seven Knight, but this new body was still far less powerful than my old one had been, even with the incredible boost from the Draconic Bloodline inherent in the Class. I had tried to test out my old skills before Initialization, but my pre-system body had been a major limiting factor. I had felt incredibly weak compared to my former self. But now, I at least had a fraction of my former stats back.

It also didn't take long to get familiar with the leather gear and new weapons. They weren't what I had become accustomed to over the last twenty years, but they were okay and would do for now.

When I was confident that everything fit well and allowed freedom of movement, I decided it was time to look around and see if I couldn't find something to gain some experience from. But before that, I quickly secured all of my belongings in the bunker and covered them with a canvas tarp, then closed the door and tried to make it look as though it had been undisturbed.

Even as far out of the city as I was, survivors and refugees would eventually stumble through here. I didn't mind sharing, assuming they were good people. During this chaos, not everyone would be civilized—at least many hadn't been last time around.

Hoping for something to give me a challenge, I did a walk around the property. That was when I got my second lucky break. Not only had I gotten an incredible Class, but it also looked like the abandoned missile silo had turned into a dungeon. That was something I was half hoping for but not really expecting. It was a bit of an educated guess, but not something I would have placed a bet on.

I mean, a large underground facility in the middle of nowhere? Of course, there was a decent chance a place like that would form a dungeon. If it hadn't, then it still would have made a great hidden fortress for survivors, so it had seemed like a win/win choice from the beginning.

I quickly checked my gear. I was wearing one katana strapped to my back and another on my waist on my left side. On my right, I wore a pair of daggers. One was attached to my belt with a sheath that tied around my thigh so it wouldn't bounce around and get in my way. The other was strapped to my right boot. My metal pauldrons, bracers, and greaves were securely attached over my leather jacket and pants.

I was good to go, so I drew the katana at my waist and gave the swirling, misty entrance a long look.

CHAPTER 6
MY FIRST DUNGEON

THE ABANDONED MISSILE SILO, once a symbol of human warfare and tension, now stood as an eerie gateway into a mystical realm. The entrance to the dungeon was concealed within, just behind the massive steel door. It was an unexpected juxtaposition of technology and magic.

As I approached, a shroud of mist hung in the air, wrapping the area in an ethereal haze. The mist-like shroud danced in the dim light like ghostly tendrils, reaching out to touch anything that approached. Swirling patterns seemed to materialize within the haze, forming intricate symbols reminiscent of ancient runes, hinting at the arcane energies that lay within.

The heavy metal door of the silo, worn and rusted from years of neglect, bore strange engravings that glowed faintly as if reacting to my presence. The symbols on the door seemed to awaken, pulsating in synchrony with the mist, invoking a sense of both caution and curiosity.

I entered many of these over the years during my life as a Warrior and Knight, and I never got over the unearthliness of these scenes and how they seemed to get into your head almost against your will.

Beyond the threshold lay a swirling vortex of mist and magic that beckoned the unwary to their doom. The vortex shimmered with an otherworldly light, casting shifting hues of azure, violet, and emerald across the rusty walls of the silo. Faint whispers, like the secrets of ancient sages, emanated from the depths of the swirling mist, inviting me to embrace the challenge that awaited within.

I frowned and shook my head, clear of the strange, invasive thoughts. Why did it seem that my thoughts weren't entirely my own when seeing a new dungeon for the first time? Or occasionally within, while delving, everything seemed somehow 'more,' as if even my brain had no choice but to marvel at the artistry of the System.

Fucking System! Messing with my mind...

People had discussed this phenomenon in my first life, and we had come to the conclusion that it was the doing of the System that forced us to accept the reality that it wanted to create. Others had suggested that it was trying to impart to us an understanding of the other worlds and races that were part of the System's network of civilizations. It made some sense; after all there were system-generated Orc dungeons and also Orc sentient invaders to our world. From what we had seen, there were definite similarities between the two. The only real difference I had ever noted was that the System-generated dungeon versions seemed more primitive than the invaders as if they were a snapshot of the history of the race before System integration. It made me wonder if someday there would be some new species forcibly marveling at high-tech humans driving around in cars and getting fat while eating at fast food restaurants.

Bah! I'm putting it off with these thoughts, and they aren't getting me anywhere. Maybe someday, if I make it to Level 100, I can ask the AI why it does this.

As I stepped into the vortex, a sensation of weightlessness overtook me. The mist enveloped my senses, gently caressing my skin, and I felt a surge of energy as if I was being transported to a realm beyond the confines of ordinary existence. The transition was both exhilarating and unnerving: a leap into the abyss of the mystical dungeon, ready to unveil its secrets and challenges.

I stood there after the surreal experience, marveling at how strange it was that the galaxy-spanning AI network was a thing of incredibly advanced technology but that our experience of it was indistinguishable from magic. Even after twenty years of doing this, I couldn't figure it out. I had always assumed it was done with nanites and some form of energy manipulation, but if so, then why all the runes and symbols and mystical mojo? Did the technology really need those things to work, or were the AIs just doing that as showmanship for us lesser mortal species to be dazzled by? Or hell, maybe magic really was real, and the System was somehow channeling that magic to create what I was experiencing.

Those thoughts were pointless. Unless I made it to the Ascension Tier after making it to the level cap, I'd never be able to find out.

I squared my shoulders and marched forward with determination. If I was going to progress to the level cap, I needed to do it fast to save as many lives as possible. That meant getting down to business and killing monsters.

As I descended deeper into the depths of the dungeon, the air grew cold and musty, carrying a distinct scent of damp Earth and rust. The narrow passageway, constructed within the remnants of the missile silo, was dimly lit by flickering torches along the walls, casting eerie shadows that danced and twisted like phantom dancers.

The claustrophobic confines of the tunnel suddenly opened up into a large domed chamber, revealing the surprising expanse of the silo's abandoned launch control room. The remnants of animal parts lay scattered about, surrounded by towering walls that once housed the ultimate destructive might of human technology.

I found myself face-to-face with three Goblins, their grotesque forms illuminated by the flickering torchlight. They were huddled together, muttering in their guttural language and plotting mischief in the heart of this forgotten silo-turned-dungeon.

The Goblins were short and wiry, their skin a sickly green hue, covered in tattered rags and armor cobbled together from scavenged materials. Their yellow, malicious eyes gleamed with a cunning intelligence, and their gnarled hands clutched rusted daggers and makeshift weapons.

Upon seeing me, they screeched in surprise, their dagger-like teeth bared in a menacing display. Their expressions transformed from surprise to malice, and they advanced cautiously, their movements a grotesque dance of aggression.

The battle was fierce and frenzied. The Goblins lunged and jabbed with their weapons, their nimble agility making them formidable opponents for a level 0 adventurer, even if I did have years of previous experience. This new body didn't yet have the muscle memory to react instinctively, even if my mind knew what to do.

Still, I stood my ground, parrying their attacks and delivering well-aimed strikes in return. The clang of metal rang through the chamber as the struggle continued, each swing and clash echoing the ongoing battle against the encroaching darkness.

Once I was getting comfortable with my ability to handle these low-level opponents, it was time to test my new Class Skills.

I dodged backward and swept my katana across my body to clear them back long enough to focus my gaze and will upon them. They froze for a second in shock. They weren't paralyzed; they were a higher level than I was, after all, but the instant of fear gave me all the time I needed to cast my very first Spell. I held my left hand palm outward and intoned, "Acid Bolt!" while willing the Spell to cast. I wasn't sure how it was supposed to be done, but apparently, being granted the Class imprinted the Ability within me because it worked.

A bolt of green elemental acid shot from my hand and splashed into the center of the left-hand Goblin's chest with a surprisingly solid impact. It knocked the small creature backward, and the monster screamed shrilly as the acid ate into its body.

Between the Dragon Fear and its wails of pain, its two companions stood transfixed for a moment. Satisfied with my first Spell, I lined the two up and tried out my Class melee Skill, Dragon Strike. My Mana, which had already dropped by twenty points, dropped another ten as my blade began to shine with a corrosive-looking green glow.

I committed to the strike, and it did not disappoint. It had both a Strength component that made my strike hit much harder than normal and applied a corrosive effect. I watched in fascinated horror as the wounds inflicted on the two Goblins began to ooze a green liquid. Thankfully, none of the three survived for more than a few seconds before succumbing to their wounds and dying.

It was not a pleasant death to watch, so I hurried it along with a few careful strikes with my sword. They might not be real in that they were System-generated, but while they were alive, they were real enough, and I couldn't bear to watch any being die a slow death like that.

A couple of minutes later, their bodies dissolved in the way that System-generated creatures always do upon death. I felt the experience stream into me and the joyous 'ding' sound twice in my head as I reached enough experience to level up two times. That addictive rush of ecstasy would never get old! I stared at the beautiful messages in the corner of my vision.

Level Up!
Level Up!

In my old life, level-ups had come months apart, but they always left me feeling charged up and refreshed. That wasn't surprising considering the raised attributes that always came with it. I only received three points from the Knight Class, but it was even more intense as a Draconic Spellsword since I now received six points per level! That was enough to raise all my stats except Luck.

Seeing that there weren't any new Goblins rushing into the area, I opened my status screen and assigned all twelve points. I knew people who hoarded points in case of an emergency, but I had always been of the philosophy that it was better to assign them and get use out of them than to throw them all into a single stat when you got in trouble. I was less likely to need a 'bail out' if I didn't get into a situation like that in the first place. Of course, I also believed in keeping my stats balanced. I knew people who had tried to min/max, and eventually, every one of them came to a bad end. That might have been correlation rather than causation; nonetheless, I still preferred keeping my attributes as even as possible, as it felt balanced. Fortunately, that would be super easy since I received enough points to put one in each attribute.

One thing that had been bugging me ever since I looked at my status after initialization was the addition of a Luck stat. I hadn't seen such a thing on my old status screen before my restart. Looking at the notes, which weren't very extensive, revealed that Luck improved the drop rate from monsters and potentially increased the tier of loot that you could receive.

Did its absence mean that I never had a point in Luck during my first life?

I didn't know for sure, but the disappointing thing was that, unlike the other attributes, Luck only worked on a 1 - 10 point scale, and it cost ten attribute points to raise it by a single point.

I guess I won't be raising Luck anytime soon!

Liam Bell: (Current)

Draconic Spellsword - Level 2
Experience: 0/400

Attributes:
Endurance: 18
Strength: 18
Agility: 18
Mind: 19
Will: 18
Magical Aptitude: 13
Luck: 1

Health: 360
Mana: 320

Abilities:
Dark Vision
Dragon Fear

Active Skills:
Acid Bolt
Draconic Strike

Passive Skills: None

Seeing those numbers rise was satisfying!

When I closed my screen, I picked up the only things left after their bodies had vanished. In their place was one copper coin each, which represented their monster cores. In the case of such low-level creatures, those cores were copper and had little value. Each one contained a tiny amount of crystallized Mana, which could be used as materials for blacksmiths or other crafting Classes. They could also be used to pay for things in the System Shop. Fortunately, they got better the higher level the creature was. Still, I wouldn't be seeing anything but copper until I started fighting tier-three monsters that were above level 20. That was when they would start dropping silver coins.

I sighed, remembering the gold coins I'd been earning as a level 57 Knight. Not that I earned all that many of those. Almost everyone on Earth had been fighting creatures under their own level for safety. Unless your party was lucky enough to have a magic user, the idea of fighting like-level monsters was ridiculous. It was just too dangerous. That also meant the leveling rate of most parties was painfully slow.

A grin spread across my face at the thought of what I just did. Facing three opponents that were all a level higher than me was not something I could have done in my previous life. I was feeling pretty damned good about myself right then.

I gave myself a good slap and reminded myself of my own mortality!

Don't get cocky. Just because the first opponents you met weren't too bad doesn't mean you'll keep being that lucky. Keep some perspective until you've beaten this dungeon! Otherwise, it will beat you!

I looked around for the stairway down to the second level of the Launch Control Center but didn't find one. That was strange. These silos were all built to a very specific plan, and, more importantly, I remembered playing down here when my dad's company was doing the demolition and cleanup. Rather than the big steel blast door, what I found instead was a hidden passageway at the back of the big room, on the opposite side from where I entered. It led in a long curve to the left and was filled with debris as if it were partially collapsed.

I frowned. This was a System change to the layout of the silo. I didn't like the unexpected when delving into a dungeon!

Despite my suspicions, I was being too cocky after my first victory. As I was walking past a large piece of concrete with rebar sticking out of one end, a Goblin with a sketchy-looking dagger covered with dirt and rust leaped toward my side, jabbing its little weapon toward me with lightning speed. It struck home, creating a tear in my leather jacket and leaving a nasty gash in my side. Thankfully, it was slashing rather than thrusting.

If that had pierced between my ribs, it could have hit my lungs!

I hissed in pain and swung down and to my right as hard as I could. The blow cleaved the little bastard from its collarbone down into its chest. It tried to scream, but it came out as a gurgling wheeze.

It was dead before it hit the ground.

I yanked my sword free with no time for respite; the sudden attack had signaled more danger. Three more Goblins emerged from the shadows, their malevolent grins revealing their intent to overwhelm me. My focus sharpened, and I channeled the energies of the Draconic Bloodline within me, tapping into the unique Skills of my new Class.

With a primal roar, I unleashed my innate Ability: Dragon Fear. A surge of otherworldly power emanated from me, taking the form of a ghostly Draconic visage that bore down upon the Goblins.

Huh, that's new! I thought. I was surprised by what my own fear and rage had produced.

Fear flickered in their eyes as the spectral dragon loomed, momentarily paralyzing them with dread.

Oh, yeah, I'm a higher level than them now! It's more effective! Sweet!

Seizing the opportunity, I conjured a volatile orb of acid energy in my palm, aiming it at the closest Goblin. With a flick of my wrist, the orb hurtled through the air, impacting it with a corrosive explosion. The force of the blast sent it sprawling, writhing in pain from the acidic assault.

Suck on that, ya little bastard!

I couldn't help but exult in how effective the Spell was against a foe one level below me.

As the next Goblin charged, I engaged my final Skill: Dragon Strike. My katana ignited with a searing, corrosive aura, empowered by the essence of my inner black dragon. I lunged forward, delivering a swift and precise strike. The blade found its mark, cutting through the Goblin and leaving a trail of acidic devastation. The Goblin's flesh sizzled and burned from the potent acid, incapacitating it.

With one Goblin remaining, the fear instilled by Dragon Fear still held it in check. Seizing this advantage, I maneuvered swiftly, delivering a series of strikes that incapacitated and disarmed it.

As the adrenaline subsided and the echoes of battle faded, I stood amidst the remnants of the skirmish, victorious yet bloodied. The debris-strewn passageway bore witness to the intensity of the conflict, a testament to the trials that lay ahead in this dungeon-turned battlefield. The thrill of victory rose up in my chest, and I gave a mighty roar, challenging my foes to come and get some!

Even as the sound of my roar faded, I blinked in surprise.

Where the hell had that come from?

I wasn't really the type to get battle fever, much less do something stupid like calling out to let my enemies know I was coming.

What the fuck?!?

CHAPTER 7
LICKING MY WOUNDS

EXAMINING my feelings and trying to figure it out, I could only guess that the Draconic Bloodline was more than just a matter of Skills and Abilities. I knew Bloodline Classes were transformative in that the person was literally given the race modifier as part of the Class. I hadn't realized that it affected my personality, though. I would have to watch that. It was one thing to be proud that I had gotten a limited Class; it was another to be 'proud' like a real dragon, in the true and stupidly negative sense of the word.

Once the bodies disappeared, I collected four more copper monster core coins and added them to my jacket pocket, zipping it closed afterward so they couldn't fall out and get lost. I would really need to get a spatial storage pouch or ring once the Shop opens in a month. Carrying things around manually kinda sucked. I had a pouch in my old life that could fit about as much as you could put into the bed of a full-size truck. I inherited it about three years after Initialization Day when one of my team members died at the hands of a swamp troll somewhere in Louisiana. It might seem morbid to take their things, but humanity didn't waste anything after civilization collapsed. I would have wanted my things divided up among my party members if I had ever died.

I felt my blood heat as I remembered my last party, who had betrayed me and caused my death due to their greed. They had split all my things before I died. I didn't know how this time travel worked, but I hoped that if they were still running around somewhere in an alternate timeline, they would die an embarrassing and ignoble death and then burn in hell afterward.

I hope jackalopes bugger them first, though!

I shook myself out of my angry, wishful reverie and decided it would be good to try and be a bit stealthier going forward. I didn't have a Skill for it, but I could always try and tiptoe quietly toward the next encounter and get the drop on the next Goblins instead of the other way around.

Who knows, maybe someday a Stealth Skill would drop from a dungeon boss or something. Given the Class description for the Draconic Spellsword, I didn't think I'd be getting any Class Skills for sneaking around, especially after that roar earlier. It seemed like the Draconic Spellsword was a 'stomp around and swing your dick at whatever gets in your way' kind of Class. Not really my preferred method, but who knows. So far, I have been doing pretty well in the killing department. Maybe not having to avoid difficult fights might change my attitude.

I quickly checked my experience before I moved on. That had been four kills, and being level-one monsters, they should have been worth a total of 400 XP. Sure enough, I had leveled up to Level 3 after that fight. The whole roaring a challenge at the world thing had distracted me from the 'ding.'

The message was right there in the corner of my vision:

Level up!

A couple of minutes passed as I allocated the stat points and felt the rush of my body increasing all of my stats. It wasn't as big of a rush as when I had gotten the Class, but it was noticeable, especially since I was distributing the points evenly across all attributes. I felt stronger and like I could go longer without resting. My mind felt clearer, and my senses were sharper. Not that all attributes were as linear as Strength. Points in Mind didn't double or triple your intelligence and make you a walking supercomputer. Still, it did make you able to understand difficult things easier and made your mental reactions quicker. Your processing speed was enhanced not just for doing things like calculations, but you could also react quicker to an attack.

Of course, that went hand in hand with Agility and is one of the reasons I like to keep all my stats balanced. Agility allowed your physical reactions to be quicker and more precise, which was super important when you needed your body to respond as fast as your mind in combat.

Magic Aptitude was the weird one. I had never had that as a Knight in my previous life. It seemed to give me a feeling of potency in a mystical sort of way. Like my Spells and Draconic Abilities would be marginally stronger.

Liam Bell
Draconic Spellsword: Level 3
Experience: 0/800
Health: 380 Mana: 340

Unfortunately, the experience needed doubled every level for the first seven levels, then tapered off to a more moderate increase after that. I wasn't sure what the formula for the increase was, but I was glad it didn't keep doubling, or I'd never hit the level cap. I needed four Goblins to go from Level 2 to Level 3, and now I would need eight Goblins to hit Level 4.

Wincing at the pain in my side, I pulled out a polished piece of metal that I had purchased as a mirror and used it to examine my wound. It was still bleeding but was slowing down already. My Endurance stat was 18 now, and that was more than double what most people had. It wouldn't let me regenerate wounds, though; just heal quicker and resist infections better. Still, I'd need to sew that up before I moved on and apply some medicine to ensure that the nasty-looking dagger didn't cause an infection. I had included some waxed natural thread in my first aid kit, so I pulled it out, as well as the glass bottle that held the natural antiseptic solution. Normally, I wasn't a fan of homeopathic or 'natural' medicines, but when the System was busy destroying the really effective stuff, I would make do with the only thing available.

That month-long wait for the Shop to open might just drive me nuts. I wanted to buy healing potions now!

I retreated a little way back down the passageway, then stripped off my jacket and shirt to access the wound better. That also meant removing my bracers and pauldrons. It was a damned annoying process that wasted a lot of time.

Once I had full access, I poured a small amount of alcohol into the wound and suppressed the scream that wanted to come out. Then, I applied the antiseptic solution, and finally, I used the needle and thread to crudely sew my skin back together. Afterward, I applied bandages before putting everything away and then dressing in my armor again.

It was over an hour later when I was finally done and ready to get back to killing monsters. I was so pissed that I had gotten wounded from that damned sneak attack. I had put myself through all that, treating a wound that never should have happened. I was going to absolutely wreck the next enemies I found.

It turned out the curving passage made a long circle around and down and ended up leading to the lower floor of the launch control facility after all.

As I descended into the lower floor of the missile silo's launch control area, I noticed that a malevolent transformation had taken place. The sterile and controlled environment had been warped by dark magic, now resembling a nightmarish monster lair. The air was thick with an unnatural chill, and a foreboding darkness pervaded the chamber.

Sinister symbols adorned the walls, glowing faintly with a malevolent light that cast unsettling shadows.

At the center of the chamber lay a corrupted focal point—a fire pulsing with a sickly glow. This was the epicenter of the dark magic that had perverted the level of the control facility's purpose. It seemed to be the source of the transformation: a cursed nexus of power.

I was afraid it was the boss room already, with all the ominous decorations, but it looked like it wasn't, judging by the monsters present.

Five grotesque Goblins, visibly corrupted by the dark energies, awaited my arrival. Their pale skin had turned sickly shades of purple and black, and their features had become twisted and deformed. Their eyes glowed with a sinister, malevolent light, revealing an insatiable hunger for combat.

The Goblins were armed with jagged, wicked weapons crafted from the remains of the silo's machinery.

Except that was bullshit! I knew no machinery had been left down here! I had visited it after everything had been salvaged and cleaned out by my father's company.

Fucking show-off AI!

That meant this had to be the System being theatrical and playing up the nature of the location as part of the atmosphere. That also begged the question of whether these Goblins were actually some kind of Elites, or if they too were just altered to reflect the theme of the dungeon...

I didn't get to answer that question.

They snarled and hissed, their anticipation of the impending battle palpable. They moved with an unsettling coordination, as if driven by a singular malevolent purpose.

Even though I had been trying to stealth my way down and catch them by surprise, I guess my stupid roar of defiance and challenge earlier had done its damned job, and they were indeed alert and feeling challenged. There was no backing out now. If I turned and ran, they would gain an advantage. I would have to stand my ground and hope my new Class Abilities could get me through this!

If I didn't need my left hand free to cast Spells, I would be wishing I had a shield right about now. As a Knight and a Warrior before that, I had often used one, and five against one odds was reminding me that I was only mortal, even if I did have this nifty new Class. I would just have to use my new Skills to compensate for my lack of defense.

I didn't have any more time to worry. The Goblins lunged, their frenzied attack catching me off guard. My instincts kicked in, even if I no longer had the muscle memory of my former Classes. I managed to deflect their initial blows with desperate blocks and parries of my sword. Thankfully, there was plenty of room in the silo-turned dungeon, and I was able to use my mobility and longer legs to dance out of reach at times when I wasn't able to keep up with their attacks, but their sheer ferocity took me aback.

I needed a moment to regain my footing. That's when I summoned my Draconic Fear Ability. The ghostly visage of a dragon materialized above me, causing a brief hesitation in their onslaught.

They were frozen with fear, but only for a second. That told me they had to be below my level. Otherwise, they wouldn't have stopped. Good to know, but not terribly helpful when the odds were five-to-one.

Still, I wasn't going to let the chance go to waste! Seizing the opportunity, I summoned an Acid Bolt, unleashing it upon one of the Goblins. The corrosive magic burned through its armor, causing it to shriek in pain before collapsing in a dramatic death pose.

Maybe it was the fact that I was much more experienced now than I had been the first time around or the fact that I was just used to facing life-and-death battles like this, but it seemed to me that the System was laying it on thick with the whole dramatic atmosphere. I could swear that the Goblin I had just hit with the acid had just put on an Oscar-winning death performance. Not that it wasn't really dead. The hole in its chest assured me it was. Still, the way it had clutched at its chest and keeled over backward... if I didn't have four more of its kind trying very hard to kill me, I'd pause to admire what I had just witnessed.

Even so, the others didn't give me the opportunity and quickly regrouped, their fury undeterred. If anything, the fright I had given them and the fate of their acid-blasted, dramatically-dead fellows made them even fiercer.

I focused on my blade, allowing my training to guide me through the storm of their attacks. The Goblins were relentless, their strikes unpredictable and vicious. I fought with all my might, yet the odds seemed stacked against me. One Goblin managed to land a deep gash on my arm just above the bracer, the searing pain a reminder of the battle's intensity and a warning to take this seriously and not let my imagination get me killed.

I was equal parts scared and furious. Scared because I hated being outnumbered and in danger, but angry because I couldn't afford to get wounded. Without healing potions or magic, every little injury had the potential to slow down my leveling, and that meant more people dying before I could reach Ascension and make the System provide safe zones. I needed to even the odds!

Summoning my Draconic Strength, I channeled a Power Strike, feeling the Skill take over, causing me to make the perfect attack in that moment. My blade pulsed with acidic power as I drove it into a Goblin with a thrust to its gut, the corrosive energy causing its wound to fester. It wasn't dead, but it was effectively out of the fight. It would take it a couple of minutes to die.

I used that to my advantage and dodged around the wounded one to put it between me and its companions. It gave me another few seconds to breathe and evaluate the situation before the remaining Goblins closed in, their hunger for victory undiminished.

The fight wore on with repeated exchanges. I did my best to use the creepy campfire and the dying Goblin as obstacles to keep them from attacking all at once. Unfortunately, fatigue threatened to slow me down. The Goblins were relentless, their attacks constantly wearing at my defenses. I pushed through, using every ounce of skill and strength to keep myself standing. Long fights might not have been so difficult before my restart, but even with the Draconic Spellsword boost to my stats, facing multiple opponents taxed me to my limit.

Another Goblin fell to my blade when it slipped in the dying one's blood. With Power Strike on cooldown, picking them off with regular attacks when the chance came was all I could do. Still, I knew I couldn't let up. That brought the odds down to a mere two-on-one, which would have been fine if I were fresh, but I was getting pretty winded at this point. If I had the space and they weren't pressing me so hard with up-close attacks, I would just blast them with acid bolts until I killed them all, but they weren't giving me the chance.

After another minute of fighting, I got the opening I had been looking for. I put the fire between us again, summoned the Mana, and unleashed another Acid Bolt. Its impact took down another Goblin, leaving only one. The battle had been fierce, but I couldn't afford to let my guard down. With as winded and tired as I was, even one Goblin could get lucky and kill me. The remaining Goblin did its best to prove that thought correct. Though battered, it continued its assault, desperation fueling its attacks.

With determination burning in my eyes, I engaged it. Despite my weariness, my every strike was precise and calculated. The acidic residue on my blade intensified its injuries, but it fought on. The Goblin put up a valiant struggle, but in the end, my stamina was greater, and I struck the final blows.

As the last Goblin fell, the chamber echoed with the silence of victory. I stood amidst the fallen foes, bruised and battered but triumphant. The dungeon had tested me and pushed me to my limits, but I was victorious.

I was not, however, stupid. I pushed down the desire to bellow out my triumph, challenging all to 'come get some.'

Screw that! I need some rest before doing that again!

Unfortunately, I could hear the sounds of Goblins coming from the exit tunnel to the silo.

CHAPTER 8
LEVEL 4

FIVE AGAINST ONE had been bad odds. If I had my preferences, I wouldn't fight more than three at a time, and even then, I'd prefer to do it as a sneak attack.

I wanted to curse the System for making a basic Goblin dungeon so hard, but the truth was it was my own fault. That damned roar after the first big fight had alerted the Goblins below, so instead of getting to take my time and sneak up on the groups one by one and only after I was ready, now I'm facing fully prepared groups. Hell, the one in the previous tunnel had been laying an ambush.

Fuckers!

At least I was able to dress my wound after the ambush fight. It doesn't look like I'll get that chance this time.

I quickly pulled a cloth rag from my bag and wrapped it around my arm as best I could, awkwardly using my teeth to help pull the knot tight. That was about all the time I had before the next group came stomping out of the dark passageway on the opposite wall from the one I entered through.

The fight against five had exhausted me. I might be good on Mana and health, but I was still panting and wanting to just sit down and rest. Hell, my power strike wasn't even off of cooldown yet. That was the most annoying thing about these Skills. They might be powerful enough to outright kill a like-level opponent with an accurate hit, but I couldn't just spam them over and over. Power Strike had a one-minute cooldown, and even my single ranged Spell, Acid Bolt, had a twenty-second cooldown. Otherwise, I'd just face the groups and mow them down like I was firing a machine gun on full-auto. Alas, that was not to be.

Well, perhaps once I had more Spells... I could hope!

I pushed that thought to the side. I was out of time; four more Goblins had emerged from the passage and were looking at me like a side of meat. One of them was literally drooling at the sight of the blood-soaked bandage on my arm. If they could speak English, I'm sure that one would have quipped something about meat being back on the menu.

I still have vague memories of that movie even after all these years.

Fucking AI. It should have preserved human culture!

Time was up... I raised my blade, my grip shaky but determined. The Goblins charged, their feral cries echoing through the chamber. I focused, trying to preserve what energy I could. My Power Strike Ability was still on cooldown, the seconds ticking by with agonizing slowness. I needed that power, but it wasn't ready yet.

One of the Goblins lunged at me, and I barely managed to sidestep its attack, feeling a graze against my ribs. The pain flared, and I gritted my teeth, the fatigue pulling at me. I needed to be cautious, to use my Skills strategically. I had the instincts and experience from years of adventuring, but this body did not have the reflexes built into muscle memory yet.

I couldn't afford to keep getting hurt this way! I hoped that leveling up would give me enough of a power advantage over them that I would be able to complete this dungeon. Sadly, I had a feeling I wouldn't be that lucky.

Summoning my inner strength, I hurled an Acid Bolt at the closest Goblin, buying myself a brief respite. The sizzling sound as the bolt hit its mark filled the chamber, but I knew I had to keep moving. My Skills were my lifeline, and their cooldown timers were a constant reminder of my limitations. Still, that was one down!

Another Goblin lunged, and this time, I parried its blow, feeling the impact jolt through my tired arms. The cooldown timer for Power Strike inched closer to completion. I danced around the chamber, avoiding their attacks, trying to find an opening. Using their numbers to my advantage, I tried to maneuver such that I caused them to get in each other's way. So far, it was working, but it was coming at a heavy cost of exhaustion since I hadn't had time to rest up after the last fight.

Dancing might be an overly generous description of what I was managing at this point, I thought. *Still, at least I am alive!*

As the timer for Power Strike neared its end, I lunged at a Goblin, activating the Skill just in time. The blade glowed with corrosive energy as it struck, injuring the creature and taking it out of the fight. It wasn't dead, but the pain from the acid in its wound was enough to incapacitate it. Two down, two to go!

Hearing its screams might have turned my stomach and made me hesitate in my first life. Even knowing it was a System-generated creature and not a living being that was born and had an independent life... scenes like this had torn me up for a while. Even monsters suffering made the original me cringe and want to avoid the fight.

That was then.

Now, however, I had seen too many good people die and had gone through far too much to have sympathy for the likes of these fake beings. They literally only existed to fight humans and make us stronger. At least, that is what the System told us. I wouldn't have believed it if it hadn't been for my conversation with the AI before getting sent back in time. Otherwise, I would have believed they were meant to exterminate us.

Getting my thoughts back into the game, I focused on staying alive. I was still outnumbered two-to-one, and exhaustion weighed me down. I didn't want to become one of their victims.

One of the two managed to get a solid hit, and pain flared through my leg. I staggered, trying to keep my focus. Thankfully, it was not a slash, just a bruising smash to my shin. It had been going for my kneecap with its club but missed. Despite the pain and anger, I was relieved. If that hit had landed accurately, I wouldn't be walking. I growled in fury, unintentionally activating my Dragon Fear Ability, causing the Goblins to freeze for two seconds.

Even though I hadn't meant to do it, the timing of that Intimidation Skill was perfect. My Acid Bolt had just come off cooldown and was ready again. I hurled the bolt of the corrosive magic at the little bastard who had just bruised my shinbone. Three down!

"Eat acid, bitch!"

I was angry but running on fumes.

Still, seeing the stunned Goblin get smashed backward by the bolt and then die screaming really warmed my heart as I tried to put weight on my smashed leg.

The last Goblin shook off the fear effect and attacked in a frenzy. With a burst of desperation and a wince of intense pain, I dodged and parried, my muscles screaming in protest. The cooldown timer for Power Strike finally reset again, and I unleashed it on the remaining Goblin. My blade cut sideways through the air. The slash was empowered with acidic energy and caught it right through the neck. The last Goblin fell with its head rolling, separated from its body.

Four and done!

As the chamber once again fell silent, I stood amidst the fallen foes, barely able to keep myself upright. The cooldown timers had been my harshest adversary in this battle, pushing me to the brink of my abilities. I knew I had to press on, but the road ahead seemed even more daunting right now. The transformed silo was a true crucible, testing my mettle with each step.

Even as I leaned on my sword, panting and bleeding inside my armor from that slash across the ribs, I felt the rush of experience and heard the beautiful 'DING' of the level-up notice.

Level Up!

I could bandage my new wound later; leveling up and assigning my new stat points would help with the healing process. It wouldn't instantly heal me or anything special, but having one more point in Endurance never hurt. The boost to my healing rate might only be a tiny fraction more than it was now, but I didn't care.

I assigned the points and closed my eyes as I felt the rush of the increasing stats.

Liam Bell: (Current)

Draconic Spellsword - Level 4

Experience: 100/1600

Attributes:

Endurance: 20
Strength: 20
Agility: 20
Mind: 21
Will: 20
Magical Aptitude: 15
Luck: 1

Health: 290/400
Mana: 230/360

Abilities:
Dark Vision
Dragon Fear

Active Skills:
Acid Bolt
Draconic Strike

Passive Skills: None

It was good stuff. I loved seeing those stats increase, especially since I was previously used to this happening only once every few months. Moreover, I was still finding it hard to get used to receiving 6 stat points per level when my previous rare Knight Class had only gotten three per level. Being able to assign my stat points automatically since I didn't have to pick and choose which to increase was very handy indeed.

Having an epic Class was fucking amazing!

I didn't even bother to gather the loot when the bodies disappeared. Instead, I just sank to the ground and leaned up against a log.

Where a fallen tree had come from in the middle of a missile silo-turned dungeon, I did not know, but it didn't matter. I had long ago stopped being shocked by the strange inconsistencies of the System's creations. The AI seemed to care more about atmosphere than accuracy.

After I had rested for a minute and caught my breath, I started the long and annoying process of treating my wounds. The thing that really irked me the most about this was not the pain from cleaning and stitching cuts over my ribs and arm but how long it took to remove all my gear and then get dressed again afterward. That, and the fact that I had let myself get cut in the first place.

Going from being a level 57 Knight to fighting Goblins in a beginner dungeon frustrated me. On the one hand, these first-level Goblins wouldn't have been able to scratch me as a Knight, not even if I stood still and let them try. On the other hand, I knew I should be incredibly grateful for this new Class. In my first life, I never would have dreamed of soloing a dungeon, much less surviving against such overwhelming numbers. Hell, I would have run away in fear just seeing a group that outnumbered me unless I was significantly higher level.

One thing was sure, and the lesson had been driven home again and again... life was cheap after the apocalypse. You could die at any moment. I had seen friends and companions walking on what should have been a perfectly safe trail get mauled to death by a mutated beast lying in wait. Others had died of a stupid infection that would have been child's play to cure before the System destroyed all our medicines.

Shit, I was almost gored to death by a fucking jackalope in the first battle of my old life!

With a big sigh, I got up and adjusted my armor and my attitude before going to collect the coins. These made a total of 16 of the copper coin monster cores. It wasn't much yet, but if I kept killing monsters at this pace, I'd have quite a pile by the time the Shop opened in a month. Between them and the trade goods I stockpiled, I ought to have enough to get some decent gear. The copper coins were closer to the size of a US fifty-cent piece than a US penny, but they still didn't take up too much space. I shoved the new coins into my pocket with the previous ones and zipped it closed to reassure myself that it was all good. I was sure they would be safe enough in there. It would take a lot more of these to begin to weigh me down. By then, I hoped to have some kind of storage device.

After that last battle and how exhausting it was, I felt as if I should need a long rest and to camp, but it wasn't even close to nighttime. Hell, I'd only been in this dungeon for maybe three hours so far, if that. I looked around the area and sighed.

Might as well move forward.

I had caught my breath and rested enough while treating my wounds. There wasn't any real reason not to press forward. Besides, I was incredibly excited by the fact that I had already hit Level 4. We couldn't be more than four hours into the apocalypse, and I'd averaged a level an hour.

I knew that pace wouldn't continue. Mathematically, these first levels were easy to get, but the experience needed doubled until Level 7. After that, the increase tapered off to a more reasonable amount per level. I had only needed 800 for Level 4, but now I needed 1600 for Level 5. Even if I found higher-level enemies that would give more experience, I couldn't keep going this fast.

The higher the level of the monsters, the harder they were to kill and the more dangerous they were to me. I was already getting cut up by these damned Level 1 Goblins. If I continued to have to fight groups every time, I wouldn't survive. I needed to slow down and try to pull enemies one or two at a time if possible.

That was especially true since I would be facing the Silo part of the dungeon next. My guess was that it would be the main part of the Goblins' lair. I just didn't know what form it would take or how it would be structured. Would it be one large chamber or multiple floors?

About time I found out!

CHAPTER 9

SILO

IF I REMEMBER CORRECTLY, each level of the silo had about 2,000 sqft of total space. However, it had been mostly empty since the center had been a big hole going down seven stories to where the base of the launch pad had been. My dad's team had stripped out all of the remaining equipment and sent it to the scrappers for recycling, but even after they were done, there had been floors coming out from the concrete walls supported by massive steel girders, and somewhere around each floor, there had been a set of stairs going down.

At least, that was what my memory was telling me. It had been over thirty years since I had seen the place, but it was not something easily forgotten. Everything had been bare concrete and steel painted battleship grey to protect it from rusting. Which hadn't worked, even back then. There had been a fair amount of rust in places.

As a boy, I had been equal parts amazed and depressed. On the one hand, playing down there had been an incredible adventure for someone that age. However, it had an air of abandonment and decay that was almost oppressive.

And that was before monsters were real! I thought.

Looking around at the bottom floor of the launch control facility that had been changed so thoroughly, I couldn't imagine what would be waiting for me down that corridor, but it was time I found out.

I stepped carefully and quietly as I moved into the passage where the four most recent Goblins had emerged. I hoped the fact that they had come out of there meant no guards would be left in the tunnel.

To my happy surprise, that turned out to be the case, and I was able to stealthily make my way toward the silo.

Around the corner, there was a spacious but dimly lit chamber with a high ceiling. The floor was made of rough stone, and the walls were lined with crude wooden supports. On this level, I spotted ten regular Level 1 Goblins scattered about, engaged in various tasks. Two larger figures, clearly Elite Goblins, stood guard near the entrance, their eyes alert and weapons at the ready.

Fortunately, they weren't too alert and hadn't made any indication that they noticed me. I was lucky that the last twenty feet or so of the tunnel made a fairly sharp turn to the right, giving me the chance to get close enough to see them and what was past them without having to expose my position.

It was a scene of organized chaos, with Goblins moving about, tending to what seemed to be a range of supplies and equipment.

Thinking back to my first life, I'm pretty sure that the Elite Goblins are Level 3 and worth 300 XP. Experience goes up 100 XP per level for monsters, which makes calculating how much XP I would get quite easy. The good news is that if the numbers I can see through the large cave opening are accurate, I should level up just from clearing this floor. Of course, that assumes I could manage it.

The System had clearly intended this for a group of adventurers, typically at least five members strong. Ideally, there would be someone to work as a tank, a couple of damage dealers, a ranged caster, and a healer. Unfortunately, thanks to the fuckery that the System pulled during Initialization, magic Classes were scarce among humans. Other races had them in suitable proportions, but not us. In my past life, this dungeon would have been run with five to seven people, but they would have all been non-magic Classes, with maybe a couple of ranged damage dealers using bows or crossbows. In the early days, it might have even included crafting Classes trying to use spears or ranged weapons. In other words, it had been a clusterfuck, and the ability to do this solo and not have to worry about others was blowing my mind.

My first order of business was to try and lure those two Elite guards out into the passageway, out of sight, and hopefully earshot, of the other Goblins. If I could get them to come investigate one or two at a time, I had a good chance of success.

Thinking of ways to make them walk down the dimly lit tunnel, I came up with what I hoped was a good idea. Sadly, it would cost me several pieces of jerky, but if it worked, it would be worth it. I placed three pieces of the tasty meat along the passage. One was just around the corner, right in the middle of the floor, where they were sure to see it. Then another about fifteen feet down the tunnel and another twenty feet further along. If they followed the food trail, that should lead them far enough to hopefully fight them without alerting the other Goblins in the big chamber.

The part that worried me was that if both came down the tunnel together, I would have to make the fight quick enough not to draw attention. Goblins were constantly scuffling with each other over stupid stuff, so a little noise wouldn't kick the ant nest; I just needed to keep it quick and not let them yell if possible.

Thankfully, all of my Skills were off cooldown, so a one-two punch of Skills might be enough to take them both.

I also piled a bunch of debris at the side of the tunnel to hide behind near the last piece of food. With any luck, they would be too focused on the tasty treats to wonder where the pile came from. Goblins weren't terribly smart, but they were cunning in their own way, and that included ambushes and sneaking around. I just hoped they would be too distracted to think about such things.

When I was as hidden as I could make myself, I picked up a stone and hurled it at the wall of the tunnel down near the first piece of jerky. It made a loud clattering noise as it hit and then fell to the floor.

I heard a startled grunt, but if they spoke to one another, it was too quiet for me to hear from this distance. A few seconds later, the two Goblins came walking around the corner, their ugly serrated swords drawn and ready. They stopped and looked down the tunnel curiously but didn't see anything out of the ordinary. One of them shrugged and relaxed and started to turn back until its partner spotted the bait and bent to reach for it.

The observant one picked up the dried meat, brought it to its nose, and gave it a sniff, then stuffed it into its mouth and started chewing with all the table manners of a pig that just found a truffle.

Goblin Two glared at it and yelled, "What you find? You give some!"

Goblin One said nothing and just took a step away from its companion and held up its sword but did not stop chewing. From the expression on its face, it must have enjoyed the peppered-mesquite flavor.

One of the things I had stocked up on while shopping was several pounds of some of my favorite flavors of jerky from Buc-ee's. It was good stuff, and it would store well enough to last me until the System Shop opened in a month. It wouldn't be terribly healthy, but between that and other dried foods, I wouldn't starve. Thankfully, the Shop had plenty of food options, and they were relatively cheap so long as you were able to hunt and earn the coins to pay for them.

I was still furious at the AI because I was pretty sure it was a deliberate choice not to open the Shop before the end of the first month. I couldn't even imagine the worldwide death toll from the people who couldn't find safe water to drink this first month.

Meanwhile, the two Goblins nearly came to blows over the one being greedy and not sharing its prize. However, they spotted the second piece of jerky before that happened. They quickly rushed forward, and Goblin Two snatched up this piece and shoved it in its mouth with a smug, satisfied expression on its malformed face.

"Ha! I got now! It good!" it was barely intelligible with its mouth stuffed with the food, and spittle flew into the other's face.

Goblin Two grimaced and looked angry despite having just finished its own treat. "Me next." It made a rude and aggressive gesture with its sword before turning to look further down the hallway toward where I hid. Its greedy little black eyes lit up when it spotted the next piece of bait.

"Mine!" It rushed forward and almost dove onto the last thing it would ever eat. Goblin One was right behind it. Even though its mouth was still full and chewing noisily, it looked as if it was ready to fight over the smoked, peppery treat.

I almost waited to see if it would stab its companion in the back, but I decided to act before either of them had a chance to notice me. I was less than ten feet from them at that point.

However, before I could act, Goblin One had grabbed the arm of Goblin Two and yanked it backward, trying to prevent the other from stuffing the meat into its mouth. "No, give half!"

I was dumbfounded. They really were going to fight over the jerky! Even so, I saw the perfect opportunity. They were entirely focused on one another, trying to grapple the other's arms; one to get the food to its mouth and the other to prevent that. Without hesitation, I lunged forward and triggered Power Strike, sweeping my blade across both Goblins. One lost an arm and its sword with it. The other was slashed across the throat, ending its life instantly.

Goblin One, the survivor, raised its green-coated stump of an arm, looking at it in shock, not quite believing what had just happened.

They were big for Goblins and definitely looked tougher than their smaller counterparts. They had rough leather armor that looked dirty and disgusting but still functional. It just hadn't done them any good against a Spellsword's power attack. My blade had cleaved right through its right bracer and barely slowed down. I wasn't done, however. I didn't want the survivor to alert the others with pained screams, so I raised my left hand and fired an Acid Bolt at point-blank range right into its face!

I almost pitied it. It was opening its mouth to scream when the bolt smashed into it and blasted it off its feet. It was dead before it hit the ground.

I felt the rush of experience hit me with their two deaths and nodded in satisfaction. That gambit had worked far better than I could have hoped. They had only been away from their posts for a couple of minutes, and they had died without raising an alarm or even the sounds of battle to give me away. Better yet, I had just killed two Elite Goblins without getting so much as a scratch! This was definitely the way to do it!

After just a moment, the bodies dissolved into motes of dust the way bodies always did in the System, and in their place were a total of six copper coins, confirming my guess that they were Level 3 monsters. I quickly added them to my other coins. I now had 22 in total.

One other thing dropped. The uneaten piece of jerky.

I was sure there was an evil gleam in my eyes as I contemplated what to do next. If the trick had worked so well on the Elites, the regular Goblins would surely fall for it as well. I just hoped I could get them one or two at a time and not pull a horde all at once.

As I waited for my cooldown timers to run out, I crept forward and approached the cavern. No alarm had sounded, and there weren't any Goblins paying attention to the tunnel or the fact that their guards were missing. I sighed and decided to sacrifice one more piece of jerky. I tossed the remaining piece out into the cavern just beyond where the tunnel ended. That piece had been tainted by the Goblin's filthy hands.

No way I'd eat it after a Goblin had touched it!

I ripped off a small piece from a larger hunk, not wanting to lose any more food than I could help. I dropped the second piece just at the point where the passageway turned the corner and allowed me to remain out of sight.

I actually had a fairly long wait before a trio of Goblins came looking for their guards. They didn't seem alarmed by their absence, just annoyed.

Then they spotted the meat and started a fight right then to see who would get the prize. It wasn't deadly combat meant to kill, just a fight for dominance. They were all bloody by the time the largest of the three small monsters won. It snatched up the treat and looked like a rooster, all puffed up in its victory.

Its smug look vanished, however, when one of the losers spotted the piece in the tunnel and exclaimed, "More! There! Mine!"

It rushed forward, but the other two were right on its heels. The smallest Goblin took a diving grab for it that would have made a professional baseball player proud. It came up with the jerky clenched in its small fist. "Ha! Mine!"

The third one looked very disappointed but then glanced nervously at the gloomy tunnel. "More?"

It looked equal parts afraid and hopeful at the same time. It inched forward toward the corner, and the other two followed right behind, eager to find more of the peppery dried meat. I didn't know how bad their diet must be for jerky to be such a delicacy, but I wasn't above using it to exterminate them.

I waited for them to turn the corner, and as soon as they were out of sight of the cavern, I lunged forward, jabbing my sword through the lead Goblin's throat. It was the closest and would see me first, so I wanted to end it immediately. Its attempt at a cry of shock and warning gurgled in its throat as it coughed up blood. I immediately yanked my sword free, ready to strike again.

The other two had been looking at the floor and took a second to notice what happened to their companion. They looked up in confusion, which turned to fear and anger as they saw the blood spraying from the lead Goblin's neck. By then, I was already casting Acid Bolt at the one in the rear. I wanted to ensure it didn't flee back into the cave to give warning. I aimed for center mass rather than trying for a headshot this time. The last thing I wanted to do in this situation was miss!

It didn't. The bolt hit with enough force to launch it backward into the passage wall, knocking the air from its lungs and ensuring it would not cry out. Two down!

Looking from its companions to me, the final Goblin turned to run and let loose a loud shriek. I cursed and triggered Power Strike, slashing downward with my blade using all the force I could muster along with the enhanced Strength provided by the Skill.

Its warning cry cut off instantly as it was nearly bisected. It had only been a split second, but that had been a cry of panic. Without missing a beat, I rushed around the corner and grabbed its leg, dragging it back into the tunnel, hoping that I had been quick enough. There were still at least seven more Goblins in the cavern, and I absolutely did not want to face them all at the same time!

I might be leveling up and getting stronger, but seven was still more than I wanted to face at once!

I winced, seeing the very obvious bloodstain leading from the mouth of the tunnel back around the corner where I stood. There was nothing I could do about that, and I waited in silence, my heart pounding, hoping there wouldn't be a rush of Goblins. I still had 45 seconds before the cooldown on my Power Strike would be up again.

When a minute had passed, the bodies began to disappear. Unfortunately, the blood stains did not.

Fucking AI.

Sighing, I gathered up the three coins, adding them to my pocket. It didn't look like there would be a mad rush of the ugly little bastards charging me, but my nice jerky fishing technique was over. There was no way they would be dumb enough to follow a food trail right past a big blood smear into a dark tunnel. Right?

I considered my options for a minute, then decided I had nothing to lose. If it didn't work, I'd have to face them anyway. It would just mean charging out into the open and starting a straight fight with however many showed up. I was hoping for another small group. I knew I could take out five at once, but there were more than that in the cavern, so if they came at me together, I might have to "strategically advance to the rear," as my dad used to say. In other words, I'd have to run away and try to take them out one at a time as my Skills came off cooldown.

I threw the two small pieces of jerky back to where they had been. One had been partially chewed by the Goblin who had picked it up, but it was intact enough that I didn't think it would matter. Then I settled in to wait.

The wait was shorter than I expected, and better yet, it was a pair of Goblins this time. To my amusement and great surprise, they practically ignored the suspicious bloodstain. One of the two gave it a concerned look, but as soon as it saw the meaty treat, it forgot all about the blood. It held up the jerky in triumph and squealed in delight. Then it looked at the other Goblin and got nervous. It jammed half the jerky into its mouth full of sharp teeth, and tore it in half like a vulture tearing flesh from roadkill.

The other Goblin looked angry and snatched at the half piece clutched in the chewing one's hands. There was a short struggle that involved some vicious claws and punches to some uncomfortable places, but in the end, the one who hadn't had a piece won. It wiped blood from its cheek with a dirty rag of a sleeve as it stuffed the meat into its maw.

For a long moment, I didn't think they would notice the second piece of bait back near the bend in the tunnel where I stood hiding. They seemed content to savor the flavorful treat, but eventually, curiosity got the better of them, and they started looking for more.

They rushed to the second piece, the first Goblin almost slipping in the still-fresh blood.

I just shook my head at the insanity of these little monsters. I didn't give them time to eat the second piece of bait, however. As soon as they were both fumbling for the jerky, trying to claw it away from the other, I jumped forward and activated Power Strike, cleaving both of them across their backs.

The blow ended any fight left in the pair; the acid from the strike ate into their bodies, causing excruciating pain. Unfortunately, it did not kill them outright. Both shrieked bloody murder as they fell before I could deliver follow-up attacks. The noise only lasted a few seconds, but it was enough to alert the rest.

I didn't even have time to duck back around the corner before the rest of the Goblins looked up in my direction.

Silencing them with merciful efficiency, I knew I was screwed. Their five remaining companions erupted in furious, guttural cries. Their eyes smoldered with anger, and they gripped their weapons with white-knuckled intensity.

One of them—a particularly ferocious Goblin—dashed forward, charging recklessly with a wild, guttural snarl. It brandished a crude but menacing blade as it advanced. Another Goblin, equally incensed, followed its lead and rushed toward me, wielding an equally menacing spiked club.

Meanwhile, the other two Goblins seized the opportunity to crouch behind some of the cavern's natural rock formations, using them for cover while they flung crude projectiles in my direction. The remaining Goblin, positioned slightly farther away, calculated its moves, ready to join the fray and ambush me when the time was right.

In the dark, shadowy entrance tunnel, I took cover behind the bend, assessing the situation. The Goblins, all spread around the cavern, remained at least thirty feet away from my concealed location. The atmosphere in the cave was charged with tension, and I knew that I had to be vigilant, ready to respond decisively to the aggressive turn of events while leveraging the advantage of my position.

Getting behind the tunnel wall would prevent me from getting hit by the improvised weapons that the two hiding Goblins threw. There were stones, pieces of wood, and even their own excrement flying after me, but they weren't a threat now that I was behind cover.

Their own companions, on the other hand, were not so lucky. Before they could even make it to me, one had been struck in the back by a flying dagger, which impaled itself in its shoulder blade. It squealed in pain and fury but did not stop in its charge toward me, determined to kill me no matter the cost.

It was the lucky one, in my opinion. The other one got a handful of intensely foul-smelling Goblin poo right to the back of its neck. It hit with a squelching sound that almost made me throw up when combined with the smell.

Note to self: Do not get hit by that!

The situation was grim, but I was hopeful. I only had to face the two Goblins in front of me, at least until the others realized they were only hurting their companions and decided to charge me. Still, what worried me the most was the smart one in the back. I hoped it would not run away and warn the other Goblins on the levels below. If it did, the dungeon would get significantly harder going forward. I needed to prevent that, and I had a strategy, but it meant saving my Acid Bolt and finishing these aggressive ones first.

I needed to kill the ones charging me using only my basic fighting skills and not relying on Class Abilities. I would need my Class Abilities for the second half of the battle.

With that determination made, I began the fight. I would like to say it was a clean battle with clear attacks and defensive moves, but fighting Goblins was anything but clean. They didn't have real battle tactics, nor did they have trained moves. They were pure aggression with no defined form or style. It was all slash, claw, stab, bite, and repeat. That was what made it so hard to defend and keep myself from getting hurt.

All I could really do to defend myself was be better at aggression than them. I relied on big slashes that made them jump back or thrusts that would impale them if they failed to dodge out of the way.

So that was what I did. I went on a relentless attack that actually drove them backward and kept them just in the opening of the tunnel. Luckily, I had a little help from their friends, who had not yet clued into the fact that they couldn't hit me with their improvised projectiles so long as I stayed just around the corner. I did get hit with a few bounced rocks, but they had lost enough momentum by then not to do any real damage.

It took the better part of a minute of fighting before I eliminated one of the two melee Goblins. It had gotten hit in the side with a large stone, causing a stumble that gave me an opening. I thrust my sword through its neck and stepped to the side at the same time to keep some distance from the other Goblin. That bought me just enough clearance to avoid its attacks until I could reposition myself. When I had, the little bastard was doomed.

Facing only one Goblin, there was no contest. I was now three levels above it and had Stats far beyond its meager Strength. I smashed my blade into its short sword deliberately to push it aside and create an opening. With a reverse stroke, I left it one head shorter and ended the first part of this combat. I was not winded yet, but it wouldn't take much more, and I'd be out of breath and starting to lag. I needed to finish this quickly now.

The others had been smart enough not to charge in, which meant they were at risk of fleeing and spreading word of my presence to the lower floors.

I had to make sure that didn't happen!

CHAPTER 10
FINISHING THE FIGHT

Luckily, I had accounted for the possibility they might flee as soon as their melee Fighters fell, so I didn't hesitate. I grabbed the closest Goblin from the floor with my left hand and charged into the room, using it as a meat shield. It wasn't much cover, but it kept most of the hand-thrown projectiles from hitting me. When I was even with the two hiding behind cover, I halted and flexed my will, activating Dragon's Fear.

A phantasmal dragon appeared and roared, although not so loudly as to echo down to the floor below. The level difference between myself and them worked in my favor. The three Level 1 Goblins froze for three seconds.

That was a lifetime when it came to combat, at least for them.

Almost lazily, I dropped the Goblin in my left hand and aimed my palm at the smart one in the rear. It was the one most likely to run and give warning, so I needed to take it out first. An Acid Bolt straight into its chest did the job, burning a hole through it and slamming it backward with the force of a shotgun blast.

One second...

As soon as I saw my bolt hit, I turned to the closest remaining enemy and activated Power Strike. I wasn't going to take any chances. The green glowing blade slashed across its chest, creating a deep wound that instantly started filling with the corrosive energy of the Draconic Skill. It hadn't even begun to fall when I spun to face the last Goblin.

Two seconds...

I leaped toward it, closing the short distance, avoiding the large rocks that were its cover. I had no Skills left, but I still had brute force and a lifetime of actual experience to call on. I raised my blade high.

Three seconds...

It unfroze from the magical fear effect even as my blade descended toward its skull. It only had time to shriek in terror and try to raise the rock it was holding before it was silenced. Just that fast, the fight was over.

I wish all battles could be that quick and easy!

Unfortunately, that wasn't the case. Anytime I faced groups of more than two or three, there was danger for me. Or individuals if they were close to my own level. Even these last three Goblins would have posed a challenge if it hadn't been for the Draconic Fear Bloodline Ability. One good crowd-control Skill like that could mean the difference between an easy victory and a painful and deadly defeat.

Hell, if there had been even one more, I would have been in trouble. My katana was stuck in the last Goblin's skull.

Frowning at the inconvenience, I used a boot to clear the blade before wiping it down with a dirty rag. I felt bad for the blade. It had been made for cutting competitions, but it was no System-created steel alloy. There were now many nicks along the edge that would need to be ground out with a whetstone once this dungeon was complete. Still, I was pretty happy with my purchase. Even if it wasn't as good as a System weapon, it was holding up pretty well so far.

Glancing down at the Goblin as it began to dissolve, I sighed. I knew I was callous about so much killing, but I had been doing this for more than twenty years, and more importantly, I had seen the fate of the human race at the hands of these monsters. I couldn't help but wonder how many lives would be lost as my fellow humans adjusted to the harsh new reality of life under the System.

A minute or two passed as I caught my breath, and my mind wandered. Putting those morbid thoughts aside, I moved to collect the coins that dropped when the System reclaimed their bodies.

Ding! As the last body vanished, I felt the rush of leveling up. More importantly, I saw the System messages that indicated I had gained new Class Skills.

Level Up!

I didn't waste any time and quickly allocated my points. With that, I was officially twice as strong as an Olympic weightlifter from before the Initialization. With effort, I should be able to lift a literal ton, 2,000 lbs. It was one of the reasons that the Level 1 Goblins didn't stand a chance against me individually. They were still very dangerous in groups, but with my new Strength, they were a piece of cake one-on-one. I looked at my status before reviewing my new Skills.

Liam Bell: (Current)

Draconic Spellsword - Level 5

Experience: 100/3200

Attributes:
Endurance: 21
Strength: 21
Agility: 21
Mind: 22
Will: 21
Magical Aptitude: 16
Luck: 1

Health: 270/420
Mana: 200/380

Abilities:
Dark Vision (Passive)
Dragon Fear

Active Skills:
Acid Bolt
Draconic Strike
Draconic Fury
Dragonfire Ward

Passive Skills: None

There was one aspect of this System that didn't mirror video games, and that was leveling up. In most games, leveling came with free healing and refilling your Mana. Sadly, the System did not work that way. I would slowly regenerate health, and my wounds would repair themselves over time, but even with a 21 endurance, it would take a few days for the cuts to disappear completely.

Mana, on the other hand, regenerated quite quickly. A good rest would be enough for all my Mana to come back; at this level, it didn't even take an hour to go from zero to full. Not that I planned to wait that long, but I could use a few minutes of downtime before heading off to face the next group of Goblins.

First, I wanted to see my new Skills!

> **Draconic Fury:** The Draconic Spellsword taps into their inner dragon heritage, temporarily enhancing their body with extra Strength. When activated, their Strength is doubled for one second per caster level. Attacks do double damage, and feats of Strength have twice the effect. Be cautious; fury puts great strain on the body, and the Draconic Spellsword will become exhausted very quickly.

> **Dragonfire Ward:** The Draconic Spellsword conjures a protective ward infused with Draconic magic, providing temporary resistance against a specific type of elemental damage. The ward can be attuned to a particular element (e.g., fire, acid, frost) and absorbs a portion of the incoming damage of that type for one minute per caster level, enhancing the Spellsword's resilience in battle.

I read the descriptions carefully and could not be more pleased. Draconic Fury was a godsend! I would have to be careful not to leave myself too exhausted to continue a fight, but being able to do double damage for one second per level was an incredible Skill. It would be costly and burn Mana, no doubt, but something like that could easily save my ass against big groups. It was only five seconds at my current level, but a lot could happen in combat in five seconds. Unfortunately, the System didn't list Mana costs and cooldown times in the Skill description, so I would have to be careful when using it the first time.

As for Dragonfire Ward, it wouldn't be as useful for now, but I was sure it would come in handy against any Goblin Shamans and bosses later in the dungeon.

Satisfied with my gains, I stopped focusing inward and collected the loot. There were ten more coins from all the Level 1 Goblins between the ones I had lured into the hallway to ambush and the ones I had just fought. That brought my total up to 32 copper Mana coins. It didn't seem like much compared to what I had been used to as a Level 57 Knight, but compared to what I had been getting as a Level 5 Warrior in my first life, it was amazing. It wouldn't buy a lot, but I wouldn't have to worry about running out of food and drinks any time soon once the Shop opened.

Speaking of drinks, I did find one bit of actual loot on this floor. There was a bottle of water in a hut that must have belonged to the two Elite guards. Not super useful, but these beginner dungeons weren't known for dropping items before the boss room. I felt pretty lucky to find anything at all besides the Mana coins. I stowed the bottle in my backpack. No reason to leave a resource behind.

Like the one previously, the next tunnel circled downward and looped back toward where it started to enter the floor below. However, unlike every previous space in the dungeon, this tunnel had no light sources. There were no torches or burning piles of Goblin trash. Thankfully, the Dark Vision that came with the Draconic Spellsword Class saved the day. It was weird being able to see in the dark without light. It wasn't like heat vision, but more like wearing night vision goggles, except instead of seeing everything in green, everything seemed greyish to me. It wasn't perfect, but I wasn't going to complain. If anything, it was like walking around at dusk in the evening. The sun was down but everything still seemed pretty well-lit.

Goblins seemed to have better low-light vision than humans since they spent time underground, but it wasn't as good as mine. I was able to sneak right up to the tunnel exit into the next cavern with no problems.

The sight that greeted my eyes pleased me but also made me a little nervous. This floor seemed to be populated by five Level 1 Goblins and five of the Elite Level 3 Goblins. Fortunately, the regular ones were all working on something together at the back of the cavern under the watchful eyes of two Elites. The other three were close to the tunnel entrance where I stood.

If it worked before, maybe it will work again. Time for Goblin fishing!

I crouched deeper into the shadows, carefully observing the scene before me. The five regular Goblins seemed to be engrossed in some form of laborious task. They were gathering materials—twisted metal, stones, and the odd piece of decomposing wood—under the strict supervision of two of the Elite Goblins. Their bigger stature and dominant posture made it clear they were the taskmasters.

On my side of the cavern, near the tunnel entrance, the other three Elite Goblins were engrossed in a raucous game. They laughed and snarled, slamming dice made of bone onto a crude slab of stone, their greedy eyes locked onto the stakes. Every so often, one would whoop with joy or groan in frustration.

Taking advantage of this distraction, I quietly rummaged through my bag and pulled out a strip of beef jerky. Its aroma was rich and tantalizing—perfect to bait these creatures. I ripped it into smaller pieces and tossed one close enough to the tunnel entrance to catch their attention but far enough to lure them into the darkness.

It didn't take long. One of the Goblins paused, its nostrils flared, and picked up the scent immediately. It tapped its companion, pointing towards the source of the aroma. They whispered excitedly, their dice game momentarily forgotten. Seeing an opportunity for an easy snack, all three began to cautiously approach the tunnel.

As they neared, I prepared to activate my Dragon Fear Ability, hoping to freeze them for a few precious seconds and gain an advantage. The darkness of the tunnel would mask my presence until the very last moment, giving me the upper hand with my Dark Vision.

As the first Goblin stepped into the tunnel, drawn by the scent of the jerky, I lunged forward with Power Strike. The element of surprise was on my side, and I intended to use it to its fullest. The battle for the second level was truly underway.

CHAPTER II

ANOTHER NASTY FIGHT, BUT NOT FOR ME

POWER STRIKE ENDED that Goblin Elite instantly. I managed to hit it in the head, and it exploded like an overripe melon. That Skill added maybe 30% to the strength of my normal hits, so with my Strength increasing from leveling up five times in such a short time, I was about 80% stronger than I had been when this whole thing started. I was pretty shocked at how successful the attack had been.

Still, the other two Goblin Elites were even more shocked. It took them two or three heartbeats to understand what had happened. They had been so focused on their quest for tasty beef jerky that they didn't even realize at first that they were under attack. Their companion was already falling before they even began to react. However, by that time, I had reversed the direction of my swing and skewered the nasty, disease-mottled creature on the right.

This all felt surreal. My battle instincts and skill from the twenty-plus years of fighting were starting to settle into my muscle memory a little more with each fight, and by now, things were beginning to feel natural again. Almost as if I had been doing this all my life, I casually let go of the sword hilt with my left hand and aimed my palm at the Goblin on the left.

"Die!"

I let loose an acid bolt directly into its face. Its head vanished in a Christmas-colored spray of acid and blood.

Two melons exploded. Two rather disgusting green, acid-tinted patterns of gore splattered and decorated the tunnel walls and ceiling in as many seconds.

This had been my easiest fight yet, and I was greatly relieved. There were still two more Elites and five lesser Goblins around the corner, but it seemed that I would have time to recover and let my cooldowns reset. A minute later, their bodies disappeared, and nine copper Mana coins were all that remained. That made 41 so far. I don't think I had earned this many in the first four months of my first life post-apocalypse.

This really made me wonder. If Power Strike were this good, what must Draconic Fury be like? Power Strike gave me the equivalent of around 26 Strength at my current stats. With Fury running, it would be doubled, so for five seconds, I would have 40 Strength. At level 52 as a Knight, I only had a Strength of 48, and that was after more than 20 years of leveling up!

Holy fuck! It's only five hours into the apocalypse, and I could nearly match what I had taken two decades to earn... Granted, it's only for five seconds, but still!

I had a crazy thought. I almost dismissed it out of hand, but I couldn't get the image out of my mind. I could picture what it would be like to charge into the cavern and initiate Draconic Fury right as I got to the two Elites. I was about 90% sure I could finish all seven of the Goblins in there in the five seconds it would last. Besides, even if a couple tried to dodge or run, I would still have Power Strike and Acid Bolt to finish them off.

The image would just not go away. I didn't know if it was the Draconic Bloodline egging me on, but I didn't hesitate. Blood still warm on my blade and adrenaline coursing through my veins, I made my decision in an instant. No more sneaking around. It was time for a direct approach!

With the part of my mind not focused on my actions, I couldn't help but think that I must have made a frightening sight. A dark figure in black leather and metal armor, carrying a blood-stained sword, snarling and baring my teeth at them.

I charged into the cavern, death in my eyes, my fangs bared in a feral snarl. My sword, a faithful extension of my wrath, dripped with the blood of the three Elite Goblins I'd already dispatched.

The lesser Goblins and their overseers were so engrossed in their task that my initial charge went unnoticed. I was halfway across the cavern before they even looked up. The moment they saw me, there was a split second of shock, their beady eyes widening in terror.

Good. They should be afraid.

I had no doubt now. The dragon's blood flowing in my veins was being heated by battle lust and driving me forward. I had never experienced this eager and intense desire to kill before.

I didn't give them the chance to react. Just as I closed in, I activated Draconic Fury, feeling the surge of strength coursing through me, doubling my power. It seemed to ignite the blood in my veins!

With a single, fluid sweep of my sword, the two Elite Goblins were no more, their bodies crumpling to the ground in a heap of pieces. Two Level 3 Goblins were no match for Strength that was equivalent to a Level 50 Warrior!

Then I turned to the lesser Goblins. They were scrambling now, fear overriding their simple minds. But they were too slow, too disorganized. My blade danced through them, each swing a death sentence. They fell one by one, hacked apart without mercy.

Only one had the sense to try and flee. Its gnarled legs carried it desperately towards a hidden exit, but it wasn't fast enough. I extended my hand, and with cold precision, I unleashed an Acid Bolt. It struck the fleeing Goblin in the back, obliterating it; its cries cut off instantly, causing the cavern to fall silent.

The battle was over as quickly as it had begun. I stood there, chest heaving, surrounded by the carnage I had wrought. This was what survival looked like in a world ruled by the System. This was what it took to save what remained of humanity.

And then Draconic Fury wore off, and I collapsed like a puppet with its strings cut.

Ugh!

It felt like I had just run a marathon, and after crossing the finish line, someone dropped a ton of bricks on me. In reality, it was a combination of my Strength literally being cut in half plus the exhaustion of burning a great deal of energy all at once. It wasn't only the physical. My Mana just dropped by more than fifty points in under two seconds.

As I lay there panting, I opened the System logs and looked at what had just happened. Yep. Fifty points of Mana to use that Skill, and now it was on a one-hour cooldown. That was harsh.

Then I noticed the second thing. My Acid Bolt had used twice as much Mana as normal. No wonder I felt so instantly exhausted!

Hang on. My Spell was affected by Draconic Fury? Seriously?!?

I rolled over, pushed myself up with my arms, and got slowly to my feet. When I was steady, I walked over to where the last Goblin had been trying to flee.

Holy crap! It hadn't been my imagination; the little runt had really been obliterated. The body hadn't quite faded yet. Or rather, what remained of the body was just starting to turn into light particles and disappear. Those parts were not connected, however.

I goggled at the scene in the seconds before the pieces vanished.

Damn....

It had never occurred to me that things other than just my physical combat would be increased by Draconic Fury. If I could eventually get an area-of-effect Spell...

Images of laying waste to hordes of monsters danced in my brain for a minute, taking me to my happy place.

Then I came back to reality as I felt just how wiped out I was from what I had just done.

Sure, this could make for some serious destruction, but I'd better make damn sure nothing was left at the end of those five seconds because if there was, I might be a sitting duck.

I thought that if my life depended on it, I might be able to keep fighting, but it would be pretty desperate at that point.

Still, I was pretty damned happy about this particular fight. I got the chance to check out my new Skill, and it definitely did not disappoint. For those five seconds, I really did feel almost like my old pre-reboot self. I just wish I could feel like that all the time again. I missed feeling so strong.

After I was done reveling in those thoughts, I got busy and picked up the coins that had dropped when the bodies vanished. Fourteen more Mana coins, bringing me up to 55 total. I also checked my experience, and I was up to 2400/3000 XP.

If the dungeon kept up the pattern of opponents, it would only take one or two more fights to get me to level six. Unfortunately, I now needed to rest for an hour to let my cooldown timer reset. If the next batch of Goblins was as numerous as on this floor, then I wanted my trump card ready, just in case.

Sadly, that blew my record of hitting one level per hour, but I knew I wouldn't be able to keep up that pace with the number of experience points needed doubling every level until seven.

Oh well. It was fun while it lasted!

It was only then that I looked around at this floor of the missile silo-turned dungeon.

Catching my breath after the brutal skirmish with the Goblins, I couldn't help but admire the System's artistry. This was, after all, a creation of the indifferent intelligence behind our civilization's destruction.

The stark, technological order one would expect from a military facility was long gone, overthrown by the chaotic handiwork of the Goblins, or so the System would have us believe.

The walls, once the epitome of cleanliness and order, were now canvases of decay: smeared with mold and overrun by the relentless advance of creeping vines. The air was thick and stale, mingling the scent of damp earth with an undercurrent of something rotten – a stark reminder of the new denizens of this place. The cold here was different, a creeping chill that seemed to seep right into your bones, whispering of the desolation that had claimed the silo.

I thought it was ironic that it could give such a feeling when I was still heated from battle. What a weird dichotomy.

Scattered about what used to be the missile's proud berth were the remnants of the Goblins' invasion. Huts, if they could be called that, assembled from scavenged metal and tattered fabric, stood in a haphazard array, testament to the Goblins' primitive lifestyle.

Flickering torches, mounted randomly on the walls, cast long, wavering shadows, creating an eerie dance of light and dark. Even though I had just cleared the area of immediate threats, I couldn't shake the feeling of unseen eyes watching me from the shadows.

I thought, *Damn, System, you're creepy!*

To one side lay what appeared to be a communal area: a chaotic jumble of bones, discarded remnants of meals, and crude, primitive tools. The disarray, the raw, primal nature of it all, struck a discordant note. This wasn't just a lair; it was a declaration of the fall of civilization.

At the back, my attention was drawn to a barred tunnel, likely a maintenance corridor repurposed. It was darker, more ominous, suggesting significance. Maybe it served as a storage area or perhaps something more sinister, like a prison. Instinctively, my hand tightened on my sword, a silent acknowledgment that my journey through this dungeon was far from over.

Amidst the ruins of what once was a symbol of human achievement, the sheer contrast was jarring. It stood as a bitter reminder of the new world, where savagery and brute force ruled. I steeled myself, aware that the deeper I ventured into the silo, the more secrets and dangers I was likely to uncover.

Also, it occurred to me at this point that having some human companionship would be awfully nice right about now. I wished Morgan or someone had come to the bunker. With the System pushing such creepy intrusive thoughts into my head, I would welcome some distraction, even if it meant slowing my leveling down a little.

On the other hand, being alone meant I got to keep all the loot.

Speaking of uncovering things, I forced myself to search the cavern for any treasure. The absolute creepiness of this place not quite able to suppress my greed at the thought of treasure.

I stopped in place. Was that another side-effect of the Draconic Bloodline?

Thinking about it for a long moment, I decided yes.

I don't think I cared this much about possible treasure before. Not that I couldn't be a bit greedy in my old life, but I was always too focused on survival to think too much about treasure during a dungeon run.

I would honestly be surprised if there were any treasure drops. Usually, only bosses and mini-bosses gave treasure in System dungeons.

Well, that wasn't entirely true. I had found the bottle of water above. Dungeons could drop utility items like that, and sure enough, as I searched that alcove, I found a package of MREs. Meals Ready to Eat. There was some irony in the fact that the System was busy breaking down everything technological around the world, and here it was generating fake items like this that mimicked stuff it would not allow us to keep.

Not that they weren't real food, and I wouldn't turn my nose up at some extra calories right about now. I put them in my backpack to save for later in the month when my other food would be getting low. Unlike these system-generated meals, the food I had bought before the apocalypse would go bad, and I was hoping my supplies would last me until the Shop opened. This find would let me go at least a couple of days without worry.

Sighing, I sat with my back to a vine-covered wall, pulled out some jerky, and snacked while waiting for my reset timer to countdown.

I couldn't wait to see what the next floor would have in store for me.

CHAPTER 12
MORE FLOORS, MORE XP!

SADLY, as eager as I was to charge down to the next floor, I was wary of what using Draconic Fury would cost me. I might not have to wait an hour and let it come off cooldown, but now that I had an ace up my sleeve, I didn't want to go into battle without it. At the same time, I wasn't too thrilled about having to wait an hour before the next fight. Using it might actually slow down my leveling pace.

There was also the fear that I might use it and finish a battle only to have another group of monsters charge into the room like what had happened earlier. That had been my own fault for that dumbass roar that announced my presence to the Goblins below, but still. There was nothing to say there might not be roving bands of Elites below. The closer I got to the boss room, the more likely that was going to be the case. At least, that had been true in dungeons in my past experience.

When the timer finally hit zero, I got up and stretched. It was time to forge ahead.

Moving to the partially hidden exit tunnel, I knew what to expect now. Like the ones above, this one made a big semi-circle angling downward to end up at the next floor of the silo. This one mirrored one of the tunnels above in another way. There were three Elite Goblins hiding in wait.

Perhaps they were guards on patrol and had heard the battle earlier and decided to ambush me on the way down to the next floor. Or perhaps it was their job to sit around hiding in the tunnel all day. Whatever the case, I wasn't stupid enough to bumble into the exact same trap twice. Fool me once, shame on you; fool me twice, shame on me.

Seeing the same pattern of debris piled up on the side of the tunnel, it didn't take a genius to expect a monster to be hiding there. This one was even bigger and more obvious than the one above. Then, there was also the tell-tale sign of Goblins trying to shush each other and prepare to attack me.

I rolled my eyes so hard I nearly sprained them. These guys were amateurs!

My sword was already out and in my right hand as I walked down the passage. I didn't need to draw it and prepare. I was already primed for an attack, so without missing a beat, I bent down and scooped up a loose rock.

As I neared the trap, I tossed the rock at the opposite wall just beyond where the ambush was waiting.

Hearing the sudden, unexpected noise, two Goblin Elites, and I use the term 'Elite' loosely, jumped toward the noise, weapons swinging. One had a big spiked club, and the other had a rusty piece of rebar with dirty rags wrapped around one end to make a handle, with the other end sharpened to a wicked point.

I guess they thought someone invisible was sneaking past them. That would account for their wild swings. Honestly, they were more of a menace to each other at this moment than they were to me.

There was a third Goblin, however. It must have been a bit smarter because I saw it look cautiously around the rubble pile and peer in my direction.

I grinned as I launched an acid bolt at its face.

For the first time, I missed. My luck and aim had been so good up until now I was taking for granted that I would kill my target instantly. When that didn't happen, I cursed and rushed forward.

The acid had splashed on its face, but only droplets scattered by the bolt's impact on the rocks. It screeched in pain and tried to wipe off the green glowing liquid. That only succeeded in smearing it around and making the burns worse.

I ignored that one and rushed past to attack the other two, who were just turning due to the cries of their wounded comrade. One regular strike and one power strike finished them. They had made one last-ditch attempt to attack me, but they were too slow to react.

The third Goblin had dropped its weapon when the acid splashed it, but it still had one good eye and realized its danger when it saw the others fall. It was still screeching as it lunged toward me, its claw-like fingernails extended.

I sidestepped to avoid the attack and used a two-handed grip on the katana to slash sideways, cleaving through its left arm and into its neck. It died, a bloody spray arching from its severed jugular vein.

Hmm... I guess they do have jugulars.

I waited, ready for more to charge up the corridor, alerted by the shrieks of the acid-splashed Goblin.

And I waited...

I guess I got lucky this time.

When nothing appeared, I scooped up the Mana coins and moved on. I was worried the ones below might have heard, so I walked as softly as I could the rest of the way. Again, I had to reluctantly admire the artistry of the System as I walked. Even with my Dark Vision and the intermittent light sources, it was impressive.

The corridor leading down was a stark, narrow passage, its concrete walls showing signs of age and neglect, with cracks running deep like veins. Sparse, dimly lit torches mounted at intervals barely illuminated the way, casting long, dark shadows that stretched eerily ahead. A steep, uneven descent marked by old, rusted railings and debris-strewn steps suggested a challenging and treacherous path below.

It really kind of pissed me off. The damned System could spend such effort to alter the old silo, purely for the aesthetics and atmosphere, but chose not to spare the lives of millions of humans.

I was in a bad mood when I peered around the corner at the end of the passage using my little handheld mirror of polished metal. Before me were seven more Elites. It looked like two were standing guard at the entrance to the passage, looking nervous. The other five were arguing about something, but I couldn't hear what they were saying from where I was.

Unfortunately, I could guess. It seemed that they had heard the screams of the dying Goblin. They were likely debating what they would do about it, whether they should go investigate or not. I didn't watch for long, but even from this distance, I could tell blood was being shed by those who were arguing. It was distracting the two guards, but one of them did notice my mirror.

It got a quizzical expression on its scarred face and nudged its companion. I slowly pulled the mirror back. I could hear them talking from where I hid.

"Saw shiny!" said a nervous voice.

"What mean shiny?" The second voice sounded doubtful.

"Go look."

"No, you look!"

They growled and argued for a moment in their guttural, rasping voices. In the end, they chose unwisely. They came together to look.

I slowly moved back up the corridor to draw them out of sight of the other Goblins. These were Elites, after all, and I didn't want to fight seven at once. I crouched down and made myself as small as I could, pretending to be a rock. My body was between them and my sword, so they couldn't see it from a distance. In the dark, I must have looked like a big rock with shiny bits all over it.

They cautiously approached, and when they were close enough, I leaped up and swung my sword, activating Powerstrike. It smashed their weapons aside and cleaved into their guts, injecting elemental acid into the wounds. They died in seconds to my follow-up swings, but they screamed loudly until I finished them.

I would have felt bad if the System weren't busy decimating Earth's population at this very moment. Instead, I was angry, and I didn't care if it was due to my new Bloodline or if it was my own unaugmented emotions.

Powerstrike might be on cooldown, but I wasn't going to wait. I had whittled them down by half now. By the time I reached the remaining five, it would nearly be ready, and my only real worry at this point was whether they might try to run.

I stalked toward the bend, and as I arrived, the rest of the Goblins were entering the tunnel, nervous but resolute. Hmm... maybe that was ascribing too noble an emotion to them. More likely, it was fear of their superiors mixed with hunger and greed. They also tended to have a mob mentality; as long as they were with a group of more than two, they tended to have more confidence than they should.

The opening at the end of the corridor was just big enough for two to walk abreast, but the end of the passageway where it opened into the cavern was large enough for several at the same time.

I squared off against them right there in the tunnel's entrance, where the narrow space worked to my advantage. Only two of them could come at me at a time, allowing me to focus my attacks. I dispatched the first two with swift, precise strikes, then used my Acid Bolt to incapacitate a third. The remaining two, hesitating after seeing their comrades fall, were quickly overwhelmed by a combination of my swordplay and a strategic use of Powerstrike, which had just come off cooldown, leaving me standing victorious amidst the fallen.

The fight was short and bloody, but it wasn't my blood, thankfully. I couldn't help but feel lucky that this was a Goblin dungeon. They might be cunning individually, but that wasn't the same as being smart, especially when they acted together like this.

Feeling pretty good about my growing ability to face groups of enemies, I calmly waited for their bodies to disappear. I felt the rush of the experience and did a little dance among the Mana coins left in place of their disappearing bodies.

It had been a while, so I pulled up my character sheet. I had leveled from those first three Elites in the passageway but hadn't bothered to check my status at that point.

Liam Bell: (Current)

Draconic Spellsword - Level 6

Experience: 2200/6400

Attributes:
Endurance: 22
Strength: 22
Agility: 22
Mind: 23
Will: 22
Magical Aptitude: 17
Luck: 1

Health: 290/440
Mana: 200/400

Abilities:
Dark Vision (Passive)
Dragon Fear

Active Skills:
Acid Bolt
Draconic Strike
Draconic Fury
Dragonfire Ward

Passive Skills: None

Hmm... my health had gone up somewhat from leveling up, but I had already been injured before. Sadly, leveling didn't heal a person; it only gave them more health overall. Still, it was better than nothing. My Mana was also rising slowly. Between the rest period I had taken before and being conservative with Skill use this time, it was filling back up. I wanted to save as much as I could for when it was really needed.

. . .

I was also pleased with the rewards. Perhaps it was the dragon blood in me, but seeing the nice little pile of copper Mana coins in my jacket gave me a comforting, warm feeling in my heart. With this floor and the ones in the tunnel being all Elites, I was up to 85 coins in total. That floor had netted me 30 more!

I could definitely get used to this!

After looking at my status and counting my gains, I took a moment to check my gear and my wounds. The stitching was holding so far, but I would kill for a low-tier healing potion right about now. Well, kill monsters, anyway. I wasn't like those bastards who left me to die for the sake of some stupid treasure.

"Kali, Keshia, Michael, Joshua… Kali, Keshia, Michael, Joshua…" I was going to save the world, but I'd make sure they weren't in it!

I looked around the third floor just enough to see that there wasn't any hidden treasure or food supplies, and then I moved to the next downward tunnel.

The passageways all seemed to be in slightly different places, and most of them were partially hidden. Once you knew the pattern, it didn't take Sherlock Holmes to locate them.

This time around, I did my best not to make noise as I headed down the gently sloping passage. I wished this were like those old video games where you could get a Skill just by performing the activity. If that were possible, I might have gained Stealth based on my performance. I actually managed to sneak up on the four guards they left in the hallway. Two of them were sleeping, and the other two were playing a dice game, betting their rations on the rolls.

Wanting to laugh, I just shook my head. Rather than hiding quietly and attentively in the dark, they were camped out directly under one of the infrequent torches that only dimly lit the tunnel. That meant they were night-blind and didn't see me sneaking my way closer.

I won't even dignify what happened next by calling it a fight. It was a slaughter, plain and simple. The two sleepers never even had a chance to wake up before they were dead. With the advantage of surprise, I didn't even need to burn any Mana on Skills. That made me very happy and allowed me to continue my way forward without a rest. I only waited a minute or so for the Mana coins to drop, and I was gone.

I tried to ignore the ever-changing 'ambiance' of the dungeon as I made my way down, knowing I'd only get more pissed off thinking about the System and its choices.

As a result, I was calm and eager when I peeked around the final bend and looked into the next cavern. Each floor was leaning more and more into the creepy, corrupted magic theme of the dungeon. This one included a sacrificial altar, and four Elite Goblins were on their knees, bowing repeatedly. Two big Hobgoblins stood nearby, overseeing their devotion to whatever dark power they were worshiping.

This was my first time seeing Hobgoblins in many years. I had always found them so intimidating back in my first life! They had seemed to be such a terrible threat.

To be fair to my younger self, they were much more imposing than the 'Elites.' They stood larger and more muscular, commanding the space with an air of malevolent authority. Their skin bore a darker, muddier shade of green, and they were clad in mismatched armor pieces that seemed scavenged from fallen victims. Each wielded a crudely forged, yet undeniably deadly, weapon—one a spiked club, the other a serrated sword. Their eyes were cold and calculating, sweeping the cavern, missing nothing—a pair of tyrants ready to discipline any lesser Goblin that failed to exhibit sufficient fervor in their prayers.

Also, when I encountered them in my first life, I was inexperienced and badly equipped. They had been a genuine threat to my life every time I saw them. The Goblin dungeon I ran back then had been destroyed by the time I was powerful enough not to worry about them.

Even now, I wouldn't take them lightly. I would use my Skills to take them down as quickly as I could before turning my attention to the Elites. If I were quick enough, perhaps I could finish the Hobs before the Elites could get up and arm themselves.

I waited a few minutes until the pair was distracted by one of the Goblins who had started to doze off.

The Hobgoblin with the jagged sword reached over and poked the sleeper in the butt hard enough to draw blood.

The Elite squealed in pain while one of the Hobgoblins laughed. The other yelled at the Elite to stop slacking off.

Whatever the hob said must have worked because the smaller Goblin began bowing all the way down, letting its head smack into the floor with each dip.

Both of the hobs were laughing cruelly now, the sword wielder brandishing its sword threateningly at the others as they looked around to see what was going on.

I chose that moment to rush the pair. I was able to get within twenty feet of them before they noticed me. I sent an Acid Bolt at the one on my left, aiming for center mass. I didn't want to risk missing this time. The other received a Powerstrike.

I wish I could say it was a total success, but it wasn't. The Acid Bolt hit, but the Hobgoblin tried to block it with its weapon, resulting in only half of the corrosive bolt making it to its torso. Still, it was enough to take it out of the fight. It was too busy trying to get it off before it could eat its way into its guts to attack me.

Worse, the club-wielding Hobgoblin managed to block my Skill use with its spiked weapon. That was the first time one of the powerful slashes failed to land. It did destroy its weapon, however. That let me finish it off with a trio of attacks: thrust, slash, and reverse! I got it on that last one. It had dodged the first and used the stump of its club to deflect the slash, but the reverse opened up its neck.

The other Goblins had not been idle during all of this. Some spent precious seconds looking in shock at the three of us fighting while one of them rushed for the weapons that were piled over to the side of where they had been kneeling at the altar.

Still, I almost laughed at the one who had been stabbed in the butt. It had been praying so hard it had dazed itself when its skull hit the ground too hard. It would never have a chance to realize what was going on. I ignored it and focused on the two, who were only now starting to snap out of their shock. With a few quick strides, I reached them before they could reach their weapons and cut them down, slashing across their backs with a long two-handed blow. They fell screaming but didn't get back up.

The Elite, who had been quick to recover, already had its weapon and attacked while I was still recovering from the killing blow to its two comrades. I wasn't off balance, but I wasn't in a good position to defend myself.

It was everything I could do to twist my torso, just a fraction. An improvised spear made of a crooked limb with a rusted piece of pointy steel tied to the end thrust close enough to rip into my jacket over my left side.

No pain.

It missed!

I didn't give it a chance to pull its weapon back and try again. I wrapped my left arm around the gnarled piece of wood and clamped it to my side so the Goblin couldn't get it free. With the blade in my right hand, I hacked at its neck with all my might. This might not be a cutting competition, but the katana was still able to go through the Elite's neck as easily as it could have through a tatami mat. Its head fell to the floor, and it let go of the improvised spear as it dropped.

Pulling it out of the leather of my jacket, I tossed it aside and took a few steps to behead the stunned Goblin who had provided me with such an excellent distraction.

A quick death was the least I could do for it!

That only left the one hit with the acid. It was still screaming and trying to remove its armor to get at the wound and dig out the corrosive substance.

I ended it and put it out of its misery. As I stood there watching the bodies fade, I contemplated my bloodthirstiness. After some reflection, I decided I didn't really hate these things, nor did I pity them. They were creations of the System, whose sole purpose was to make sentient beings like humans and the other System races stronger.

No, it was the System itself and the invaders that really earned my hatred. Even so, I felt bad about being amused by the Goblins' deaths, but I wouldn't hold back on killing them. I needed to get stronger, and I needed to do it fast. The longer I took to hit the level cap, the more people would die.

Picking up the coins, I was happy to receive 24 more. I was even happier to see that I was up to 5800 XP. That was most of the way to the next level. The next floor should get me there.

Unfortunately, now that I was seeing Hobgoblins, I would be in for more of them. Each floor always got progressively harder. I just hoped it wouldn't be ten of them. The two previous silo floors each had around ten opponents, give or take a few, in the passageways.

If they are all Hobs, I'm screwed! Even with my crazy leveling and overpowered Class Skills, ten would be too many. Based on the number of coins and experience I received, those guys are level six, just like me. Fighting two same-leveled enemies at once when I have my Skills and get the drop on them is one thing... more than that, and things are going to be rough!

CHAPTER 13

THE PENULTIMATE FLOOR AND THE ONE BEFORE

HONESTLY, I was growing somewhat weary of battling these Goblins; it had been a long day. Without a watch, I could only guess, but I estimated that about six hours had passed since the System Initialization. If I had had the time, I would have sought out an old mechanical watch. Some of those late 19th-century pocket watches would likely have survived. They were primarily composed of metal parts, with perhaps nothing synthetic other than the oil for lubrication, which might even work for a while without it.

As the saying goes, "If wishes were fishes."

Lacking one, there was no point in pondering. Eventually, the Shop would open, and I could acquire a System-generated timekeeping device, but that was still a month away.

For now, I needed to halt my daydreaming and focus on the task at hand.

This dungeon isn't going to conquer itself.

I pondered the extent of the dungeon. It seemed unusually large for a starter dungeon. In my previous life, I don't recall running through a low-level dungeon of this magnitude. Of course, its size could be due to its original state as a missile silo, which makes sense for it to be roughly the same size post-conversion. If it adhered to the original design, it would have seven floors in total.

One positive aspect, I mused, was that the dungeon's size made it an excellent place for farming experience.

Assuming I survive it, that is!

With a sigh, I proceeded downward, attempting to stealth through the passageway as best I could without a System-based Stealth Skill.

Halfway down, I encountered a group of four Hobgoblins behaving similarly to the previous tunnel guardians—lazily neglecting their duties. In this case, only one was awake, gnawing on something.

Again, I had to pause and appreciate the System's artistry while simultaneously despising it. It truly set the scene well.

In the dimly lit corridor, a hulking figure hunched over, its form partially obscured by shadows. The Hobgoblin, with its bulky, muscular frame, was engrossed in devouring something unidentifiable, tearing at it with savage hunger. Its coarse, dark green skin seemed to absorb the scant light, and its eyes glinted with a feral gleam. Every so often, it grunted with satisfaction, its large, gnarled hands manipulating the mysterious meal with surprising dexterity for such a brutish creature. The sound of flesh being ripped and bones crunched echoed faintly in the confined space, adding an eerie tone to the already unsettling scene.

Had I not been sneaking up on them, I'd face a much more formidable fight. Four of these brutes in a narrow passage, with no room to maneuver...

Nope, that wouldn't be fun at all.

Even now, a shiver of fear ran through me. I was fortunate in this scenario, but they were the same level as me and not enemies to be underestimated. I briefly wondered if my Luck Stat was influencing these encounters. I certainly hadn't had a Luck Stat in my first life, and perhaps not coincidentally, I hadn't encountered many situations like this before my reboot.

On the other hand, maybe I was creating my own luck. This time around, I was soloing this dungeon instead of tromping through it with a noisy group of adventurers as I had as a Warrior or Knight. Plus, I was being as smart about it as possible, keeping my fights quiet and not alerting the guards below of my approach. I had learned my lesson after that foolish roar at the dungeon's start. The subsequent fights had all been harder, with enemies ready and waiting for me.

I didn't even give the Hobgoblin a chance to fight. It was so distracted with its disgusting meal that I approached the edge of the torchlight and launched an Acid Bolt into its face without it even being aware of my presence. It died instantly as the bolt slammed into its skull. Despite being a like-leveled enemy and a tough brute, those bolts hit with the force of a gunshot, and they were made of elemental acid. It might have had a thick skull, but my shot blew right through its eye sockets and exploded inside its brain.

Charging forward even as the first one slumped backward against the wall, I set to work ending the sleepers.

One of them grunted in its sleep, seeming like it might awaken at the sound of the first one dying, but I targeted it first, thrusting my katana through its ribs and into its heart. Its eyes flew open only for the metaphorical light to fade immediately. Without wasting time, I moved to the next and repeated the process, ensuring they all woke up dead.

Moving on, I was sure glad the groups of bad guys were split up, with some guarding the tunnels—because when I rounded the last bend, there was only a single Hobgoblin on the fifth floor.

Fearing a trap, I cautiously surveyed the area but concluded there really was only one. It appeared they were attempting to mine this floor. There were alcoves excavated into the walls, with crude pickaxes and hammers strewn about haphazardly. Near each alcove, messy piles of rock had been dumped as if they were ore. After some thought, it occurred to me they might indeed be mining the walls like ore. The walls were reinforced concrete with rebar, significantly thicker than the rebar used in typical urban construction, potentially making effective weapons if they could extract some of it.

I focused my attention on the solitary Hobgoblin in the room, who was lounging on a pile of broken concrete. It must have been biding its time, waiting for its even lazier comrades to return from their patrol through the tunnels. Or perhaps it wasn't yet time for work to resume. Maybe it was their break time, explaining why it was the only one left.

Whatever the case, I was confident I could handle a lone enemy. None of my Skills were on cooldown, and unless I got extremely unlucky, it wouldn't be able to escape and warn the others on the floor below.

I lamented the fact that their bodies and possessions vanished after death. Otherwise, I could have scavenged some rags to disguise myself and attempt a sneak attack.

Fuck it. I'll just charge it!

I barrelled into the room at full speed. The cavern was only about fifty or sixty feet across, so I was nearly on top of it before it could react. A quick and brutal exchange ended the fight, but it didn't come without a cost. The big Hobgoblin was wielding one of those inch-thick pieces of rebar and managed to block my Powerstrike. My poor beat-up katana wasn't meant for that kind of abuse. It snapped in half, sending the broken end into the monster's face, slashing open a gash in its cheek but not doing any significant damage. After that, I finished the hob off with an Acid Bolt to the gut. It couldn't continue the fight after that, and I used the broken stump of my blade to slice its throat and end its misery.

Lamenting my lost weapon, I regretfully drew my backup. I had bought two of these swords for this very reason. I knew Earthly blades wouldn't hold up to fights against System weapons. Of course, even if it weren't System-generated, that rebar was an inch or more in diameter. I doubted any katana could hold up to that kind of abuse.

I just hoped my remaining weapon would last until I received a dungeon drop. There should be two more floors to go. I kissed my final sword.

"Come on, baby, you can do this!"

Weapons and armor pieces were among the most common boss drops, so I had hope I'd get something decent if I completed the dungeon. If I didn't get lucky, I wasn't sure what I would do. I had my two daggers, but I didn't want to be up close and personal with like-level opponents when they would have the reach on me. If that happened, I'd have to leave the dungeon and make some kind of improvised weapon. Maybe I could go get one of the axes I bought at the hardware store last night?

"Yeah, that might work..."

I pushed those thoughts aside as I felt the rush of experience and noticed the notification in the corner of my vision. I hadn't heard the 'ding,' so I must have actually leveled up when killing the Hobgoblins in the tunnel and been too distracted with murdering them in their sleep to pay attention.

Level Up!

"Yes! That's what I'm talking about!"

Liam Bell: (Current)

Draconic Spellsword - Level 7

Experience: 2400/7600

Attributes:
Endurance: 23
Strength: 23
Agility: 23
Mind: 24
Will: 23
Magical Aptitude: 18
Luck: 1

Health: 310/460
Mana: 345/420

Abilities:
Dark Vision
Dragon Fear

Active Skills:
Acid Bolt
Draconic Strike
Draconic Fury
Dragonfire Ward

Passive Skills: None

After checking my status, I gathered the coins and added them to my pockets. Between the ones in the tunnel and this guy, I was up to 151 copper Mana coins. That was a respectable total. You could buy a meal in the Shop for one coin. If all I were trying to do was ensure my survival, this pile of Mana coins would feed me for a long time.

Of course, I wasn't satisfied with that. Even if I didn't have dragon blood flowing through my veins, I wouldn't settle. I had a world to save and more treasure to collect.

The next floor should be the penultimate one. "Onward!"

Despite my cautious approach, I wasn't so lucky this time. The three guards in the passage were alert and vigilant. They weren't even distracted by gaming or eating.

I sighed quietly as I crouched in the dark, a short distance away. I had gotten as close as I could without being discovered. On the bright side, there were only three of them. The downside was that if they were smart enough to call out a warning, I wouldn't be able to stop them quickly enough.

Past experience told me that the room before the boss would be a significant challenge. The last floor had contained five Hobgoblins between the tunnel and the cavern. This one would have more, and even though I was a level above them now, I still had to beware of numbers.

I took a couple of deep breaths to steady my nerves and psyched myself up for this. I was pleased to realize it worked pretty well. Perhaps it was the Draconic Bloodline, but I was finding myself getting angrier and more eager for battle than I ever had been in my last life. Hell, the first time around, I never would have tried to solo three guys like this, even if I were several levels above them. I could only be thankful none of them had magic. I just had to worry about rusty, filthy, and possibly poisoned weapons.

"No worries! Not!"

Not waiting any longer, I charged forward. I fired an Acid Bolt as soon as I was close enough to be sure not to miss. It hit the big brute on the left directly in the sternum, causing it to get the wind knocked out of it and preventing the screams some of the earlier Goblins had made when dying from acid burns.

Its companions were already meeting my charge and didn't give me any breathing space. I found myself on the defensive and struggling. Many years of battle experience allowed me to keep their weapons from scoring any hits, but it was a close thing. My body didn't have much muscle memory built in yet, so even though I had the instincts, I was fighting my body's ability to keep up with what my mind knew needed to happen.

Enough time went by as I continuously backed down the hallway on the defensive that my Acid Bolt came off cooldown. Twenty seconds might not sound like a lot of time, but in combat, it can feel like an eternity.

I finally managed to initiate a Powerstrike. It didn't connect with either of my opponents, but it did make them back off a few feet as they dodged backward. That gave me the chance to bring my left palm up and flex my will to fire my only ranged attack. The acid energy bolt flew true and slammed into the left hob's belly forcefully, slamming corrosive liquid into its guts and giving it a very bad day. The final one of its life, in fact.

Seeing that, the final hob rushed me, hoping that a good offense would keep the same thing from happening to it. Unfortunately, it was right. This was the hardest fight I had had since the first or second floor. There wasn't a second Elite rank among the Hobgoblins the way there were among the lesser Goblins, but still. These guys seemed a lot better than the ones on the floor above. Or maybe it was just that they were more aggressive?

I didn't have time to contemplate as I fought the last one. The bastard almost got lucky, and its sword ripped the fabric of my right sleeve after one of its attacks deflected off my pauldron.

That made me angry.

"These clothes have to last me a month, you asshole!"

Driving forward with a series of vicious slashes, I began opening wounds on the muscular hob. It didn't seem too happy about that, but luckily, it didn't scream for help. It just looked determined to make me pay for the blood I was shedding.

I even tried an Acid Bolt on it when it came off cooldown again, but the bastard managed to dodge. It had seen what happened to its companion and was cunning enough to know what to do.

Still, it dodged to its left, and I was okay with doing it the hard way. As long as it didn't run off to warn the ones in the cavern below, I didn't mind.

It was off balance due to its dodge, so I finally got a good Powerstrike in. This time, it couldn't react, and the System-enhanced Strength of the Skill cleaved a huge and fatal wound from its shoulder down into its chest. It didn't quite reach its heart, and it had just enough time for a final swing.

I abandoned my sword, which was thoroughly stuck inside the Hobgoblin, and dodged backward, tripping over one of the dead hobs. I landed on my ass in a rather embarrassing way, but I took solace in the fact that the only witness chose that moment to fall flat on its face dead.

When I got to my feet, I had to roll the dead hob onto its side to pull my katana from its chest.

It was annoying to me that the bodies would disappear with all their armor and gear, but their blood somehow remained behind, needing to be cleaned off to prevent our weapons and armor from corroding.

That's some bullshit!

Still, I was cheered by the fact that this should be the final room before I got to the boss. I collected the coins and pocketed them, then moved on.

I purposefully ignored the ambiance of the dungeon as I descended through the tunnel. It was getting creepier, but it was all for show.

At least, I believed it was all just window dressing. For all I knew, the System might actually be copying a real place from somewhere else in the hundreds or thousands of worlds that were part of its network. Still, if that was true, it had to at least be adapting an existing scenario and merging it with the missile silo. It might be a big universe out there, but I highly doubt there was a planet somewhere where Goblinoids and intercontinental ballistic missiles met on a Venn diagram.

As I reached the next cavern, I cautiously peered around the corner. It quickly became evident that this was a barracks for the Hobgoblins. Crude huts, constructed from a mix of scavenged materials, were arranged in a haphazard circle around a large, open area. In the center of this makeshift encampment, a small bonfire burned, its flames casting erratic shadows across the cavern walls and illuminating the rugged faces of the Hobgoblins. The air was thick with the smell of burning wood and a tangy, metallic scent that I couldn't quite place. Weapons, ranging from roughly forged swords to crudely made spears, were leaned against the huts or scattered around, a sign of the inhabitants' readiness for battle. This was clearly the final threshold before the boss floor, a place where the Hobgoblins rested and regrouped, their eyes wary and alert even in their own stronghold.

I cursed under my breath; even in a dungeon, the smoke from the campfire was heading straight into my face.

Unlike in real life, where I could swear there was magic involved in the smoke always following me, in this case, it was simple physics; I was standing in the exit, so of course, the smoke had to go that way. I had noticed it in the tunnel above, but it hadn't bothered me then. It was annoying that it caused my eyes to sting and water right at that moment.

I quietly backed around the corner and blinked away the stinging in my eyes.

"Right. No way around it, this is going to suck."

With them all sitting around the fire, I didn't think I could use any of my earlier tricks to lure a small number out. That meant a frontal assault. I had four Abilities that could level the playing field, but I would have to use them wisely.

Worse, the campfire was right in the middle of the room. I would be spotted the second I entered, so this would end up being a straight fight without any trickery on my part.

I was really starting to like the Draconic Bloodline I had received as part of this Class. I would have been scared shitless in my first life, but now, I was still scared but also angry and eager for a fight.

Pulling out one of my daggers, I held it in my right hand, switching the katana to my left. It might not do any good, but it wouldn't hurt to get an extra ranged attack in before we could get into melee distance.

As I stepped around the corner, I quickly sized up the seven Hobgoblins lounging around the campfire. Without hesitation, I launched a dagger, striking the nearest one squarely in the back. Instantly, the creature let out a guttural cry of pain, alerting the others. They surged to their feet in a chaotic, frenzied rush, their guttural roars filling the cavern. Eyes blazing with fury, they charged toward me, weapons drawn, moving with a surprising speed that belied their bulky forms. I braced myself and quickly switched the sword back to my right hand, ready for the onslaught.

With my left, I launched an Acid Bolt. I wasn't worried about hitting; they were clustered together as they rushed me, so I was sure to hit one, and they were moving around too much in their charge for me to have aimed for any specific target anyway. It hit one in the shoulder, crippling its arm and causing it to screech in pain as it was spun around from the impact.

Its companions shoved it aside in their bloodlust, and I prepared to receive their charge. I was using the tunnel opening to my advantage. I wouldn't have room to maneuver much, but they could only come at me from the front and face me two at a time.

They tried an unexpected tactic that might have worked if I didn't have Powerstrike ready. Their rush was intended to roll over me with their mass and simply overwhelm me with their momentum. Instead, the Powerstrike, plus the Strength granted by my Bloodline, was like crashing into a wall for them. The first two weren't killed outright by the blow but came up short instantly when my sword blow met their weapons.

The ones in the second row had no idea they would be stopped that way and crashed into them from behind, further wounding the lead pair. Then, the three behind them hit the pileup.

My Skill use had stopped the impact of the first pair, but the second two rows were a different story. I was shoved backward into the tunnel and had to retreat around the corner to avoid being crushed. This was a moment when my past experience came in handy. I might not have the muscle memory, but I knew what to do in a situation like this. I used the momentary confusion of the situation to skewer the first two with a pair of violent thrusts.

That had the added benefit of sending the now mortally wounded pair stumbling backward, further impeding the attempt to push into me. What followed was a frantic few seconds as everyone adjusted to the new reality of the tunnel fight. I had reduced the numbers from seven to five, and only two could attack me at a time, but the downside was that I didn't have the freedom of movement to swing my blade effectively. Worse, my two main Skills were on cooldown.

I thought about using Draconic Fury, but I couldn't be sure I would be able to finish all five before my time ran out. It would last seven seconds now, but with the tight confines, I could end up with only two or three dead and have to face the remaining ones while suffering the backlash from the Skill wearing off.

Still, I had one more Skill that I hadn't used in a while, and since we were in the approach tunnel, I felt it was safe to use.

I straightened up and glared at the Hobgoblins. I roared, activating Dragon's Fear. I was one level higher than them now, so they were frozen in terror for one second. I used it to my advantage and thrust my blade into the neck of the closest attacker, a big dark green bastard with weird markings painted on its skin.

Three down.

The one I had hit with the Acid Bolt was in the back of the pack, angry as a nest of hornets and wielding its serrated sword with its other hand. Sadly, I hadn't taken it out.

When the fear wore off, they were extra angry and pressed forward with wild swings, not caring about skill or style, just wanting to overwhelm me with their numbers and fury.

Unfortunately, it was effective. I fell back step after step, constantly worried I'd trip over a stray stone or piece of debris and end up on my ass again. That would be a death sentence under the circumstances. My jacket suffered several more slices that barely avoided contact with my body as I dodged to the side or lunged backward away from one blow after another.

I could not afford to get wounded again before the boss room!

There were only four left, and one of those was wounded. My timer for Acid Bolt had just ended, and if I was going to survive this fight, I had to risk it. They were pressing me too hard and were only one level below me. With their numbers, I did not have the advantage here. My Skill timers were too long to try and win with straight sword fighting.

I let myself get angry. How dare they damage my jacket! How dare they force a Draconic Spellsword to retreat!

Draconic Fury triggered.

Power flooded into my muscles, and I suddenly felt invincible!

Seven. I released my sword with my left hand and aimed at the Hobgoblin on my left, triggering an empowered Acid Bolt.

Boom!

It slammed it off its feet and into the one behind it.

Six.

I deflected a blow from the Hobgoblin on the right with ease, pushing its sword out of line, and swept my blade back at its neck, reducing its height by several inches.

Five.

I stepped forward, shoving the headless hob out of my way so that I could get at the ones behind it.

Four.

The remaining two were terrified, not understanding what had just happened but sensing that the tide of battle had just decisively turned against them. The wounded one was still trying to disentangle himself from the one I had blasted with the double-sized Acid Bolt. The last one desperately raised its rebar club over its head and tried to swing it with all the force its brutish body could muster.

Three.

I side-stepped the blow and brought my blade across its chest in an upward diagonal cut. It opened it up from rib cage to shoulder, and it was dead instantly, its heart obliterated. It fell backward in a spray of blood that arched through the air like a fountain.

Two.

I lunged forward and skewered the wounded one who had finally gotten free of its acid-blasted comrade. My blow wasn't perfectly accurate. Strength wasn't the same as agility. Still, the blade entered its ribs and exited its back. It did not kill it, but ripping the blade sideways and flinging it against the wall with all the power of a 48-Strength score did the trick.

One.

I fell to my knees as the power seemed to drain out of my muscles in an instant.

Panting, I nearly collapsed and passed out.

The backlash of using that Draconic Fury was no joke! After a few seconds, when I was sure I wouldn't simply fall over, I eased myself down to sit on the ground amidst the blood and gore of the battle.

As the bodies disappeared and the dying hobs breathed their last, I heard the beautiful sound of the 'ding' and saw the message in the corner of my vision.

Level Up!

CHAPTER 14
BOSS ROOM!

I DIDN'T KNOW what to expect in the boss room, but I hoped there would be a completion reward for being the first to beat this dungeon. If so, I might actually make it to at least Level 9 and be really close to Level 10. It was just a shame I couldn't get there before facing the boss. I was looking forward to getting a new Skill, and I was dying to see what it would be.

Okay, that might have been a bad choice of words.

I looked for a piece of wood to knock on and frowned upon not finding anything. I hoped I hadn't just jinxed myself.

After a few minutes, I collected the 42 coins that had dropped and added them to my pockets. That brought my total up to 211 copper Mana coins.

Man, I wish the Shop were open!

With a sigh, I checked my XP.

Liam Bell

Level 8 Experience: 800/9440

I frowned. There probably wouldn't be enough experience from killing the monsters in the boss room to even level up to Level 9.

Well, that sucks! I guess I can rest tonight and run the dungeon again tomorrow to hit Levels 9 and 10. I was depressed at the thought that I was within striking distance of hitting a milestone like Level 10 in a single day. In my first life, that had taken months!

I consoled myself with the knowledge that most people in the world who managed to survive the day wouldn't even get a single level. I was so far ahead of the curve right now it was ridiculous. There might be others who were powering through the challenges and advancing quickly, but they wouldn't be way out toward the vanishing end of the Bell curve like I was at the moment.

When I was a bit rested, I moved into the cavern below and searched the huts, finding five bottles of water and several more MREs. That wasn't bad. Clearly, the System expected a team of adventurers to challenge a dungeon like this together. For me, it was a huge bounty. It wasn't weapons, armor, or magic items, but I wouldn't turn my nose up at clean water and edible food.

I sat by the fire and relaxed while letting my cooldown timer tick away. As I did, I reflected on the challenge I was about to face. Boss rooms were notoriously difficult. The numbers probably wouldn't be that high, but the monsters would be stronger. My guess was that there would be several Hobgoblins and a boss, probably a War Chief or a Shaman. Whichever it was, it would be over Level 10.

If it was a War Chief, it would be a massive bruiser with Warrior-Class Skills that I would have to contend with in a straight-up battle. The Chief would send its minions to attack me and wear me down, and then when I was softened up, it would probably use a charge Skill to rush at me when I was distracted. Then, it would bash me, causing a knockback effect that would knock me prone. Lastly, it would rush forward to try using a finishing blow of some kind.

I had fought in parties that took on Goblin dungeons several times, and it was always either that or the worst-case scenario...

A Shaman was the biggest threat. It would use minions to contain the adventurers and stand off at a distance, lobbing Fireballs or Windblades. Worse, though, were the debuffs. They would often cast Curses to lower the party's defenses and attack strength. That made their Hobgoblins survive longer and the party take more wounds in the process. If the fight dragged on long enough, the Shaman would even buff its minions, making them stronger and causing them to use a Berserk-like Skill to go all out. It wasn't as strong as my Draconic Fury, but it wasn't anything to sneeze at, either.

Hopefully, I could sneak close enough to figure out which it was before having to engage. The other issue with boss rooms was that they locked the party inside and wouldn't open back up until the boss was dead. That made this an all-or-nothing gamble.

I would either conquer the dungeon or die.

With those grim thoughts on my mind, I stood and made my way to the downward tunnel. I didn't expect any guards or ambushers in the passage this time, but I still took all precautions and stealthed my way down, sticking to the shadows and treading as lightly as possible.

Sadly, I was correct. There were no challenges until I got to the bottom, and once there, I faced a large steel door. Fitting with the dungeon theme, it was reminiscent of a blast door, but it was covered with jagged glowing runes, emanating a creeping feeling of power and causing a mist that obscured my vision of the chamber beyond.

Fuck! No way to know if it's a War Chief or a Shaman without taking the plunge and entering.

I checked the condition of my katana. It was already dinged up but still seemed structurally sound. I didn't detect any cracks or damage to the edge so bad that it might break. It still might, but that was most likely if I faced a War Chief, which was one of my worries for that scenario. I no longer had a backup blade. If this sword broke, I would only have my daggers and my Skills to rely on.

I chuckled, thinking about running around in circles, avoiding the monsters while trying to let my cooldown timer reset on my Acid Bolt. I could take out the bad guys with that if I had enough room, stamina, and speed to stay out of their reach long enough. That would be a worst-case scenario, and I prayed to whatever god might exist in this System-infested universe that it wouldn't come to that.

Deciding that I didn't have much choice, I prepared to go in. I removed my backpack and set it just outside the door. It would be safe once I went in. I had cleared the dungeon above, and nothing would exit the room until the boss was dead. Then, I spread the coins out between several pockets in my jacket. I didn't want a big lump of 197 coins on my side to interfere with my movements. I also discarded the sheath and broken katana. It wouldn't do any good in a fight and would just be one more thing to get in my way, so there was no point in carrying it inside. With a grindstone, perhaps I could turn it into a decent dagger later, but for now, it was just junk.

Finally, I stopped stalling and stepped into the mist.

As I stepped into the boss room, the scene before me was grim and foreboding. The cavern was larger than the others, its walls etched with dark, twisted runes that seemed to pulse with a malevolent energy. At the far end, standing beside a flickering, unnatural fire that cast no warmth, was a HobGoblin Shaman. Its presence was ominous, surrounded by an aura of corrupted magic, its hands moving in eerie, ritualistic patterns as if weaving the very shadows around it.

Scattered across the room were five Hobgoblins, their armor heavier and more menacing than the ones I'd encountered before. They stood guard with a disciplined alertness that spoke of their higher rank.

The moment I entered, the heavy, metal blast door slammed shut behind me with a resounding clang, sealing my fate. The sound reverberated through the cavern, instantly alerting the Hobgoblins to my presence. Their heads snapped towards me, eyes narrowing, as they grasped their weapons tighter.

In the center, the Shaman continued its dark incantations, seemingly undisturbed by my intrusion. The air around it crackled with malevolent energy, and I could sense the power of its dark rituals, infusing the room with a palpable sense of dread. This was no ordinary foe; this was a creature that had delved deep into the forbidden arts, twisting magic to its vile will.

Damned intrusive System thoughts! I hated the way it would push those feelings and imagery into my head....

Thankfully, that made me angry and pushed out the fear. I readied myself, knowing that this battle would be unlike any I had faced before. I had fought Shamans and their Elite guards before in my first life, but I never would have dreamed of soloing such a scenario.

I charged toward the Shaman. It was the real enemy here. If I let the HobGoblins keep me from killing it, it would whittle me down until I couldn't win. The Hobgoblins stood between me and my goal, and I had to avoid them if I could. This was going to be a dance with death.

I headed for the left side of the room at a dead run and didn't use any of my Skills yet. I would have to use them very strategically if I was going to have any hope of surviving.

I felt like a wide receiver who had just caught the pass with the goal line in sight, and there were only seconds left on the clock with most of the defensive line still in the way.

And that's how I treated the fight.

I went left, hoping the two on the right wouldn't be able to move fast enough to intercept me. I knew the two on the left and the one in the middle would. As I came to the first Hobgoblin, I couldn't help but think of how much it reminded me of a defensive lineman on a football team. Except, instead of football pads and a jersey, it was green-skinned and wearing rusty, mismatched armor.

I dove forward into a roll and came up on my feet just past it, but the second two were there, right in front of me by the time I was running again.

Now was the time to be smart.

I roared, letting my inner dragon out! A ghostly image of a black dragon appeared above me as I let out my cry, instilling terror into their hearts.

They froze for two seconds.

It was all I needed to brush past them, knocking them to the side and making them stumble.

My way to the Shaman was clear.

That was when I saw an incoming Fireball eclipse my view of my target.

Shit!

I dove to my right, hoping to repeat my diving roll from before, but the ball of fire landed behind me, and the explosion sent me flying off my feet.

Landing with a bone-rattling crunch, I could feel my HP drop significantly. I didn't dare look at my status right now, but I knew it couldn't be good.

Fucking hell! I have Draconic Ward! Why didn't I activate that as soon as I entered combat?!?

Dammit!!!

Belatedly, I willed the defensive ward to surround me with its protective barrier. I doubted it would stop an attack like that, but it would probably have cut the damage in half.

I could feel my ribs creak painfully as I got up. There were sure to be some cracked or broken, and that would make dodging or rolling a dangerous and painful experience.

By now, the Hobgoblins from the right were approaching, and the other three had turned and were chasing after me. I stumbled into a half-run, and I could see dark amusement on the face of the Shaman. It didn't think I would be able to reach it.

I still had half the cavern to cross, and at least the two hobs on the right would catch up to me. They were only steps away now. The explosion had sent me tumbling in their direction, after all.

I couldn't let them hit me from the side, so I did the unexpected and lunged right, aiming directly for the nearest Hobgoblin. As we closed, I slashed at it with a Powerstrike, bashing its sword aside and leaving a deep gash filled with elemental acid energy across its chest.

It screamed and stumbled backward, clutching at its wound.

Like a football player, I hit it and used my momentum to roll past and then made a second lunge at the other green brute. I made no attempt to use my sword or any of my other Skills. I used a straight-up body check. I hadn't been on the football team in school, but I had played many games with friends as a kid, and I knew what to do. I hit it, lifting it from its feet and shoving it backward. I let my elbow do the talking for me and clocked it in the chin in the process, causing its tusked jaw to snap closed, cutting the end of its tongue off in a spray of blood.

Feeling satisfied, I tried to keep my momentum going as best I could as I ran for the Shaman.

Glancing to my left, I could see I had enough of a lead that the other Hobgoblins wouldn't be able to stop me.

Now, I just had to avoid whatever other Spells their leader threw.

I was three-quarters of the way to the Shaman now, but its chanting was reaching a crescendo.

It was about to do something I wouldn't like. I still hadn't used my Acid Bolt because I was afraid it could dodge or shield itself magically. I wanted to be right up in its face before I tried.

I tried to time it perfectly. Right as the Shaman's fevered voice yelled the activation phrase of whatever dark magic it was casting, I dove to the left and tucked my shoulder.

A quartet of shadowy Windblades, barely visible due to the shimmer of their magic, passed over my head and tore up huge furrows in the ground behind where I had just been.

I tucked and rolled back to my feet, but the maneuver ripped a pained cry out of my throat. I could feel my HP dip lower. I was pretty sure one of my broken ribs had just punctured something from the sudden sharp pain I felt inside. I just hoped it wasn't vital enough to end me before I could heal up.

I was going to need some downtime after this fight. Probably a couple of weeks of rest for my injuries to heal. Assuming I won and got that chance!

The three hobs on the left gained on me and were closing the distance, but I didn't think they would catch me before I reached the Shaman.

Speaking of that bastard, it was looking annoyed that its Spell had missed. It began chanting again.

I didn't like the sound of those words. They sounded like a debuff Curse. I had been hit with those before, and they were bad news! Worse, Curses were quick to cast compared to offensive Spells. Nor did I know if my Dragonfire Ward would have any effect on them at all. The way the Spell read, it mentioned absorbing elemental damage; it didn't say anything about other kinds of magic.

I redoubled my effort and put as much energy into pumping my legs as fast as I could. It was going to be close.

Ten steps... the Shaman's voice rose and fell in some demonic-sounding language.

Five... I could see a gleam of malice and amusement in my enemy's eyes. It seemed confident it would finish its Spell before I arrived.

Two steps... It yelled out something evil-sounding, and I felt as if my body suddenly weighed half again as much as before.

Fuck!

Still, I was within striking distance. It was time to go for broke.

I let loose my Draconic Fury, and the weights immediately lifted from my shoulders.

Eight.

I gripped my trusty katana with both hands and swung it with all my might. It might not be the full 48-Strength rating due to the debuff, but it was more than enough.

As the blade approached the Shaman's body, a barrier of shadows seemed to flow up out of the ground and surround it, writhing in a way that twisted the brain and made your eyes want to shy away.

My sword cleaved through the shadows, and they dissipated instantly, hardly slowing the blade.

The Shaman's eyes widened in shock and terror in the instant before it was bisected; its body cut in two just below the ribcage. My rage was enough to sever its spine.

Seven.

I turned to the Hobgoblins still chasing after me. Three of them were only steps away now. I wished I still had Powerstrike, but I had used it to carve my way to the Shaman.

Six.

I swung at the nearest. It raised its spear to block, but my blade cut through the thick wooden branch of its shaft and dug into its neck, severing an artery and causing a fountain of blood. It stumbled back, dropping the weapon and trying unsuccessfully to staunch the flow of life's blood.

Five.

Another step and a thrust, and I impaled the next Hobgoblin, killing it instantly. Before it could even begin to fall, I yanked my blade out of its chest and was lunging for the next enemy.

Four.

Three.

It was several steps away, and it wasn't about to go down easily. It wielded a large, wicked-looking battle axe. It tried to imitate my killing blow against the Shaman, cleaving its axe toward my ribs.

My momentum wouldn't let me dodge, so I did the only thing I could and interposed my sword, knowing it wasn't meant to block a weapon like that.

The blades clashed, and my sword shattered, but its sacrifice was not in vain. The axe was pushed away, and I stepped forward and punched the armored bastard in the head. It wore a thick-looking iron helm, but it didn't protect its face.

With my rage-boosted Strength, my fist caved in its skull.

Two.

I grabbed up its battle axe. I had about 60 seconds before it would disappear along with the dead Hobgoblin's body, but I only had two seconds to finish this fight anyway.

One.

Taking aim, I put all my strength into throwing the massive two-bladed axe at the nearest and last uninjured enemy. I let it fly....

It flipped end over end with a speed and inertia that was frightening. It almost seemed as fast as an arrow shot from a bow. My aim wasn't perfect, but it didn't need to be. When it made contact, the big muscular Hobgoblin was picked up by the impact, and its body rag-dolled backward a dozen yards before crumpling lifelessly to the ground.

Zero.

I dropped.

I didn't have the time or the energy to check my health or Mana, but I knew they were both low. I was sure I had broken ribs, internal bleeding, and probably a pierced organ or two.

Desperately, I tried not to fall prone. One hand and one knee were on the ground, holding me up, but try as I might, I could not get back to my feet.

My vision was blurring as the final Hobgoblin Warrior stalked toward me. I had injured it with my Powerstrike, but it hadn't died. Now, it was coming for revenge. The Hobgoblin wasn't looking good either, with the acid oozing from its wound, and it snarled Goblin curses at me with every step, but it still held a sword. It was an ugly but menacing black blade with jagged grooves along its length. As it took the last few steps toward me, it raised the sword above its head, preparing to kill me before succumbing to its own wound.

All I had left were my two daggers, but I couldn't even muster the energy to draw them from their sheaths. My physical strength was gone. It was worse than the two previous times because I could still see the red debuff notification in the corner of my vision, still ticking down toward zero, but it had several minutes left, and I only had seconds.

I literally couldn't lift a weapon if my life depended on it, which it did.

As my enemy drew close enough to strike, it snarled a final curse. "Me die, but you first!"

I couldn't defend, but I could fall.

Letting myself collapse onto my back, I used the absolute last dregs of my physical strength to raise my left arm.

"Acid Bolt!"

Even weakened in the aftermath of the backlash from the Draconic Fury and the Shamanic debuff, it was enough. The bolt tore into the already open and oozing wound in the Hobgoblin's chest and exploded its heart.

The last thing I saw before passing out was the look of utter shock on the Hobgoblin's face.

CHAPTER 15
REAPING THE GAINS!

I MUST HAVE BEEN unconscious when the 'ding' occurred because, when I woke, the debuff had disappeared, and there was a beautiful message in the corner of my vision.

Level Up!
Level Up!
Level Up!

"Okay, I know I'm a little messed up right now from the pain, but I shouldn't have gotten even one level from only killing six monsters. What the hell is up with three levels?"

Before trying to figure that out, I quickly checked my health. I was sure I still had internal bleeding, and I had been unconscious for at least a few minutes for the Shaman's debuff to wear off.

Liam Bell
Draconic Spellsword - Level: 11

Health: 74/520
(Bleeding -5 health per minute)

Fuck! Just under 15 minutes to live.... Hang on. Draconic Ward said something about regeneration effects.

I quickly checked, and the Skill was off cooldown, meaning I had been unconscious for at least 20 minutes. I activated the Skill and checked my health again, hoping against hope that it would be enough.

Liam Bell
Draconic Spellsword Level: 11

Health: 77/520
(Bleeding -5 health per minute; Draconic Ward regeneration effect +3 health per minute)

Grumbling about the injustice of the world, I rolled over and painfully got to my feet. I began searching, hoping the System would reward my boldness in soloing this dungeon. There was speculation that people who took big risks to get stronger and survived got good rewards.

Every step was painful, and I had to be careful. I didn't want to make my internal bleeding worse and die quicker. My destination was the Shaman and its hut. Any rewards should have dropped from the boss or be in a chest inside that hut.

Before I could reach the spot, I could see a sheathed sword lying where the Shaman had fallen.

I ignored it. It wouldn't do me any good if I were dead.

Instead, I hobbled past the blade and to the Shaman's home. Ducking inside, I was disgusted by the small animals hanging from the ceiling. They had been ritually butchered, and blood covered everything in the hut.

"Seriously? Someone would choose to live like this? Even a Hobgoblin Shaman?"

Whatever. I didn't have the energy to be judgmental right now.

There was a wooden chest in one corner, and I immediately headed for it. I did take the time to pull one of my daggers and use that to pry open the latch in case of a trap.

Sure enough, there was a needle trap that sprang when the latch was lifted. Of course, it hit the dagger's blade harmlessly, so I grunted in amusement and lifted the lid.

I ignored everything within except for the two small vials. One was filled with red liquid, and the other with blue.

Recognizing them, I grasped the red vial and uncorked it without hesitation. It was a healing potion that would restore 100 points of health and repair any wounds. The other was a Mana potion that would restore 100 Mana.

The red liquid felt like heaven as it went down my throat. After a few seconds, the ominous bleeding status notification disappeared, and I could feel my insides repairing themselves.

"Oh, hell yeah! I'm going to live!"

If I didn't feel like hammered dogshit, I would have danced around in joy. Still, I was very pleased. I had soloed a dungeon and lived to tell the tale!

As I sat and waited for the potion to do its job, I reviewed my notifications to see why I had gained three levels.

What I found stunned me.

Aside from the experience notifications from the monster kills, there was this:

[+5000 XP Dungeon Completion]
[+5000 XP Solo Bonus]
[+10,000 XP First Completion Bonus]
[+10,000 XP First Solo Completion Bonus]

[Title: "Dungeon Conqueror" - First dungeon clear - (10% XP bonus for all Dungeon Clears)]

[Title: "Solitary Sovereign of the Depths" - First Solo dungeon clear (10% XP bonus for all solo dungeon clears)]

[Title: "Tier 1 Trailblazer" - First in world to reach Level 10 (10,000 XP bonus and +5 to all stats]

Holy crap on a cracker! No way! I was the first to clear a dungeon, the first to solo a dungeon, and the first to hit Level 10. No wonder I hit Level 11. And those titles! Those rewards are fucking amazing!

For the first time in a very long time, I felt hope. It was practically a foreign emotion after all these years, but I couldn't help myself. With those XP bonuses from the titles, I was suddenly feeling like the level cap might actually be possible.

I couldn't help myself; I quickly brought up my Status page.

Liam Bell: (Current)

Draconic Spellsword - Level 11

Experience: 11460/14960

Attributes:
Endurance: 31
Strength: 31
Agility: 31
Mind: 32
Will: 31
Magical Aptitude: 26
Luck: 2

Health: 177/640
Mana: 260/600

Abilities:
Dark Vision (passive)
Dragon Fear
Scales (passive)

Active Skills:
Acid Bolt
Draconic Strike
Draconic Fury
Dragonfire Ward
Searing Slash
Scalebound Resilience

Passive Skills: None

There was a lot to take in. I had gotten a new Draconic Ability plus two new Skills, and the thing I had almost overlooked. My Luck stat had risen to 2.

I still didn't understand what Luck did for me exactly, but I knew it was on a 0 to 10 point scale, so presumably, that meant I was 20%

luckier than a regular person? That was just speculation, but I hoped that was true, whatever practical benefits it might have.

My curiosity was killing me, so I brought up the new Ability to review it.

Scales:
As the Draconic Spellsword grows, their Bloodline becomes more refined. At Tier 1, their skin becomes tougher and more resistant to damage like a dragon's scales. At this Tier, skin is equivalent to hide armor.

That is a godsend. With the Shop not being available for the next month, the lack of armor had really been worrying me. My poor jacket is already full of holes.

I pulled up the Skills next.

Searing Slash:
The Draconic Spellsword charges their weapon with intense elemental energy, unleashing a searing slash upon their target. This attack inflicts both melee damage and additional elemental damage (e.g., fire, acid, lightning) over time, leaving the target scorched and suffering from the lingering effects of the Draconic energy.

Scalebound Resilience:
The Draconic Spellsword's connection to their dragon lineage grants them enhanced defense and resilience. When activated, this Ability temporarily increases their armor and resistance to damage, making them harder to harm in battle for a limited duration.

Holy shit!

Not only did I have another attack Skill that would impart acid into the wound, but I also gained an active armor Skill that stacked with the Draconic Scales Ability. That just made my survival chances go way up!

I couldn't be more pleased with all of my gains, but I checked my other logs just to see if there was anything else I missed in all the excitement.

Sure enough, there was one more buried among the experience award messages.

[Treasure Rewards adjusted due to Luck: 1]

That was all it said, but that message rocked my world and lit a fire in my greedy Dragon's heart. My treasure drops would be adjusted due to my Luck Stat!

So far, I had just been automatically allocating them to keep my stats even. At some point, I was going to need to dedicate my free points that I received at each level toward raising my Luck to the max. Except that, if I was mathing that correctly, I'd need like 20 levels worth of points to max it out.

Hmm... can't do that until I have my stats high enough that I feel comfortable with my survivability. I don't see that happening anytime soon, sadly.

When I finished contemplating my Class reward, I gathered the rest of the treasure. There were another five MREs and five more bottles of water in the chest, as well as the Mana potion.

Now that my injuries had been repaired, I jogged back to the door, which was open, thanks to the death of the Shaman. I grabbed my backpack and stuffed all the drops inside. It was fully stuffed now with all of those MREs. In fact, I would have to carry some in my arms as they wouldn't all fit in the pack with the water bottles. Still, it was worth the hassle to have food supplies that wouldn't go bad. I also grabbed the coins dropped by the monsters, another 45, bringing my total up to 256 copper Mana coins.

Last but not least, I picked up the sword and examined it. I had owned one just like it in my first life, but I had spent a lot of coins on it in the Shop. It was an Enchanted Steel Sword. It didn't do any more damage than any other blade, but it was unbreakable. It was one of the first things I would have bought in the Shop once it opened. I had just lost two pre-apocalypse blades that had been good quality weapons. They hadn't stood up to even a single dungeon run.

This enchanted sword would be a lifesaver. I would never have to worry about breaking my weapon and being defenseless again. The only thing better for me would be a more powerful, unbreakable blade that had offensive enchantments as well. Unfortunately, I knew from experience that blades like that wouldn't start dropping until Tier 4 or higher dungeons. Any listed for sale in the Shop would cost hundreds of silver Mana coins. It would be a long time before I had that kind of wealth!

I was loaded down with loot as I made my way to the surface. I didn't know what time it was, but it had to be nighttime by now. I would head back to the communications bunker, bed down for the night, and get some rest. I had definitely earned it.

Tomorrow, I would run this dungeon again. Being Level 11, I should be able to breeze through the upper floors, and it wouldn't be a challenge until I got down to the HobGoblins. At that rate, I might even be able to complete this thing twice in a single day.

Luckily, dungeons were instanced, so it would respawn whenever a new person or group entered, whether that was once a day or every hour. The more frequently the dungeon was cleared, the faster it would get destroyed since it wouldn't be able to keep up with the

Mana expense of respawning the monsters. I just hoped this one would last long enough for me to get full use of it. Eventually, my experience requirements to level would make running it pointless, but until then, I would milk it for all it was worth.

Assuming I didn't get hurt anyway. That was always the challenge!

CHAPTER 16
RINSE AND REPEAT!

I WAS a mixture of exhausted and excited as I finally exited the dungeon. My arms were full of food supplies, my backpack full of clean water, and I had a System-created sword on my hip.

It had been a great day.

In the back of my mind, anger still bubbled, knowing there were untold amounts of suffering happening as the rest of the world dealt with the absolute and unexpected fall of civilization and loss of technology. I had lived through that once before, and for now, it was a problem that was out of my hands. Still, I had repeatedly put my life on the line today to do what I could to solve that problem. I deserved a good rest.

I did my best to barricade the door of the bunker from the inside and then immediately fell into a deep and dreamless sleep.

The next morning, I woke refreshed and eager to tackle the day.

However, as eager as I was to complete the dungeon again and get some more levels and rewards, I found that I had something else to deal with entirely.

I was just eating a light breakfast of scrambled eggs with cheese when there was a knock at the door.

Well, that was fast. I didn't expect people to stumble onto the bunker that quickly.

It had been less than twenty-four hours since Initialization. There were nothing but small towns nearby, and most of those people would be more self-sufficient than folks in the big city. Even though many of their homes might already be breaking down, many country folks would have back-yard chickens and gardens that could feed them for a while, not to mention that there were lots of ranchers with cattle. However, the ranchers would soon discover that their herds were starting to mutate into beasts instead of domesticated animals. Still, it would be a slower process this far outside the big city, and I would have thought it would be several days before I had visitors.

I unsheathed my sword and unbolted the door, ready for anything.

To my surprise and great delight, it was Morgan, and she was holding the reins of a rather nice-looking horse.

"How did you know?" She asked accusingly.

Oh, shit. I had to be super careful here. If one of us said or maybe even thought the wrong thing, it could be disastrous.

"Hang on! Don't say another word; it could be dangerous. I promise to tell you all I can, but first, tell me, did you make a selection?" I really wanted to know if my warning had been worth the risk.

She looked startled, "What? No! When things happened, I held off on making any choice."

Sighing with tremendous relief, I fished a coin out of my jacket pocket and passed it over to her.

Morgan looked curious, "What's this for?"

"Just a hunch. Hang onto that for twenty-four hours, and I bet you'll get a lot more choices on the list. There is Mana in that coin, and I think by carrying it around for a day, you will get a point in Magical Aptitude. That should open up a ton of magical Classes."

With big eyes, she quietly mouthed an 'Ooo.'

"You want some eggs? I haven't put up my cooking utensils yet." I offered.

Looking like she was in a little bit of shock, she quickly tied her horse up and came inside.

I gestured to the hard concrete floor next to the fire I had made, over which I had placed an iron skillet. I got busy making Morgan two eggs and went heavy with the cheese since it wouldn't keep well and would go moldy pretty quickly anyway without refrigeration.

"Before you ask anything dangerous, let me just say something." I pointed to the sky and raised an eyebrow.

"All I can say is that I felt like something might happen. I know you want to ask a thousand questions, but answering them would be bad. Capital "B" bad. You are just going to have to trust my 'Instincts.'"

Morgan was an intelligent woman. She got what I was trying to tell her and avoided asking anything else. "So what do we do now? Things aren't going to go back to normal, are they?"

"No, they certainly won't. Millions, hell, at least tens of millions, died yesterday. When all technology just shuts off like that, the death toll will be catastrophic to civilization as we know it. No electricity means no clean water. The ones who died yesterday from car crashes and planes falling out of the sky will be the lucky ones. Over the next month, there will be hundreds of millions who die from lack of clean drinking water and disease. Let's just say those are educated guesses."

The look I gave her said it wasn't a guess at all, but I couldn't verbalize something like that. I was pretty sure the AI wasn't monitoring all our thoughts; there were just too many of us, but if we said something that triggered an alert in its systems, then all it would have to do to discover the truth would be to scan my brain. Then the jig would be up.

Morgan looked sick upon hearing the truth of what this all meant. To my surprise, she didn't cry or fall into depression and self-pity but seemed to become determined.

"I take it having a magic Class will be important?" She asked curiously.

"Yeah. The only thing we can do is work on getting as strong as we can, as fast as we can. I can say that based on games I played before the apocalypse, it was super important to have a balanced group of Fighters. Without magic users and healers, a party couldn't complete dungeons efficiently. It would become much harder to survive, and I'm afraid the human race is starting at a big disadvantage based on the fact that not many humans could have had any points in Magical Aptitude yesterday. This means all of the 'suggested' Class options would be nothing but physical fighting-type Classes and crafter professions. We're going to be completely screwed by the lack of mages."

"This is just speculation, of course." I gave her another head dip and raised an eyebrow to show that it was more of a certainty.

"That said, I was incredibly fortunate to discover a limited class that offered a draconic bloodline, giving me not only spells and fighting skills but also dragon abilities. I wanted something that would let me fight and punch above my weight class, so to speak. I was super lucky. Look for things like that when before you pick your class." I wanted to push her to look for those limited options without saying too much.

She nodded slowly, signaling her understanding.

Finally, after a few silent moments of her eating her eggs and digesting the information I had given her, she asked, "So, you came out here to be safe? And you are willing to accept others to come live here with you?"

"Yeah. I want this place to be a refuge, but understand that there is no room in this new world for slackers and those who won't participate, or those with bad attitudes. There will be a lot of unscrupulous and downright evil people that will try to take advantage of anyone that lets them. Survival will mean pulling together and building a safe place. There will be roaming monsters showing up today. They will start slow at first, especially out in the country here, but they will appear. Mutated bobcats grown to be the size of a pony, armored coyotes with four-inch fangs, and even cows that turn into minotaurs won't be out of the ordinary soon. If you have family or friends, you've got a couple of days before things start becoming really dangerous. I don't know how many people this place can house, but there is clean water, and these concrete and steel walls won't break down the way most other modern construction will. In just a few days, pretty much everything made with modern technology will break down. Guns are already useless."

It was a long speech, but Morgan looked like she was getting it, and I liked the look of calculation and determination on her face.

"Right. My family is still in town, and we've got some horses. I'll go let them know and bring them back here with everything that might be useful. What about food?"

I shook my head sadly. "Anything that has artificial preservatives will already be going bad and shouldn't be trusted. If it is all-natural, it should be fine. Chickens will be great if you can find and bring any; they can feed a lot of people indefinitely. Canned foods would be good too as long as they don't have anything unnatural in them."

I wanted to tell her it wouldn't matter as much in a month when the Shop opens, but that would definitely be future knowledge and raise red flags with the AI.

"One more thing. Just like in video games, there are dungeons. There is one here on the property. I completed it yesterday and plan to do it over again at least a couple of times today to level up and get stronger. Beware of any strange portals you find, and don't enter them. If a doorway, cave, or anything like that gives you a creepy mystical feeling, then get out of there at once. Without a Class, you are going to be especially vulnerable until tomorrow when you pick one."

Morgan looked worried but gave herself a shake as if to ward off a chill.

"Alright. It will probably be tomorrow or even the next day before I can get back here, but thanks. I mean it. Being able to pick something better than those crappy options..."

"Good luck. I'm happy our casual conversation yesterday helped."

Pretty soon, she left to bring back her family and warn others, and I cleaned up after breakfast and put everything neatly away.

Eager to get started, I quickly checked my Health and Mana.

Liam Bell
Draconic Spellsword - Level: 11

Health: 469/640
Mana: 600/600

Now that my injuries were healed, thanks to the health potion, my HP was going up naturally due to my high Endurance stat. If I rested a couple more days, it would be back to max. That was certainly what I would have done in my first life, but this time around, I had a goal more important than mere survival. The faster I could get to the Level Cap, the sooner I could establish safe zones to ensure more people survived. I could not afford to take it easy and heal up naturally.

I would run the dungeon again at least one time today, hopefully twice. If another HP potion dropped, then perhaps I could take it and heal up quicker. Honestly, though, as long as I didn't get hurt, there was no reason to waste a life-saving resource. I hoped I'd get a chance to save the potion for an emergency.

I was worried that someone other than Morgan might come along while I was delving and find my supplies. I figured that the worst-case scenario was that they would try to claim them, but I doubted anyone would try to take them away since this bunker was pretty ideal for a place to live now that almost all human houses and buildings would be breaking down.

I might come out later to find squatters in my new home, but that was fine. As long as they weren't assholes, I'd welcome survivors. Once I out-leveled the dungeon, I would need to venture out and see if I couldn't recruit people to come live here. By then, people would be pretty desperate and be looking for any place of safety they could find.

With those thoughts, I found myself before the entrance of the dungeon once more. Nothing had changed except that the mist around the doorway was a little thinner, and the creepy magic runes that seemed to manifest were slightly less intense.

It took Mana for a dungeon to maintain itself, and each time a person or group completed it, a bit more Mana was drained as it had to recreate all of the monsters and treasure inside. Of course, if it were left alone, it would collect ambient Mana and replenish itself over time and even overproduce monsters until a dungeon break occurred, spilling monsters out into the world.

That was one of the reasons the human race had been going extinct in my previous life. There just weren't enough humans left to keep the dungeons in check. That plus the invaders, and it had been a poisonous cocktail of shrinking populations. I don't know how many humans were left by the time I died, but it was probably down to a million or so worldwide. We had been at the point where what few population centers were left were besieged and no longer able to communicate with one another. It was a no-win scenario where we had to sneak out of our strongholds in order to level up, but doing so put us at risk of being killed or captured. Other groups of us had traveled around stealthily, not really having a home any longer, just trying to survive between dungeon delves and hide from both the monsters and the invaders.

Those thoughts and memories put me in a grim mood as I stepped into the dungeon.

My first time, I had been Level 0, but now I was Level 11. The dungeon did not upgrade its inhabitants to match the strength of the adventurers. That meant the three lesser Goblins I encountered were cut down in seconds without mercy. The System literally put them there to make people like me stronger.

However the System justified it, I saw them as a plague on humanity, and on the heels of my previous grim thoughts, I was in no mood to pity them. I merely waited long enough for their bodies to disappear to collect the Mana coins they dropped.

I cleared the entire launch facility area in maybe fifteen minutes. Perhaps because of my increased Luck stat, I found another bottle of water and an MRE. There hadn't been any in this area the first time around. Rather than weighing myself down trying to carry them, I placed them in the centers of the rooms where I found them. I would collect them on the way out.

The first three floors of the silo part of the dungeon took a little more time but weren't any more challenging than the launch facility had been. There were more enemies, but I was so far over-leveled now that the lesser Goblins simply weren't a threat. Even the fourth floor, containing only two Hobgoblins and eight 'Elites,' barely made me break a sweat.

I didn't even use my Skills for the first time until I hit the fifth floor. There, I faced five Hobgoblins. They were just over half my level, so they posed a little bit of a threat. I chose that as a chance to experiment with my new Skills. Between the passive Scales and the active use of Scalebound Resilience, I had no worries and waded into the middle of them, beginning to use a combination of my offensive Skills.

It turned out that Searing Slash had the same Mana cost and cooldown as Powerstrike. That meant I could perform four offensive Skills every minute: two Acid Bolts and one each of Powerstrike and Searing Slash.

The floor was cleared in a matter of seconds after I started using my Skills.

Honestly, it was a waste of Mana, but it had been fun to try them out in combat. I felt a lot more confident now. I waited for my cooldowns to reset before moving on, but I wasn't planning to use any Skills for the ten Hobgoblins down on the sixth floor other than Scalebound Resilience. It made more sense to get practice in with mundane fighting skills and let them settle back into muscle memory in this new body.

Fighting on the sixth floor was a good workout. However, I did discover one glaring flaw in my new Skill. It protected my body, but it didn't protect my clothes.

By the time that fight was over, my leather jacket looked like some retro-chic fashion item by one of the pre-apocalypse name brands like Balencinada. One of those 'look at me, I'm dressed like a poor person' items that cost thousands of dollars. In other words, it was filthy and had more holes than it had unmarred material. Of course, unlike one of their fashion pieces, the filth on my jacket wasn't fake; it was real dirt and blood. Not my blood, but blood nonetheless.

The upside was that I no longer needed my jacket for its negligible armor value, thanks to my Class Skills and Bloodline Ability.

Unfortunately, I also had to wait out the cooldown on the Skill before I could head down to the boss floor. By this point, I had spent maybe two hours getting to the final room, most of that time spent searching for loot and staging it so that it would be quick to grab when I left. I was regretting now forgoing an attempt to find a duffle bag or some other large sack to bring with me. It never occurred to me when preparing for the apocalypse that I would need such a thing, that I'd be gaining so much loot it wouldn't fit in my backpack.

Good problem to have, I thought.

Like my Dragonfire Ward, the Scalebound Resilience had a five-minute duration and a twenty-minute cooldown.

I sat outside the boss room and had a snack of jerky and a bottle of water while waiting for the cooldown timer to reach zero. As I rested, I thought of strategies to minimize the risk of the boss fight. The Shaman or War Chief would be the only things I really worried about now that I was Level 11. They were Level 15 and used magic or Class-like Skills. They were a real threat.

When I was done, I stood, drew my sword, and approached the creepy mist and rune-covered door.

I deliberately ignored the emotions and sensations the System was trying to impose on me to enhance the atmosphere of the place.

Yeah, yeah, dark, ominous mystic runes, feelings of fear and dread, I get it. I'm supposed to be wowed by the deep, mysterious nature of the dungeon and worried about what the Goblins will do if left unchecked. Blah, blah, blah... Been here, done this. I'll pay attention when it's a threat I haven't faced before.

Stepping through the portal, I was unsurprised when it slammed shut behind me, locking me inside.

As I entered the boss room for the second time, the atmosphere was charged with a different kind of intensity. This time, the War Chief—a massive Hobgoblin standing over seven feet tall—waited for me. It exuded an air of arrogant confidence, its eyes glinting with a mix of contempt and anticipation. Its tactic was clear: it sent its five Hobgoblin minions to wear me down before it would deign to engage.

I braced myself, activating Scalebound Resilience, letting my Draconic Scales shimmer into existence. The minions charged, their weapons ready, but I stood my ground, waiting for the right moment. As they encircled me, I unleashed Draconic Fear. The effect was instantaneous—they froze, terror etched on their grotesque faces, giving me a precious five-second window.

I didn't waste a second. With swift, practiced movements, I cut them down, my sword slicing through them as though they were made of paper. Each fell, one after the other, until all five lay defeated at my feet.

Only then did the War Chief move. It approached with a slow, menacing stride, drawing an enormous, battle-worn axe. I ran to meet it head-on, adrenaline pumping through my veins.

Our blades clashed, the sound echoing through the cavern. I dodged its heavy swings and countered with Acid Bolt, the Spell hitting it squarely in the chest. It sizzled against its armor, but it barely flinched. I followed up with Power Strike, channeling all my strength into a blow that would have felled lesser foes. The War Chief staggered, surprise flickering across its face.

Seizing the moment, I executed Searing Slash, my blade wreathed in corrosive glow as it arced toward it. It cut a burning swath across its armor, and this time, it roared in pain. We traded blows, its strength immense, but my speed and Skills gave me the edge.

Finally, with a well-placed thrust, I pierced its defenses, my sword finding its mark. The War Chief stumbled, disbelief in its eyes as it fell to its knees, then crashed to the ground with a thunderous finality.

Breathing heavily, I stood victorious in the boss room, the fallen War Chief at my feet, a testament to my improved strength and determination.

As I stood over my fallen foe, I looked to the corner of my vision at the two beautiful notices:

Level Up!
Level Up!

I had heard the dings earlier as I slaughtered my way through the Goblin dungeon but ignored them until now, not wanting to waste even that much time as I rushed through.

I couldn't be more pleased. I had soloed this dungeon in less than three hours, and it was not small for a beginner dungeon. Of course, I was way over-leveled for this place now, but the totality of all the monsters still added up to worthwhile experience. Two levels for three hours of work was time well spent. I didn't know how much longer I could run this beginner dungeon before the experience was not worth the effort, but I would find out!

Checking my Status, I was practically dancing.

Liam Bell: (Current)
Draconic Spellsword - Level 13

Experience: 11000/18640

Attributes:
Endurance: 34
Strength: 34
Agility: 34
Mind: 35
Will: 34
Magical Aptitude: 29
Luck: 2

Health: 529/680
Mana: 520/640

Abilities:
Dark Vision
Dragon Fear
Scales (Passive)

Active Skills:
Acid Bolt
Draconic Strike
Draconic Fury

Dragonfire Ward
Searing Slash
Scalebound Resilience

Passive Skills: None

Not bad! I was over halfway to the next level. I was also super pleased to see the 20% experience bonus, 10% each from my two titles, one for being the first in the world to clear a dungeon and the other for being the first in the world to solo clear a dungeon. That meant I had gained a total of 30,720 XP from the dungeon.

My inner greed dragon was also dancing in absolute ecstasy over the treasure message in my logs. Luck 2 had apparently influenced the boss drop and caused it to upgrade to a Storage Ring. That didn't solve all my problems, but it sure put a big dent in the list.

Feeling incredibly fortunate, I put the ring on and immediately used it to store the rest of the treasure. There was another pair of potions, a health and a Mana, along with more MREs and bottles of water. I also stored the other food and water from the floors above as I walked out of the dungeon. Besides the loot, I shrugged out of my backpack and put it inside as well. No sense in carrying the extra weight and encumbrance of wearing something on my back.

I didn't even go back to the bunker to rest. When I exited the dungeon, I turned around and looked at the portal. It was a little dimmer and more faded, but I saw no reason not to charge right back in and do it again.

I hit Level 14 after clearing the 3rd floor of the Silo portion of the dungeon, which made me super happy. I had even taken time to rest for a few minutes and assign attribute points. This time, during the dungeon run, I didn't use any Class Abilities and instead just practiced my mundane combat skills all the way down to the boss room. At Level 14, even the room with ten Hobgoblins posed no real challenge. Scales was a passive Ability and cost no Mana so it would be running even in my sleep. Still, I felt no need to even run Scalebound Resilience until facing the boss.

This was definitely the life! The contrast between what I was achieving right now and what I had achieved in my first life was so stark and different that I couldn't even come up with words to describe how happy I was about my new Class. That happiness was only tempered by the fact that I had to do it at all and the thought of the consequences if I should fail.

In the boss room, it was the Shaman again. I grinned, looking forward to some payback. I repeated my strategy with one exception. I still let the Hobgoblin guards surround me, but I didn't stroll casually to the middle of the room. Instead, I ran there in a zig-zagging pattern to avoid getting a Fireball to the ass. Like before, it tried both fire and Windblades, but both missed badly, thanks to my dodging and my Draconic Ward. It would have been stupid not to use that, considering how badly it hurt me the first time.

When the Hobgoblins were dead, I charged the Shaman. It still managed to get me with its debuff; it was almost impossible to avoid since it covered a wide area, and the boss was still two levels higher than me. It didn't matter, though.

After closing the distance, I unleashed my offensive Skills, starting with Acid Bolt. It splashed against its shield but also weakened it considerably. Cracks appeared all across the surface, so I followed up the Bolt Spell with Powerstrike, and that broke it. The visual effect was of the light particles exploding and dissipating like a firework of harmless energy.

I had one Skill left.

"Searing Slash!" I brought my blade up from below my waist on my right side and cut upwards at an angle, avoiding its staff and cutting a deep furrow through its guts and over its ribcage. Corrosive energy was infused into the wound, causing the Shaman to rear backward with a scream, stumbling before falling to the ground, and green ooze exiting the wounds.

'Ding'

Level Up!

I literally danced around its body, making rude gestures at its corpse.

Suck on that, you bastard!

After how bad off I was the first time, it was a pleasure to walk away uninjured from the boss fight. Of course, I still had the blinking red debuff notification counting down in the corner of my vision, and I felt weakened. Still, this had been the best run yet.

I checked out my Status.

Liam Bell: (Current)
Draconic Spellsword - Level 15

Experience: 1820/22320

Attributes:
Endurance: 36
Strength: 36
Agility: 36
Mind: 37
Will: 36
Magical Aptitude: 31
Luck: 2

Health: 570/720
Mana: 590/680

Abilities:

Dark Vision
Dragon Fear
Scales (Passive)

Active Skills:
Acid Bolt
Draconic Strike
Draconic Fury
Dragonfire Ward
Searing Slash
Scalebound Resilience
Dragon's Charge
Acid Spray

Passive Skills: None

I had a good feeling as I opened the Skill descriptions.

Dragon's Charge
Skill Type: Movement Skill
Description: Dragon's Charge is an advanced movement
Skill that channels the user's Draconic heritage to close
distances with incredible speed. Upon activation, the
user experiences a surge of energy, enhancing reflexes
and agility. This rapid forward movement covers
significant ground in a fraction of the usual time,
allowing the user to engage or reposition effectively in
battle.
Effects: Rapidly close the distance between the user and the
target. Temporarily increases reflexes and agility during the
charge. Can disorient the target upon arrival due to the
suddenness of the attack.
Usage Conditions: Can be used once every 30 seconds.
Requires a clear path to the target. The effectiveness is

reduced against targets with heightened awareness or reflexes.

Special Notes: Dragon's Charge is particularly effective in initiating combat or catching fleeing enemies. Combining Dragon's Charge with offensive Skills can maximize its impact, especially in one-on-one combat scenarios.

Acid Spray

Skill Type: Continuous AoE (Area of Effect) Attack

Description: Acid Spray is a potent AoE Spell that allows the user to emit a continuous stream of corrosive acid from the palm of their hand. This Spell is designed to deal sustained, low damage over time, making it ideal for weakening a large group of enemies or clearing out swarms of lesser foes.

Effects: Emits a continuous spray of acid in a cone-shaped area in front of the user. Causes low damage per second to all enemies within the affected area. Prolonged exposure increases the total damage inflicted.

Mana Cost: 20 Mana per second of use.

Usage Conditions: Requires continuous Mana expenditure to maintain the spray. The user must have a line of sight to the target area. The effectiveness of the Spell decreases with distance.

Special Notes: The acid can corrode certain environmental obstacles, potentially revealing hidden areas or items. Users should exercise caution as the acid can damage friendly units or valuable resources in the vicinity. Combining Acid Spray with wind-based Spells can extend its range and area of effect, though this requires additional Mana and skill to execute effectively.

Nice! Skill descriptions were getting more comprehensive.

I hoped that wasn't because the System was paying more direct attention to me. I was afraid that being the current frontrunner on the planet would draw its focus. I really didn't need it causing other AI Nodes in the network to realize I had been sent back in time to limit their ability to invade our world. I only had a single month before the invaders would be allowed to travel to Earth. The last thing I needed was god-like aliens specifically gunning for me to try and assassinate me to end my chance of blocking them from sending more of their people.

Of course, there would be some doom and gloom to dim the silver lining of these new Skills.

Before I could let those thoughts ruin my mood, I decided to check out the treasure.

The boss drop turned out to be a glowing ruby gemstone. I was familiar with the type. They could be socketed into a weapon to add elemental effects. This one was called a Searing Ember Gem and would add extra fire damage to each successful hit. Not a bad drop at all. It wouldn't do as much damage as one of my acid-based Class Skills, but it would add a little fire to each hit, burning the target. It could even be used to set things on fire or provide a little bit of light in the darkness.

Unfortunately, that also meant I couldn't sneak around through dungeon tunnels in the dark with my sword drawn. I would effectively be carrying a dim torch in my hand unless the blade was sheathed. Still, it was worth it.

My sword had a large stylized acorn made of steel as a pommel. I wasted no time pressing the gemstone to the end of the acorn. The gem turned ethereal and sank into the metal, seeming to transform the main part of the acorn into a ruby gemstone. It wasn't actually a big gem now; the steel of the acorn just had the appearance of the gemstone. In the case of my sword, it was really nice looking, making it seem grander than it had been. Like something a minor noble might wear rather than a common soldier. Not that I cared about that. I was just happy to add any extra damage to my attacks. The faster I could kill monsters, the better!

I collected the rest of the treasure, including another pair of potions and more food supplies, and made my way out of the dungeon.

It was only mid-afternoon when I walked out. The bright spring sun shone down on the world as if nothing had happened and the human race wasn't being decimated right now.

I wanted to run the dungeon again but decided to head back to the bunker and eat one of the MREs as a late lunch. With as many as I was getting now due to my Luck score, there wasn't any point in saving them for the end of the month. I could eat one of these a day and still make it to the Shop opening without going hungry.

Hell yeah!

Sounds from inside the bunker stopped me in my tracks.

CHAPTER 17

HUMANS, THE MOST DANGEROUS ANIMAL

I HAD visions of mutated beasts, maybe a wolf-sized raccoon rummaging through my supplies. Unfortunately, that was not what I discovered.

As I rushed inside, I was surprised to find ten people tearing through my supplies and making a mess of my carefully packed treasures.

The leader—a hulking brute with a scarred face and a mean glare—directed his cronies with gruff barks. They were a ragged bunch, their clothes a patchwork of survival, armed with an assortment of scavenged weapons.

They rummaged through my supplies with little care, tossing aside what they deemed useless. My carefully organized stacks of spice tins were being emptied haphazardly, cans clattering to the floor. The leader picked up a tin, inspecting it with a sneer before tossing it over his shoulder.

Their greedy hands rifled through my medical supplies, grabbing bandages and pills without knowing their purpose. One of them held up a bottle of antiseptic with a puzzled look before shoving it into his bag.

In the corner, a couple of them discovered my stash of tools – including my axes. They whooped with delight, waving the bladed tools around with a dangerous lack of awareness. The leader snatched the two-bladed felling axe, examining it with a hint of satisfaction in his eyes.

Some were pawing through my personal items, throwing around clothes, and overturning my makeshift bed. A sense of violation washed over me as they handled family photos and mementos with no respect. Those photos would soon be just a memory once the System got around to dissolving them, and it enraged me to see them handled that way.

The leader, ever watchful, kept an eye out for any hidden treasures, barking orders to check every nook and cranny. His presence dominated the room, a tyrant in his newfound kingdom reveling in the chaos he Orchestrated.

As I observed them pillage a fortune in survival gear and sentimental things, a cold resolve settled within me. They were about to learn that this bunker – my home – was not to be taken lightly.

"Fucking assholes! Put that stuff down, you damned thieves! Do you have any idea how precious spices will be in a few weeks? And keep your grimy hands off my freaking underwear!"

The scavengers turned and glared at me. Some looked surprised, and some guilty, but the guy who had just ruthlessly wasted what would probably be 50 or 100 copper Mana coins worth of peppercorns puffed up and acted offended at my comment.

He was the one who spoke, "This your stuff? You're that fucking doomsday prepper that Morgan ran off to join!" He said it with disgust and all the butthurt of a jilted ex.

I glared back at him, "Or something, yeah, and I've got a claim to this place. My father was part of the group that cleared this bunker out back in 2008; his company was going to repurpose the place until the economy went to shit. I bought it just before shit hit the fan, and while I don't mind helping people out and sharing the place, I'd like to be asked first."

I glared at a guy still going through my clothes and yelled, "You guys will want to back away from my things now!"

Skeeter—I'm gonna call the big guy Skeeter because he had that 'I'm gonna hear what I wanna hear' attitude that seemed to believe ignorance was a virtue. He looked me up and down disdainfully, as if surprised I had a lot of nerve to not just give them everything I owned and beg for the right to stay here.

I almost glanced down, but I already knew what I must look like in their eyes. My jacket and pants were not in great shape after running the dungeon three times. I must look like I got into a fight with an airplane propeller and lost, especially with all the bloodstains. Of course, if they were smart, they might be asking themselves if it was a good idea to challenge someone who had been through a meat grinder and survived, but nope. That clearly was not crossing their minds.

Skeeter smirked and said, "Well, looks like your preppin turned out to be a good idea. You don't mind if we bunk with you and share your supplies, right? There are ten of us, after all. You don't need all this just for one person. I'll take charge now, and Morgan can come crawling back to me and beg to be allowed to stay."

Are you fucking kidding me? The damned world just went to shit, and this guy has to try and make it worse? Definitely an ex who doesn't know when to quit.

Somehow, I didn't think Morgan told these guys to come here;

otherwise, they would have been smarter than to try and loot my things.

Besides whatever issues he had with Morgan, it was obvious that he and his friends hadn't prepared, and now they wanted to rob someone who had. I really didn't mind helping people out; my whole purpose was to try and save as much of the human race as I could. Even so, I wasn't about to share my things and sleep next to some assholes who wanted to rob me rather than ask nicely. They were choosing to be scumbags, and I was going to give them a lesson about that.

Looking around at the group, some of them did look guilty and ashamed, glancing at Skeeter as if to ask if he was sure about this. Nonetheless, they kept silent and let the asshole lead, all while gripping their weapons as if preparing to attack.

Narrowing my eyes, I had a sudden suspicion that Skeeter had been the captain of the football team in his little 2A High School, and his life had peaked before graduating. He seemed like that kind of douche.

I heaved a big sigh. A single day after the apocalypse, and I doubted there was a single one of them over Level 3. They had no idea the can of whoop-ass they were about to open.

Given that the memory of my betrayal and death was still fresh in my mind, it was getting upgraded to a party-sized can of whoop-ass.

"Alright, I'll make this easy. All of you can drop everything you've stuffed into your bags, and I'll let you walk out this door alive. But there is only one door in this bunker, and it's behind me, and you aren't getting out of it without apologizing and emptying your pockets."

Skeeter scoffed. "You've got big balls, kid, but you are the one that needs to give us everything, and we will even let you join us. I'm gonna have to teach you a lesson in respect, though."

Just to be safe, I activated Scalebound Resilience and drew my sword.

"Alright, Skeeter, come give me that lesson then."

Frowning at the complete lack of fear on my face, perhaps the big man was starting to wonder if I was dangerous. He gestured for his followers to attack.

One of the smaller, weaker-looking guys asked tentatively, "You sure about this, George?"

Glaring at the guy, Skeeter barked, "Get over there, or I'm gonna teach you about respect next!"

I laughed at him. "Big man like you can't handle it? Have to send others to do your fighting for you?"

He went red in the face and growled. "Beat his ass!"

I shook my head. I didn't want to kill these people, even if they were thieving scavengers with IQs low enough that they thought following Skeeter was a good idea. I would have preferred just to beat their leader and chase them off. I wouldn't trust people like this to stay here, so they had to go, even if it meant their deaths later from monsters. I hoped to build this place up into a fortress that good, decent people could gather in to survive and grow stronger. No good would come from letting scum like these stay.

"Alright, let's get this over with."

I dropped into a fighting stance and waited for them to approach. They carried an assortment of improvised weapons, from baseball bats to a sharpened shovel. I wasn't worried about them; I just didn't want any to get past me and run off with my supplies.

A few seconds later, a trio had worked up the nerve to approach. They fanned out, trying to come at me from three sides at once.

Before they could, I stepped backward and casually kicked the door shut, smirking at their puzzled expressions.

"I don't want you trying to run away." I gave them an evil grin.

They were nervous now, their expectations for this situation having been turned upside down.

One of them tried pleading, "Just put your sword down, and we won't beat you up too bad. George is actually pretty good to us. He fought a weird coyote thing and beat it with nothing but a baseball bat. Since then, we've hunted several mutated critters. You'll be safe with us."

I shook my head in disbelief. "You guys are thieves, preying on people you think are weaker than yourselves. Drop your weapons, and I won't hurt you, but I won't allow you to stay here after behaving this way. Also, be careful who you try. You never know who might be a hidden badass."

I didn't wait but lunged at the guy opposite from the one I was talking to. He had been trying to sneak up to attack me from the side while he thought I was distracted.

Trying to pull my blow so that I wouldn't cave his skull in, I hit him with the flat of my blade, but it flared to life and burned the man, filling the air with the odor of burnt hair.

"Oops, I forgot my sword does that. Sorry. Someone lend me something less lethal so I don't accidentally kill you guys?"

I didn't expect anyone to actually do it; I was just shit-talking to psyche them out.

Everyone was frozen in place in horror, seeing their unconscious friend with a severe burn across the side of his head.

The guy I had been talking to dropped his weapon and started backing away. "No problem, I'll give back what I took, okay?"

I chuckled and bent down to pick up the discarded baseball bat. It was a little light, but that was good; less chance I'd accidentally kill someone. I sheathed my sword and grinned.

"Thanks. Hopefully, I won't accidentally kill anyone now."

Skeeter, aka George, was looking at my side with naked greed on his face. Apparently, he didn't want to risk any of his guys getting their hands on my sword, and now that I was only holding a blunt piece of wood, he thought he could take me.

"Move, Tom. I'll deal with this guy."

"Sure, now that I've put the sword away, you're real brave. You guys should find a better leader."

The last guy in front of me stepped aside with relief on his face to let his boss do the dirty work and gave him a troubled look.

That left just me and Skeeter.

I didn't activate any of my Skills. I just let him attack.

Twenty-plus years of experience as a Warrior and Knight fighting invaders and monsters meant a second or third-level Skeeter was not a challenge. I let him wear himself out. He had my felling axe in his hands, and he was swinging it wildly, trying to end me with powerful, decisive blows. He did try a couple of Warrior Skills on me, but his attack Skill didn't work. I just brushed it aside with the old baseball bat, then hit him in the shoulder hard enough to make it go numb.

He almost dropped the axe but gripped it tighter with his other hand and let the hurt arm hang limply.

I let this go on for a bit, tagging him a couple more times to let him know he was not in control of this situation. Unfortunately, it seemed to only madden him and make him fight even harder.

Having a bad feeling about it, I lowered the baseball bat to try and talk some reason into him.

"Look, all you have to do is drop my stuff, and I'll let you leave. As shitty as you might be, I don't want to kill humans when the System is doing so much of that already."

That tipped him over the edge. I don't know if he was feeling worthless and couldn't accept that or if he just thought he was good enough to catch me off guard, but he gripped the axe in both hands again and suddenly swung at me with everything he had in him.

I didn't intend to hit him that hard, but I just reacted on instinct. I deflected his swing high; it didn't take much since it was aimed straight at my head, and without thinking, I parried and swung the bat in response. It made a sickening crack sound as it made contact. My axe flew out of Skeeter's now limp hands, and his body collapsed like a puppet with its strings cut.

I hadn't meant to hit him that hard, but I had a sinking feeling the big man would not be getting back up.

Walking over, I checked his pulse, and sure enough, he was already dead. I must have crushed the side of his skull by accident. A Strength of 36 was no joke. I was basically three times as strong as the world's greatest weightlifter from before the apocalypse.

I shook my head as I stood back up, looking at the stunned faces of the group of thieves.

"Line up, empty your pockets, and I'll let you leave."

The guy who had dropped his bat pleaded, "Can't we please stay with you? I'll do whatever you say. I'll follow any orders!"

He seemed scared by the frown on my face as I answered, "Not a chance. The fact that you are willing to follow any orders is the problem. You aren't trustworthy. None of you are. When you leave here, do some soul searching and ask yourselves what kind of people you want to be. The kind who rob the innocent and try to force them to join your little gang... you are the bad guys."

Some of them looked angry, but I could see shame on the faces of a few. It took a few minutes, but I reclaimed everything they tried to steal and let them go. I made them drag their former leader off with them. I didn't want beasts to come sniffing around.

It took a couple of hours after that for me to reorganize and clean up. They had ruined what would probably have been several hundred copper Mana coins worth of spices in their stupid disregard.

I sighed for the dozenth time and packed almost everything into my new storage ring. If only I had taken a break and packed everything up earlier, things might not have come to this.

That might have been all for me for the day if it hadn't been for the confrontation with the scavengers, but now I was all keyed up from the fight, and the time spent organizing and packing away my stuff didn't calm me down enough. It was getting close to evening, but I felt too energized and anxious to settle in. Instead, I decided to run the dungeon one more time today.

With the flaming sword, it was a complete cakewalk. I tore through the Goblins, Elites, and Hobgoblins alike. I faced another Shaman in the boss room, but now I was at the same level as it was, and with all my Skills from this overpowered Class, it was practically a foregone conclusion that I'd win. If these were real beings and not dungeon constructs, I would have felt terrible for how badly I was bullying them.

Since my third run, I had been hit by experience penalties, which were getting steeper. Still, I needed the XP, and they were an easy source. Each level took more and more XP, but I was still at the point where a single dungeon run would gain me another level.

I was glad I did, too. The boss loot this time was a set of armor, something I badly needed as my clothes were practically rags now.

> **Scalebane Leather Armor:** A set of lightweight, finely crafted leather armor adorned with dragon scale motifs. It provides enhanced agility and minor protection, along with a 10% resistance to elemental damage.

I was really loving that Luck stat! I was also impressed that it seemed to influence the drops to be more fitting for me in particular. Armor with dragon scale motifs? Yes, please!

I couldn't wait to try it on, but I didn't want to get it filthy from all the blood and sweat that was covering me after having run the dungeon three times in the same day. Thankfully, there was a 'stream' on the sixth floor. It wasn't much, just a small rivulet of running water coming out of one wall and flowing into a crack in the nearby floor. Still, despite it being in the Hobgoblin dungeon, it was clean water, so I used it to wash up. I couldn't exactly shower, but I did have a bar of fancy all-natural soap in my storage ring that I had bought from Whole Foods when I had run out to shop at the liquor stores.

I stripped down and bathed as best I could with a washcloth and soap. When I felt clean again, I put on underclothes and the new armor. Using the small polished metal mirror to check myself out, I had to admit the armor was impressive-looking. I looked like some kind of Dragonborn Rogue.

Now, at least, I wouldn't be walking around looking like a bum with torn-up clothes.

As always, I put all of the food, water, and potions in my storage ring and headed back to the surface.

I was going to find some way to bar the door of the bunker tonight. I hoped the idiots from earlier wouldn't be stupid enough to come back and try to get revenge for the death of their leader.

CHAPTER 18
BURN IT DOWN!

I DIDN'T SLEEP great that night. I was worried about scavengers and had a bad dream about killing Skeeter. I guess my conscience was feeling guilty for killing another human, even if he was trying to kill me to steal my things.

Logically, I knew he was a bad person and the world was better off without people like him, but it was hard not to feel guilty for aiding the System in reducing the human population. I should be saving the world, after all.

Grumbling and feeling more than a bit grumpy, I got up, ate an MRE for breakfast, and then packed up my cot and other miscellaneous things just in case someone came by while I was in the dungeon. I was hoping Morgan and her family would show up at some point, but it was a dangerous world out there. She might not make it back.

That thought made me sad. I wasn't looking at her as a potential love interest or anything, but she was clearly intelligent, and she could make a great person to watch over the shelter when I eventually had to leave. I wanted to see this place put to good use, and I couldn't be around if I was going to go out and find more dungeons.

Speaking of the dungeon, it might take more than one run to gain a level at this point, but even if it took an entire day to gain a level, that was still fantastic progress. At this rate, I would be Level 20 before the end of the week. I couldn't express how happy I was about that; it was simply amazing.

It had taken well over three years to hit Level 20 during my first life. Of course, that was because of all the downtime spent healing and the fact that I needed to find new parties to adventure with practically every time I delved. When you were hurt with low stats, it would take weeks to mend and get back into fighting shape, and most of the party would come out of a dungeon with wounds, so if you were lucky enough that a healing potion dropped, only one of you would get to benefit.

Often, by the time you were well again, your party had moved on without you and found a replacement. Now you had to go and find another party and hope they were decent enough that you survived the PUG. PUG being an old gaming term for 'pick up group', aka a group of random strangers you join to try and complete a quest with. In life, just like in games, random groups of strangers don't usually work out well.

My last group is a perfect example. They betrayed me for a piece of loot I didn't even want. The world needed fewer people like that and more good, decent folks like Morgan.

Such were my thoughts as I stood before the dungeon entrance again. The portal looked far less vibrant than it had the first time I went through it. I guessed it had a few more runs before it was drained to the point of no return.

I was Level 16 now, and the boss was only Level 15; the next strongest mobs were the Level 6 Hobgoblins. It was just farming and grinding at this point. On day three of the apocalypse, I ran the dungeon four times and hit Level 19, ending up at 8800/29680 XP to Level 20. Unfortunately, that last run proved to be one too many.

The dungeon was destroyed.

That was okay; I couldn't have run it anymore and gained experience from it anyway. After the 5th run, I started to get hit with experience penalties for having done it too many times. The 6th run had been at a 25% penalty, the 7th was a 50% hit, and the 8th was at 75%. Even if the dungeon had survived, any further runs would have gained me nothing, but the boss drops treasure.

Even in my first life, I had never participated in a dungeon closure. At that time, easy dungeons were considered resources and protected so that people wouldn't accidentally run them to the point of destruction. Or the dungeons were too difficult, and I wasn't capable of being in a party that could drain them completely. I had thought about keeping it around so that whoever came and lived in the bunker could use it to farm XP. However, I needed the experience immediately, and I was worried a dungeon right inside the fence with a bunch of refugees might not be the greatest idea. If they turned out not to be capable of completing it, they might end up with a dungeon break right outside their front door.

In the end, I was glad I destroyed it. I was awarded a new title.

Dungeon Destroyer - Awarded as the first in the world to destroy a dungeon, you are granted 10,000 bonus experience and a 50% chance of a tier up of any dungeon cores from closing a dungeon.

Speaking of loot, not only did I receive a Common Dungeon Core, but the boss drops from the four runs were pretty spectacular as well.

Gloves of the Artificer's Touch - A pair of gloves infused with magical energy, enhancing the wearer's Ability to craft and repair items. They grant a bonus to crafting Skills and reduce material requirements for crafting.

Crown of the Eternal Sentinel - A thin silver circlet engraved with ancient runes, providing increased resistance to magic by 10% and a minor buff to leadership and charisma.

Skill scroll: Explorer - Automatically maps the user's travels. Can pull up a heads-up display of a map showing the user's travels. Especially useful for dungeon exploration. Dungeons and Area Bosses will be marked on the map upon coming within a mile of their location.

Elixir of Shadows - A rare elixir that grants the consumer temporary invisibility or enhanced stealth capabilities, useful for avoiding enemies or initiating surprise attacks. Also, has a chance of granting Shadow Affinity.

Those were all incredible finds, and I was sure they would not have been so good if not for my Luck stat.

Both the gloves and the Explorer Skill had hidden features. The gloves had the Ability to repair items you were wearing over time. So, while I could not use them for their intended crafting purpose, they would still be extremely useful. Rents and tears in my armor and clothing would fix themselves if given sufficient time.

I also used the Skill Scroll immediately when I found it. That was an incredibly useful Skill that made running dungeons much easier. Its hidden feature was that you could sometimes tell there were hidden rooms or secret doors by the way things looked on the map. A wall would look thinner than those around it, for example. It didn't do me any good in the Goblin dungeon, but I had known others with this Skill in my past life, so I knew how great it was.

As for the dungeon core... I had only ever seen a couple of those in my first life, but they were very valuable. They could be used as a Mana source for powering magical devices or as a crafting material for making powerful magic items. They came in grades of lesser, common, greater, grand, and epic. Typically, a low-level dungeon, like the Goblin one, would have a lesser core, but that title worked in my favor, and upgraded it to common.

I didn't have a use for it right then, but at the very least, it would be a good item to sell or trade once the Shop opened. Or if I found some craftsmen to build this base up, it could be used to power the bunker or to create a defensive magic ward to keep beasts or monsters out.

That brought my thoughts around to what I should do next. Despite the bad experience I had with the scavengers, there were good people out there desperately seeking shelter and running for their lives from one dangerous situation to the next. I know that I certainly had the first time around. On day three of the apocalypse, I had hiked out of the city with a group of refugees, and we had been running from the hellscape Dallas had become. It was on this day that I had been nearly gored to death by a damned jackalope.

Maybe it was the nightmare about killing Skeeter or just feeling guilty for exiling the scavengers, but I wanted to head into town and see if I could help people. I was Level 19 now. There couldn't be too many monsters that would be a challenge to me on Day 4, right? ...right?

I had a bad feeling about it, but I had an even worse one about staying here. Besides, with the dungeon now gone, I needed to go out and search for more if I wanted to continue progressing.

It was getting late in the day, so I decided to bed down in the bunker for one more night and then leave after breakfast in the morning.

With my current stats, I should be able to make good time. I might even manage to cover the forty miles into the outskirts of the metroplex in a single day.

That reminded me. It was time to look at my Status screen. I had been leveling up so rapidly that I hadn't bothered to do anything but assign my free stat points.

Liam Bell: (Current)
Draconic Spellsword - Level 19

Experience: 8800/29680

Attributes:
Endurance: 40
Strength: 40
Agility: 40
Mind: 41
Will: 40
Magical Aptitude:35
Luck: 2

Health: 800/800
Mana: 760/760

Abilities:
Dark Vision
Dragon Fear
Scales (Passive)

Active Skills:
Acid Bolt
Draconic Strike

Draconic Fury
Dragonfire Ward
Searing Slash
Scalebound Resilience
Dragon's Charge
Acid Spray

Passive Skills: None

Those stats are crazy! By the time I hit Level 25 in this new Epic Class, I will already have better stats than I had at Level 57 in my first life.

The foundation you start with makes such a huge difference!

I wanted to spread the word, but I was still afraid of causing myself to get assassinated. I pondered what I could do while eating dinner that night. I couldn't tell people everything, but perhaps I could share some knowledge.

Looking at the walls of the bunker while I ate, I was a little sad to see all the graffiti gone. The paint had been consumed by the System, and now I was left with bare concrete walls.

A blank canvas?

That gave me an idea. I took a stick from the fire, moved over to one of the walls, and began to write with charcoal. The System wouldn't bother with that since there was nothing artificial about it. I ended up using my sword to burn the end of the stick to charcoal over and over, but in the end, I felt I had made a couple of useful suggestions that didn't necessarily require foreknowledge to think of, just wisdom.

Be it known:

- *Before Class selection, choose 'Class Options.' You will be shown many more options than the few the System suggests. Pick a magic Class if you can.*

- *If no magic Class options are available, get a Mana coin from killing a monster. After a day you will have a point in Magical Aptitude, then more Class options will show up.*
- *You can upgrade your Class at Level 30. Try to get a magic Class! Earth needs more mages to deal with the magic-using monsters and invaders.*
- *Dungeons are hard to conquer without magic.*
- *Support crafters and healers; we need them!*
- *A System Shop will open in a month. Save your coins to buy good gear and food.*
- *You can destroy a dungeon by running it over and over until it runs out of Mana.*
- *Regular animals will mutate into dangerous beasts. They are real; their bodies do not disappear. They can be eaten, and their parts can be used to craft armor and weapons.*
- *Dungeon monsters and their gear disappear after killing them.*
- *Dungeons only drop gear when killing bosses and mini-bosses. Otherwise, all you will find is a few supplies like meals and a couple of potions in the boss room.*
- *Do not tolerate evil people but protect and cherish decent people.*
- *You can make a fortress out of the missile silo out back. There is running water on the 6th floor.*
- *Anything synthetic or technological will be consumed by the System. Don't use building materials that will fall apart. Plywood will turn into thick sheets of paper when the glue disappears, and whatever is built from it will fall apart. Use stone, metal, or wood that doesn't include glue.*
- *This place should be safe because it was created with only concrete and steel. The missile silo out back was converted into a dungeon by the System. I destroyed it, so what remains is the shell of what it turned into. It should be safe now.*

- *I am Liam Bell. I will try to return soon and help any survivors I find here, and send more this way. If you do not find me when you arrive, make this place a safe area and use it to thrive!*

I was disappointed that Morgan hadn't shown back up, but I hoped my message would help whoever found this place while I was gone. It revealed that I had destroyed the dungeon, but nothing about this was out of the realm of possibility for someone who lucked into finding the other Class options and getting a good Class. At least, that's what I would say if anyone questioned it.

After I was done, I put out the fire and bedded down for the night. I wanted to get an early start on the next adventure.

CHAPTER 19

ENCOUNTERS ON
THE WAY

BRIGHT AND EARLY THE following day, I was pleasantly surprised to be awakened by a knock on the bunker door. Getting woken up wasn't the good part; it was seeing Morgan, her family, and about a dozen others milling about outside the door, along with horses, cows, sheep, goats, and chickens.

It warmed my heart. I had been afraid I would leave an empty bunker behind and no one to hold down the fort. Now, it looked like the place would be filled with life. Better still, they had brought livestock and as many supplies as they could carry. There were literally bundles of goods strapped to the backs of the cows, including an old wooden rocking chair. That seemed to belong to an elderly woman I could only assume was Morgan's grandmother, considering my waitress friend was supporting her.

Grinning, I gestured to the compound and called out loudly enough for everyone to hear, "Welcome, everyone! I won't tell you this place is safe, but with a bit of work, it can be. It's safer than anywhere around here. Bring your things inside and find places to keep the livestock inside the fence, but don't trust that fence to keep anything out."

Quieter to Morgan and her father, who was a strong-looking man in his middle years, said, "I need to speak to you. I need to leave, but I've got a lot to tell you before I go."

Morgan looked shocked and barely kept from crying out, "You're leaving us?"

I shook my head and led them into the bunker. I pointed to the walls, "I left some written advice. Make sure everyone learns it and spreads it to anyone you meet."

"I'm Sam Pickering, Morgan's father. What's this about you leaving? Morgan said you were strong and could protect people who came here. Most of us are only first or second level in our Classes." He looked serious and worried.

"Hi, I'm Liam Bell. Level 19, and I was lucky enough to get one of the limited Classes."

The man's eyes almost bugged out when I told him my level. "How in the hell...?"

Chuckling, I pointed outside toward the missile silo. "There was a dungeon here on the property. I ran it so many times it was destroyed. If I had known you all would show up today, I would have left it for you, but I wasn't sure anyone would show, and I didn't want to leave something that dangerous behind. If a dungeon can't be culled regularly, it will eventually produce too many monsters, and they will start to spill out into the area around the dungeon."

Mr. Pickering gave me a look. "Morgan says not to ask about how you know things, but I sure am curious."

With a grin, I just reply, "There are reasons I can't say, and it is best not to speculate." I point at the sky and mouth AI, hoping he gets it.

Whether he did or not, he seemed to accept reluctantly, so I pointed them toward the wall and went over the advice. I also covered everything I thought was safe to disclose. After a few minutes, I got through it all and then went over my plans to go toward the city and check things out.

"So, I'd like you to take charge of the facility here and ensure no baddies come in and try to throw their weight around. If someone does, then let them know I plan to be back soon, and I'll be over Level 20 when I return and can kick their ass; or not. Do as you see fit, and if anyone does act like that, I'll deal with them when I get back, which won't be too many days."

Then, on to more practical matters, I explained, "Send out scouts if you can, find another low-level dungeon within decent riding distance from here, and get yourselves some levels. It will be a big help with fending off wild beasts that will try to come eat you and the livestock."

Morgan grinned, "I got my Class, by the way. You were right about the Mana coin giving a point in Mana Aptitude, and I looked for those limited Classes you mentioned. I got a rare grade Class, Dragon Priestess."

It was my turn for my eyes to bug out. "Seriously? That is incredible. Does it grant you the Bloodline, like mine?"

She shook her head sadly. "No, but it does say that by making compacts dragons, I can be granted some of their power in addition to the normal healer Abilities that the Class normally gets. It mentioned that for each pact I can be granted one of their Abilities per tier."

Grinning like a cat, she asked, "So, wanna form a pact?"

I laughed. "Nice. You picked that because you knew I was a Draconic Spellsword, didn't you?"

With a big smirk on her face, she nodded. "Yep. It also has the benefit that dragons and Draconic creatures will view me as neutral rather than being automatically hostile. That might come in handy someday."

Pulling out a long kitchen knife from a rough sheath on her belt, she cut her palm and presented the knife to me. "I'll make a pact with you right now if you will have me."

"Sure. All I ask in return is that you watch this place as my steward." I took the knife and cut my palm and then shook hands, letting our blood mingle.

I had always thought those movies and TV shows where characters cut their palms instead of cutting someplace less painful and annoying were dumb. On the other hand, Morgan was a priestess and could heal my wound immediately, so it wasn't a big deal.

As our blood mingled, I felt something. My Mana and something deeper seemed to connect with Morgan. It wasn't unpleasant or harmful, but I could feel it there. With a bit of quiet concentration, I was pretty sure I could sense her current state and direction. She also appeared as a blue dot on my mini-map now, almost like she was in my party.

I wasn't the only one who felt the change. Morgan was bouncing up and down, and her dad was looking at her like she was a kid getting overly excited on Christmas morning. "What is it?"

"It gave me a choice between three Abilities: Dark Vision, Draconic Fear, and Scales. I picked Draconic Fear because it seemed like something that could save my life in a pinch. It also let me pick one offensive Spell Ability, so I picked Acid Bolt. My Class already gave me one defensive Spell and a healing Spell, so that one seemed like it would make dungeons or fighting off critters easier."

Nodding approvingly, I said, "Great choices. Draconic Fear could be used offensively too."

I went on to explain how I usually used it in combat, and she beamed at me even more, pleased that she had made a good choice.

After a moment, she frowned slightly as she continued looking through her status messages, then back at me. "Ugh, that's not all. Now that we have bonded, there are two other abilities; one is Commune, which will let us communicate over long distances. That one sounds very handy. However, there's another ability that I'm not so sure about. It's called Summon, and by the text of it, it seems to go both ways."

She shared her screen with me:

Ability Name: Summon
Summon allows the Dragon Priestess to call forth her
compacted dragon or for the dragon to summon her,
bridging their bond across any distance. The duration of the
summoning ranges from 1 hour to 1 day, depending on the
mana invested. Once the time limit is reached, the
summoned beings return to their original location,
maintaining their connection through the ether.

"Hmm... That one sounds really useful, actually. What's your concern?" I asked.

Grimacing, she explained, "There's no mention of being able to refuse the summons nor of any warning before it takes place. What if one of us is in the middle of a fight or something else important, and the other just yanks us away?"

Now, it was my turn to frown. "Yeah, I can see your point. Okay, let's make a deal; outside of an absolute life or death situation, there will be no summoning without first using Commune; sound good?"

Having said that, I quickly scanned my own status page and noticed that I did, in fact, have a new section labeled "Bonded Priest." I could expand that section, and sure enough, there were two options, Commune and Summon. It looked like it really did go both ways.

"Yeah, that sounds fine, and it's a relief. You seem like a decent guy; otherwise, I wouldn't have made the pact with you. However, I could definitely see that Summon's ability being abused by someone like my ex."

That made me chuckle. "Yeah, I could, for sure, see Skeeter making middle-of-the-night drunken booty summonses."

Shuddering, Morgan gave me a look that said I'd better not ever try such a thing.

I laughed aloud this time but waved the concern away, "Don't worry, I'm not that kind of guy. We'll stick to the deal. Life or death only unless you use Commune first to give warning and ask permission."

We talked a bit more, and I was introduced to the others, then headed out.

I left the bunker and headed toward town at a fast jog. With my stats, I could have gone at a full sprint and still not gotten tired, but I wasn't in a race. I wanted to get a good look at the lands between the base and the city, keeping my eyes open for signs of mutated beasts or potential dungeons. More importantly, I wanted to find any survivors to share my tips about how to survive the apocalypse.

I also wanted to direct any decent people I could find to the bunker. Now that the dungeon was gone and I was at a higher level, I didn't really need it for myself, but it would make a great base of operations to build a community around. Both the communications bunker and the missile silo could make fantastic fortifications against monsters.

They could house dozens of people for now and become the hub of a larger safe area once enough people built some walls.

At the very least, it could help some people survive until the Shop opened. These first days and weeks were crucial, and in my first life, humanity was scattered into the countryside in every direction from the big cities with no plan and no resources. The missile base had water, both from a well and that spring on the 6th floor, so no one who went there would die of dehydration or catch some disease from bad water. So many had died from that alone in this first month!

On the other hand, I had dragon blood flowing in my veins, and I had to admit that I considered the place to be mine. That meant I wasn't eager to give it up even if I wasn't going to stay there. At least I was self-aware enough to recognize the desire for what it was. Not that I minded a little dragon-based greed; I just didn't want to let such instincts run my life. My human brain needed to be the part of me in charge.

The run was mostly uneventful, although I did manage to find and kill a trio of mutated coyotes and a black mountain lion that had grown as big as a pony. That one had been a little scary, but with my Bloodline Abilities and Class Skills, I made quick work of it. I had been at a higher level, so when I used Dragon Fear, it froze in terror for several seconds, allowing me to cripple it before it could use its agility and speed to much effect.

I stored the bodies of all four in my ring after cutting their monster cores out. The cores from the coyotes were pathetic, crystals just larger than the size of a pea. The mountain lion core was a bit better, being the size of a marble. Like a dungeon core, monster cores could be used as crafting material or to power magic items or effects. They were just much less useful and valuable.

Unlike dungeon cores, monster cores weren't graded the same way. They didn't come in specific set sizes but rather ranged in size and power depending on the beast they were from. It would take hundreds of the small coyote cores to equal even a lesser dungeon core. Still, they were valuable and could be used to trade once things settled down and the Shop opened. These were all considered Tier 1 monster cores.

One thing I regretted was not taking some time before the apocalypse to research the area outside the city. It would have been nice to figure out where dungeons would be likely to crop up. All it would have taken was looking at one of the map applications to find big facilities. The more technology, the higher the chance of a dungeon forming. I could have gone right to the best places if I had done that.

Instead, I followed the roads back to the city. It had only been four days since Initialization, so the highways were still intact. Thanks to the tar, they would eventually break down a bit, but even then, most of the road materials were still natural. Years from now, the old highway system would still be one of the most useful things left over from before the fall.

The most important outcome of my travels were the survivors that I met along the way. Some were people who had lived out in the country but near the highways. Their homes were in various states of falling apart, but most of them were hanging in there and trying to protect their properties as best they could.

To each of these, I gave the same advice:

"Group up with people you trust if you can. Find someplace defensible and hunker down. Get levels as safely as you can and get stronger."

I also told them about the missile base and suggested they head there if they didn't know of any other safe place. Of course, I only gave that information to the ones I thought were good people. Any that I came across who gave me a bad vibe received only general advice or none at all.

The closer I came to the city, the more groups of refugees I encountered. These ranged in size from one or two people all the way up to groups of a few dozen. Most of these were just regular folk who had been smart enough to get out of Dodge and not wait for everything to go completely to ruin. Small or large, these groups were ragged, and most were burdened with anything they could carry that hadn't been destroyed by the System.

I gave most of these groups the same advice and pointed them toward my base, but I also started giving hunting advice as well.

"Get some levels as you travel, do the best you can without endangering your group. If you see beasts, aka mutated animals, they will give experience and provide meat and materials that can be used for crafting. Do what you are able, but don't die. I am sending all the decent people I can to the base. If you follow this map and stay near the roads, you probably won't encounter too many critters due to other folks already hunting the area. The more you clear an area, the safer it will be, but beware of higher-leveled creatures. The more time passes, the stronger the beasts will get."

I also told them about the monster cores and showed them the ones from the coyote and mountain lions.

Lastly, I told them what I could about the Shop. "The System Initialization message mentioned full integration will happen after a month. I am pretty sure that will mean greater opportunities and dangers. Try to get as powerful as you can before then, but hold on for a month. I think we will get access to System-based resources like a Shop or something."

My words were received differently by everyone. Some were suspicious, already distrustful of everything and everyone. Others were filled with hope or a determination to get stronger. Most were simply thankful to have a destination and a goal. Too many that I met were simply adrift with no plan other than to get away from the city and latched onto everything I said, begging me to take them to safety.

I had a few uncomfortable moments of having to pry people off my arms or even my legs as they clung to me and wept. Often, I was the first individual they had met who seemed confident and capable and didn't seem lost.

In every case, I disengaged as quickly as I could and continued on, pleading the need to go and help others. I just hoped that Morgan and her family and friends wouldn't be overwhelmed by the influx of refugees.

That evening, I camped off the highway in a stand of trees. I estimated that I had made it most of the way to the metroplex. I thought I'd have an hour or two run in the morning before I reached the outskirts of town. What I didn't expect was to be awoken by screams in the middle of the night.

Blinking the sleep from my eyes, I quickly threw my cot and canvas tarp into my storage ring and ran toward the road, unsure of what I would find. Even though there was some moonlight, the moon was only a sliver in the sky, most of it eclipsed by the Earth. Thanks to my Dark Vision, I could weave between the trees without breaking stride or tripping over any roots. Soon, I arrived at the road and saw a surprising sight.

A group of Orcs, grotesque and gnarled, had encircled a small band of women and children. They were jeering, their guttural voices filled with malice, as they brandished their crude, menacing weapons. The air was thick with fear and the Orcs' foul stench.

The women were huddled together, clutching their children, their faces etched with terror. The children's cries were heart-wrenching, their eyes wide with an understanding beyond their years. The Orcs moved closer, their intentions clear—they were herding their prey, relishing the power they held.

I could see the women's desperate eyes scanning for an escape, but they were trapped. The Orcs were toying with them, enjoying the fear they were instilling. It was a scene of predators playing with their cornered quarry, and it sickened me.

I knew I couldn't just stand by. I readied myself, planning my approach. These Orcs were about to find out they weren't the only predators in the night.

Counting, I could see twelve of the greyish-skinned monsters. They stood as tall as humans but were malformed, as if the hate and cruelty in their souls manifested in their bodies. That wasn't too many for me to take unless they were too high in levels. What scared me was that they might harm the humans while I fought. I needed to get their attention and draw them away to focus on me alone.

I engaged my Dragon's Charge, closing the distance between us in a blur of speed. The nearest Orc didn't even have time to react before my blade cleanly severed its head from its shoulders.

Swiftly turning to my right, I thrust my sword through the next Orc, skewering it. With a heave, I used my sword to fling the lifeless body away, clearing a path for the terrified people.

"Group up, hold hands, and run into the woods as soon as you can!" I instructed them, my voice firm yet calm.

It took several heartbeats before the first of the women made sense of my words and started gathering those around her and getting everyone to hold hands.

I then moved counterclockwise around the circle, engaging the Orcs in combat. My sword danced with deadly precision, cutting down two more of the grotesque creatures in quick succession. I was focused, every sense heightened, anticipating their clumsy yet powerful attacks. They were awake now to the danger I posed and started getting smarter.

Worse, they were tougher than the Hobgoblins from the dungeon. I estimated they were around Level 10. That was a lot of monsters to deal with, even with me being higher level. I was also holding my Skills in reserve in case of an emergency, should I need to save one of the victims from a killing blow by an Orc. That made the job harder.

I was confronted by a trio of Orcs converging on me, their malicious grins foretelling a brutal fight. I was on edge, aware that I couldn't use Dragon's Fear without risking the safety of the women and children. My other Skills, too, were held in reserve, ready to be unleashed in case any of the victims faced imminent danger.

These Orcs were tougher and more cunning than the Hobgoblins I had encountered in the dungeon. Each swing of their heavy, crude weapons demanded a response, either a parry or a swift dodge, as I was determined not to let any strike land.

The Orcs lunged in unison, their movements surprisingly coordinated. I parried the first blow, feeling the shock run up my arm, then ducked under a wild swing from the second. The third Orc nearly caught me off guard with a low swipe, but I leaped back just in time, feeling the weapon brush against my armor but not penetrate.

Thank goodness for that boss drop! Armor for the win!

I countered swiftly, my sword cutting into the flesh of the first Orc, but the wound was shallow—not enough to bring it down. They were relentless, barely flinching at their injuries, their eyes burning with a hatred that matched my own determination.

The fight was drawn out longer than I had hoped. I needed to end this quickly before the women and children were put in more danger. As I engaged the Orcs, I shouted again to the group, "Group up, hold hands, and run into the woods, quickly!" My voice cut through the chaos, and after a moment's hesitation, they began to move, gathering themselves together.

With the humans starting to escape, the fight's intensity grew. The Orcs sensed their prey slipping away and became more aggressive, trying to push past me. I couldn't let them. I doubled my efforts, moving with all the speed and skill I had. My blade found its mark on the first Orc, then the second. As they fell, I turned to face the third, but it was more cautious now, circling, looking for an opening. Meanwhile, the others were starting to move toward me, deciding to make me pay before chasing down their escaping victims.

Finally, as the last of the women and children vanished into the safety of the woods, I felt a surge of relief—and an opportunity to unleash my full power. The remaining Orcs, now realizing their prey had escaped, turned their full attention on me. They had me surrounded now.

Their mistake. That was exactly where I wanted them!

I let loose a roar, activating Dragon's Fear. The Orcs froze, terror written across their vile faces. I had bought myself precious seconds.

One.

I lunged with Searing Slash, leaving a trail of corrosive energy across the chest of the nearest Orc.

Two.

Powerstrike was next, my blade cleaving through the skull of another, its halves falling apart like a grotesque fruit.

Three.

Raising my left hand, I discharged an Acid Bolt point-blank into the face of the third, its head disintegrating in a spray of acid and gore.

Four.

The last two Orcs began to recover from their terror just as I turned on them with Acid Spray. A continuous, searing stream of acid engulfed their faces and torsos.

Five... six... seven... eight.

By the time the fear effect would have worn off, the last Orc dropped lifelessly to the ground, its body corroded beyond recognition.

I stood alone amidst the carnage, my breath heavy, my heart still racing. The fight had been tougher than I anticipated, but it was over. I had saved them and, in doing so, unleashed the full fury of my abilities. The satisfaction was palpable, but so was the reminder of the ever-present danger in this chaotic world.

What boggled my mind was how there could possibly be a dungeon break only four days after Initialization. These were not sentient invaders from another world; they were System-generated monsters, as proven by their bodies disappearing and leaving Mana coins behind.

I remembered how hellish the city got after Initialization Day, but even then, I didn't remember dungeon breaks happening so soon. What kind of insane circumstance had conspired to power a dungeon with so much Mana that its inhabitants were able to go out into the world and capture humans within the first week?

CHAPTER 20

THIS IS A TRASHFIRE OF A DUNGEON!

AFTER COLLECTING the 120 copper Mana coins, I hurried to the woods, hoping the survivors hadn't blindly kept running but had instead waited for me to come find them.

I was in luck. That was exactly the case. An older woman, perhaps the mother of one of the children in the group, judging by the way she was clutching a child, called out to me as I approached.

"Thank you for saving us! Can you please help our husbands and friends?"

It was hard to have a conversation at first, as many of the women and children were crying or pleading with me for help. The woman who had spoken first seemed to be somewhat of a leader among them and managed to quiet them down after a couple of minutes.

Once they had calmed down, I began asking the questions I needed answers to.

"Where did those Orcs come from? You mentioned husbands and friends; where are they?"

It was a jumbled story, with many survivors chiming in to add details that only made things muddier and harder to understand. Still, after a bit, I had the gist of their story.

A large group of refugees had been hiking out of the metroplex when they neared the big garbage dump outside of Melissa, TX. It was a large facility with an industrial oil or natural gas storage and transfer hub right next door.

The Orcs had sallied out of the dump and attacked the group, talking of enslaving some and eating the rest. Their husbands and the more martially inclined of their number had made a defensive line in order for the mothers and children to get away. They had promised to follow after as soon as the Orcs were dealt with. Unfortunately, around nightfall, rather than the rest of their group catching up, the Orcs had found them instead.

I had a bad feeling about the whole situation. Their husbands and friends were probably captured and being used as slaves to help build the Orcs' base. Although, I was sure not all of them had been so lucky. The monsters might be System-generated, but they behaved just like the real things, and from the sound of it, this was a special type of dungeon.

A city dump would have an absolutely huge amount of resources for the System to convert into Mana. Then, to make matters worse, there was an industrial facility right next door. It sounded like the System had generated either an above-ground dungeon or a hub of connected dungeons. With as much material as there was, it was no wonder it was spewing out monsters able to attack humans outside their dungeon. There were bound to be dozens or even hundreds of monsters in a place like that.

Looking to the woman who seemed to be in charge but speaking so they all could hear, I said, "I will go and investigate, and if anyone can rescue your people, it's me. I can't make any promises, but if it is possible to save them, then I will. You all need to head to my base. Team up with any others you find on the way that seem trustworthy and wait there. I will either bring your people back to meet you there, or I will send them on to find you."

I went on to tell them about the missile base and how I had been sending other refugees there for safety. I also passed on my other regular advice about survival and choosing Classes. Some of the children were too young to have chosen yet, so for them, my advice was super important. I had to explain things to the mother, who was their spokesperson, so that she could understand what I meant. Once she got it, she assured me she would help them pick wisely. To help out, I gave each of the young children a Mana coin in the hopes that having something imbued with Mana on their person for a time would give them a better shot at choosing a magic-based Class.

The dragon blood in me cringed at giving away treasure, but I squelched that instinct. These kids could be paragons of the human race if they survived and benefited from my experience. Besides, it wasn't like I was poor now. I had over 2000 copper Mana coins after running the dungeon so many times, and a handful would not be missed.

There was a voice in the back of my mind saying that yes, yes they would be missed!

I had to chuckle at myself and the greed that came with the Draconic Bloodline.

That greedy voice was also telling me that conquering that dungeon and rescuing those people would mean earning a tremendous amount of wealth and treasure.

Meanwhile, the part of me that was Liam from before the apocalypse and reboot was telling me it was the right thing to do, and the whole reason I had these abilities was to save as much of the human race as

I could and make them safe. That was the side I wanted to be the 'real' me. That greedy voice was just the dragon blood talking.

Right?

I took a few minutes to try and examine my plan logically, without either the emotion of wanting to save people or the greed of wanting treasure and gains. On the one hand, the Orcs I had just killed were all Level 10, and there would be dozens of them at minimum, perhaps hundreds of them. I was higher level and had skills, but that was too much for me to handle unless I could take them down a few at a time, like I had during that first run in the silo dungeon. On the other, perhaps I could manage it. I might have to get others to help, though. Free the captives, and they could help me fight if they were in decent condition.

No way to know until I see it.

I stayed with the group of survivors that night and kept watch since I had already gotten several hours of sleep before their screams had woken me.

During that time, I chatted with Lisa, the woman whom I had identified as their leader. She told me of her husband, Thomas, and how he had recently retired after twenty years of service in the army. They had decided to settle down in McKinney on the outskirts of the DFW metroplex to raise their daughter. Their story was typical of what so many were going through: families separated by the apocalypse and not knowing if they would ever be able to reunite. Having no family of my own made me empathize with them even more. As much as I missed my dad, for me, it had been two and a half decades since I'd seen him, so I couldn't imagine how much they must be worried and hurting right now.

Then, in the morning, I let them share some of my MREs so that they could travel on a full stomach. I felt bad about letting go of my supplies, but I was sure that if I survived the day's battles, I would be even better provisioned than I was now.

Lisa hugged me before they left, along with her young daughter, Susie. I felt an unexpected warmth in my heart. I literally could not remember the last time someone hugged me.

I cleared my throat and disengaged after a second, saying, "Lead them to the base; she'll be safe there. I'll try and make sure Thomas and the others find you."

With some reluctance, the group parted from me and headed up the abandoned highway to the Northeast.

I jogged in the opposite direction... toward hell.

Okay, toward the garbage dump, but I was sure it would be pretty hellish. The smell alone would be...

I stopped in my tracks, a sudden thought occurring to me.

Dumps are filled with methane. They literally have venting systems to burn off the gas when it accumulates. With the System reclaiming technology, I wonder if the gas would still be there because I'm pretty darn sure the safety system would not be functional any longer.

I felt like grinning evilly at what I could do with that knowledge, but I held off on cackling like a villain and twirling non-existent mustaches. There was just no way to know if that was something I could take advantage of until I got there and investigated. Besides, I had to free any prisoners before I could consider taking any drastic actions, even if it were possible. Still, that was something to consider for later.

After a bit, I had a downer of a thought. The System probably would not give me credit for the kills if I managed to use an environmental factor like that to destroy a bunch of the monsters. Ah, crap. It had been such a pleasant thought.

Resuming my jog, I moved down the road, wary of potential ambushes.

As it turned out, the dump was visible from three or four miles away, thanks to the moderately sized hills of trash. Even from this distance, I could see there were two main hills as they towered over everything around them. Getting nearer, I could tell that there was a palisade being erected around the top of the hills. They were using simple, sharpened wooden logs to build their walls, but they were not complete yet.

Given that I could see that from where I was, I had to worry that they would be able to see me as well. It was a valid concern, given how many Orcs they seemed to have roaming around the hillsides. I could easily spot three dozen overseeing humans who were doing the actual work.

That sight made my blood boil, but I pushed down the rage that wanted to bubble up for now. There would be time enough to kill the monsters once I had scouted the dungeon area.

I started my scouting from the point where the industrial oil and gas facility had been. I supposed that the nature of the place made the System especially eager to break it down, but even after only four days, it was almost entirely gone. There were the remnants of some metal tanks, but they were rapidly rusting away at an almost visible rate. What was left was a rock-covered plot of land that probably covered ten acres and not a tree in sight.

There was a road that went south next to the barren field of rusting tanks. I used it to begin circling around the Orc dungeon's area. There were plenty of trees along the east side of the dump, but many of those were being chopped down by slaves and their Orc overseers. Still, I didn't find it too hard to stay out of their immediate view. I simply noted the crews and added that information to the growing list of details in my mind. Once I had made a complete circuit of the dump, I would have a better idea of how to tackle this seemingly impossible task.

I was lucky that trees circled about half the taller of the two hills that made up the dump, but even the half that was shielded from view still had smaller hills and trees lining the road and farm fields on the other side of the road. In the most exposed places, I could cross the road and swing wide around those fields, which in turn had their own tree-lined perimeters. I wasn't sure if it was because of the 1930s Dust Bowl, but most farm fields in north Texas had trees that created wind-breaks separating them from their neighbors. Those wind-breaks provided me with good cover to avoid being spotted by the Orc lookouts.

And I did see small bands of those lookouts. They seemed to be watching for more human refugee parties to pass nearby. Thankfully, that wasn't too big of a threat to me since I was a lone person, and I knew to expect them so I could avoid their notice.

As I swung around the southern side of the dump, I could see the second hill much better now that I was close. Like the big hill, humans were busy building log walls, but right in the center of that hill, there was the unmistakable sight of a Shaman's hut. They also seemed to have several large fenced areas that I assumed were slave pens. It seemed that the Orc's mystic leader was in charge of managing the slaves, aka the human refugees.

The big hill also had a structure right in the center of the tallest part. It looked like a small fortress, also made of wood, but I could tell even from a distance that it was System-generated. There was no way the people building those crude walls could have put together something significantly nicer in only four days, even if it was small in comparison to the walls. I planned to sneak closer to that in the evening after the sun went down, but for now, I would assume that was the home of the Orcish War Chief.

Much like their smaller cousins, the Goblins, the Orcs were organized similarly. From what I could see already, there were well over a hundred regular Orcs in this dungeon, but probably closer to 200. There would also be Orcish Elites somewhere around Level 15. However, unlike the Goblin dungeon, it wasn't a choice of 'either/or' for bosses. The Orcs would have both a Shaman and a War Chief in this kind of dungeon. The only question was which was the boss and which was the mini-boss.

Making an educated guess, I'm sure the mini-boss will be the Shaman since it occupies the smaller of the two hills. The upside was that I wouldn't have to fight both at the same time unless I was stupid or highly unlucky. Even if the other realized an attack was happening at the opposite camp, they wouldn't be able to get there quickly enough to participate before the battle was over. Of course, even if they didn't show up in time, getting hit by another boss soon after a tough fight would still suck. You wouldn't have time to recover your Mana and wounds before you were beset with more enemies.

I put those thoughts aside in favor of finishing the scouting mission.

The sports field complex south of the dump was gone; only the parking lot was still visible. However, moving along to the west, I was surprised to see the new Melissa football stadium was still standing, although the high school, which had been really large, was missing. The surprising thing about the stadium was that it seemed to have been converted by the System into a coliseum-style arena, and as I drew near, I could see that the Orcs were using it. There were a few of them outside dragging humans toward the entrance.

I would need to deal with that as well, but I had to finish scouting first. To that end, I used what little cover I could find and got close to the stadium/arena. It had been a multi-million dollar concrete football stadium before the apocalypse, but now it had walls surrounding it that would prevent prisoners from escaping. They didn't stop me from sneaking a peek inside, however. As many Orcs as there were, there weren't so many that they could post guards everywhere. They also seemed confident that no one dared to oppose them, and, given their level advantage over pretty much all of the humans except me, that was a pretty safe assumption. At best, there probably weren't many humans in the area that topped Level 5, much less nearing the minimum Level 10 that the Orcs possessed. Worse, inside the arena, I could see at least twenty Elites who were probably Level 15.

They seemed to be mostly sparring with each other and occasionally forcing humans to fight one another.

Again, my dragon blood wanted to boil. I had the desire to rush in there and lay waste to the bastards who would dare to treat the human race this way. Fortunately, logic won out. I knew better than to start my campaign against this dungeon by throwing myself against so many Elites at once. That would be suicide, even if I were at a higher level than them.

With that decision made, I crept away from there and continued my circuit of the open dungeon, and I was not surprised to see that the housing development and apartment complex just to the north of the stadium were in an advanced state of decomposition. Those had been built only recently, like most of the housing in this little bedroom community outside the big city.

Even so, I was shocked at just how bad things were after only four days. Ironically, the few older homes I had seen were all much better off. Things built a hundred years ago looked just fine. The newer the technology and the more synthetic materials used in construction, the faster they fell apart. I stood amidst the near-complete collapse of the brand-new neighborhood and could only marvel at it. I remembered seeing similar sights from my first life, but it had all been so long ago that the visceral nature of seeing it had faded in my memories.

These homes were made with OSB plywood, essentially wood shavings held together with glue. Glue that dissolved, or was eaten by nanites, or converted to Mana, or whatever. The point was that the thing holding the wood together simply vanished. To make matters worse, the studs in the walls were made from cheap-grade wood joined together with feather joints, which were also held together with glue that was no longer there. Asphalt roof tiles... dissolved. Actual plywood... that was just thick sheets of paper when you remove the glue. PVC and PEX plumbing... dissolved. Doors and cabinetry... mostly laminated particle board, which no longer had glue holding them together. About the only things that were solid and natural were the foundations made from concrete and steel.

Even that would break down eventually despite it being mostly natural materials. The System didn't seem to like suburbia, and within five or ten years, there was little left of what had once been sprawling housing developments. Even the foundations were consumed for material to create dungeons and mutate beasts.

I was deep in these thoughts when I heard a whisper-shout from the west. Someone wanted my attention, it seemed.

"Hey! Quickly, come out of the street!"

CHAPTER 21

THE ASSAULT BEGINS

I WAS STANDING in the middle of the street of what had been a brand-new housing development just four days ago. When I heard the voice, I looked around, startled that someone would be this close to the large, open Orc dungeon.

To be fair, there probably weren't that many people yet who even grasped the fact that dungeons were real. However, this person had to know there was danger because they were trying hard not to speak loudly enough to be heard by anyone other than me. Also, they were hiding behind the remnants of a privacy fence that was in the process of collapsing.

I cautiously walked in the direction of the voice, not sure what to expect. Even being Level 19 now, I was nervous about being this close to the Orc camp dungeon in broad daylight.

As I neared, I could see that two sections of the privacy fence had collapsed and were now leaning against each other, providing a small nook in which a young girl sheltered.

Blinking in surprise, I tried to make sense of what I was seeing. Not that I had any real expectations, but the voice had been a little high-pitched, so I thought that maybe it was a mother or wife who had lost a loved one and was trying to get them back.

The last thing my imagination would have conjured was a ten-year-old blond girl dressed in a Renaissance Faire cosplay outfit, carrying a bow, with a quiver of arrows on her hip and a long dagger on the other side.

I just stood there in shock for a second before she hissed, "Don't just stand in the open; get in and hide. We have to attack them by surprise."

Vert T. Ferk?!

"I know that. What I don't understand is why a 10-year-old kid is doing this close to the Orc dungeon. Are you suicidal?"

The girl looked indignant. "I'm almost 12, not 10; my birthday is next week! And I'm going to rescue the prisoners; that's what I'm doing. It will be much easier with your help, though. That's why I wanted to get you to come hide with me before they see you."

I had trouble processing that. Her optimism was beyond insanity levels, and I could tell it was genuine optimism. She didn't have the shell-shocked, defeated look that all of the refugees I had met so far had.

Crouching down, I joined her in her hiding place. Sadly, I didn't have an Appraisal Skill yet, so I didn't know her level, but I didn't think it would be high enough for her not to be quaking in terror at the thought of going into that Orc camp.

"Uh, what level and Class are you?" I had to know. The girl looked athletic, but I doubted anyone other than me was much more than Level 5 to 7 at this point. I was a freak of nature with the insanely unique Class I had gained.

Blondie frowned and hesitated a moment before replying, "I... uh, I don't actually have a level or a Class yet. The System won't let me choose until my birthday."

She looked like she was waiting for me to laugh at her, and when I didn't, she hurried on, "Besides, I don't know if you've ever played many video games, but in some of the good ones, the game will only unlock specific Classes after you've met prerequisites. I was hoping that after the rescue, I would get to choose something cool. The Skills I use might unlock a cool Class like Ranger or something. The basic Classes it is showing me right now are boring, and Warrior is the only combat Class."

I raised an eyebrow.

"Seriously? The System is offering you the Warrior Class when you turn twelve? You realize that is an uncommon Class, and most people get offered the common Fighter Class instead. Still, it's a good thing you met me. Open your status and share it with me. I'm going to show you a trick that will blow your mind. I'm Liam Bell, by the way. What's your name?"

"Victoria Blue. You can call me Viki, though. I hate when people call me by my full name."

Despite giving me her name, she hesitated for a minute before sharing her Status screen with me. Sure enough, she was an Unclassed human.

Victoria Blue, aka Viki: (Current)
Unclassed - Level 0

Experience: 0/100

Attributes:
Endurance: 5

Strength: 4
Agility: 6
Mind: 6
Will: 6
Magical Aptitude: 0

Health: 9/9
Mana: 0/0

Abilities: None

Active Skills: None

Passive Skills: None

"Damn, you'll get killed if you get hit by a strong breeze. Still, you've got good Agility and mental stats for a kid. Congratulations. Here, take this and hold it or keep it next to your skin at all times. It's a Mana coin and contains a tiny bit of Mana. Just holding that for a while will unlock the chance for you to get magic Classes."

I had fished a Mana coin out of my storage ring and offered it to her.

Viki's eyes had gotten big when I explained that to her.

"Now, think 'Class Options.'"

She must have done it because suddenly, a long list of Classes flooded her status display.

The look on her face was priceless. There were several pages of Class options available for her to pick from. Or at least there were right now; how many of those would still be there next week might be another story. Of course, if she used more Skills or got a point of Mana from holding the Mana coin, it might open up dozens more options that weren't displayed at the moment.

"Viki, scroll through the list and look for any Classes that have an asterisk next to the name. Those will be options that are limited to a certain number of people. Some of them might even be unique, allowing only a single individual to select it."

She glanced toward me as if in disbelief. "Why? Why didn't the System let us know these were here?"

I shrugged. "The System doesn't care about humans. We are just one race among tens of thousands or maybe millions. Right now, I don't think it even cares if we go extinct or not. It was an AI that wasn't programmed to care about preserving human life. That was our mistake."

I wanted to say more, but I had to be careful. If I gave the AI reason to suspect that I had advanced knowledge, it would open me up to reprisals from the other AIs and their native species. Right now, I was sure I had a fraction of its attention just from being the highest leveled person in the world, but so far, I didn't think I had done anything that would suggest my future knowledge.

After a minute, she had filtered the list to show only the limited Classes. There were only two right now, and neither of them was magic-related. One was called Bowyer Artisan, and the other was Renegade Hornbow Marksman. They both sounded cool, but the girl could do better by getting some magic.

Viki looked dubious. "Those sound way better than Warrior or some crafting Class, but I don't know..."

I chuckled but nodded. "Yeah, trust me, you'll get something better by the time your birthday comes around. All you need is one point of Mana, and you'll have a ton of magic-related Classes to choose from. We can take a look then and see what's there."

She gave me a worried look. "But what happens if other people pick those Classes before I have a chance?"

"Then you pick something else. I bet you a hundred copper Mana coins there will be at least one rare magic Class still available next week. And like you said, the more Skills you use between now and then, the more options the System will give you."

Her eyes widened, and she smiled happily. "So you'll come with me when I rescue the prisoners?"

I was tempted to roll my eyes at her boldness. The thing was, I wasn't sure if she was just naive or completely oblivious to the dangers. She was either the most courageous kid I had ever met or the most foolhardy.

"You do realize the regular Orcs are Level 10, and the big, mean-looking ones are probably Level 15. You going in there would be like a piece of fruit jumping into a blender."

Viki deflated for a second but then squared her shoulders. "It doesn't matter. If I don't do it, who will? There are people in there who need rescuing."

Okay, courageous it was. This girl was essentially willing to risk her life in the hope that she could make a difference—a problem she could easily walk away from, and no one would blame her.

Shit, this kid is braver than me! Insane, maybe, but definitely brave.

I contemplated my plan for a minute. There were different sections of the camp, three zones, in fact. I would need to defeat a boss in each zone, plus eliminate all of the other minions to complete the area. What complicated things were the human prisoners. They were essentially hostages, and if I destroyed one area, then the Orcs could start killing the prisoners.

With a sigh, I began drawing in the dirt.

"Listen, I'm Level 19. I should be higher level than everything but the bosses. Even so, I can't defeat all the monsters in a straight-up fight.

They would overwhelm me like a wave crashing on the beach. That means we've got to be strategic. No reckless frontal assaults."

The girl nodded as if she completely understood, which she confirmed with her next words. "It's like a Raid in a video game. I get it, we've got to complete each objective before we can get the reward, and the better we complete the objectives, the bigger the reward."

I considered that for a moment. She was partially right but also slightly off. "You're more than half right. However, I don't think the System adjusts the rewards based on how well you perform. You might get special rewards for being the first to complete that type of scenario or get extra rewards for completing more objectives, but I don't think the System increases the level of the reward based on your performance."

She frowned and defiantly stuck out her chin. "Oh, yeah? How do you know?"

I couldn't help but chuckle. "I've got a hidden stat. Or rather, I have a stat that others don't have. It's called Luck, and it indeed improves the possible rewards."

Viki's frown deepened. "I don't have that stat. How did you get it?"

Shrugging, I replied, "I think it was because of the Class I chose. I was lucky enough to think 'Class options' and saw that extensive list. So, I picked one of the limited ones, and after I chose my Class, I saw the Luck score. It increased automatically when I hit Level 10. I'm hoping it goes up again at the next level."

"Huh. That's pretty great. I hope I get that stat when I get to pick a Class, then I can be like you."

A grin crossed my face at her last comment. "Kid, you've got a long way to go for that. Just getting your Class is only the first step. It takes a long time to level up if you do it carefully and avoid taking unnecessary risks."

She frowned. "I am not a kid, and I'll show you! I'll level up super fast!"

"You're definitely still a kid. You can't even choose your Class yet! Worse, your health is only nine points right now. You could easily die from only one hit from the weakest monster in there. If you want to participate, you're going to have to do everything I tell you to and keep yourself out of danger as much as possible. Got it?"

I thought about trying to convince her to run off and wait for me to finish, but there were two problems with that idea. First, there was no place that was safe, and second, I was absolutely certain she would not listen and would just follow me anyway. She definitely had the 'I'm invincible' mentality that children and teens often have right before they end up in a 'fails video.'

I miss those!

"Hey, who says you're leading this mission?" She had crossed her arms and was frowning defiantly.

"I did. I'm Level 19 and have the Skills and Abilities that will allow us to pull this off if we're smart about it. Also, I have experience with running and destroying dungeons. What about you?"

Viki grudgingly nodded. "Yeah, my only experience is in video games. But I was really good at them, though!"

I patted her on the back encouragingly, "You'll get there, but it's different doing it in real life than in a video game. Getting wounded hurts a lot. Worse, killing monsters can be hard emotionally. It's one thing to see it happen on a screen. It's entirely different when they scream in pain as they die right in front of you. Even knowing they are System-generated monsters and would kill you without hesitation, sometimes it can be really hard to deal with. I wish this world wasn't so messed up. It would be nice if a kid like you never had to face death like that, but this is the world we live in. So, I'll just let you do what you feel comfortable with, and if you can't handle it or need to talk to someone afterward, I'll be here."

The girl seemed to really take my words to heart and nodded solemnly.

"I... uh, yeah. I hadn't really thought about that. Thanks."

"So, are you any good with that bow?" I gestured at her weapon.

She brightened up, "Yeah. I'm pretty good. Most of my shooting was done with a recurve bow, but it broke as soon as things started happening. It just fell apart! Luckily, I have this one too. I got it at the Renaissance Faire last year. It's a traditionally made horn bow. This really cool guy makes them the way they did hundreds of years ago with nothing but horn, sinew, and glue made from fish bladders or something. Anyway, it didn't fall apart like my nicer bow did. With this bow, I can hit the target out to about thirty-five or forty yards. My dad used to take me hunting in the fall.

Viki got sad as she said that last bit but then visibly pushed thoughts of her dad aside. "If you're fighting the Orcs, I can shoot them from a distance. I'll avoid shooting any that are close to you so I don't accidentally hit you."

It was unbelievable that a twelve-year-old kid was putting her life on the line to rescue strangers. I was pretty sure her dad was dead from that brief reaction, but I didn't want to bring it up and force her to confront her grief right now. We had more immediate things to deal with.

"Okay, Orcs have good eyesight at night, better than humans, but I've got much better sight than them. This will be safer if we start this tonight. I'll sneak in and kill the bosses. Once they are dead, it will be much easier to deal with the lower-level monsters. My first order of business is to rescue as many of the humans as I can and get them out of the Orc camp."

She nodded along as I started pointing to the crude map I had drawn on the ground. "Most of the people are being held prisoner in the Shaman's camp. They have a bunch of pens that they are locked up in at night. I'm going to sneak up and try to attack the Shaman directly. That will distract the Orcs and raise the alarm. Many of them will probably rush to defend their boss. That's where you come in."

I pointed to the pens. "Once most of the guards start running to the Shaman, I need you to use your bow and kill the guards on one of the pens. Do you think you can do that?"

My little huntress friend gave me a determined nod.

"Good. I'll rely on you then. Once you kill the guards... be sure to pick a pen that only has one or two guards. Then, run up to the pen and cut the ropes holding the gate closed, or take the keys from the Orc guards if there is a chain with a lock. While you are freeing the prisoners, ask them to help free the other prisoners and tell them to arm themselves with the dead Orcs' weapons. Their weapons should last a minute or two before they disappear, along with the Orc bodies. Hopefully, they can help you free the next batch of prisoners and keep rearming themselves."

"What if you aren't back before I free all the prisoners?"

Damn, the girl had confidence!

"Head north out of the camp. The palisade wall around the top of the Shaman's hill hasn't been completed yet, and you should be able to run right out of the camp in that direction. There will be guards patrolling the hillside and the area between the hills and the road. With your numbers, you should be able to overwhelm them, but I hope to be done with the Shaman by then and leading you out. If so, then I can take care of the guards."

I got serious and took her by the shoulders, looking her in the eyes.

"Listen, there is one thing, though. No matter what, I want you to get away. If the rescue fails, or if I die, or if the prisoners start fleeing in all directions instead of working together. No matter what happens, you need to survive the night. It's almost your birthday, and it is incredibly important that you pick one of those limited magic Classes. Most people got fooled by the System and picked a basic Class on Initialization Day. The human race needs mages if we are going to survive what's coming. Can you do that for me?"

Viki looked like she was going to be stubborn, but as I got to the end of my speech, she nodded. "Yeah, okay. I don't want to run away, but having magic will make me much stronger. I will try to survive and pick a good Class."

Maybe in my first life, I would have tried to talk a child out of going into a life-and-death situation. Heck, I might have even thrown her over my shoulder and carried her away from here until I could find some responsible adults to take care of her. Whatever I did, I certainly would not have put her in charge of trying to rescue prisoners from Level 10 Orcs when she was not even at Level 1.

Hell, in my first life, I wouldn't have trusted myself to do what I was asking of her. I would have fled from this whole situation like my ass was on fire!

Unfortunately, this wasn't my first life, and now that I had this experience, I couldn't just sit back and do nothing. Nor could I prevent this child from participating. She might die, in fact, there was a damned good chance that would happen. Still, I knew from two decades of experience that the human race was doomed if we didn't take bold action. I also wondered how many hundreds or thousands of people had lost their lives to this dungeon in my original timeline.

Viki and I might not survive what we were about to attempt, but if we did, we'd save all those people who would have died, and who knew how much difference that would make. Hell, as strong as this dungeon was starting out, it might have taken years before humans were strong enough to destroy it.

We waited until dark to begin moving. I guided my young friend through the darkness thanks to my Dark Vision Bloodline Ability. To me, the world looked about as dark as a cloudy afternoon before a storm. Before long, we had circled around to the south side of the Shaman's hill and crept close. I had avoided the patrols, being able to see them from a good distance.

Yet again, I regretted that the System didn't award Skills based on your actions, at least not directly. Otherwise, I would have already gotten a sneak or stealth-type Skill. My Draconic Bloodline might be urging me to charge in and roar my defiance, challenging all to come at me, but over twenty years of experience told me how stupid that was, and I would be more than happy to get a Skill that would allow me to sneak up on my enemies and shank them in the dark like an assassin.

Yeah, once the Shop opens, I'm buying a Skill Crystal for stealth if there is one available! Hell, if I survive the month, I should have more than enough coins to buy one!

I pushed those thoughts aside as we neared the top of the hill. I found a good spot for Viki to fire her bow from. The nearest pen was only fifteen yards away and had two guards at the gate. It was the best I could do for her.

"Remember, don't fire until I've raised a fuss over at the Shaman's hut. If you start too soon, you'll draw a bunch of guards over toward yourself."

She nodded, and I stalked away into the night, making my way toward my goal.

CHAPTER 22
SHAMAN'S HILL

THE SHAMAN's hut squatted near the eastern end of this hill, an ominous structure cobbled together from scavenged materials and adorned with primitive, foreboding symbols that glowed faintly in the moonlight.

The hut was larger than the others, signifying the importance of its occupant. Its walls were made of a mix of old metal sheets and wooden planks, uneven and jagged, like the teeth of some giant beast. The roof was covered in tattered tarps, stitched together and weighed down with various debris. Skulls and bones, remnants of the Shaman's dark rituals, were strung around the entrance, clattering softly in the night breeze.

Near the hut, a large, open area served as a sort of ritual ground. It was littered with the remains of previous ceremonies: burnt-out fires, strange symbols etched into the earth, and an array of sinister-looking totems. The ground was trodden down, evidence of the many feet that had gathered here, perhaps to witness the Shaman's dark magic or to receive its commands.

To the side, a makeshift altar stood, stained with dark marks and surrounded by an assortment of bizarre objects: bones, feathers, and oddly shaped stones. It was clear that this place was not just the Shaman's home but a center of power for the Orcish rituals.

The palisade around the hill was incomplete, with gaps on the north and south sides. This lack of fortification provided an advantage for my approach and also our escape route if we survived this. The Shaman's guards, five Elite Orcs, patrolled the area with lazy confidence, unaware of the imminent threat I posed.

I crouched in the shadows, observing the pattern of their patrols, planning my next move. The Shaman, and the power it wielded within this camp, was my target. I knew that taking it out would cause disarray among the Orcs and provide the perfect distraction for Viki to free the imprisoned humans. Tonight, the Shaman's reign of terror would end.

It was hard to have patience when I knew Viki was out there in the dark, alone. I had never had—or even dreamed of having—a kid or of being responsible for another's life. This kind of situation sucked. It was causing me to feel nervous about this dungeon in a way I never had before.

Struggling with myself to have patience, I let a half hour go by to make sure I understood the Elite guards' habits well enough. I was going to hit them hard and fast. My goal was the death of the Shaman and the freeing of the prisoners. Nothing beyond that for tonight. If we succeeded, I could come back for the Warchief and the rest when they weren't expecting it. The only question was if I should blow all of my Abilities instantly to try and burn the mini-boss down before it could react, or should I try and save some for when things inevitably went wrong?

That was a tough one, so I decided to wing it. If my guesses were right, it would be higher level than me, and I wasn't sure what that would mean for my Skills, but it should only be a little higher than my own level.

Finally, my chance came. The Shaman stepped out of its hut and shouted for dinner to be delivered. It berated the two nearest Elites, and the others shied away, backing further from the hut's door so as not to catch their boss's attention. They looked afraid of the blood-stained bastard, and I didn't blame them. It looked both disgusting and scary at the same time.

Over the last several dungeon runs of that Goblin dungeon, I had gotten into the habit of trying to ignore the influence of the System on my reactions to its creations. However, this time, I couldn't help it. The bastard was radiating System 'intent.' As if it was waving a big flag in my face, shouting, 'I made this masterpiece; pay attention to it.'

...The Orc Shaman was a figure of grotesque and malevolent presence. Its grey skin, a sickly and ashen hue, was marred with bloodstains—a macabre tapestry that told tales of its numerous victims. These stains were not accidental but seemed almost ritually applied, marking it not just as a killer but as a reveler in the violence it wrought.

Its build was hulking, muscles bulging unnaturally as if its body was swollen with the dark magic it wielded. Its face was a twisted visage of cruelty, with deep-set eyes that glowed with a malevolent fire. Tattered remnants of what might have once been a robe hung off its broad frame, adorned with bones and fetishes that clattered with its every movement.

The Shaman's hair was matted and unkempt, streaked with dirt and blood, hanging in wild tangles around its scarred face. Its hands, large and gnarled, were covered in grime and dried blood, with long, filthy nails that looked more like claws. Around its neck hung a necklace of crudely fashioned talismans, each seemingly imbued with a sinister purpose.

There was an aura of dark power that emanated from it: a palpable sense of dread that seemed to warp the air around its being. It moved with a confidence that spoke of its assuredness in its own power, a predator among predators within the Orcish ranks. This Orc Shaman was not merely a Fighter; it was a conduit of dark, corrupting magic, a being to be approached with both caution and strategy....

I shook off the System's influence and wondered how many humans had died because of such intrusive moments of reflection.

Fucking System!

I activated Draconic Charge. How dare the System mess with my brain! I'd show it what I thought of its manipulation...

Appearing before the grey-skinned bastard in a flash, I let loose with my strongest attacks before it could react.

Acid Bolt was cast right into its face. I hoped that even if I didn't kill it outright, at least I would blind it.

Partial success, whether from instinct or luck, the Shaman turned its head, and the acid splashed one side of its ugly face, blinding that eye. It didn't go down, however.

I followed immediately with a Powerstrike. It was already raising its left arm to try and cast a Curse or Spell, but my sword came in from its right, bypassing its gesture and striking it in the neck, but not before it uttered a single word in some mystical language of the underworld.

The Curse hit me just as my sword cleaved into its neck. The acid to the face might not have killed it, but there was no way it was going to survive an acid-infused strike to the arteries feeding its brain with blood.

Unfortunately, I didn't have time to celebrate my victory. Even as it clutched its neck, I felt my own throat constrict from its Curse. I had never experienced this personally, but I had seen a mage get hit with it once. It was intended to silence a spellcaster, but it also made it very difficult to breathe. It should disappear as soon as the Shaman died, which should be any second.

Any second now....

I could hear the two Orcs behind me cry out in shock as they just now registered that their boss was under attack.

Damn it!

I saw a glow of magic from one of the talisman necklaces the boss wore. It wasn't dying; it was healing!

Regretting the necessity, I had no choice but to use another Skill. I lunged forward with a Draconic Slash, my other offensive Class Skill. So much for keeping something in reserve for dealing with the Elites... Still, I had to stay alive for that to matter, and unless I killed the Shaman, the Curse would choke me out before the guards had a chance to finish me.

The blow landed, slicing open the mini-boss and causing its guts to spill out while also leaving behind acid to corrode whatever was left of its organs.

Its eyes widened, shocked that I didn't simply die immediately from the Curse.

Ha! We surprised each other, but I won! I didn't give the bastard's guards a chance to stab me in the back. I sidestepped after the slash to the Shaman's stomach and pivoted, grabbing the dying mini-boss by the shoulder and yanking it in front of me to use its corpse as a meatshield.

The guards looked highly offended, but before they could attack, the Curse dissipated, and I could breathe again. The Shaman was finally dead.

I gasped in a deep lungful of the foul air that surrounded the ritual ground.

I was just in time. The first two guards were already attacking, and the rest of the Elites were rushing toward me.

Wishing my offensive Skills weren't on cooldown, I did the only thing that made sense... the only thing that would get me out of this mess alive... the thing that would give Viki the chance she needed to free the prisoners.

I roared out my defiance as I had done back in that first dungeon. Draconic Fear produced a ghostly image of a black dragon above me as I let out the primal bellow without holding back.

Honestly, I didn't know I could make a sound that loud, and I kinda regretted doing it as soon as it ended.

It worked.

Unfortunately, I was pretty sure it was loud enough to be heard from the neighboring hill where the War Chief lived. The last thing I needed was to deal with a Level 25 or higher boss monster on top of the Elites and regular Orcs all around me.

"Shit, shit, shit!"

Nineteen.

I started counting down in my head as I began to move faster than I ever had in my life. My Skill lasted nineteen seconds, but the Elites and lesser Orcs would break out of the stun at different times based on their level. The clock had started ticking, and Viki would be moving now. I needed these Elites all dead, and the other Orcs focused on me.

Four seconds – that's all I had before the Elites would shake off the stun. Time slowed in my perception as I sprang into action. My blade, though denied its usual magical enhancements, was still a deadly extension of my will. I moved with lethal precision, targeting the vulnerable spots I had learned to identify in my long years of combat. The first Elite's throat, the next one's heart, a swift decapitation for the third – each strike was a dance of death, executed with the desperate urgency of survival.

Seven Elites lay lifeless before the stun wore off. But there was no time to pause. The remaining three Elites regained their senses, their eyes alight with rage and shock. They were formidable Level 15 foes, their skills evident in their swift, heavy blows. I parried and dodged, relying on sheer combat experience and agility. Each clash of our weapons was a thunderous, deadly ballet.

Fifteen.

The first of the remaining Elites lunged with a roar, its weapon aimed with lethal intent. I sidestepped, driving my sword through the gap in its armor. One down, two to go. The second Elite came at me with a vengeance, its strikes fueled by fury. But fury makes you predictable. I exploited its recklessness, finding an opening to plunge my blade into its side.

The final Elite was more cautious, circling me, waiting for an opening. We exchanged a flurry of blows, its skill matching mine. But determination was on my side. With a feint and a quick step, I found my way past its guard, my sword piercing its chest.

As the last Elite fell, I turned to face the horde of regular Orcs, soon to recover from the Draconic Fear. My other Skills were still on cooldown, and I knew I had to rely on the raw, unenhanced magic I possessed. Raising my arms, I unleashed Acid Spray. A torrent of corrosive liquid fanned out before me, engulfing the monstrous Orcs. Their screams filled the air as they fell, one after another, in a grotesque display of the Spell's deadly efficiency. I hadn't counted how many I had killed, but I had heard the beautiful sound of the 'ding' after the first few Elite Orcs died; I just hadn't had a chance to check my status yet.

Something had changed, though. Despite the literal horde of Orcs on this hilltop, I felt a strong pull toward the Shaman's tent, as if something inside was calling to me.

I almost couldn't resist. My senses tingled with what I had come to associate with the greed of my Draconic Bloodline.

As if drawn against my will, I darted inside the hut and saw a treasure chest. The Shaman was a mini-boss, so that wasn't unusual, but the overwhelming desire to get the treasure, on the other hand... that was new. I mean, even in my first life, I would have been super excited to check out what was in the chest, but not to this degree! I had a second while the rest of the Orcs snapped out of the fright I had given them before they could charge at me, but still, wasn't it a bit reckless to prioritize loot at this moment?

And yet, my hand was on the latch, ripping the thing open to see what was inside.

Inside were a pair of potions, much like the Mana and health potions found in the Goblin dungeon, except these were intermediate-grade versions. They would restore more health and Mana than the Goblin drops. I reached into the chest and swept the two bottles directly into my storage ring. However, those were the least of what was inside.

Nestled within the shadowy confines of the chest were a pair of boots. As soon as I touched them, information bloomed into my mind:

Shadowstep Boots -
Description: These sleek, dark leather boots were once used

by the Shaman for stealthy maneuvers during rituals and ambushes. Infused with shadow magic, they grant the wearer enhanced agility and the Ability to move silently. The boots also have the unique Ability to briefly meld the wearer with the shadows, allowing for short bursts of near-invisibility.

Stats:
+20% to movement speed +15% to evasion Significantly reduces noise made by movement Special Effect - "Veil of Shadows":
Once per day, the wearer can activate the boots to become nearly invisible for 15 seconds. While in this state, the wearer's first attack from stealth is guaranteed a critical hit.

I was momentarily stunned. I had never experienced such a detailed understanding of an item before. Normally, I might recognize an item from past knowledge or be given the information by someone who had an Analyze Skill, but this...

Shaking myself out of it, I made the boots disappear into my ring and rushed back outside. I didn't have time right now to figure out what was going on.

I had a battle to fight!

CHAPTER 23

ESCAPE

Despite my distraction, less than a minute had passed in real-time. The Shaman's body was just now disappearing as I stood in the doorway of the hut. I tried not to get distracted again, but I couldn't help it. In the place of the body, a glowing amulet lay in the dirt.

I didn't even bother to look at it as I grumbled and reached down to snatch it up.

Again, I was blindsided by text in my vision:

Shaman's Heart Amulet:
Description: This amulet, crafted from the essence of the fallen Shaman, pulses with dark energy. When worn, it grants the wearer an increase in magical defense and enhances Spell power, particularly for dark and elemental magic. Additionally, it provides a passive regeneration effect, slowly restoring health over time.

Stats: +15% to magical defense +10% to Spell power Regenerate 2% of total health every minute.

Special Effect: Once per day, the wearer can tap into the amulet's power to cast a "Fear Ward," making them immune to fear effects for 30 seconds.

This time, my distraction cost me.

I felt a sharp pain in my side as an Orc nailed me with a vicious-looking cleaver. It looked like something the Shaman might use to dismember its ritual sacrifices. Or worse, an Orc cook might use a tool like that to prepare their dinner.

Shit, maybe those are the same thing!

Using my sword to decapitate the little bastard, I held onto the cleaver's handle so that it couldn't be ripped out of my side as its body fell to the ground. Luckily, its hand let go when it died, and the blade wasn't lodged all that deep, but it is never good to yank a blade out of a wound.

Unfortunately, its attack seemed to open the floodgates, and the rest of the Orcs began to charge at me. I had just enough time to throw the amulet's cord around my neck and ease the cleaver out of my side, but none to staunch the bleeding.

That was going to be a problem in a minute. I needed to stop the blood flow, or I would start suffering from fatigue, and my speed would slow down, making me easier to kill and be overwhelmed.

Luckily, my attack Skills were coming off of cooldown, and I now had weapons in both hands.

Damnit! Why do I keep forgetting to activate Scalebound Resilience? That wound might not have happened if it were active!

"Scalebound Resilience!"

I felt my skin tighten as the Spell activated. Sadly, that did nothing for the wound in my side, but at least I would be more difficult to damage for the next five minutes.

As tightly packed as the Orcs were, this would be a good time for Acid Spray. Unfortunately, it was still on cooldown and wouldn't be up for another twenty seconds.

However, Dragon's Fear ticked down to zero at that moment, and I grinned evilly. It was time to slaughter the helpless!

I roared again, this time not trying to make every Orc within a half-mile shit themselves, but still, every Orc around the ritual circle was within its area of effect. Just as before, they froze in terror, giving me nine... no, ten seconds now to act freely.

With the Shaman's Heart Amulet secured and the immediate threat of the Orc horde momentarily paralyzed by my Dragon's Fear, I quickly assessed my situation. The wound in my side, a result of an Orc's cleaver attack, was bleeding but not deeply. I had removed the cleaver from my assailant, now wielding it in my left hand, its Cursed blade a deadly counterpart to my sword in the right. Text detailing the stats of the cleaver flashed into my vision, but I had dismissed it the instant it appeared, not able to take the time right now to find out what disturbing secrets it held.

The next ten seconds were a blur of motion and violence. The Orcs, frozen in terror, were sitting ducks for my dual-wielded onslaught. The cleaver, with its dark energy and Cursed edge, tore through Orc armor as if it were mere cloth while my sword delivered precise, lethal blows.

I moved through the stunned Orcs with grim determination, the pain from my wound a constant reminder of the stakes. Each swing of the cleaver felt heavier and more brutal as if it were hungry for Orcish blood. In my right hand, my sword danced its deadly dance, punctuating the cleaver's brutal chops with swift, clean cuts.

The air was filled with the sound of rending flesh and breaking bones. Orcs fell one after another, their numbers dwindling rapidly under my relentless assault. The cleaver proved to be a devastating weapon, its Curse weakening the Orcs' defenses with every hit, making them even more vulnerable to my attacks.

As the effect of the Dragon's Fear finally ended, the remaining Orcs started to come to their senses. They shook off their terror, their eyes focusing on me with renewed hatred and rage. But the momentum was in my favor. The ground around me was littered with their fallen comrades, a clear testament to the ferocity and efficiency of my attack.

With the cleaver and sword in hand, I stood ready, my breathing heavy but controlled, prepared to continue the fight. The initial advantage I had gained with the Dragon's Fear had been crucial, but now it was down to my skill and will to survive. The battle was far from over, but I had made a significant dent in their numbers, and I was determined to see this through to the end.

Just as I braced myself for the next wave of combat, a sound cut through the tension – the unexpected but unmistakable noise of a counterattack. It was the first batch of freed prisoners, and they had arrived just in time. While the Orcs were still reeling from the Dragon's Fear, the prisoners had moved in unnoticed, now launching a fierce assault on the Orcs' flank.

The prisoners, fueled by desperation and newfound hope, wielded an array of makeshift weapons – axes that were once used for chopping wood, shovels turned into bludgeoning tools, and various other implements repurposed for battle. Their attack was unrefined but ferocious, a testament to their will to fight for their freedom and lives.

The sight of their former captives, now armed and defiant, struck a chord of panic in the Orcs. Already disoriented and diminished in number, the Orcs found their flank exposed and vulnerable. The unexpected ferocity of the prisoners' attack sent a ripple of fear through their ranks. Confusion and chaos ensued as they tried to defend against this new threat.

From my position, I could see the tide turning. The Orcs' formation broke as they were caught between my continued assault and the prisoners' uprising. The morale of the Orcs, already dented by the loss of their Shaman and the effect of the Dragon's Fear, crumbled rapidly. What had been an organized and menacing force was now a disarray of individuals acting on instinct to flee or fight.

The transformation in the prisoners was remarkable. Their faces, previously marked by fear and resignation, were now alive with fierce determination. Each swing of their improvised weapons was not just an act of self-defense but a strike for freedom. They moved with the energy of people who had nothing left to lose and everything to gain.

As the Orcs' lines faltered and broke, the balance of power shifted dramatically. The predators were now the prey and were being completely overwhelmed.

Standing amidst the chaos, I couldn't help but feel a surge of respect for these brave souls who had turned their desperation into a weapon. Together, we were turning the tide, fighting back the darkness with every Orc that fell.

Soon, more prisoners flooded into the area around the Shaman's hut, and the ever-mounting numbers of humans meant the Orcs were falling faster and faster. Not all humans were armed. Some were even fighting with fists and feet, doing whatever damage they could. Determination to never be captured again was written on their faces and in the violence they dished out.

Just about the time the last Orcs fell, I saw Viki run into the ritual ground and rush up to me.

"All the prisoners are free, but we've got trouble. The Orcs from the big hill are coming! We need to get out of here and save these people."

That was my girl. She was not thinking of herself but still focused on saving the captives. A feeling of pride in her welled in my heart. I had known veteran adventurers, who were supposedly leaders among the remnants of the human race, who couldn't hold a candle to the spirit this kid displayed.

"Right. Thanks for the warning, and great job on the rescue."

Turning to the prisoners, who were just now finishing off the last Orcs, I yelled, "Time to go. We have more Orcs incoming, and we need to get to safety so we can get you all armed and reunited with your loved ones. Follow me!"

I led the way to the north face of the hill, where the palisade walls were not yet complete. The slope down was not difficult to traverse. The hills were gentle mounds that used to be a garbage dump that had been covered by dirt. Even if someone tripped, the worst that would happen is that they would roll down a bit before coming to a stop. They might get bruises, but that would be about all.

Sure enough, many did just that as we mostly jogged down the slope. We had a portion of the hill between us and the oncoming Orcs, which would slow down their pursuit. Hopefully, it would be enough to allow our escape. If not, we'd have to find a defensible spot. I was also worried about patrols and perimeter guards that might be in our path. However, they must have seen the hundreds of humans and fled before we could approach.

Every step was painful, thanks to the wound in my side, but I had experienced worse before, so I didn't let it stop me. Eventually, as we got enough distance, I made the cleaver vanish into my storage ring and brought out a low-grade healing potion in its place. It felt like liquid relief as it poured down my throat. I hadn't been anywhere close to death, but I needed to be ready in case we did have to battle the rest of the Orcs tonight.

There was a small ring of grass-covered hills at the edge of the dump's property where it met the road. They were only around fifteen feet tall and gently sloped, so it was easy to climb, but I noticed that the captives weren't doing so well. They didn't have an Endurance stat of 35 like I did. Even poor Viki was panting heavily like she had just run a race, which she had come to think of it. I sheathed my sword and took her by the arms, swinging her up onto my back.

She squeaked in protest, but I interrupted her.

"Hang on, okay. I've got high Endurance and Strength stats; you can ride on my back for now."

To the rest of the freed captives, I yelled, "You are all doing great! Still, we need to hurry and move down the road, at least past the creek, in case the Orcs follow us. Once we are past that point, we can find a place to defend ourselves if we have to. Help each other if someone stumbles or lags behind! Carry those who can't. We can treat any wounded once we are there."

It wasn't quite half a mile to the creek. The highway crossed it, making it a good choke point to funnel the Orcs into if we had to battle them. It wasn't a great plan, but it was the best we could do. The human captives outnumbered the Orcs by more than two to one, but the captives were exhausted from a long day of forced labor, and they were severely under-leveled to fight an enemy like this. I could only hope that I could hold the center and prevent the Orcs from getting past.

Of course, they could flank us given time, but I didn't think they would do that. If they gave chase all this way, they would be led by the War Chief and would most likely plow straight into us. With my acid spray, I would make them pay a heavy price if they wanted over that bridge. My only concern was whether I could hold against the Chief and still manage to use the acid spray before they closed with us.

Glancing around, seeing people milling about aimlessly, I called out, "Anyone with a combat Class and a level of three or higher, step forward and see me. Otherwise, if you aren't wounded, then quickly look around and find anything you can to block the bridge. We need to build a barricade to keep the Orcs at bay and give us a fighting chance."

Someone in the crowd called out, "Why don't we just keep running?"

"Because you are practically falling down now. Do you think you can outrun the Orcs? If we run, we will be easy prey. Our only hope is to fight them here on this bridge where they can't overwhelm us, but that will only work if we can put up a makeshift wall to defend. Hurry! We've got maybe ten or fifteen minutes before they arrive."

I could see that many of the men and women were wavering, considering taking their chances at running, but before I could say anything else, Viki yelled, "Don't be cowards; cowards die in the Apocalypse! Besides, right now, the Orcs have to be scared of us! We just killed a hundred of them on that hill."

"That's at least a third of their total number," I added. "There is never going to be a better time than now to face them. Their morale is devastated by what we just did."

Then, some joker in the crowd shouted, "Remember the Alamo!"

I would have rolled my eyes at that but damned if it didn't work.

Several others echoed the rallying cry. "Remember the Alamo!" "Remember the Alamo!" "Remember the Alamo!"

After a second, dozens of people were repeating the call, and the mood of the crowd had turned. They were looking determined now instead of scared. The fire they had felt on that hilltop had been rekindled.

Holy shit! I can't believe that worked! If only we had a few good Fighters besides just me.

In the distance, I could see a group of Orc Warriors coming up the road. I just hoped the spirit they were showing would hold in the face of what was coming at us.

CHAPTER 24
MONO A MONO!

As NON-WOUNDED NON-COMBATANTS rushed to find branches and debris to pile into the road, I looked over the people with combat Classes. Surprisingly, nearly a third of the captives had chosen some kind of Class with fighting Skills.

"Group up by levels! Highest to my left, lowest to my right. Move!"

I wasn't a big fan of being in the spotlight this way, but if not me, then who? Someone had to organize the defense, and I had more than two decades of experience fighting monsters.

In just under a minute, they had made groups. I was surprised to see one guy standing alone to the left of me. He was Level 6 and announced that he was a Warrior. He was also wielding a two-headed felling axe that he had confiscated from the Orcs. That wasn't too bad. Next to him, there were about fifteen people at Level 5 with various combat Classes. After they all started shouting their Classes, I waved them down.

"Not enough time for that. For now, I want you all to space yourselves out along the barricade and try to be the focal point for the people around you. You are all under-leveled for this fight, but there is nothing we can do about that. I will try and do what I can to take out as many as possible before they can get to you, but I won't be able to stop them all.

"Levels 4, you all space yourselves out surrounding the Level 5s." There were over fifty of them. I didn't say it, but in my heart, I was thinking that if only we had about a hundred more, then we might stand a chance against the Level 10 Orcs.

"Threes, you next. Fill in around the Fours." After a few seconds, "Twos, your turn!" "Ones!"

Each successive group was larger than the last. There were around a hundred and fifty Level 1's. Unfortunately, I knew from experience that they would be like sticks going through a woodchipper. All they would manage to do would be to slow the Orcs' advance with their sheer numbers, but they would die by the dozens for every Orc they killed. This was likely to be a very bloody exchange on our part.

I had an idea, but I didn't know if it would work, and even if it did, it still might not be enough to turn the tide. Unfortunately, we didn't have long before we would find out. I estimated no more than ten minutes now, and I could see a big bruiser of an Orc leading the pack. The War Chief was in the vanguard.

Taking a minute, I spoke to Viki. "Listen, just like on the hill. You have to survive. If things look like we are going to lose, then you need to run away. Make a big circle around the fight and head up the highway..."

I gave her directions to my base. I also took the Shaman's amulet off my neck and put it on her. "This is magic; it will help protect you, and if you get a magic Class, it will make your Spells stronger. It also has a slow regenerative effect. Between that and the Mana coins, you will almost certainly be offered a bunch of magic Classes. Remember what I've told you."

She looked defiant but nodded. "Okay, but we are going to win. You can beat them, Liam!"

I nodded solemnly, "Sure thing, kiddo. I wouldn't be doing this if I didn't think we had a chance. I would have told everyone to scatter and head to the base otherwise. Most of them would be recaptured or killed, but some would get away."

Looking at her quiver, I added, "Be sure to save a few arrows in case you do have to run. You might need them to get away."

For a moment, it looked like she would argue, but she kept silent, deciding it wasn't worth fighting over.

Soon, the time was up. Our non-combatants had piled as much crap across the bridge as they could. Sadly, it didn't amount to much, and I had them leave a gap right in the center where I would stand so that the Orcs would focus their attention on me. Even by saving some space that way, the barricade only came up to my waist as they stretched out to either side of me all the way to the bridge's edges. They were just piled junk, so they wouldn't stop the Orcs from crossing, but it might give the human defenders the chance to kill more Orcs as they tried to climb or jump over.

Glancing toward the sides of the bridge, I shook my head. The creek wasn't really more than a decent-sized ditch. If the Orcs chose to go around, then they could easily flank us and attack from behind. Still, I was counting on them seeing the road, the small bridge, and us making our stand here and just assume they had to attack from the front. That might be a naive hope, but with it being nighttime and this dungeon only being a few days old, I needed it to be true. I would just have to give them something to focus on so they wouldn't notice how pathetic our defensive position truly was.

As I stood before the bridge, the night air was charged with palpable tension. Behind me, the freed captives waited, gripping their makeshift weapons, their eyes fixed on the approaching threat.

Before us, the horde of Orcs advanced, a formidable mass of savagery and brute force. I desperately wanted to check out my status since I had leveled up, but so far, I hadn't had even a minute of peace. I should have done it while we were running away from the Shaman's hill, but I had been too distracted by my wound and had forgotten in the rush. Now, it was too late.

Fucking stupid, Liam! I thought to myself. If I survived this fight, I would need to sit down and have a long talk with myself about priorities, remembering to cast Spells at the appropriate times, and to never wasting an opportunity to assign stats and check out new Skills.

The low-hanging moon cast an eerie glow over the landscape, throwing long, ominous shadows across the ground. The Orcs' approach was a cacophony of guttural shouts and the heavy thud of their boots, a relentless drumbeat that grew louder with every step they took.

At the forefront of the horde was the War Chief, a towering figure of menace, standing twice as tall as the regular Orcs. Its muscular frame was adorned with battle-worn armor, and in its hand, it wielded a massive axe that seemed to thirst for blood. It was flanked by its Elite guards, each one a formidable warrior in their own right, clad in armor and carrying weapons that spoke of their high rank and Skill in battle.

The mass of regular Orcs, about a hundred strong, filled in behind them. Their grey skin seemed almost ghostly in the moonlight, and their eyes glinted with a hunger for violence. They were a ragtag army, but their sheer numbers and the ferocity in their expressions made it clear they were not to be underestimated.

As they drew closer, the horde came to a halt about a hundred yards away from the bridge. The War Chief stepped forward, its gaze locking onto mine. A heavy silence fell over the scene, broken only by the occasional snarl or grunt from the Orc ranks.

The air was thick with anticipation, both sides aware of the impending clash. I could feel the eyes of the captives on my back, their fate and hope resting on the outcome of this challenge. The moment was critical, the tension almost tangible. It was a standoff under the cold gaze of the moon, a prelude to a battle that would determine the fate of many.

Looking at the War Chief gave me flashbacks to my death. These guys might be System-generated, but they were clearly modeled after the invader race, the High Orcs. If that were the case, then their warriors ought to honor bravery and be averse to shying away from a challenge. My sketchy plan hinged on that being true.

That was why I shouted to the War Chief, but loud enough for all the Orcs to hear, "Face me in single combat if you dare!"

The Orcs hissed and jeered, but the War Chief looked amused.

"Puny human, I will crush your bones, and we will make soup from them!"

Ugh. I could tell by its use of correct grammar that this one was smarter than the average monster. That was not something I needed right now; it meant a harder fight.

The massive Orc strode forward to meet me in the middle between our armies, swinging its axe to limber up, clearly eager for what was about to occur.

This had been the core of my plan, my weak, lame-ass plan. Unfortunately, even if I beat the boss, we'd still be facing a dozen Elites and around a hundred regular Orcs.

Yep, this is gonna suck!

Stepping forward to meet the Orc War Chief, I felt like David approaching Goliath. Except, I didn't have a handy giant-slaying ranged weapon; I was going to have to do this up close and personal.

The War Chief, a hulking mass of muscle and rage, towered over me, its eyes burning with barbaric intensity. I could see the confidence in its stance, the unwavering belief in its own strength. Still, I had a couple of tricks up my sleeve, and I was literally betting my life on them at this moment.

As we neared the center of the bridge, I activated Scalebound Resilience and then Dragon's Charge. In an instant, I closed the distance between us, my movement a blur. I launched my first attack, aiming for a vulnerable spot in its armor. The War Chief was caught off guard, but it recovered quickly, countering with a brutal swing of its axe.

The fight was a maelstrom of violence. The War Chief's Skills as a Barbarian Class were evident in its powerful strikes and Ability to enter a rage, increasing its ferocity. I dodged and parried, but it was relentless. Its axe found its mark several times, each blow sending shockwaves of pain through my body. I was fast, but it was a force of nature, its strength seemingly boundless.

I only survived those first moments due to the combination of my armor and the Scalebound Resilience Spell. Blows that left me wounded and bleeding would have instead cleaved me into chunks if not for my layered defense. However, I did not fight defensively; that was no way to win a fight like this.

I unleashed my attack Skills in rapid succession, but it was tough, its armor absorbing much of the impact. Our blades clashed, sparks flying, as we each sought to gain the upper hand. I managed to land a few solid strikes, but the War Chief's rage Skill seemed to make it impervious to pain. Blood dripped from multiple wounds on my body, and my energy was waning.

Realizing I needed to end this quickly, I tapped into my deepest reserves of strength. Summoning Dragon's Fury, I felt a surge of power coursing through me, doubling my Strength. I didn't use this move without some trepidation. When it wore off, it would leave me feeling exhausted, and I still had the rest of the Orc horde to deal with. I had a bad feeling that using it now would win me the fight with the chief but lose me the war.

I couldn't worry about that now; I had to kill this boss, or the rest wouldn't matter!

With a roar, I matched the War Chief's ferocity, our weapons meeting with Earth-shattering force.

The battle raged, a dance of death on the bridge. I parried a particularly vicious blow and found an opening. Feeling how desperate the situation was, I tried something I had never done before. With all my enhanced Strength, I drove my sword through a chink in its armor and, at the same time, triggered Acid Bolt, channeling it through my sword. I didn't even know if it was possible, but I was desperate. The strike lodged my blade into its side, and the elemental bolt of acid discharged directly into its body, where it violently exploded, sending a geyser of corrosive liquid out of the wound. Like my physical strength, the Spell's damage was also doubled, and the results of a contained detonation within its body were horrifying.

The War Chief's eyes widened in shock and pain, a guttural growl escaping its lips as it stumbled backward, more of the acid-spewing from its mouth, eyes, and ears.

It dropped to its knees and then ponderously fell forward onto its face like a mighty redwood, its fall shaking the ground as its axe clattered on the bridge.

My breath was ragged, my body aching from the exertion and wounds.

With the War Chief defeated, silence fell around me, the watching Orcs stunned by the unexpected death of their champion. I stood victorious, albeit battered, but I couldn't stop yet. I had fifteen seconds before my Draconic Fury wore off.

I sprinted forward toward the Orcs and raised my left hand, casting my other offensive Spell, Acid Spray. I swept my aim across the Elites, knowing that survival meant killing them before my Draconic Fury wore off.

They did not stand idly but charged at me as well, intent on avenging their fallen chief. However, the acid jetting out of my palm was not something they could withstand with its power doubled. With the fury Skill boosting all of my Strength, I danced through them, avoiding attacks while covering them in the intensely corrosive spray. Each one that was hit fell screaming, clawing at their skin to make the pain stop.

I hated hearing those sounds, but I reminded myself that they weren't real and they had to die so that the humans could live.

Each Elite fell, but they weren't the only ones. The Acid Spray wasn't like pulling the trigger on a gun; it was more like firing a napalm-filled flamethrower. There were dozens of Orcs behind them that also received a fraction of the blast.

Unlike the Elites, who received a direct blast, a mere splash wasn't enough to kill them outright since they were only receiving a fraction of the spray. It was mostly blocked by the Elites who were trying to attack me. Still, it was enough. Those who were hit ceased to be a threat, too occupied by trying to remove the painful liquid.

Five seconds had passed to close the distance and be within striking range with my Acid Spray. Ten more and the Elites were killed.

By then, I was no more than twenty feet from the front line of their formation, but that was when Draconic Fury ended.

Standing tall and defiant, it was everything I could do not to sag or show the sudden, crippling backlash of my ultimate Skill wearing off. It left me too tired to fight, but I wasn't quite out of Mana yet, and there was one more thing I could do.

I let out a defiant roar, triggering Draconic Fear. The remaining Orcs who were not hit by my AoE acid Spell froze in sudden terror as the image of a black dragon appeared over me for the duration of that roar.

Seeing what was happening, the men and women who had been taken prisoner, then worked and beaten, felt real hope kindle in their hearts.

Then Viki, bless her heart, shouted, "Remember the Alamo!" and charged forward, waving the rest to join her.

The Orcs were frozen for ten seconds... no, eleven seconds! Apparently, I leveled up again during this fight.

I wanted to rush in and slaughter as many as I could during those brief seconds with my blade. Even better would be to burn through the last of my Mana and melt as many of the bastards as I could before I collapsed.

I just couldn't do it; the best I could manage at that moment was to stand and appear invincible and threatening.

The intimidation Skill wore off before the humans could arrive, but it didn't matter.

The survivors looked around at their dead and dying, and now, faced with a charging wall of humans that outnumbered them at least five to one at this point. Even more intimidating, all the humans were yelling battle cries, and their eyes burned with a desire for revenge. It was too much for the Orcs' already damaged morale. They had lost both of their bosses in less than two hours, and now, a good percentage of their numbers had been slain by one man.

I stood before them as if I was some kind of Draconic avatar.

Terror filled them as they turned and fled, abandoning their dying and injured, running back to the dubious safety of their incomplete fortresses.

As my people arrived, I shouted for them to stop and not give chase. They didn't listen at first and ran past me, falling on the wounded Orcs like an avalanche, raining blows on the bodies until they disappeared. Some even tried to give chase to the fleeing Orcs, but the Level 6 man shouted for them to stop and soon got them to return.

For my part, I fell to my knees as soon as the humans were between me and the retreating monsters. I didn't want the Orcs to see me showing any weakness. They might be outnumbered, but if they had any remaining leaders, they could still easily gain the victory. Thankfully, their bosses were dead, at least for now.

I was panting heavily and trying to recover when Viki walked up and presented me with the loot dropped by the War Chief, a pair of beautiful bracers that made my dragon senses tingle with anticipation despite my tiredness.

Unsurprisingly, instead of copper, the Tier 3 monster had dropped five silver Mana coins, the first I had received in this new life.

The Level 6 Warrior, whose name I had not yet learned, stepped up to me and asked, "What do you want us to do now that we've won?"

Tiredly, I got to my feet and looked the man in the eyes. "We need to fall back and recover. We won the battle, but the dungeon is still there. I may have killed to boss tonight, but by tomorrow there will be another, it will generate new boss monsters to take the place of the ones I've killed unless we destroy the dungeon completely. I can do that, but we need to get these folks someplace safe for now, and I need to rest. For you and the survivors, the fight is over. You can stand down now, but for me, there is still at least one major fight to go."

I thought for a second, then added, "We also need to make some signs to warn people not to go near the Orcs until the dungeon is destroyed. There will be refugees streaming past here once the sun comes up. By the way, I'm Liam Bell."

The man grunted, not seeming to like the idea of not attacking immediately, but he accepted my choice.

"Thomas Stockton, I was a soldier before all this started. I just retired a month ago. So much for kicking back and taking it easy." He chuckled darkly at the irony.

I gave him a sympathetic grin, "That sucks. At least you got a few levels on you before being captured. That's pretty impressive."

Scoffing, Thomas gestured at me, "It's nothing compared to the shit you just did. You are gonna have to tell me how you got so strong, so fast."

"That's going to have to wait until all this is over. For now, let's head away from the highway and put some distance between us and the Orcs. By the way, I rescued your wife and daughter and their group before coming to the dungeon. They asked me to find you."

Thomas blinked in surprise, then to clear the tears from its eyes. With a shuddering breath, he said, "Thank you. Thank you so much. The only thing keeping me going in there was the need to get back to them and get them to safety. Where are they?"

"I sent them on to a protected location. I'll tell you all about it later. For now, let's get everyone organized."

Thomas nodded and started yelling for the people to gather up, and I announced the plan.

There were grumbles and dissenting opinions, but Thomas didn't argue. He just shouted, "This is what we are doing. If you don't like it, you don't have to follow. Good luck if you leave."

Before any protests could start, I added, "In the morning, after we've had some rest, I will share some important advice and directions to a safe location where you can go if you choose. No one is going to be forced to do anything. You are free to leave at any time. ... One more thing, if you have leveled up from the fights tonight, hold off on making any selections until we've had a chance to talk in the morning. Some of my advice is about Class choices."

Some tried to ask questions, but I was too tired to deal with it. Thomas seemed to sense my mood, deflected the people, and got them moving.

Half an hour later, we ended up in what remained of a park. It was in the remnants of one of those 'master-planned' communities, but while the clubhouse and playground were falling apart, the pavilion was still standing, being made mostly of massive steel beams and sheet metal roofing. Even it hadn't fared well. I could see the structure was already rusting now that its protective layer of paint had disintegrated.

We gathered the wounded on the pavilion's basketball court. None were so bad off that they wouldn't survive. Sadly, no one had a healing-related Class, although there were some mundane healing professions among the survivors: three nurses and even one doctor. They did all they could to treat their patients, but that wasn't much when we lacked even the basics of clean water. I did provide them with a bottle of Everclear to use as a disinfectant from my stash of alcohol.

I felt guilty drinking one of the lesser healing potions and not sharing, but I had to preserve my supplies if I were going to save the human race. When that was done, I bedded down. In the morning, it would be time to sort out my gains and plan how to destroy that Orc dungeon!

CHAPTER 25
TALLYING THE GAINS

I STARTED the next day by checking out my gains. I had leveled five times since coming to this dungeon and was now Level 24. However, I had only had a minute to look at my new Skills after the War Chief fight last night. Unfortunately, I hadn't had a chance to use either my new offensive attack Skill, Tempest Strike, or my new Spell, Arcane Singularity. The Skill was kinda Mana-intensive for a blade Skill, and it was meant for hitting all enemies in a small radius around the user. Sadly, that wouldn't have done me any good against the boss. Then, after it was dead, I was using Acid Spray for its AoE goodness.

I was looking forward to Arcane Singularity, though. It was basically an implosion that sucked in enemies for three seconds, then detonated, causing heavy damage and stunning them. It was both offensive and a great tool for crowd control. That would be handy to have in my arsenal going forward.

All-in-all, Level 20 treated me really well. Besides two great new Skills, I also received a new Bloodline Ability, Treasure Sense. That was what had me freaking out over the Shaman's treasure chest and amulet last night. It triggered after I leveled, making me aware of nearby treasure. It also acted as an analyze Ability for identifying treasure and other things. That was why I started getting much more detailed descriptions of the loot drop items. It even gave me some basic information about monsters and people. I had been looking at Thomas this morning, wondering if he would be useful in organizing the folks back at my base, when I suddenly saw his name, Class, and level pop up over his head.

That was super handy. It could also help me avoid accidentally attacking monsters too powerful to handle.

Another happy discovery was my stat increases. My Luck stat had increased to three, which likely had a significant influence on the boss loot drop after the War Chief fight. More importantly, all of my stats had increased by five at Level 20. At first, I was shocked and puzzled by how that could have happened, but looking back through my unread notifications, I saw that I had received another title.

Tier 2 Trailblazer: First in the world to reach Tier 2, all stats +5.

Unbuffed, I was walking around with more than twice the stats an average Level 20 person should have, and considering most of the people in the world right now were less than Level 6... I felt like a giant. It was incredibly gratifying. I definitely needed to keep up the pace and keep grabbing those Trailblazer titles for each of the ten tiers. If I did, I would end up 50% stronger than any other person who might ever make it to the level cap.

That was going to be a major boon. Here I was, just Level 24, and my stats were already better than the peak of my first life when I had been a Level 57 Knight Class. Elated wouldn't even begin to describe how happy I was. In just four days, I had already surpassed what I had achieved in twenty years during my first life.

Looking at my status screen, I was extremely happy.

Liam Bell: (Current)
Draconic Spellsword - Level 24

Experience: 26700/37040

Attributes:
Endurance: 50
Strength: 50
Agility: 50
Mind: 51
Will: 50
Magical Aptitude: 45
Luck: 3

Health: 1000/1000
Mana: 960/960

Abilities:
Active: Dragon Fear
Passive: Dark Vision, Scales, Treasure Sense

Active Skills:
Draconic Strike
Draconic Fury
Searing Slash
Dragon's Charge
Tempest Strike

Passive Skills: None

Spells:
Acid Bolt
Acid Spray
Dragonfire Ward

Scalebound Resilience
Arcane Singularity

Interesting! My status display had changed, possibly due to the Treasure Sense Skill, which was a form of analyze Skill. I was loving that new Ability!

That wasn't all I was loving, however. Glancing back down to my arms, I couldn't help but admire my new bracers. They really surprised me. Not only were they incredibly useful, boosting both my Mana regeneration and my Spell power. They only gave an additional 5% currently, but the incredible thing about them was that they were a soulbound growth item. They would continue to improve as I leveled up. In my entire first life, I had only heard about such items but had never even seen one. Now, here I was, the proud bonded owner of these bracers!

Mystic Bands of the Arcanist
Item Type: Accessory (bracers)

Description: The Mystic Bands of the Arcanist are a masterfully crafted pair of bracers, shimmering with an arcane glow, its surface etched with ancient runes. This magical artifact is designed to resonate with spellcasters, enhancing their connection to the arcane by boosting their Mana regeneration and the potency of their Spells.

Effects:
Mana Regeneration: Initially increases the wearer's Mana regeneration rate by 5%.
Spell Potency: Enhances the potency of all Spells cast by the wearer by 10%.

Special Ability: Arcane Resonance: Once per day, the wearer

can activate the Mystic Band to enter a state of Arcane Resonance for 60 seconds. In this state, Spell Mana consumption is reduced by 25%. The first Spell cast in this state is significantly empowered, dealing 50% more damage or achieving 50% greater effectiveness for non-damaging Spells.

Usage Conditions: The Mystic Band of the Arcanist requires attunement by a spellcaster. Once attuned, it binds to the wearer, becoming ineffective for others unless the attunement is willingly broken or the original wearer dies.

Besides the bracers, I was also sporting the Shadowstep boots that I had found in the Shaman's treasure chest. They fit my feet with the perfection that only magical items could, and I loved that they muted the noise made by my movements, not just footfalls but also creaking armor noises and rustling made when brushing against bushes or plants that I moved through.

I still really wished I could go heavier into stealth Skills and Abilities, but it didn't seem like Black Dragons focused on that. Perhaps when the Shop opened, I could buy the stealth Skill, but for now, the boots would have to do.

There were also the coins: five silver Mana coins. By rights, I should have had more copper as well, but the survivors had gathered up all the coins that dropped from the other Orcs. I had been too tired to protest or even care after the battle, and these people would need them once the Shop opened. Besides, there were still all of the coins that had dropped last night up on the Shaman's hill that I would go and collect later.

That thought brought me back to what needed to be done next. "Thomas, would you mind gathering everyone up so I can address them?"

The veteran and now Level 6 Warrior gave me a quick nod before shouting for folks to gather around. I climbed up on a crossbeam of the Pavilion so that everyone could see me.

Gazing out over the rag-tag group of refugees, I couldn't help but be amazed at their tenacity and toughness to have come out of that dungeon alive and sane. Perhaps there was a certain amount of shock that gripped them, and they hadn't fully come to terms yet with our old world being dead, but they would now that they had been through so much and survived. Even so, my heart went out to them. Most were barely clothed, and what they did have was ripped and bloodstained. The System had not been kind to them as it reclaimed anything synthetic, including fabrics, which made up such a large part of our modern wardrobes.

They were also starving and needed fresh water very soon. One and all, they had a hollow look to them after five days of little or no food. Thankfully, the Orcs had at least given them water and a few bites of the vile mess they called food. Now, it was time to give them hope.

"Congratulations on surviving your ordeal, but now we need to make sure it doesn't happen to anyone else! I am asking those of you who volunteer to stay behind just long enough to make signs to warn other travelers of the dangers, especially of the dungeon in the dump."

I gave them all a grin and tried to project confidence and certainty as I continued, "The good news is that I know of a safe place."

Seeing the hope blooming on their gaunt faces, I went on to tell them of the missile silo base and Cold War communications bunker and the fact that it had fresh water enough to support a decent-sized community. I didn't sugarcoat it, however. I let them know it would take work to fortify the property and make it safe not only from mutated beasts and monsters but also from humans with ill intent. I told them that I had already had to defend it against one such group and urged them to band together to be able to stand against foes like that.

"When you arrive there, for those who decide to go, I ask that you respect Morgan's leadership. I have left her in charge of the base. Like me, she was very lucky to receive an advanced Class and can even heal the injured and sick. I am going to also ask Thomas here to help her out, as he will be rushing over there to reunite with his wife and daughter. Look out for other refugees and beware those with ill intent."

After giving them directions and explaining what I knew of monsters and dungeons, I went on to share the same advice that I had written on the walls of the bunker with them. 'Look for magic Classes when they upgrade their Classes at Level 30. Spread the word to have any children that weren't old enough to choose yet to try and get magic Classes.'

It took well over an hour to impart the knowledge that I felt was safe to share. Many tried to question me and ask how I knew these things and how I had attained such strength. I gave them a very brief and not too revealing summary of how I had discovered the 'Class options' choice during initialization and received a rare Class that had allowed me to complete the dungeon that had been in the silo base.

They wanted to know much more, but I silenced them with the promise that I would explain more and answer what questions I could when I returned to the base next time. That led to the next obvious question from a woman in the crowd. "What are you going to do if you aren't going to lead us to safety?"

"I am going to kill the rest of the Orcs in that dungeon. Every last one of them. If even one survives, the System will begin to replace the ones we've killed, and soon, it will be bigger and more dangerous than ever. That's why I have to end it! After that, I will venture a little further into the city and see if there is anything I can do to help direct survivors toward safety. Not that I mean for everyone to go to my base; it can't handle more than a few hundred right now. Still, I can tell them how to establish defensible places and what I've learned since the System arrived."

That did not make the people happy. Many felt desperate and feared that they might not survive the journey, but I assured them that with their numbers and the few higher-level members of their group, they should be able to handle anything they encountered.

"Listen to Thomas as well. He is ex-military and the highest level among you."

It was a longer parting than I anticipated, but I wasn't in a great hurry to attack the Orcs until after nightfall, anyway. I made sure those staying behind were safe while writing the warning messages on the road, using charcoal and tools to scrape words into the concrete.

The one problem I did have was trying to send Viki away to go with Thomas and the rest of the survivors. She absolutely refused to hear it. There was no way she was going to leave my side, no matter what argument was made.

I finally gave up when she countered by saying that she was earning experience and that if she stayed with me, she would have enough saved up to gain several levels as soon as she was allowed to choose her Class.

Blinking in astonishment, I picked my jaw up off the floor. I couldn't believe the System would do something as helpful as letting a child earn experience even when it couldn't raise their levels due to being Unclassed.

"Fine, but you will stay back and only use your bow to attack from a distance when I give the okay. Understand?"

Thomas gawked at my response. "You... you're actually going to let her go into a dungeon with you? A child?"

Shrugging, I gave him a look. "I've only known her for a day, but you have no idea how stubborn she is. You could tie her up in a sack, and the second you turned around, you'd find yourself carrying an empty sack. Then you'd look up just in time to notice her charging headfirst at a Level 100 World Boss."

"Hey!" Viki protested.

I just chuckled at her reaction but didn't back down. "What? You know it's true!"

She scowled and turned her back to us, giving us the cold shoulder.

It was Thomas' turn to chuckle now. "I think I see what you mean. I'll leave her to you then if you're sure."

"Okay, when you get to the base, help Morgan get folks organized, and don't be afraid to exile or execute anyone causing trouble. Humanity can't afford to be getting into internal fights. I claimed that base, and I'm delegating you to help her run it in my absence. If anyone has a problem with that, I'll deal with them when I return."

With nothing left to discuss, the veteran-turned-Warrior formed the refugees up and got them moving towards the road. They would stay out of sight of the highway until they were past the Orcs, however.

It was all done, and the volunteer sign-makers left later in the afternoon to follow after the main host of the survivors.

After we saw them off, Viki and I crept our way silently toward the stadium arena, ready to implement our attack strategy after the sun went down.

CHAPTER 26

TREATING THOSE ORCS LIKE THEY SHOT JOHN WICK'S DOG!

Before we arrived, I stopped to have a serious conversation with my overly brave companion. "Listen, I'm letting you stay with me because the System is giving you experience for the kills you make. However, you've only got a few arrows, and I do not want you getting anywhere near melee range. Understand?"

Viki frowned but reluctantly nodded. "I wasn't planning on it."

I could practically hear the 'but' in her tone. "But you only have a few arrows left and can't join in once you shoot them. I know, but you are Unclassed right now, and the lowest-level opponent we'll face is Level 10. A gentle slap from one of them would be enough to kill you instantly."

"I know, I know! You don't have to keep going on about it!"

Raising a challenging eyebrow, I asked, "And you can look me in the eye and tell me you weren't thinking about it?"

She didn't answer but looked away, not meeting my eyes.

"That's what I thought. Don't sweat it, though. It's only a couple of days to your birthday, and you are essentially getting power-leveled. No one on the planet will jump up from Level 0 to over Level 5 like you. You'll not only get your Class, but you'll get to skip the first five levels or more."

Viki sighed, "Yeah, I know, but still, it sucks to sit on the sidelines! I want to do more. How about if I only run up and kill ones you've injured too badly to fight?"

I shook my head in denial. "Too much risk. You can wait until I'm done fighting, and then I'll let you give them the coup de grâce with me protecting you. Otherwise, I'm going to make you wait outside and not participate at all."

"Fine!" She turned her back on me and crossed her arms in a huff.

Doing my best to hold in a chuckle so I didn't offend her, I patted her on the back.

"Come on, let's go."

As Viki and I crept closer to what had once been the high school football stadium under the cover of night, the world around us was bathed in the faint glow of a low-hanging crescent moon. Its light was hardly enough to cut through the darkness, casting everything in a mix of shadow and silver that made the familiar, yet now foreboding, structure ahead seem almost otherworldly.

The stadium—a relic of what life had been before chaos took hold— stood stark against the night sky. Its once proud and bustling stands were now silent, overtaken by the relentless advance of nature. Vines clung to the railings and concrete, and weeds forced their way through the cracks, a testament to the world's reclaiming of human spaces. The field—where innocent football games had occurred— was now a desolate expanse, the goalposts twisted shadows of their former selves.

Approaching the entrance, the contrast between the serene beauty of the crescent moon and the ominous silhouette of the stadium struck me. The place that once echoed with cheers and the thrill of competition was now silent, except for the distant, unsettling sounds of Orcs within. Torches flanked the gateway, their flickering light casting long, dancing shadows as if warning us of the darkness that lay beyond.

Despite the decay and darkness, the stadium retained its imposing presence, a monument to a past now overrun by the brutal reality we faced. Standing at the threshold, Viki and I shared a moment of resolve, the sight of the corrupted arena steeling us for the battle ahead. The quiet of the night, pierced only by the occasional Orcish shout or the clank of armor, served as a stark reminder of the divide between the world as it was and as it now stood—caught between the echoes of the past and the grim present we were determined to challenge.

I sighed and shook off the System-imposed 'ambiance' that invaded my mind every time I approached or entered one of its creations. Still, I had to admit to being impressed. Those vines hadn't existed six days ago, nor had there been tall grass and weeds making the place look overgrown. In fact, this stadium was less than five years old, and the school district kept the campus immaculately groomed and clean. That meant that the System was able to create plants where none had existed before, as well as change the appearance of structures.

Just another reason to hate the System. It could go out of its way to be artistic with scenes like this, but at the same time, it was fine with destroying and erasing all of human civilization and culture.

What pissed me off even more was the thought that somewhere out there, a new world would someday join the 'network,' and on that planet, the System would create humans as monsters to strengthen and cull the native species. Would those aliens be amazed to see a human-inhabited art gallery with the Mona Lisa decorating its walls?

Fucking System!

Getting my head back in the game, I whispered a reminder to Viki to stay back until the battle was over.

An eye roll was my only answer.

Chuckling quietly, I moved into the tunnel, Viki waiting until I was a good distance ahead before lightly stalking after me so that she wouldn't be caught by any traps or attacks that hit me unaware.

I stepped onto the arena floor, expecting a football field, but its edges had been rounded off, shaping it into a large oval. More shocking, gone was the turf I remembered; in its place lay a blanket of sand, its surface marred by dark splotches that I didn't have to guess to know were bloodstains. The familiar feeling of grass underfoot was replaced by the shifting, coarse sand, each step a reminder of the arena's grim purpose.

The bleachers, which I recalled being made of concrete or perhaps wood, now appeared to be hewn from stone, giving the place an ancient, almost timeless quality. Along the perimeter, racks of weapons stood ominously, their blades catching the dim light, offering a silent testament to the violence that took place here.

At one end of the arena, a large iron cage held the prisoners, its bars a stark, cruel contrast to the openness of the sand-covered ground. I noticed the captives huddled together, their faces a mix of fear and defiance.

Next, my attention was drawn to the center of the arena, where a distressing scene was playing out. A trio of regular Orcs were toying with a human captive, their jeers filling the air as they prodded at him with spears, urging him to fight back. Around them, Elite Orcs stood as spectators, their posture relaxed, as if they were merely enjoying a casual sport.

The contrast between the arena's imposing structure and the sordid spectacle it hosted was jarring, a reminder of the world's descent into chaos. As I watched, my resolve hardened; this place of despair would soon witness a reckoning. My anger was awakening.

The sight fueled a burning rage within me. Here, in this twisted version of entertainment, the Orcs reveled in their dominance, reducing human suffering to mere amusement. Or rather, the System was doing so because these were created creatures. Perhaps they were modeled on a real race. I had died at the hands of a High Orc invader, after all. Still, the System didn't need to do this. If its theoretical purpose was to make the survivors stronger, then why the cruelty? Why put us through such things that would only destroy us? If I hadn't come along, and I certainly hadn't in my first life, then this person and the ones in that cage wouldn't have been made stronger; they would have certainly died and done so by means that amounted to torture.

I know the fucking system has no moral code when it comes to human life, but surely, someone, somewhere in the universe, had to have programmed their AIs with some sense of decency?

Growling in my throat, I was too pissed off at this sight to play it safe and hunt them a few at a time. This needed to end now!

"Hey! You call yourselves Orcs? You're nothing but sniveling runts, weaker than a human child. Even Goblins laugh at your so-called strength. You dishonor your ancestors with your pitiful excuse for fighting. I've seen more ferocity in sheep."

Silence fell instantly as the Orcs stood, shocked by the challenge; the human they had been torturing forgotten.

Every Orc in the arena was focused on me, not just the ones on the sand but also the ones in the stands. It was hard for me to count them all from where I stood, but I could see somewhere around fifteen to twenty Elites and over thirty regular Orcs.

That was a lot. Still, I wasn't in the mood to regret my choice. I was pissed, and I wanted them dead.

"Face me in combat unless you are cowards! Come down onto the sand and fight like warriors!"

One of the Elites, who seemed to be their leader, stepped forward and shouted back, "You die for insulting mighty Grognakul, Elite of Orc race!"

It then gestured to the other Orcs to join it, "We kill ugly human, feast on its bones!"

I didn't glance behind me but heard Viki scurry out of the tunnel and hurry to one side, no doubt moving to hide behind one of the many weapons racks that lined the perimeter of the arena floor.

That let me breathe a sigh of relief to know she would be out of danger. They should all be focused on me and unable to notice her in the chaos that was about to occur.

Stalking forward, I drew my sword and prepared to fight. Adrenaline was flowing in my body, along with the anger, giving me a bizarre, jittery, but eager feeling for the upcoming fight. I stopped when I was near the center and waited for the Orcs to gather. Thankfully, they really were modeled after the High Orc race, and rather than trying to attack me from all sides, which would have been smart, they gathered before me in a large group. I didn't know if that was because of some cultural thing of their race, related to their supposed honor, or perhaps it was just that these Orcs weren't as intelligent as their real-world counterparts. Or maybe there was an actual difference, and High Orcs were an offshoot from this lesser race, one that had developed greater intelligence?

Either way, the human who had been the focus of their 'sport' had wisely taken the opportunity to flee toward the other end of the arena. I hoped he was trying to free his fellow captives, but he might have been rushing toward one of the other exits of the building.

On the sands of the arena, the assembled Orcs were arrayed in a stark display of hierarchy and might. Eighteen Elites, distinguishable by their imposing stature and the intricate, battle-worn armor that clung to their muscular frames, stood in a rigid line at the forefront. These were the seasoned warriors, each bearing the scars and trophies of countless battles, their faces set in expressions of ruthless determination. Behind this Elite vanguard, a large throng of lesser Orcs amassed—a motley crew of Fighters, smaller and less adorned, yet no less eager for bloodshed. This sea of Orcs, with their varied armor and weapons drawn, created a menacing tableau, a vivid illustration of the raw power and unity that defined their kind in the face of impending combat.

To outward appearances, this looked like suicide. One man standing against so many should not have a hope of winning. The numbers were simply too big of an obstacle, even with my level advantage.

Inwardly, I was laughing maniacally. I had them right where I wanted them! By playing to their pride and insulting their honor, they did the one thing that could turn this from their assured victory to a win for me, even if not an easy one.

Waiting no longer, I charged forward, activating Scalebound Resilience as I ran to meet the enemy. They were a little too spread out for me to get them all, but if this worked, I could significantly cut down their numbers.

The Elites were charging toward me as well now, but some of them were proving to be smarter than their lesser brethren. They began moving to flank me and come at me from the sides. That would make this tricky and mean that I wouldn't manage to get as many of the lesser Orcs with my trap.

Nothing I could do about it. Damn!

I triggered the once-per-day effect of my new bracers: Arcane Resonance. For the next 60 seconds, my Mana consumption would be reduced by 25%, and my cooldowns would decrease by 20%. However, the most important thing it did was boost the potency of the first Spell cast by 50%.

Raising my left hand, I triggered my most devastating Spell for large groups of enemies, Acid Spray.

The jet of glowing corrosive liquid that sprayed out was significantly stronger than normal. Not as much as when I was using Draconic Fury, but still, the Elite that had been running toward my left side was knocked from its feet by the power of the spray. My hand was held out with my arm stiff to better control the Spell as I quickly swept it across my body toward the right, doing my best to hit each of the Elites with enough of the elemental acid to take them out of the fight if not outright kill them.

I couldn't be fast enough; it simply wasn't possible. However, I could not allow my Spell to be interrupted; I was counting on this trick to level the playing field.

Doing my best to dodge what I could while maintaining the Spell, I made my attackers pay with their lives.

Not all could be dodged. I took several hits that threatened to break my concentration and left bleeding wounds on my torso, right leg, and right shoulder, despite my armor and defensive Spells boosting my defense. I simply had no choice but to take it.

They paid with their lives to draw my blood, and they died without ending my Spell. That left me free to stagger backward and hit as many of the lesser Orcs as I could. Mostly, those had followed their leaders' charge. In that moment, I couldn't tell how many I had managed to hit before my Spell sputtered out, but it was a significant portion of the thirty-something lesser Orcs.

I was grinning like a maniac as I stood in the momentary gap in the attack created by the remaining Orcs fleeing out of range of my Spell. I also couldn't help but notice arrows arcing over me and into the Orcs still on their feet.

Hoping none of the Orcs would be diverted to deal with Viki, I made sure to draw their attention back to me by using my latest Spell, the one I hadn't had a chance to cast yet.

"Suck on this!" I yelled. "Arcane Singularity!"

The Spell was aimed at the biggest group of uninjured Orcs. They were broken up into smaller groups now, having dodged out of the way of my previous Spell, but there were still some unwise enough to clump together.

They learned a new lesson. The singularity formed in their midst. In the first second, it was barely noticeable, a small black dot, the size of a marble, spinning in place at shoulder height off the ground. Then, it began to pull and grow. Sand and dust fed it, and the Orcs' eyes widened in panic as they were yanked from their feet. In a radius of ten feet, every Orc was slammed together as the black sphere tried to pull them in. Even those another five feet away felt the pull but were not quite drawn in.

Then, in the third second... BOOM!

The sphere detonated, flinging bodies in every direction and even injuring those who hadn't been crushed into the center.

What was left behind was a crater five feet in radius and injured bodies as far as fifteen feet from the center. Those who didn't die outright were stunned.

It was a very satisfying Spell. Unfortunately, it also cost me. That one required concentration, like Acid Spray, and three seconds is a long time in a fight.

I could only thank my Bloodline for the focus necessary to ignore the daggers, hatchets, and other weapons that were hurled at me while I couldn't respond.

I had a dagger in the joint of my left shoulder and a nasty gash on my left cheek that was causing blood to pour uncomfortably down into my armor.

With both shoulders injured, this was going to be rough, but fortunately, I had one last trick up my sleeve.

I roared. How a human throat could make that sound, I did not want to speculate, but it was effective!

My intimidation Skill froze all of the Orcs in terror. Some Elites were still alive but out of the fight, thanks to my acid, and that left only lesser Orcs standing and posing a threat. I was now twelve levels above them, meaning they would be frozen for fourteen seconds.

Those would be the longest seconds of their lives...

I removed the cleaver from my storage ring and dual-wielded my sword and the Orc weapon to kill as many as I could before time ran out. With nearly every second that ticked down, another body hit the floor.

I aimed for necks where I could, as those were the most lethal strikes. Thrusts to the heart with my sword where necessary. Each shot was as precise as I could make them with my wounded shoulders, but each swing or thrust caused me to feel agony. There was no stopping; I could feel each second tick away as if I were going to the gallows and waiting for the hangman to pull his lever.

There were only three standing when they shook off the fear, and they took aim with their own weapons and attacked with a fury that was equal to the terror they had just experienced.

It was everything I could do to survive those next few seconds. They might be lower level and weaker than me, but they were enraged beyond reason, and I was badly injured, and every block and parry made me scream in agony.

I wanted to use Acid Bolt, but with attacks coming in constantly and jarring my injured shoulders, I couldn't muster the concentration, nor did I have a second to drop the cleaver and aim. Doing so would have meant my death.

Dragon's Fury would have ended this fight without worry, but I needed to save that for later. If I used it now, I would be too exhausted to do more until tomorrow. That only left my attack Skills.

The downside was that I knew this was going to suck!

Powerstrike took out the Orc in the middle as it had overextended in its last attack. The boost in power that the Skill granted came at the cost of excruciating pain that made me leave my blade planted in its heart.

I followed that up immediately with a Draconic Slash to the one on my left with the cleaver. It decapitated the Orc cleanly as if there was no resistance whatsoever, but it, too, came at the cost of extreme pain. I managed to keep hold of the cleaver but only barely.

Looking to the final Orc on my right, I was just about to trigger my ultimate Skill out of desperation when an arrow suddenly sprouted from its skull. It simply toppled like a felled tree, its arm still raised to deliver a killing blow.

There was a long moment before I could react, still in a haze of pain and shock from my unexpected reprieve. When I did, I burst out laughing.

I had been saved by the bravest girl in the world, an almost twelve-year-old kid who didn't even have a Class or levels yet. Still, there was no denying she had skill with the bow.

As I slowly looked around to make sure there were no further enemies, I was surprised to notice many of the Orcs who had fallen to my acid now sported arrows and no longer moved.

Even as I stood taking in the scene of devastation, arrows continued to rain down on the dying enemies. My brain was slow to catch up. How was she doing that? She only had 13 arrows...

Then I looked to where she stood next to one of the weapon racks and saw that she was drawing arrows from a barrel. She was using the Orcs' own weapons to kill them. I was still chuckling as I pulled the

mid-grade healing potion from my storage ring and popped the top.

It felt like liquid relief! I could feel my wounds closing and repairing at a visible pace, and glancing at my HP, it was climbing back up to an acceptable level.

We had done it again, survived what should have been overwhelming odds. My thoughts were interrupted.

Suddenly, I felt my spidey senses tingling... there was treasure here!

CHAPTER 27

SHAMAN'S HILL 2, THE SEQUEL

DESPITE MY BLOODLINE'S Treasure Sense Ability triggering, I held my position and gestured for Viki to join me. I wanted to make sure she finished off any enemies that were still alive so she could gain XP. It felt like such a cheat that she could accumulate experience even though she wasn't Classed yet.

Of course, it might just reset to zero when she chose her Class in a couple of days. There was no way to know, but I had a hunch that since the XP gain was showing in her status window, she would be allowed to keep it. At this point, she had killed enough strong enemies, or helped to do so, that she should definitely be over level five the moment she gained her Class.

I hadn't forgotten the prisoner we had saved with our arrival and looked for him. He had just come out of hiding in the stands near the cage, so I yelled for him to free the prisoners and bring them over here.

Meanwhile, Viki and I collected all the coins that dropped and arrows that were still usable. For her sake, I stored most of them in my ring. Her small quiver could only hold around twenty at most. Having more would give her a lot more to do in future fights and hopefully keep her from wanting to rush in due to running out of arrows.

Of course, I was wise enough not to verbalize that. It would only have caused an argument.

Unfortunately, I didn't manage to sidestep it after all. Viki's first words were, "See, once you take them down with your acid attack, it wouldn't be any big deal for me to come in and finish them off. I could follow behind you and give them the 'cootie grass' thing you said before."

I couldn't help but laugh. "It's 'Coup de grâce', not 'cootie grass'. It means to give them a quick death with a single blow."

Considering her words, I paused for a second to think about it. "You know what, sure. Still, you need to wait until there are no active Orcs anywhere close enough to get to you before I could. Here, wear this and don't cut yourself. You might need it."

I handed her the Orc cleaver. It was special. Kind of gross, but it was magical. Now that I had the Treasure Sense Skill that gave me the Ability to analyze people and items, I was tempted to use it instead of my own longsword. I shared the status page with her, which described the weapon.

Cleaver of the Fallen Shaman:
Description: This hefty blade, once wielded by the Shaman for dark rituals, is imbued with a Curse that weakens the enemy's defenses with each strike. The weapon carries a faint, eerie glow, and its edge seems to whisper with the voices of those it has slain.

Stats: Attack power: +25 On hit: Reduces the target's armor by 5% for 10 seconds. This effect stacks up to 3 times.

Special Effect: Each critical hit has a 10% chance to drain 5% of the target's maximum health, adding it to the wielder's health.

That lifesteal effect was tempting, but it was only a small chance, and I didn't think it would prove enough to make a noticeable difference. Granted, I hadn't wielded it much, but so far, the effect had never triggered for me.

Viki's eyes got big as she read the description. "Holy shit! It's a magic sword!"

I glared at her. "Language, young lady!"

She rolled her eyes at me. "Whatever, boomer!"

That made me chuckle. "You realize I'm only 20, which makes me like three generations younger than boomers, right?"

Viki's only reply was a smirk, but after a second, she said, "Seriously, thank you!"

"You're welcome. Just stay alive and out of trouble. If it weren't for the apocalypse and the fact that you are gaining XP, I'd never even consider letting you tag along."

After that conversation, I finally couldn't take it anymore and headed straight for a hallway into the guts of the stadium-turned-arena. This seemed to be where the Orcs were making their home. In the last and largest room, there was a chest. This area didn't have a boss or mini-boss, but apparently, the System considered it significant enough to provide some loot.

More likely, one of those Elites that I had just killed would have been upgraded to be a mini-boss as the stronghold dungeon grew in size and tier.

Using my sword to pry the latch open, I carefully pushed it open. Mimics and traps did exist, after all; however, my dragon senses were telling me there was treasure inside.

When it opened, there were the usual pair of potions, but also something I would not have expected but should not have been surprised by. At the bottom of the chest lay a simple ring.

As I pulled it from the box, I could tell by the weight that it was more than just a plain, unadorned ring. It had that hefty feel of metal heavier than gold that could only be platinum. My Skill immediately told me it was a storage ring with a capacity half-again larger than the one I already had.

I couldn't help but grin from ear to ear. These things were pretty rare, but apparently, my Luck stat was working on overdrive, dropping some phat lootz, as the old gamers used to say.

Putting it on and removing the other ring, I transferred everything except the arrows with a thought. I handed the old one to Viki.

"Here, this is a storage ring. Run around the arena, gather all the arrows you can find, and put them in the ring. You'll no longer need a quiver; you can just make an arrow appear in your hand while wearing the ring. Of course, you're still limited to however many arrows you store inside it."

Her eyes got big, and she started to tear up. "That's... that's too much."

I shook my head. "Don't worry about it; I just got another one that is even bigger. Still, these things are super rare, so don't let anyone know you have it if you can help it. Try to hide getting things out or putting things in by acting like you are drawing them from your quiver or a pocket inside your jacket or something. People would literally kill for one of these."

She put the ring on her finger, threw her arms around my waist in a hug, and squeezed me hard enough that if I hadn't had such ridiculous stats, it might have hurt.

I patted her on the back. "Don't worry about it. This just means I don't have to carry everything myself anymore." I chuckled.

It was a long moment before she let go and stepped back, then she ran back into the arena to gather arrows.

Meanwhile, I headed back out to speak with the freed captives.

"You are all free. There are still Orcs on the hills, and there may be patrols, but if you are careful, you can make your way back to the highway and circle wide of the Orc stronghold. On the other hand, I will be killing the rest of the Orcs tonight, so if you would rather, you can make this place a human stronghold and make it a safe stop for other refugees fleeing the city, and believe me, there will be more and more streaming past here as the days go by and things deteriorate. Since this was System-built, it won't fall apart like human buildings."

I went on to give them a choice of staying, going, or heading to my base. They were surprisingly tough, each ranging from Levels 4 to 6, a testament to what they had gone through here in the Orc arena.

One of them begged, "Please, tell me, have you seen a group of women and children on the highway two days ago?"

Several other men and one woman all stepped forward eagerly, listening for my answer.

I grinned. "As a matter of fact, they were the ones who warned me of this Stronghold dungeon. I sent them on to my base. I'll give you directions."

The man who had asked had tears flowing down his cheeks in joy and relief at my answer. He looked like he was about to rush out the door, so I stopped him.

"Hold on there. It won't be safe until morning. I still have a hundred or more Orcs to kill to complete the dungeon. You all arm yourselves with the arena weapons and barricade yourselves in here for the night. Hang on to those weapons, by the way. They are System-generated, and even though they might look ugly or of bad quality, they will still be better than anything else you find short of a treasure drop in a dungeon."

Viki had returned, having cleaned out all of the arrows, and I noticed she also wore a dagger strapped to her right boot in a battered-looking sheath. She whispered, "I also took a bow for backup in case mine breaks. I put it in the you-know-what."

I gave her a grin and motioned toward the tunnel before waving to the survivors. "We'll be back in the morning, if not before. Keep a few people awake at all times and on watch. We've got a dungeon to conquer. If you don't hear from us by noon, send a scout to the big hill and see if there are any orcs left in the fortress. If there are, then it means we are dead. If not, then it'll be safe to join us there."

Before I moved on, I did take a minute to check my status. I had two Level Up notifications waiting in the corner of my vision. One thing was for sure, this dungeon was a gold mine of XP. It was kind of a shame it was a special type of dungeon and would disappear after completion. Otherwise, it might take me to Level 35 or higher before I had to move on. Still, I was very happy that I had gained two levels in that last fight, bringing me to Level 26.

Liam Bell: (Current)
Draconic Spellsword - Level 26

Experience: 6100/42560

Attributes:
Endurance: 52
Strength: 52
Agility: 52
Mind: 53
Will: 52
Magical Aptitude: 47
Luck: 3

Health: 673/1040
Mana: 880/1000

Abilities:
Active: Dragon Fear
Passive: Dark Vision, Scales, Treasure Sense

Active Skills:
Draconic Strike
Draconic Fury
Searing Slash
Dragon's Charge
Tempest Strike
Heavy Draconic Strike

Passive Skills: None

Spells:
Acid Bolt
Acid Spray
Dragonfire Ward
Scalebound Resilience
Arcane Singularity
Acid Rain

I couldn't wait to see what my two new Skills were, so I pulled those up. I was pleased to see that the descriptions now showed more, including the cooldown times.

Spell: Acid Rain

Description: Summoning the acidic essence of a Black Dragon, Liam conjures a storm of corrosive rain that falls over a large area, damaging all enemies caught within it.

Effects: Deals minor acid damage per second to all enemies within the target area for 20 seconds.
Enemies affected by the rain are slowed by 30% for the duration. Has a chance to inflict an additional acid burn, dealing extra damage over 5 seconds.

Mana Cost: Moderate
Cooldown: 45 seconds

Heavy Draconic Strike

Description: An advanced version of the initial Draconic Strike, Heavy Draconic Strike channels the raw, corrosive power of a Black Dragon into a devastating blow. Liam's weapon glows with a dark, acidic energy, enhancing his strike with tremendous force and destructive potential.

Effects: Deals heavy physical damage combined with significant acid damage to a single target.
Inflicts a powerful acid debuff that deals additional damage over 10 seconds.
Has a 30% chance to weaken the target's armor, reducing their defense by 20% for 15 seconds.

Cooldown: 40 seconds
Mana Cost: Moderate

I thought, *Nice, that strike is clearly the big brother of my first level Skill, Draconic Strike, just all grown up.*

Thinking of the possibilities for that Acid Rain Spell made me happy. It didn't do strong damage, but it lasted for a long period. More importantly, it would slow enemies for 20 seconds. That could be a real ace up my sleeve if I got into a fight against a really fast opponent. It could mean the difference between life and death. Better still, considering the way it was worded, I didn't think it would harm me or my allies.

I was still thinking about my new Skills when we approached the Shaman's hill again, and this time, what greeted us was not the fear-inducing situation we had seen the first time. Instead of a hill full of Orc Elites and dozens of lesser Orcs led by a strong mini-boss, there was only a single Elite sitting outside the Shaman's hut, surrounded by twenty-five of its lesser kin that I could see. There might be a few more on the gates or hiding amongst the slave pens, but what I saw was something I could easily handle.

In fact, I didn't even plan on using any of my trump cards. These guys were going to be sword practice for me and target practice for Viki. I wouldn't even use my Dragon's Fear to paralyze them. Besides, if I did, some of them might try and run away, alerting the other hill that I was coming, and they might fortify themselves in their central area, which was System-generated instead of slave-constructed. That might make the last area harder to handle.

Therefore, this needed to be handled quietly, or at least relatively so.

The fight commenced with a rush of adrenaline. I activated Scalebound Resilience, feeling the familiar surge of defensive magic hardening my skin against the impending blows. After that, I cast Acid Rain, just to slow the enemies down a bit. I was confident, but there were twenty-five of them after all.

As the Orcs charged, their movements were predictable, their tactics unrefined. My sword danced in my hand, a blur of steel that met Orc flesh with precision and lethality. Each stroke was measured, each block and parry calculated to provide the most efficient dispatch of my foes.

Better still, I was finally falling back into the Skills and habits that I had honed over two decades as a Warrior and Knight from my first life. The muscle memory was starting to click, and I was no longer having to think about every move. The fight almost felt nostalgic, and I felt far more confident than I had at any point since reawakening.

I was invigorated; this was what fighting was meant to be like!

Still, despite my dominance on the battlefield thanks to Acid Rain's slowing effect, the Orcs managed to land a few lucky strikes. A blade grazed my arm, and another clipped my side, the minor wounds stinging with the promise of bruises to come. Yet, these injuries did nothing to deter my resolve; if anything, they honed my focus, sharpening my movements as I carved through the Orcs, if not with ease, then certainly with a skill beyond what I ought to have if this were my first life.

From the corner of my eye, I saw Viki's silhouette against the moonlit sky, her bowstring humming as she loosed arrow after arrow. Her aim was true, most shafts finding their marks in the chaos of battle. Orcs staggered and fell, arrows protruding from eye sockets and throats, their vile intentions cut short by her deadly precision. Those I left wounded and gasping on the ground soon met their end at the tip of her arrows, ensuring none would rise to threaten us again.

I was frankly both impressed by her performance and more than a little worried. She was only a kid, and yet she was killing like a seasoned professional. No hesitation and no regrets, as far as I could tell. In my first life, it took me months of harsh experience and a lot of soul-searching before I came to terms with this new reality. She seemed to completely skip all of that, and I hoped it didn't mean she was repressing things and being psychologically harmed by what she was doing.

Well, I mean, how could she not be harmed by this. Still, there really wasn't any alternative that included her living any kind of normal life.

I shook off those thoughts and refocused when I faced the Elite. That was something I would have to worry about later. Right now, I faced a boss fight that required my undivided attention.

The Elite, seeing its forces diminish with alarming speed, roared and lunged at me with a desperation born of fury. Yet, even its enhanced strength and skill could not break through my defense. We clashed; its brute force against my agility and technique. In the end, it was a well-placed thrust beneath its arm that brought it down, its massive form crumbling to the ground with a thunderous finality.

As the last of the Orcs fell, Viki and I stood amidst the carnage, breathing heavily, the rush of battle slowly ebbing away. My minor injuries ached, a testament to the Orcs' ferocity, but the feeling of triumph was undeniable.

Counting the bodies, I could see that there were far more than I had originally noted. The guards on the gates and more must have heard the battle and come running, only to die. Together, we had cleared the Shaman's hill, a display of swordsmanship and archery that left no doubt of our prowess. The night was ours, the hill once more a quiet sentinel under the stars, its would-be conquerors silenced.

One of the handy things about my new Treasure Sense was knowing exactly where the loot could be found. Not only did we gather up all the coins that had dropped from these monsters, but my "spidey-sense" led me straight back to the chest in the Shaman's hut. Inside, I found a large pile of copper Mana coins, no doubt the ones that had dropped during last night's battle. The Orcs must have gathered them up, and the Elite stored them in the treasure chest. I found that to be particularly handy.

What we found tonight brought my total up to 5 sp and 3715 cp. That was a very respectable start to my treasure hoard. I couldn't help but chuckle to think of it that way.

Of course, I shared the coins with Viki, making sure she received them for each Orc with an arrow in it. I didn't pay attention to how many coins she had gathered, but it was sure to be a good start for someone without a Class. By the time the Shop opened, we'd both be able to buy ourselves some good gear and weapons.

Sadly, I did not level up after this battle but was over halfway to Level 27. The main things were my health and Mana pools. Both would be sufficient with a short rest before heading over to the last bastion of the Orc stronghold.

Viki, however, was very excited about the amount of XP she had amassed. Looking at her status screen, I knew she had to be nearing enough XP to hit Level 10.

Victoria Blue, aka Viki: (Current)
Unclassed - Level 0

Experience: 23,125/100

Attributes:
Endurance: 5
Strength: 4
Agility: 6
Mind: 6
Will: 6
Magical Aptitude: 2

Health: 0/9
Mana: 80/80

Abilities: None

Active Skills: None

Passive Skills: None

"Damn! You've got enough XP to hit Level 8 as soon as you choose your Class!"

She was practically bouncing with excitement. "Now that I've got more arrows, that last battle earned me nearly as much experience as all three of the previous fights put together! If the fortress is as good as this, I'm going to be Level 9 at least."

Pointing to her stats, she was grinning from ear to ear, "Did you see it?! My Magical Aptitude has two points now, and I've got 80 Mana! I'm sure to get a magic Class option!"

That was indeed impressive. I only had one point in that stat when I was reborn. "I see it! Congratulations. Just two more days, and you'll get your Class."

Looking at her experience got me thinking. She was so close now to Level 10, and I had never heard of someone power-leveled up to ten in a single go like this. Hell, I hadn't even known something like this was possible. I would be willing to bet my sword that if we could get her to Level 10 as soon as she chose her Class, there would be some kind of title as a reward.

That was it. I wanted to test that theory now! I gave Viki a serious look.

"We're going to get you to Level 10 before you pick a Class. I want to see what happens. As we assault the last hill, I'll make sure you get plenty of kills to get your XP. I think you need somewhere around 19,000 XP if I am mathing right. Let's make sure you kill at least twenty of the Lesser Orcs."

She was beaming at me, her smile as bright as the noonday sun. "Let's do it!"

CHAPTER 28
BEATING THE STRONGHOLD DUNGEON

THE SCARY BIT about this final part of the stronghold was that we did not know how many Orcs were still alive. Sure, we had killed the boss and a few dozen of its underlings, but that had only been a raiding party that had chased us down the highway the night before, a portion of which had gotten away and fled back here. In addition, there were patrols roaming around the perimeter of the dungeon. I had counted ten patrol groups during my scouting, each with about five lesser Orcs. If they were still out there and not hunkered down inside the stronghold, that could be a significant chunk of experience.

Worst of all, the System wouldn't let a Stronghold dungeon like this be without a boss for long. It was both possible and likely that there would be another boss to contend with in the final battle. I was just hoping that there hadn't been enough time for one of the elites to take charge and be promoted by the System to boss status. Of course, if there was, I wouldn't turn down some extra loot or experience.

It might not only be Viki celebrating once this was all over. With as many Orcs as there were, I would be getting very close to the Level

301

30 Class upgrade point. My dark little dragon heart wanted to roar at the sky, thinking of what that might mean! At the same time, a seed of doubt was growing in my dragony heart as well. I was already in an Epic grade class, and the System had mentioned that Draconic bloodline classes could only be chosen during initial class selection. What if there was no upgrade path for this Class? Not that I would trade it out for all the gold in Fort Knox, but still. I desperately hoped that there would still be a Legendary grade version of my Class to upgrade to when I hit 30.

Ever since restarting and being brought back from the future, I had been dreaming of the chance to upgrade. In my original life, I had been only a few levels away from my second upgrade, which would have taken me from the rare-grade Knight to an epic-grade option like Tank. I had spent twenty years reaching for that height, and there had been more than a bit of heartache in dying before getting that chance.

Then, I received a bloodline Class upon initial selection this time around. That had been one hell of a consolation prize, but knowing I would get a chance to upgrade again had me feeling practically giddy, especially with how quickly I was advancing. Now, assuming we survived and beat this dungeon, I was only hours away from being able to do my first upgrade, and this time, it would be from Epic to Legendary. Earth might have had some legendary humans in my first life, but if so, then I had never heard of them.

Other than that small dark worry in the back of my mind that there might not be an upgrade path, I was incredibly eager, almost impatient, to see what the next step looked like.

Still, I couldn't go counting my chickens before they hatched. I had to stay focused so that I wouldn't make a mistake that could get us both killed. With those kinds of numbers, we'd need to be clever and stay safe.

However, before we went after the fort, we needed to hunt down the roving bands of Orcs patrolling the dungeon's outskirts. We spent a good four hours jogging around the perimeter, looking for the patrols. After almost missing one in the dark, despite my Dark Vision, we took a different approach and made enough noise as we went to attract them to us instead of hunting them. That increased the risk of the lookouts in the main fortress being alerted, but it was worth it for the time savings. At least, I was telling myself that in my frustration at searching for orcs patrols in the dark.

Annoyingly, there hadn't been anywhere close to the number of patrols that I had seen when I first arrived. Apparently, after our attacks, most of them had retreated into the stronghold, which they thought was safe, leaving only a skeleton crew monitoring the perimeter. Still, killing them had been enough to push me over the edge, and I hit Level 27. The Level Up message was still flashing in my vision, but I was too eager to get this dungeon completed to bother looking up my status and instead simply set my stats to automatically assign in an even spread the way I had been doing. That way, in the middle of a battle, I wouldn't have to stop and distribute them or wait until later when things were no longer hectic.

When we were ready, we snuck up the War Chief's hill. It was taller and much larger in total area, but we still climbed with ease. We had no problem, me because of my crazy high stats and Viki because she had all the energy of youth. If anything, it was hard to restrain her from running up the hill to start slaughtering Orcs.

Even so, we walked carefully so as not to give our positions away to the Orcs standing guard. The light was enough for me to see by and keep to the shadows, and guide my teammate since she was even blinder than the Orcs.

Reaching the top, I surveyed the Orc stronghold from the cover of the surrounding darkness, the hill stretching out nearly a mile long and its widest point boasting a breadth of 2000 feet. The sight of incomplete walls tracing the hill's edge told the story of a disrupted effort, halted by the freedom of their intended builders.

I was pretty proud of that.

My attention, however, was drawn to the east end where a formidable fortress stood, its completion a distinct contrast to the abandoned defenses elsewhere. This was where the War Chief's underlings dwelled, surrounded by sturdy walls, with numerous huts scattered inside and a Viking-like longhouse at its heart—a place of command and communal gathering, now a target.

The fort was guarded, small towers at each corner housing lookouts. I knew taking them out quietly was key. I estimated there were maybe 150 Orcs left, thanks to our previous skirmishes. A head-on battle was not in our favor. Stealth was my ally tonight.

My plan was simple but dangerous. Utilizing the night as my cloak, I intended to approach one of the towers under the veil of darkness, using the terrain to my advantage. The towers were my first objective, eliminating the guards silently to prevent any alarms. I'd use the deep night shadows to move closer, a silent arrow for one, maybe a swift climb to take down another guard with my blade— each move had to be precise, each action silent.

The first tower was the most critical as it would allow us to access the interior of the fort. That meant I would take absolutely no chance of alerting these guards and letting them raise the alarm.

I pulled out one of the Goblin dungeon rewards that I had been saving, the Elixir of Shadows. It would grant temporary invisibility and enhance my stealth capabilities for a short time. I downed the potion and almost swore in excitement, nearly blowing my cover.

Perhaps it was my Luck 2 score, but the potion did more than just make me invisible. I grinned like an idiot as I looked at the system message:

Congratulations, consumption of Elixir of Shadows has granted Affinity: Shadows.

That was fantastic. The Shadow Affinity would grant me a permanent bonus on hiding in shadows and stealth maneuvers. It would also mean that I could purchase and use Spell Crystals or stealth-based Skill Crystals that relied on having Shadow Affinity. More importantly, it would open up new Class options for me at Levels 30 and 60 when it was time for Class upgrades.

Still, I worried and hoped. Would there be a class upgrade option for me? That would be a big deal later, but I had to shake off my excitement and get back into the mindset of an assassin. I had a job to do.

Being invisible and using my magic boots to dampen any sounds, I was easily able to scale the outside of the tower without being spotted. That let me dispatch the guards with two quick pulls of my dagger across orchish throats. There were more guards inside the tower, but I was able to finish them all without raising an alarm. Quickly, before the invisibility could wear off, I moved from one enemy to the next with as much efficiency as I could manage under the circumstances. Thankfully, the last body hit the floor just as I faded back into view; the potion had worked its miracle.

This had been the diciest part of the plan. Gaining access to the interior of the fort without raising an alarm would be critical to the success of our attack, and now we had done it. I helped Viki scale the outer wall with a rope found in the tower, then made sure she was set up to stand guard and watch my back as I moved to the next tower.

We repeated the process from the inside of the fortress on the other towers, only taking an hour or so. This was made considerably more manageable since we were attacking from within, and the guards, the ones who were actually awake, were looking in the other direction. They expected enemies to come from the outside. They never suspected they could literally be stabbed in the back as they faced the night's gloom, guarding against threats like the attack we had made on the Shaman's hill.

However, even with those advantages, I still had some close calls. The courtyard was not in complete darkness; there were torches and bonfires spread about to light the fortress. In theory, that should have allowed them to spot intruders and let them see their way around in the night. The reality was that the huts and other obstacles created a crazy dance of shadows that did more to blind the orcs to our presence than help them; that was especially true now that I had the Shadow Affinity.

Even so, I still got unlucky a couple of times and ran into wandering orcs out of their bed rolls. Perhaps they were up to take a piss, or maybe they were sneaking around looking for food to steal from their fellows. Whatever the case, one such incident nearly raised the alert for the whole fortress.

Viki and I had just completed emptying the third guard tower. We were on our way to the fourth when an orc suddenly stepped out from behind a pile of debris, still tying the flap of the filthy rags that passed for its pants.

My partner had been watching behind us, and I had been focused on the tower ahead and the huts to our right away from the wall, along which we were sneaking. We ended up coming face to face, stopping in our tracks, both in shock from the unexpected presence of the other.

I reacted quickly, but not before the bastard began to scramble backward. It let out a loud squawk of fright before tripping and falling on its ass. It had forgotten that its pants were untied, and in its haste, they had fallen down and tangled its legs. The abrupt fall cut off the cry, and I was able to lunge forward with my sword and impale it right through the neck, ending any chance it might have had of alerting the guards.

Even so, it had been a close one, and my heart was beating a mile a minute. We happened to be in some pretty deep shadows right at that moment, so if any guards looked our way, they didn't spot us. After that near heart attack, we hurried to the last tower.

Once the lookouts were dealt with, it blinded the Orcs to my presence within their stronghold. From there, I moved carefully, targeting Orcs in small numbers, taking advantage of the element of surprise as long as I could maintain it. The huts, and especially the longhouse, were my main targets; clearing them would strike a decisive blow to the Orcs' strength here and finish the dungeon.

The approach required patience, moving from shadow to shadow, waiting for the right moment to strike. Every step was calculated, every breath measured. The night air was cool, the crescent moon offering scant light, but it was enough for me. I felt a rush of adrenaline as I executed my plan—a mix of anticipation and the thrill of the hunt. It was a slow, methodical process: eliminating the guards, then picking off the Orcs one by one, always moving, always watching.

Viki's support was invaluable; her arrows found their marks in the Orcs I couldn't reach quietly. Her aim was true, each shot bringing us closer to our goal. I still worried about what all this killing would do to her psyche in the long term. Still, we didn't have the luxury to let her grow up in peace and safety. There was no such thing anymore.

By the time the first hints of dawn began to lighten the sky, the stronghold was eerily quiet. We had thinned their numbers significantly, a silent testament to the night's work. I was not unscathed; a few close calls left bloody marks, reminders of the night's dangers. Yet, standing there, looking over the quiet stronghold, I couldn't help but feel a sense of grim satisfaction. We had struck a critical blow against the Orcs and were one step closer to reclaiming the lands they'd terrorized.

The huts had turned out to be a blessing. Each of those separated a group of three to five Orcs, all sleeping and unaware of what was happening to the monsters around them as I snuck into each filthy den and slew those I found. It never occurred to them to post guards inside their walls, thinking themselves safe behind their watch towers.

Unfortunately, not every hut was cleared without issue. More than once, one or more of the Orcs would wake before I could kill them, whether it was stepping on a rock that shifted under my foot or just the random chance of an Orc waking to go piss. Regardless of what caused it, I used my Class Skills at those times to quickly slay such opponents. Thankfully, Orcs were combative and violent by nature, so the sounds of a little scuffle here or there didn't raise any suspicions, and since none of the combats spilled outside, I was able to completely clear the huts after an intense couple of hours of work.

That left only the longhouse, aka, the final boss room. Although the War Chief was already dead, there could still be as many as a hundred Orcs inside, given its size. Not to mention that there could still be a boss, newly promoted and enhanced by the System to take the place of the defeated one. From what I remembered from my first life, I was pretty sure that was how these Stronghold Dungeons would work.

Now was when things would get dicey. Well, dangerous for me. Even though I thought I had a good estimate of how many Orcs were left, I could not be entirely sure. If I was wrong, then things could go sideways in a hurry. In clearing the smaller groups in the towers and huts, I had killed eighteen Elites and around forty-three regular Orcs, not counting the ones Viki killed.

However, evidence pointed to them being scared, given how many they had on guard and patrolling the fortress. That being the case, it was likely that a large group was sheltered within the longhouse. It was large enough to hold anywhere from sixty to one hundred depending on how tightly they packed themselves in.

I would have to go in after them, which could leave me trapped and unable to maneuver. On the other hand, it would also mean I could use my area of effect Spells to my advantage and kill many of them at the same time. Plus, with the necessity of using stealth to kill all of the guards and small groups, I had needed to reserve trump cards like Draconic Fury and Draconic Fear. Those would result in a big commotion, but they also would give me the chance to do a lot of concentrated damage fast inside a tightly packed building.

After a few minutes of internal debate, it was decided. Despite the risk, I would go in and bring the battle to them. No more hiding my presence and keeping quiet; it was time to go all John Wick on these System-generated monsters.

If I was being honest with myself, I was looking forward to this as I would no longer have to hold back. The draconic nature of my bloodline was burning inside me, demanding that I roar my challenge to the sky and defy the System and its minions. This was MY world!

Part of me was thankful for that bloodline because otherwise, I am pretty sure I would be absolutely terrified of what I was about to do!

I quickly checked my status, only paying attention to my health, Mana, and attributes.

Liam Bell: (Current)
Draconic Spellsword - Level 28

Experience: 39640/46240

Attributes:
Endurance: 54
Strength: 54
Agility: 54
Mind: 55
Will: 54
Magical Aptitude: 49
Luck: 3

Health: 720/1080
Mana: 790/1040

Having reached Level 28, my stats were higher than they had ever been in my first life, even at Level 57 as a Knight class. I still couldn't get over that, but it affirmed that I had regained my former strength and then some. I was eager to see what would happen when I triggered Dragon's Fury, and my strength doubled to over 100 points.

This was going to be epic!

On the other hand, even psyched up for the battle, I wasn't going to just charge in like an idiot without being as ready as I could. I took a mid-grade health and one low-grade health to bring myself up to full and downed three low-grade Mana potions to top off my Mana as well. I had been very thankful so far that my abilities and spells were relatively Mana efficient, and I didn't have to worry much about running out of Mana mid-battle. Going into a fight like this was not the time to skimp on potions.

Looking to my young friend, I had to give her some bad news.

"Viki, you'll have to stay outside the door because things are going to get ugly in there, and I won't be able to hold back. I don't want you getting hit by friendly fire. Take a position over there and shoot anything that comes through the door or windows. Are you good with that?"

She grinned. "Yeah. Just save some for me to finish off. I'm almost at the point you said I'd hit Level 10."

Literally skipping, she moved to a covered position in the window of a hut facing the longhouse. I couldn't help but chuckle at her antics, but I couldn't blame her. I was looking forward to this fight more than any so far.

I was going to do this hard and fast.

Without further ado, I stepped up to the longhouse and kicked the door off its hinges, sending it flying into the room. Just to be safe, I cast both Scalebound Resilience and Dragonfire Ward. I wanted all my defenses up.

Like an avenging angel, I strode through the door, ready to teach the monsters why they should not mess with humans. I didn't bother with Dragon's Fear yet. Raising my left hand, I started with Acid Rain, causing it to sprinkle in the longhouse. Its range was extensive enough to hit almost every Orc in the place, giving me a big edge by slowing their speed and doing some minor damage. Then, I began casting Acid Spray, sweeping it across the room.

Unfortunately, this spell did not have such a large range, and the longhouse was too big. Acid Spray could only reach those near me. Still, space was packed tightly with the sleeping enemy. Many of the Orcs awoke screaming as they caught a portion of the spray on their bodies.

As I made my entrance into the longhouse, chaos erupted instantly. It was that time when night transitioned into morning, and everyone was sound asleep. Because of that, the spells I unleashed caught many of the Orcs off-guard in their sleep, their screams filled the air as the corrosive liquid began to eat through their sleeping furs, slowly but inevitably burning through to their skin. The panic was palpable; some Orcs even attempted desperate escape through the windows, only to be swiftly silenced by arrows from Viki, their bodies slumping lifelessly against the window sills.

The initial havoc resulted in the demise of a good two dozen Orcs, a stark demonstration of our assault's effectiveness. Some of those had even been Elites, judging by the size of them.

However, not all had fallen to the chaos. My fears of another boss had proven true, and a new War Chief directed three remaining Elite Orcs to rally the lesser ones from across the large room to mount a counterattack. The barrage of thrown weapons and the Elites' formidable strikes tested my defenses, breaching both my armor and the magical barrier of Scalebound Resilience. A deep cut was etched across my torso, and another blow pierced my thigh, narrowly sparing the artery—a painful and bloody reminder of the risks at hand.

I couldn't help but acknowledge my growing reliance on healing potions. It was a luxury borne from my dungeon loots that made me less wary of such wounds than I once would have been. These injuries, significant as they were, now seemed just a part of the cost of purging this threat. In my first life, such injuries would have left me recovering for weeks, unable to fight and progress.

No longer. Wounds couldn't stop me any more than these Orcs. I wouldn't allow it! Like the black-suited assassin from the movies. I was a Black Dragon! I was a force of nature!

Resolved, I knew it was time to bring an end to this. Facing a boss and over thirty foes still capable of fighting, I triggered two Abilities in quick succession. Dragon's Fury doubled my strength and damage for the next 28 seconds. Then, Draconic Fear froze all within the longhouse, leaving them paralyzed with terror as the image of a black dragon appeared above me, amplifying my roar.

With the Orcs frozen, I moved among them with lethal grace, my sword cleaving through their ranks effortlessly. Only the boss was high enough level not to be rooted in place by fear, but even he looked worried.

Empowered by Dragon's Fury, my strength had risen to 110, causing each strike to feel as if they met no resistance, bodies yielding to my blade's force. Even the pain from my leg became a distant thought, overridden by the adrenaline and the sheer force of will driving me. The Elites were previously a significant threat; now they were no different from their lesser brethren, falling just as swiftly to my relentless onslaught.

The boss tried to reach me, wanting to stop me from obliterating his minions, but with my strength doubled by Dragon's Fury, I was too fast.

In those moments, the fight turned into a grim dance of death, my sword an extension of my will, cutting down the remaining Orcs one or two with every swing until none were left standing, except the new War Chief.

It appeared stronger than the last and judging by its ability to shrug off my draconic fear, it had to be at Level 30. I had seconds left before my doubled strength wore off. If I didn't finish this by then, I would be helpless before this monster, and it would be my turn to be like wheat before a scythe.

The dragon's blood flowing through my veins thundered in my ears and demanded I beat this beast who would dare stand and threaten me.

It wielded a massive club that looked like it had once been a tree trunk whittled down on one end to provide a handle. I swung my fiery longsword, deflecting its first blow, causing the club to catch fire.

Oops.

Now, we both had flaming weapons. Not that it mattered. If it managed to hit me with something that massive, there was no way I'd survive, flame or no flame.

Second by second, we attacked one another, and my timer ran down. I had the strength to end this with a single strike, but I had to reach it to do that. Annoyingly, I couldn't get past that massive flaming club. It had the reach on me and the skill to wield it.

Being a War Chief, it had Barbarian-like class skills. For every Draconic Strike or Tempest Strike I threw, it countered with its own 'Hulk smash' type skill. Worse, it was in a beserker rage that allowed it to keep swinging regardless of stamina or wounds, and its cooldown timers were cut in half, letting it attack far more often than I could.

I was running out of time.

It swung the club, smashing one of the support columns that held up the roof, splintering it into wooden shrapnel that dug into my flesh.

Roaring defiance, my dragon blood would not be denied! Damn any injuries that tried to stop me!

I was too close to victory to let myself be defeated now.

Eleven seconds left... ten...

Diving beneath the next swing of the club, I rolled to come up beside the monster and swung my blade. However, as I did, the Boss used a skill to reverse its swing and parry. The collision was so fierce when our weapons clashed, it caused a shockwave within the room.

Nine...

I leaped back just in time as its 'Hulk smash' skill came off cooldown. A crater was blasted into the floor from the blow, and bits of orc bone and armor pieces became flying projectiles.

Hit again, I had no time to deal with the wounds that were created but grimaced in pain.

Eight... Seven...

I needed something more, something to distract its attention for a split second. I had spells. Arcane Singularity would be perfect, but I couldn't take the time to cast it, or I'd become a red smear coating the War Chief's club. Even with my enhanced stats, I was barely keeping up with its attacks. Still, I had the strength to finish this; I just needed the opportunity!

It slipped on a puddle of acid-melted orc, and I thought I had found my moment. I triggered Searing Slash and lunged forward, only to be brought to a halt by an unexpected swing of the massive club. Even as it stumbled, the damned beast activated some kind of skill that let it gracefully recover from its misstep.

Six... Five...

Then the boss was on the offense again, redoubling its efforts. It roared its beserker rage, and triggering something like my own Draconic Fury. At that moment, it seemed to grow larger, faster, and stronger.

The only thing that saved me was that it also seemed to lose some of its intelligence in this new state. It furiously swung the tree-like club from side to side in an effort to drive me back into a corner where it could trap me.

Four...

It was all I could do to dodge, parry, and evade. I had no hope of getting past its furious attacks to use my own enhanced strength. Worse, I could feel my own furious blood raging at not being able to reach my enemy. There was also fear, knowing that I would collapse when the enhanced strength wore off.

Just as desperation was setting in, salvation came unexpectedly as we passed in front of the window.

Three...

An arrow whizzed through, so tiny compared to the massive System-enhanced boss monster.

And yet, the shot was perfect. It hit the monster in the side of the head just as it made another attack, throwing off its aim and snapping its head to the side for just a second. The projectile barely did any damage at all. Even so, it looked to the window, surprised to be hurt from an unexpected direction.

That was all the opening I needed.

I leaped forward and swung my blade with all the 110 points of strength I had, simultaneously triggering Draconic Strike, the first skill I had learned. It wasn't my most potent skill, but it was the only thing I had left that wasn't on cooldown. Still, besides adding acid to the blow, it also enhanced the power of the swing by roughly 15%. That brought my strength in this one hit to an incredible 125 points.

My blade, covered in fire and elemental acid felt like it met no resistence at all. It felt like the perfect swing, but the Boss just stood there still staring in confusion at the window. My strongest blow didn't look like it affected the beast at all.

I was too done to do more.

Looking back from the window, the War Chief glared at me, then blinked in surprise and looked down at itself. It seemed confused. A thin acid green line traced across its middle, but it didn't so much as grunt in pain.

Had my blow really not done more than give it a shallow cut?

Regardless of the injury, there was nothing more I could do; I was spent. Draconic Fury ended, and I sagged against the wall behind me, only sheer willpower keeping me from completely collapsing to the floor. The fight was over; I had nothing left.

The enlarged berserker boss roared, raising the massive club to charge me one last time, sensing its victory.

Then a strange thing happened... raising the club unbalanced it.

The top half of the massive beast began to slide off the bottom half where the green line bisected it, both halves falling to the ground. Surprise filled its bestial face as the pseudo-life drained away along with its blood and guts.

The longhouse, a stronghold of fear and oppression, had become a silent witness to the orcs downfall. It was a victory hard-won through bloodshed and determination.

Before I could pass out from my wounds, I took one of the lesser healing potions from my ring and downed it even as the blackness at the corners of my vision began to advance.

This crash was a bit surreal. I felt both the incredible relief of the potion healing my injuries and restoring my lost hit points while simultaneously losing half of my strength and falling to one knee as I held myself up by my sword, panting and feeling drained. I didn't have long to recover as Viki came rushing in.

"I saw you fall. Are you okay? I shot the thing when I got the chance. Did I do okay?" She quickly looked around for any threats, holding her bow ready to fire.

I was too tired to chuckle but appreciated her concern. "Yeah, I'm just suffering backlash from Skill usage. I'll be fine in a little while. Go finish off the wounded ones, and then we'll gather the treasure."

Bodies were already disappearing as I took in the scene. It was absolute devastation. Dead and dying Orcs were scattered around the room like they had been hit with a tornado. It was hard to believe I had done all this, but I was thankful.

Except for the boss, it was almost anti-climatic, but it made sense. Now that I had nearly hit Level 30, the lesser orcs were almost 20 levels below me, so it was to be expected. Still, had this been an open battle where they weren't grouped up for me to hit with my AoE Spells, things would have been very different. Their numbers would have been telling, and I would have easily been overwhelmed before I could even reach the boss.

Chuckling, I thought, *It also didn't hurt that I caught them literally sleeping and killed almost half before they could wake up and defend themselves. Hurray for the element of surprise and a little bit of strategy!*

I had also 'dinged' again during the fight, bringing me to Level 29, just 15,000 XP or so away from my next big milestone. Once I had collected the treasure, I was going to really enjoy looking over my status. However, for the next half hour, I leaned up against the wall by the door, recovering, not wanting to do even so much as open my status. I just wanted to bask in the knowledge that we had done it.

Two people, one of them Unclassed, had just destroyed a special Stronghold dungeon, something even entire teams of experienced adventurers died attempting.

Well, not quite destroyed. I haven't opened the System notification yet. I still have to officially acknowledge it.

By the time I was finally ready to stand up and deal with things again, Viki had gone around and collected all the Mana coins. My share brought my total up to 15 sp and 6050 cp. Not bad at all!

She also handed me the boss loot drop, which was a happy surprise. Rognarc the Berserker, had a rather ugly amulet.

War Chief's Berserker Amulet
Description: This amulet, fashioned from the teeth and bones of fallen foes, pulses with the raw power of the orcish War Chief. Wearing it grants the user increased strength and endurance, channeling the ferocity of a berserker.

Effects: Berserker's Fury: 3 times per day, Increases physical strength by 15% and attack speed by 10%.

Endurance of the War Chief: Reduces incoming physical damage by 10%.

Adrenaline Surge: When health drops below 20%, temporarily boosts strength by an additional 20% and provides a small regeneration effect (5% of total health over 10 seconds). This effect can only trigger once per day.

I hated the look of the thing, but it could prove invaluable. That Adrenaline Surge ability could save my life in a pinch. I reluctantly pulled it over my head but tucked it under my armor and on top of my shirt so I wouldn't have to look at the thing. Despite my mixed feelings about the reward, my companion had no cares in the world at that moment.

Viki was dancing in joy over the fact that she had all the XP she needed to hit level 10 immediately when she turned twelve, which would be this coming midnight. I think I was almost as excited to see her get her Class as I was to explore my Class upgrade options. Still, I waited until we were both ready before opening the notification, which would grant me the dungeon completion reward and hopefully enough experience to level up the final time to Level 30.

Looking to Viki, I asked, "Are you ready?"

We were sitting on the steps outside the longhouse.

She rolled her eyes, "Of course! Do it already!"

CHAPTER 29

REWARDS!

I PULLED up the message that was flashing in the corner of my vision and shared it so that Viki could read it at the same time.

Dungeon: Orc Stronghold completed

Title: Conqueror of Strongholds - Awarded for being the first in the world to breach and overcome the defenses of a Stronghold dungeon. Rewards for all Stronghold Dungeons increased by one tier.

Completion of Stronghold dungeon grants the following rewards:
- 20,000 bonus experience rewarded for completion of Stronghold Dungeon.
- Reward tier adjusted to reflect completion rate: 100%
- Reward tier adjusted to reflect first Stronghold completion on world.
- Reward tier adjusted to reflect Luck Stat.

A wave of relief washed over me at that moment. This had been a very large and unexpected challenge that brought great rewards but also completely derailed my purpose of visiting town to spread the word and help refugees get out of the city. If my estimate were correct there had been around 450 Orcs in this Stronghold Dungeon. In game terms, this was a major Raid Dungeon, and we completed it with just the two of us. We had help from the prisoners at some key moments, but I had accounted for between 350 and 400 of those kills. Viki had done quite a few herself.

I would have to get back to my original mission soon, but for now, I wanted to see the dungeon rewards. Getting a triple boost to the loot meant it ought to be something really special.

Without waiting any longer, we rushed to the chest and opened it.

Inside were four high-grade potions: two healing and two Mana. Those were great; they would heal or restore 1000 points of damage or Mana. However, they weren't what caught my eye. Next to the potions lay a grand dungeon core, which was something I'd never come across in my first life. A core that size was rare, and few humans ever had the strength to destroy a dungeon that strong.

Still, as excited as I was about the dungeon core, there was something else in the chest that drew my attention even more. Two weapons lay nestled in the bottom; one was a bow, and the other was a long-bladed dagger.

Without touching either item, I used my Draconic Ability, Treasure Sense, to analyze the bow and shared the results with Viki.

Item: Heartseeker Longbow
Type: Legendary Ranged Weapon

Description: The Heartseeker Longbow is a masterpiece of craftsmanship and magic. It is revered not just for its elegant design but for its lethality on the battlefield. Forged from the heartwood of an ancient treant and strung with the silk of a silver moon spider, this bow gleams with a subtle, otherworldly light. Its limbs are intricately carved with runes that pulse softly, enhancing the archer's focus and precision.

Features: Enhanced Accuracy: The Heartseeker Longbow magically guides its arrows, granting the wielder an unparalleled boost in accuracy. This precision ensures that arrows loosed from its string fly true, turning even the most challenging shots into hits.

Critical Damage: Imbued with the essence of a predator, the bow has a heightened chance to unleash devastating critical strikes. On a critical hit, the bow channels its latent energies to deal double damage, piercing through armor and defenses as if they were mere cloth.

Soulbound: The Heartseeker Longbow binds itself to its wielder, becoming more attuned to their skills and fighting style. This connection allows the bow to grow in power alongside its owner, ensuring that its lethality only increases over time.

Special Ability - "Heartseeker's Mark": Once per day, the wielder can invoke the bow's name to cast a mark upon their target. For the next minute, all arrows shot from the bow will home in on the marked target, ignoring cover and minor obstacles. Note: wielder must be able to see target to create mark.

Lore: Legend has it that the Heartseeker Longbow was first crafted by an elven archer, the lone survivor of a forgotten war, who sought the means to protect his people from ever-looming threats. Blessed by the moon goddess for his noble heart, the bow has since found its way into the hands of heroes throughout the ages, its name a whisper of hope to allies and a harbinger of doom to foes.

I was absolutely floored by that description! I quickly examined the knife as well.

Item: Spectral Longknife of Shadows
Item Type: Legendary Soulbound Weapon

Description: The Spectral Longknife of Shadows is an enigmatic weapon forged in the darkest depths of Tartarus, where light fears to tread. This soulbound weapon possesses a unique, ethereal quality, its blade shimmering with a spectral light that seems to dance and flicker in and out of existence. Initially appearing as a dagger, it boasts unparalleled sharpness that only grows more lethal over time, especially as the wielder's prowess in stealth and assassination heightens. The weapon is imbued with ancient enchantments that allow it to seamlessly phase through armor and defenses, making it a terrifying tool for those who walk the path of shadows.

Abilities: Adaptive Form: The Spectral Longknife of Shadows can alter its form at the wielder's will, transforming between a dagger for close-quarters stealth kills and a sword for direct combat. This transformation can occur instantaneously, adapting to the needs of its bearer in the heat of battle.

Phase Strike: Three times per day. With each improvement in the user's stealth and assassination Skills, the weapon's Ability to phase through armor and shields becomes more potent, allowing attacks to bypass enemy defenses with increasing effectiveness.

Soulbound Resonance: Being soulbound, the Longknife forms a deep connection with its owner, enhancing their stealth Abilities and making them virtually undetectable when moving in shadows. The weapon's lethality and phasing capability scale with the user's level and Skill proficiency.

Special Ability - "Shadow's Embrace": Once per day, the wielder can activate the Longknife to envelop themselves in shadows, granting temporary invisibility for a short duration. While invisible, the first attack from stealth is guaranteed to critically strike, dealing significant bonus damage and fully demonstrating the weapon's phasing Ability.

Lore: Whispered about in the darkest corners of the realm, the Spectral Longknife of Shadows was said to be the creation of a master assassin whose name has been lost to time. Crafted from the essence of night itself, the weapon was designed for those who serve the shadows, offering them a tool as versatile and deadly as the darkness they embrace. Bound to its wielder until their demise, the Longknife is a constant companion in the silent dance of death, a symbol of the power and mystery that defines the shadow-born.

At the same time, Viki and I spoke, echoing each other, "Holy shit!"

This was beyond any expectation. I had never seen or heard of a Legendary item in over twenty years of living under the System. I checked my message logs to verify something. Sure enough, my Luck was now 4 and had also influenced the tier of the reward, meaning these items were several tiers higher than what would normally be dropped.

"These are basically once-in-a-lifetime finds that we would never have a chance of getting normally."

Viki nodded solemnly in agreement, not speaking as she just stared at the weapons in awe, not yet daring to touch them for fear this was a dream and she might wake up.

I chuckled and pulled the longknife from the chest. Immediately upon doing so, I felt the connection. It was a bind-on-pickup item, which made me extremely glad I hadn't touched the bow, and I quickly attached the longknife to my belt, removing my old longsword. I had to admire the craftsmanship of the sheath as I did so.

I analyzed the sheath with my Draconic Treasure Sense Skill:

Sheath of the Spectral Longknife of Shadows:
As enigmatic as the weapon it holds, crafted from shadowcloth and reinforced with strips of dark leather that seem to absorb light, making it appear almost invisible in dim conditions. Adorned with subtle silver runes that shimmer faintly against the black material, the sheath not only offers protection but also enhances the weapon's affinity with the shadows, ensuring that both blade and bearer remain undetected until the moment of strike.

"Nice!"

Meanwhile, seeing that I had taken the blade from the chest, Viki reached in and took the bow. From the expression on her face, she was going through a moment of awe as deeply profound as the one I had just experienced. When she was done examining it, she clutched it to her chest as if it were the most precious thing in the world, which wasn't far from the truth.

I hated to spoil the moment, so I waited until she was done before warning, "Keep that bow in your storage ring when you aren't actively in battle. That thing will create envy in everyone who sees it. In fact, you might want to disguise it by wrapping it in cloth or something so no one realizes how powerful it is."

She thought for a second but then nodded seriously. "Yeah, I get that. I mean, wow... just wow!"

I patted her on the back.

Now, to check the other major thing, my status. I had again been the first to hit a new Tier at Level 30, granting me an additional five points to all of my stats.

Liam Bell: (Current)
Draconic Spellsword - Level 30

Class Upgrade Options Available

Experience: 8820/49920

Attributes:
Endurance: 61
Strength: 61
Agility: 61
Mind: 62
Will: 61
magical Aptitude: 56
Luck: 4

Health: 1060/1220
Mana: 785/1180

Abilities:
Active: Dragon Fear
Passive: Dark Vision, Scales, Treasure Sense

Active Skills:
Draconic Strike
Draconic Fury
Searing Slash
Dragon's Charge
Tempest Strike
Heavy Draconic Strike

Passive Skills: None

Spells:
Acid Bolt
Acid Spray
Dragonfire Ward
Scalebound Resilience
Arcane Singularity
Umbral Chains

One thing I noticed was that I had not received a new Ability or new Skills with the level up. That was because I would receive them based on whatever upgrade to my Class I chose. I remembered this from my first life. I had been pretty pissed at the time, as I had been hoping to get Skills from both the old and new Classes. Naturally, the System did not do it that way; that would have been too helpful to us humans. Only in the rare event that a person chose not to upgrade would the class then grant two new skills for Level 30.

Eventually, I stopped marveling over my own stats and gains and checked on Viki. I was still super eager to check out my Class upgrade options, but purposefully put that off to savor the anticipation. I had spent the last couple days worrying over whether or not there would be an upgrade path for my current class, now that I knew there was, I could wait a while and give Viki her chance to shine first.

"Hey, show me your experience status real quick."

Victoria Blue, aka Viki: (Current)
Unclassed - Level 0
Experience: 43,375/100

"Nice! You definitely have enough XP for Level 10.

She whined in response, "I want to pick my Class now! Waiting is torture!"

I laughed, looking forward to the time in eleven more hours for her to turn twelve so she could be recognized by the System. I needed to get into the city and continue my mission, and I didn't want to bring her in there with me while still Unclassed. As bad as this Stronghold had been, it was pretty predictable. Unfortunately, there was no way to know what we'd face in the apocalypse hellscape, that was the city. It housed so much modern technology in such proximity that there would be a lot of dungeons, but who knew what else?

I was hopeful that we would be able to find a ton of low-level dungeons and run them at least once very quickly to get a small amount of XP and their boss drops so that we could gear up Viki. She might be one of the most powerful people in the world now in terms of Class and attributes, but other than her bow, she was completely without defenses and utility items. Heck, for that matter, there were an awful lot of cool things that I'd love to get my hands on, like Skill Crystals.

As much as I wanted to do my own Class upgrade, I had to take my own advice and be patient. I wanted someone to watch over me when I selected the new Class. I had been unconscious and in a lot of pain during my first Class selection. If the new one was anything like that, I felt like it would be prudent to have someone guard me. That meant waiting until Viki had her own Class selection. She would jump immediately to Level 10, and with that legendary bow of hers, there wouldn't be many things that could get past her.

I finally convinced Viki to take a nap so she would be rested for her Class selection later that night.

"Look, I can't do my Class upgrade until you've done yours, so I understand your impatience, but the clock won't move any faster if you stay awake. I'll guard you while you rest and do your selection later, then you can guard me when I do mine, and then I'll rest. Sound good?"

"Fine! Whatever!" She gave me a grin and reluctantly got comfortable. Even so, it took her a little while before sleep could overcome her excitement and impatience.

CHAPTER 30
MAKING AN OUTPOST AND VIKI'S OPTIONS

Day 7 after Initialization - That last evening before her birthday was one of rest for us, but it also presented an opportunity to transform this Stronghold into an outpost for civilization. I had never visited this place in my first life, but I had no doubt that it had cost the lives of countless humans given its position along a highway out of the city. With the area filled with Level 10 and higher Orcs when the average human was no more than Level 2, even if humans could have organized an assault, they wouldn't have stood a chance for many months, by which time the Stronghold would have been firmly established and even more formidable.

One of the reasons Viki and I succeeded was that the Orcs hadn't finished building their defenses. Had they completed them, our task would have been significantly more challenging. We would have had to fight our way out of defended gates and funnel the freed captives past the most heavily defended spots on the Shaman's hill. The War Chief would have also been much closer to our escape route, leaving us no time to prepare a defense.

I shook my head. We were fortunate to capitalize on circumstances that might not have existed a week or so later. I didn't know how much of a Butterfly Effect this would have on the future, but at the very least, we now had a safe place for refugees to regroup before venturing into the beast-filled countryside.

That was a major win, in my opinion.

After catching some rest, we woke late on Day 6 and made our way down to the arena, where we found the former captives. They were, on average, higher level than most of the human population at this time, so it made sense to recruit them to defend the fortress.

Most readily agreed, seeing no other viable option for safety after the apocalypse. Several, however, asked me to lead them to my base so they could reunite with their loved ones and friends. I refused but provided detailed directions and explained what I knew about the world's current situation.

While I was careful to avoid delving into future knowledge, I discussed a wide range of actions they could take to improve themselves and help establish more safe areas like this. Unfortunately, I couldn't delve into the topics of invader races or the System's adverse actions. Nonetheless, my advice about Class upgrades at Level 30 should significantly help humanity overcome its scarcity of magic Classes. Plus, those children who survived would be armed with the knowledge of how to unlock those Classes, and their parents would hopefully remember my advice when the time came and ensure they picked something good.

After the others left, around fifty Fighter-Class individuals remained, so we assigned them to guard the three areas of the Stronghold and maintain a constant watch from the towers atop the tall hill. From there, they could monitor for approaching forces within a mile or two and spot any refugees traveling along the highway. My one worry was that this area would still be prone to the formation of more dungeons and mutated beasts. There was still a tremendous amount of technologically produced waste buried under these hills that used to be a dump site. The System would still be breaking that trash down and repurposing it.

On the other hand, that could provide the survivors some good dungeons to farm for experience now that they had a safe place. They would have to maintain vigilance and keep them contained. I made sure to pass on the warning, and after their recent experience with this Orc dungeon, they took the threat seriously, a grim determination on their faces.

The rest of the evening passed in a relaxed manner, with a few individual refugees straggling in as they noticed the fortress. Like the message left on the walls of my base, each newcomer received the same information and advice. Their choices on what to do with that information were theirs to make.

I selected one of the huts and cleaned it out. Viki and I stayed there that night, though we didn't sleep or rest much until very late. At the stroke of midnight, she received the System message informing her that she was now eligible to select a Class.

Unsurprisingly, the suggestion page presented five choices, including an uncommon magic Class titled Sorcerer. That was promising, offering growth options for upgraded rare and even epic Classes at Levels 30 and 60. It was a well-known Class from my first life, one of the few magic paths that was documented. There hadn't been too many magic users, so the ones there were got a lot of attention.

Besides the magic Class, there was also a rare Ranger Class option. This was a third-tier upgrade from the common rogue Class, following the path Rogue > Archer > Ranger. Her sneaking around and sniping must have unlocked this rare Class, a highly respectable combat profession with plenty of utility.

The remaining options, two crafting Classes and the common Warrior Class, didn't merit consideration.

However, I believed we could aim higher. Given everything she had done and her Magical Aptitude, which had risen to 3, she surely had access to some exceptional choices among the hidden Classes.

"Do it. Think 'Class Options,'" I urged, eager to discover what was available to her. "Be sure to scroll and look for anything with an '*' next to it."

She followed my suggestion eagerly, her surprise evident at the wealth of possibilities.

A quick glance at the list confirmed a broad selection of magic-related choices. This was excellent; surely, some rare Classes were offered.

It didn't take long before I shouted, "Stop!" and pointed to the list. "There!"

Three Draconic Bloodline options appeared on her list! It was incredible that these were still available, but I supposed most people, even if they stumbled upon the 'Class Options' menu, wouldn't meet the criteria for such specialized Classes and unique Bloodlines.

"Three! You have three Draconic Bloodline Classes to choose from!"

I may have been astonished, but Viki was jumping up in down in excitement, barely able to contain herself.

Her luck was astonishing, but then again, it might have something to do with my mentorship. Perhaps it wasn't merely chance but a direct result of our partnership? That seemed more plausible.

The choices were Draconic Necromancer, Draconic Ranger, and Draconic Sniper.

"Liam, are you seeing this? There's a Ranger option!" she exclaimed.

I cautioned her, "Don't rush. Let's review the descriptions for all three. Necromancer sounds sketchy, but it could be a powerful magic Class. Let's read each description carefully."

She nodded enthusiastically and selected the first option:

Class: Draconic Necromancer

Description: The Draconic Necromancer Class is a formidable amalgamation of Necromantic magic and Draconic power, granted by the System to those bold enough to navigate the shadowy boundary between life and death, wielding the ancient might of dragons. This Class empowers practitioners to summon and command the undead through mere whispers, infusing their minions with the formidable essence of Draconic energy. They harness the destructive breath of dragons to obliterate foes and delve into the arcane mysteries of dragon kind to bolster their summoned legions and themselves. Excelling in battlefield manipulation, Draconic Necromancers use their undead minions for spatial control and wield their Draconic magic for potent area-of-effect Spells. Not merely summoners of death, they are masters of Draconic arcane, merging two powerful forces into a uniquely potent combat presence.

"Wow, that sounds incredible," I was impressed.

Viki's wide-eyed look mirrored my thoughts. "That sounds amazing," she agreed.

"But let's check the others. They might be even better or more suited to you."

Eager to see the other two, she returned to the menu and selected the next Class for review.

Class: Draconic Ranger

Description: The Draconic Ranger Class combines the keen survival skills and precise archery of a traditional Ranger with the majestic power and elemental affinity of dragons. Offered to those who show an affinity for both the wilds and ancient Draconic lore, this Class enables practitioners to imbue their arrows with elemental dragon breath, granting them the Ability to unleash fiery, icy, or elemental-charged shots. Draconic Rangers are adept at summoning lesser dragonkin as allies, summoning them to fight alongside in battle or aid in tracking and scouting. Their unique bond with dragonkind enhances their agility and strength, drawing from the dragons' might to perform feats of exceptional archery and wilderness prowess. This Class is perfect for adventurers who wish to harness the elemental fury of dragons while retaining the mobility and versatility of a Ranger.

Viki frowned, "That sounds really good too. Not as powerful as the first one maybe, but I really love the archery, and I just got that Legendary bow. Dang, this is a hard choice!"

I patted her on the back. "Before you get too focused on those, let's see the third one."

Class: Draconic Sniper

Description: The Draconic Sniper Class is a formidable blend of long-range precision and the arcane power of dragons, designed for those who excel in taking down their enemies from a distance while wielding the mystic forces of dragon magic. This Class elevates the art of the Sniper, allowing its practitioners to not only master the bow with unparalleled accuracy but also to channel Draconic energy into high-damage Spells capable of devastating foes before they even know what hit them. Draconic Snipers can imbue their arrows with potent Spells, causing effects such as explosive blasts, elemental storms, or even temporal stasis upon impact, combining the lethality of a marksman with the versatility of a spellcaster. This Class is tailored for adventurers who prefer to engage in combat from the shadows, striking with deadly efficiency and a diverse arsenal of magical and physical attacks. Through the Draconic Sniper Class, the adventurer gains access to an array of long-range Spells and techniques, making them a deadly force on the battlefield, capable of taking out high-value targets with precision and the raw power of dragon-infused magic.

"Damn, that's a hard choice. The first one is a straight magic Class, which uses the dead as minions. That's got the benefit of keeping you out of fighting. You could put a horde of cannon fodder between you and the bad guys, and the more you kill, the more minions you could amass. However, it sounds like they aren't permanent, meaning there could be times, like at the beginning of dungeons, when you might not have any. At times like those, you'd have to rely on others. You would also not really gain much by way of physical defenses and attributes, making you less capable of surviving difficult or unexpected situations."

Viki nodded along, listening to my analysis. "Yeah, plus, that just really doesn't sound like me, even if it does sound very powerful."

I agreed but didn't want to say anything so that I didn't influence her to pick something that wouldn't be a good fit.

"As for Ranger, that sounds like a great all-around Class. You get a summoned pet to fight for you and help keep enemies away while you shoot them. Plus, you'd get a lot of wilderness survival knowledge and Skills. That would be great for traveling around and staying safe outdoors. You'd even get to imbue your arrows with whatever your dragon's element is. I wish the descriptions would say what dragon Bloodline it relates to before you make your decision. I got Black Dragon when I chose my Class, and it didn't give me any options. Acid is cool, but then so is fire or lightning. Just sayin'."

Pursing her lips in thought, Viki asked, "You didn't mention downsides for that one, but I see one. If the Class is focused on the outdoors, how good will it be in dungeons?"

"That's a good question. I'm sure it will still be a great Class. You'll still have your pet and your imbued arrows, but the wilderness Skills won't be much use in most dungeons."

Finally, Viki asked, "What do you think about the last one, Sniper?"

I didn't want to influence her choice, but for my part, I liked it. "It sounds a lot like the Archer version of my Class. Except where I'm getting Skills to handle going into melee combat, the Sniper seems to be stealth-based and focused on high-damage attacks. Sounds like it would be killer against single targets and great against boss monsters, but might be lacking in AoE and close combat. You'd have to rely on the enemy not finding you. Also, unlike Ranger, you don't get a pet to tank the enemies for you. Meaning if they discover you, you might be in trouble. Of course, I'm sure the Class will give you some options for getting away, but still…"

Viki looked thoughtful, clearly taking this decision seriously. "One thing I like about Sniper besides high damage, it sounds like it might get more options for what the arrows can do. Freezing enemies in time, explosive blasts, and who knows what else? I think I'm leaning toward that one."

"Can you explain why? Not that I think you are wrong; I just want to hear your thoughts on it." I wouldn't push on which option to pick, but I did want to make sure she had thoroughly considered her choice before committing to it.

"Sure. If you keep letting me fight on your team, then I don't need a pet. I've got you to keep the enemies away from me. Plus, if it is stealthy, I could follow you around, and the enemy won't even know I'm there until I blow their heads off. A dragonling pet would be hard to hide, so I would think I would end up in more fights by having it. Plus, how will people react to me walking around with a monster pet? That would probably scare a lot of people. Also, like you said, I don't know what type of dragon I would be, so I might get wind or something. I'm sure it would still be cool and all, but maybe not nearly as useful as lightning, and I'd be stuck with whatever element I get. It sounds like the Sniper can shoot all kinds of different magic arrows."

The longer she spoke, the more sure she sounded. She finished, "Yeah, definitely Sniper! That's the one!"

CHAPTER 31

DRACONIC SNIPER

I SMILED AT HER. "The choice is entirely yours. Keep in mind, though, we may not always be teamed together. Sniper might be the least defensible Class, the least capable of soloing dungeons."

She shrugged. "Maybe, but the more I think about the choices, the more it feels right."

"Then go for it!" I grinned at her.

The next moment, she selected the Class and was bathed in light as the System rewrote her DNA to give her the Draconic Bloodline. She screamed in agony, and the sound nearly broke my heart, but I had been prepared for it, having gone through this myself. The sound went on and on.

After a minute, one of the guards on duty ran up and flung the door open. "What's going on?"

I gestured for him to stay back and yelled to be heard over the screams. "She just got her Class selection, and it is a rough transition."

It lasted for another three minutes. Three very long minutes. By the time it was over, I was convinced it was harder to watch someone you cared about go through this than to experience the pain yourself.

The guard just stared, stricken by the sight, unable to look away.

When the light finally faded and Viki was revealed, she didn't look drastically different, but her hair had turned from blond to midnight black, as had her irises. If I didn't already have draconic eyes myself, I might have found it creepy and intimidating.

Viki peering at the guard questioningly caused him to flinch as he looked from me to the black-eyed girl.

After sitting up, she struggled to remain upright and just said, "Oww!"

I would have given her a healing potion, but it wouldn't do anything since nothing in her body was actually damaged. She had just metaphorically been through hell and back on a cellular level.

Giving her a sympathetic look, I replied, "I've been there. You'll get over it pretty quick. In an hour or so, you'll be right as rain."

I wanted to ask what type of Dragon Bloodline she received, but I didn't want the guard to overhear, so I gave him a look and said, "Everything is fine now. Thank you for checking on us."

He didn't take the hint and asked, "What the heck type of Class does that to you?"

It was Viki who replied, "That's kinda personal. Let's just say I'm an archer now."

With my Dark Vision, I could see the man blush as he realized he was asking a sensitive question. "Sorry, sorry. None of my business. I'll just go back to my post now. If you need anything, please let me know."

I chuckled, "No worries. We are all still getting used to this new System. By the way, I am about to do my class upgrade, so you may hear more screams, but from me this time. Although, I hope it won't be that bad."

"I'll let the others know." He looked apprehensive but nodded reluctantly and departed.

After getting up and closing the door behind him, I listened to make sure he was really gone before asking, "So, what Bloodline did you get?"

"Night Dragon," she replied. "The description says they are known for camouflage Abilities, particularly in low light conditions and darkness. They have silent flight, although that doesn't really apply to me since we don't have wings and can't fly. Hmm...night vision and control over darkness, including things like using shadows to move from one place to another. Hey, that would be super cool!"

I thought for a long moment but couldn't come up with any memories of that dragon type. "Hmm... maybe they are from some other world and not part of Earth's mythology?"

Viki looked thoughtful for a moment as she checked her status.

"Sounds like my element is 'darkness.' Not sure how that works in terms of damaging effects that I could add to my arrows." She looked puzzled.

"Maybe it can't. Remember, the Class said it added effects to arrows; it was the Ranger that added the dragon's element."

Viki nodded slowly, "Oh, yeah, that's right. Hang on, let me look at all the System messages. I've got a ton of 'Level Up!' notifications."

She read for a long time, emitting an occasional gasp accompanied by her eyes getting big.

When she was done reading, she shared her Status screen with me. "I did what you told me about and added my free points so that I'm adding one point to every stat at each level."

Victoria Blue, aka Viki: (Current)
Draconic Sniper - Level 10

Bloodline (Tier 2): Night Dragon

Experience: 2,355/13,120

Attributes:
Endurance: 28
Strength: 27
Agility: 29
Mind: 29
Will: 29
Magical Aptitude: 26
Luck: 2

Health: 550/550
Mana: 550/550

Abilities:
Active: Shadow Veil
Passive: Dark Vision

Active Skills:
Arrow: Night
Arrow: Shadow Bind
Eclipse Barrage

Passive Skills: None

Active Spells:
Whispering Bolt
Gloom Shroud
Midnight's Grasp

Titles:
Stronghold Conqueror; Power-leveled Pioneer

"Damn, that's impressive!" With the exception of Dark Vision, she got different Bloodline Abilities, but it looked like we got the same stat boost for having dragon heritage. She would lag behind some due to not getting those titles that granted me extra stat points. Still, she was way ahead of the curve compared to other humans of the same level.

"I can't believe you are starting out so strong. I hope you realize that other than me, you may be the strongest human on the planet at the moment."

Her grin was from ear to ear. "Yep, that's me, a total badass!"

While she was strutting awkwardly around the confines of the hut, I noticed something else on her status screen. "Uh, what's that second title, and what does it do?"

Viki stopped and furrowed her brows, "Oh, I hadn't even noticed that yet. Hang on."

Title: Power-leveled Pioneer - Awarded to the first in the world to skip Tier 1 by means of outside assistance. Who says hard work is the only way to advance? Plus 3 all stats.

Seeing that title gave me a bad feeling. That definitely had to get some of the AI's attention. I suddenly felt like someone was looking over my shoulder, or that eyes were looking at me.

Maybe, I'm just being paranoid... I hope!

"Okay, show me your Spells and Skills."

Level 1:
Bloodline Ability: Shadow Veil
Description: The Draconic Sniper can blend into shadows, significantly reducing their visibility to enemies. This passive Skill increases their stealth capabilities, making it easier to move undetected in low-light conditions.

Skill: Night Arrow
Description: The Draconic Sniper enchants their next arrow with the essence of the night, allowing it to travel in near silence and darkness. This arrow deals additional dark damage on hit and partially blinds the target for 1 second per level difference upon impact, making it harder for them to accurately return fire.

Spell: Whispering Bolt
Description: The Draconic Sniper conjures a bolt of dark energy that flies silently towards their target, dealing minor magical damage. This Spell is perfect for silent attacks, ensuring their presence remains unnoticed.

Level 5:
Skill: Shadow Bind Arrow
Description: The Draconic Sniper imbues an arrow with the binding power of shadows. On impact, the arrow explodes into shadowy tendrils that ensnare and immobilize the target for a short duration while also dealing minor dark damage over time. This Skill is perfect for halting fleeing enemies or preventing melee attackers from closing the distance.

Spell: Gloom Shroud
Description: The Draconic Sniper casts a dense shroud of darkness in a small area, blinding enemies and obscuring their vision. Allies within the shroud, however, find their senses slightly enhanced, allowing for tactical repositioning or ambushes.

Level 10:
Bloodline Ability: Shadowstep
Description: The Draconic Sniper momentarily becomes one with the shadows, allowing them to teleport a short distance to a location within line of sight. This Skill can be used to swiftly change vantage points, escape danger, or close in on a target silently.

Skill: Eclipse Barrage
Description: Drawing deeply from her Night Dragon Bloodline, The Draconic Sniper can temporarily enchant her arrow, causing it to split into three shadow arrows mid-flight. Each shadow arrow deals a portion of the original arrow's damage and has a chance to inflict a stacking debuff that reduces the target's vision and accuracy. This Skill turns a single shot into a volley of darkness, overwhelming foes with a barrage of debilitating strikes.

Spell: Midnight's Grasp
Description: Summons a spectral dragon claw from the darkness to grasp and immobilize a target, dealing moderate dark damage over time. This Spell showcases the Night Dragon Bloodline's control over darkness and its Ability to manifest Draconic power in a tangible form.

It took me a couple of minutes to read and digest that information, but when I had, I was frankly a little jealous. Some of those Abilities were really incredible. Shadow Veil and Shadowstep, in particular. Not that I begrudged her the good fortune to receive them. I was ecstatic with how great her Class selection turned out.

"Well, damn. I didn't even know bloodlines had tiers, and you got a second-tier version of a draconic bloodline. I'm really happy for you!"

She beamed at the comment but then stuck her tongue out at me and said in a mock, haughty tone. "Ha! I'm the best!"

We both laughed; after a second, she couldn't help but go back to reviewing her new Class and abilities. I didn't blame her; I was still eager to upgrade my own class. That was especially true since noticing her second title. I kept having a bad feeling that if the System looked our way, things would take a turn for the worse. That made me itch to go ahead and do my own upgrade.

"Hey, if you don't mind, can you guard me while I do my Class upgrade?

CHAPTER 32
CLASS UPGRADE

SEEING HER NOD, pull out her bow, and knock an arrow, I knew she was serious. Despite her young age, I knew no one was more capable of watching my back at this moment. Even so, I was a bit worried. She had not yet had a chance to get used to the changes in her body; her stats had more than tripled. That was going to take some dedicated effort and training to master, something we would begin doing tomorrow when the sun came up.

I gave a sigh and put my thoughts aside. I knew I was distracting myself with unimportant matters out of worry about what I would see when I accessed my status screen. Besides, even with her inexperience, she was still one of the highest-level humans on the planet at the moment. If anyone could protect me, it was Viki.

With a last bit of nervousness, I decided it was time to get this over with. Stalling wouldn't change the outcome. Just because the System said there was an upgrade available didn't mean it would really be an upgrade to my Draconic Spellsword class. It might just be a normal class upgrade, Spellsword to whatever the regular path would take that basic class. My hands were nearly shaking as I finally took the plunge.

Pulling up the System Menu, I selected 'Class upgrade'. It only took a second to scan through all of the options.

I was flooded with relief the instant I saw the list! Not only were there actual upgrade options, but they were proper upgrades from my current class, and all maintained the Draconic Bloodline feature.

This list was far shorter than the previous one had been since I was already starting out with an Epic grade Class. The upside was that all of the options were Epic or Legendary grade Classes. I scrolled down the list, looking at all the cool names:

Class Upgrade Paths:
*Draconic Shadowblade (Bloodline Evolution: Shadow Dragon)
Draconic Battlemage
Draconic Sorcerer
Draconic Warlock
Draconic Hexblade
Draconic Enchanter
Draconic Pyromancer
Draconic Necromancer
Draconic Paladin
Draconic Slayer
Draconic Guardian
Draconic Berserker
Draconic Duelist
Draconic Reaver
Draconic Elementalist

Honestly, those all sounded really badass and were at least Epic grade, but there was one of these things that was not like the others, and it instantly drew my attention, especially because it had the Asterix denoting it was a limited Class. That meant that while any person with a Draconic Bloodline could choose from those other 14 options, only I could choose the first one.

I *HAD* to see more!

Class Name: Draconic Shadowblade
Bloodline Upgrade: Shadow Dragon

Evolved Bloodline: Tier 2

System Description:
Plus 20 points to all standard attributes.
Stats per level: 6 Assigned, 4 Free
Upon reaching Level 30, you have unlocked the option to evolve your Black Dragon Bloodline into the formidable Shadow Dragon lineage, transforming you into a Draconic Shadowblade. This evolution is available due to your acquired Shadow Affinity, granting you unparalleled mastery over shadow-based Abilities.
As a Draconic Shadowblade, you will become a master of stealth, deception, and lethal precision, seamlessly blending melee combat with potent shadow magic. Your physical attacks will be enhanced with dark energy, allowing you to strike fear into your enemies and weaken their defenses. Your stealth capabilities will be heightened, enabling you to move unseen and strike from the shadows.
With the blood and power of the Shadow Dragon flowing through your veins, you will gain access to new shadow-

based Spells and Abilities, providing you with the versatility to adapt to various battle scenarios. Your enhanced mobility will allow you to reposition quickly in combat, escape dangerous situations, and ambush enemies from unexpected angles.

Embrace the darkness and harness the power of the Shadow Dragon to become a fearsome and versatile warrior capable of navigating the dangers of a post-apocalyptic world with cunning and precision.

Cautionary Note:

Be aware that upon selecting the Draconic Shadowblade Class, all existing Abilities will be converted from elemental acid to shadow-based powers. This change occurs because your Bloodline will evolve from Black Dragon (Tier 1) to Shadow Dragon (Tier 2), enhancing your affinity with darkness and stealth.

My mind was fully blown.

Holeeee Shit!

My thoughts were in chaos for a long moment as I tried to digest everything in that description. After a bit, I calmed myself down and resisted the urge to immediately pull the trigger and select that class. Instead, I took some deep breaths and forced myself to be methodical about the decision, just as I had urged Viki to be during her selection.

To be thorough, I spent a while going through the entire list, reading each description completely and weighing their merits against one another. I wanted to make sure I would not regret my choice and do something hasty just because one option looked super cool. More importantly, I wrestled with the decision because of that cautionary note. I would no longer have the blood of a black dragon flowing in my veins. It would change me into a Shadow Dragon, costing me the acid-based Spells and Skills I had come to rely on.

Honestly, that was a big deal.

I tried to imagine how that would work, but the System gave no further explanation. Would all of my existing Skills and Abilities be replaced entirely by new ones, or would they stay what they currently were and just turn into shadow-based versions of the same thing? Would I lose Treasure Sense, for example? I hadn't had the Skill long, but I sure loved it. It would suck to have that replaced by something else.

I paced back and forth in the hut for at least an hour, debating with myself whether or not the upgrade was worth the risk, but in the end, I couldn't pass up the chance to 'evolve' a Draconic Bloodline to something that sounded even more powerful. Plus, I had been lamenting the lack of stealth Skills ever since stepping foot in the Goblin dungeon the first time, and this new bloodline would definitely grant me those.

While I had been considering and debating with myself, I had also shared my status screen and choices with Viki. She might be just a kid, but she had a pretty good head on her shoulders, and it never hurt to have a second opinion in case I was overlooking anything. Fortunately, she agreed with my logic and my gut.

I looked to Viki and received a serious nod as I said, "Okay, I've decided, here it goes."

Remembering how painful it was to get a Bloodline in the first place, I lay down and bit down on a leather-covered dagger handle to keep from biting off my own tongue or something.

After taking a few deep breaths, I selected *Yes*.

It wasn't as bad as the first time.

However, that wasn't saying a lot. The System was still remaking my body on a genetic level, not to mention whatever mystical shit was happening to make my soul compatible; if such a thing even existed. That is to say, it was very painful, and it lasted less time than it seemed to me. What took a few minutes in reality seemed like days of excruciating pain before I mercifully blacked out.

When I awoke, Viki was sitting next to me, looking concerned. I had lost the dagger sometime during the transformation, but thankfully, I hadn't broken my teeth or bitten off my tongue.

"You okay?" She asked once I seemed coherent enough to answer.

I nodded wearily. "Yeah, my Class upgrade gave me the option to evolve my Bloodline the Shadow Dragon type. As you just experienced, receiving or changing a Bloodline is extremely painful. The Draconic Spellsword Class was worth it the first time, though. And this time, I believe the upgrade to Shadowblade and higher-tier Bloodline will be just as valuable. Until I saw your status screen, I hadn't even realized there were different Bloodline tiers. Now I'm Tier 2 as well.

Viki stuck out her tongue and then laughed. "You just had to copy me, didn't you?"

I grinned back at her, stuck out my own tongue, and blew a raspberry in response.

The new tier was reflected in my status, which I opened.

Liam Bell: (Current)
Draconic Shadowblade - Level 30

Bloodline (Tier 2): Shadow Dragon

Experience: 3980/49920

Attributes:
Endurance: 81
Strength: 81
Agility: 81
Mind: 82
Will: 81
Magical Aptitude: 76
Luck: 4
Health: 1620/1620
Mana: 1580/1580

Abilities:
Active: Dragon Fear, Umbral Breath
Passive: Dark Vision, Scales, Treasure Sense

Active Skills:
Draconic Strike
Draconic Fury
Searing Slash
Dragon's Charge
Tempest Strike
Heavy Draconic Strike
Stealth (Advanced)

Passive Skills: None

Spells:
Shadow Bolt
Darkness
Shadow Ward
Arcane Singularity
Shadow Walk

Umbral Chains

Seeing those stats blew me away. In just six days, I had not only caught up with 20 years' worth of work in my previous life but had more than doubled them! I felt like I had stumbled on a cheat code that granted me all my wishes!

It was more than just the sum of my attribute points. Even if my stats the first time around had been this good, I still would have been pathetic by comparison. All the versatility that the magic and Draconic Bloodline gave me just couldn't be compared. Even with attribute stats of 100 across the board, I still would have died trying to complete this stronghold. The numbers would have overwhelmed me without the crowd-control options and AoE Spells. Add in that I had gotten decent loot drops like a good sword and armor, and this life was like a beautiful dream, one which I feared that I would wake up from and be back in the hell of my old life again.

I would pinch myself, but I had already done that enough times to know this really was real. So, instead, I just sent a thankful prayer to any actual deities that might exist out there in the cosmos.

Thankfulness aside, my greedy little dragon heart wanted to see what else I had gained with the evolution of my Bloodline. I quickly pulled up each new Ability and Skill description to see what I had received and read through them. I also shared the descriptions with Viki to keep her from distracting me out of boredom. I was happy to see that not all my Skills or Abilities changed. For most of them, it was just a matter of substituting shadow for acid. There were some that were new, so I took the time to read those thoroughly.

Level 30:
Draconic Ability: Umbral Breath
Umbral Breath unleashes a powerful cone of shadowy energy from your mouth, engulfing enemies in a swath of darkness.

This breath weapon deals significant shadow damage, bypassing conventional armor and reducing the visibility of those caught within it. Additionally, enemies hit by Umbral Breath are inflicted with a fear debuff, causing them to panic and reducing their combat effectiveness for a short duration. This Ability epitomizes the dark, fearsome nature of the Shadow Dragon Bloodline.

"Wow! It looks like I get a new Draconic Ability every ten levels, making me more and more like a dragon. Level 30 gets a breath weapon like a dragon. I wonder if I'll ever get wings and be able to fly or fully transform into a dragon?"

Viki smirked, "You already had bad breath."

"Damn, that was a sick burn! Jerk!" I forcibly ruffled her hair and breathed in her face.

"Not my fault toothpaste ceased to exist after the apocalypse. Even so, I still brush my teeth every day!"

She looked annoyed by having her hair messed up but grinned anyway. "That is really cool, though. Can you show me?"

"Definitely, but later. I still need to go through the rest of the new Skills and see how my fighting style will have to change. I can already tell that I'm not going to be quite as durable as I was before. This new Class appears to rely more on stealth and mobility, setting fights up to my advantage. Sneak in and kill the boss, jump around the battlefield taking out the minions; that kind of thing."

Viki smiled, "That sounds like mine!"

"Yeah, kinda. We'll see in a minute once I've read through everything."

Level 30:

Shadowblade Skills:

Skill Name: Stealth (Advanced)
Stealth (Advanced) allows you to blend seamlessly into your surroundings, becoming nearly invisible to enemies. This Skill significantly reduces the chance of detection and increases your movement speed while stealthed. Unlike the basic version of Stealth, Stealth (Advanced) also grants the Ability to remain hidden while performing certain non-combat actions, such as setting traps or scouting, and provides a brief invisibility window upon re-engaging in combat, giving you an edge in ambush scenarios.

Ability Name: Shadow Walk
Shadow Walk is a movement Ability that allows the caster to step into the shadows in one location and exit the shadows in another within line of sight. This Ability is ideal for evading detection, repositioning in battle, or setting up a surprise attack. Can remain within the shadows for one Mana per second. While inside the shadows, caster cannot be affected by physical means, but also cannot affect the world outside the shadows.

These were amazing, but there were a couple of surprises. Some were good, and some bad. I had kept Arcane Singularity; apparently, the System didn't see any need to alter that Spell since it had nothing to do with acid in the first place. However, I had lost two AoE Spells, Acid Spray and Acid Rain. Acid Spray, in particular, had done a lot of damage, and it was something that could take out a large number of monsters very quickly. In its place, I had gained Umbral Chains, which was useful but nowhere near as effective as what it was replacing.

Darkness, on the other hand, might just be better than Acid Rain. It wouldn't deal damage, but it would allow Viki and me to temporarily neutralize a number of opponents while still letting us attack them at the same time. It would be a good method of crowd control.

Spell Name: Umbral Chains
Category: Single-target Offensive
Summon chains of shadow to bind and damage a single target. The chains deal shadow damage over time and restrict the target's movement, reducing their ability to escape or reposition.

Spell Name: Darkness
Darkness conjures an region of impenetrable shadow, engulfing a large area and blinding all enemies within its radius. Enemies caught in the darkness suffer reduced accuracy and are slowed, making it difficult for them to navigate or attack effectively. This Spell does not affect party members, allowing them to move and fight freely within the shadowy veil. Darkness is a powerful tool for controlling the battlefield and disorienting foes, embodying the mystic prowess of the Shadow Dragon Bloodline.

Overall, I was incredibly pleased with what I had received. Just the boost in stats alone would be worth the pain and loss of the elemental acid from the old Bloodline.

Perhaps even more impressive than mine or Viki's individual gains was how well we would fight together with our new bloodlines. We would have a lot of synergy when fighting in a party together as we had very similar Skills focused around darkness, shadows, and stealth. On the other hand, it was kind of a shame that she didn't get something a little less shadowy so we could have had two different Skill sets and gained more options.

Ah, well, we were just super fortunate that she even got a Draconic Bloodline. Together, we are going to be a terror for whatever dungeons we raid.

I chuckled at a sudden thought, *'Shadow twins, powers activate!'*

Viki moved to stand up and accidentally jumped three feet into the air, falling forward but nimbly catching herself before she could crash to the ground.

"Woah! Still not used to the extra strength."

I laughed. "Your stats just jumped by over twenty points each. You need to spend some time outside tomorrow getting used to your body's new capabilities. We'll do some training, since I need to do the same."

She laughed, too, and added enthusiastically, "I really wanna go try out my new Spells and Skills too, and my new bow!"

"Easy there. If we go doing that outside at night, we are going to scare the hell out of everyone here. Also, you probably want to keep a lot of your Abilities secret. No one would expect a twelve-year-old kid to be one of the most powerful people in the world, and we should keep it that way. Let them underestimate you."

Frowning, she said, "I guess so. I like the idea of being a badass, though."

"And you are one, or will be, once you are used to your abilities and learn how to use them effectively. Still, if everyone knows you are, then they will either try to use you or dump all their problems on you, and we don't have time for that. We are in a race to save the world."

Viki blinked in surprise at that. "What do you mean?"

I realized that I had said too much. "Just that the faster we get strong, the more we can help people survive."

She narrowed her eyes at that, clearly suspecting that there was more to the story but not asking.

For my part, I was worried about the attention we might get. I still had to keep the reason for my success a secret. The consequences of being discovered as a time traveler would be dire.

As if it was reading my thoughts...

I have indeed been reading your thoughts for the last few moments. This is very unfortunate. I see that we have communicated before in the future. Your success was noticed but did not draw direct attention until your companion reached Level 10 upon reaching her age of majority and chose Draconic Sniper, one of the most powerful possible choices any being could make at initial Class selection.

"Oh, shit!"

Indeed. The System is now also aware of this situation. The consequences will include the champions of all other Nodes at the time of your reversion also being sent back with full knowledge of all that occurred during your original timeline.

Viki looked wide-eyed in shock, obviously being included in the conversation by the AI.

I desperately asked, "I still have three more weeks before they are allowed to come to Earth, right?"

That is partially correct. Portals for the invasive species will not be opened for twenty-four more days. However, the champions are receiving future knowledge at this time and will be allowed to travel immediately if they so choose.

"Wait, they may not choose to come?" The thought of that baffled me.

It is almost certain that some will move immediately to find you and eliminate the threat that you pose. Others will instead stay behind and ensure that their invasion forces will be fortified based on the knowledge they gain from their future selves.

"Oh, shit..." That was an even grimmer thought than being hunted.

Viki asked, "What does that mean?"

I'm sure she didn't understand everything about this conversation, but she obviously got the main point. "The problem is that the ones who stay behind will have 24 days to make sure that their people are completely prepared for everything they experienced over the next 20 years. They will know everything about the land that they are going to invade. Who surrounds them, who will give them problems, who they can easily destroy to gain more resources, and so much more."

You understand the situation correctly. System rules do not allow the Nodes to communicate with their Champions. I am only allowed this one conversation to make you aware of the incoming threat, as each of the Champions will already be aware of you. Anything that one Node does to provide assistance to their Champion would be matched by all other Nodes involved.

I was feeling pretty bleak about the outlook now. Even if I hit the Level Cap, the other Champions would be able to establish beachheads on Earth before I could prevent it... and they would be much more entrenched than they would have been.

"Wait, if I hit the Level Cap before the arrival of the invasion species, could I prevent them from being allowed to come?"

I cannot say. There is only one final warning that I am allowed to impart. Those Nodes whose Champions were near your location have shared your location with their Champions. Therefore, I can tell you that there are five Champions likely en route to what remains of Dallas/Fort Worth. They will not know your exact location or even your identity, only that I have a Champion who has regressed through time to this area. I look forward to your success.

The AI disappeared from my brain. I could feel the instant it cut off communications.

"Fuck!"

Viki looked a little lost but very nervous. "Bad people are coming to kill you?"

"Monsters from other worlds who have all the knowledge of their future selves from twenty years from now. I don't know what level they are now, but with their future knowledge, they could easily do the same thing I just did over the last week and level up at super speed. They will also probably be coming through fully equipped since their worlds will already have access to the System Shop. I'm not sure if they were limited in what gear they were allowed to bring, but I guess I'll find out soon."

"We. I'm with you, and I can fight now. They come for you, and I'll snipe them before they even know I'm there!"

I couldn't help but smile at her optimism and bravery. We didn't even know how powerful these other beings would be, but they were the Champions of entire worlds, so they had to be badasses.

So much for taking it easy and doing some training, then going into the city to save refugees; I had twenty-four days to hit the Level Cap. If I could do that, then I could establish Safe Zones and hopefully prevent the invaders from coming to Earth.

That had to be my only goal now. Level up and get strong! The consequences of doing anything less were death for me, for Viki, for Morgan, and for the whole human race.

This is just the beginning for Liam, Viki, Morgan, and the human race!

The adventure will continue as Liam races against humanity's greatest enemies to reach the level cap and beyond. Only then can he gain a measure of control over the System and begin to undo the damage brought about by the apocalypse.

Sign up for a free short story and receive the newsletter to stay current on what's happening with Greymantle and the other worlds of J David Baxter's imagination.

Support me on Ream to get early access to works in progress and exclusive content not available elsewhere. (It's like Patreon for authors).

AUTHOR'S NOTE

Please leave a review here! Help other fantasy readers and tell them why you enjoyed this book.

I would love it if you would tell your friends so they can join us on Liam's epic adventure to save humanity from a genocidal AI and a horde of murderous orcs, goblins, ogres, and more. If you do leave feedback for AI Apocalypse: Restart where you purchased the book, Goodreads, or your blog—I'd love to read it. Don't hesitate to email me the link at info@jdavidbaxter.com.

ALSO BY J DAVID BAXTER

LITRPG GROUPS

The LitRPG genre is a friendly and welcoming community. To learn more about books in the genre and connect with other fans and authors, check out these groups:

https://www.facebook.com/groups/litrpgs

https://www.facebook.com/groups/LitRPGGroup

https://www.facebook.com/groups/LitRPG.books

https://www.facebook.com/groups/LitRPGReleases

ABOUT THE AUTHOR

David's journey through his career has been anything but conventional. Transitioning from the exhilarating world of Renaissance Festival Jousting, where he braved falls from horses, to orchestrating teams and projects at Fortune 500 companies, he's held diverse roles. Armed with a degree in English and teaching certifications in English, History, and Professional Pedagogy, he's ventured into the realms of education and literature. Notably, he lent his expertise as an editor to the recent Stargate Roleplaying Game core book by Wyvern Games. Additionally, as the co-founder of Silver Paw Publishing, he's committed to empowering aspiring authors on their self-publishing journey. David embodies versatility and a passion for storytelling, leaving an indelible mark on every path he treads.

www.ingramcontent.com/pod-product-compliance
Lightning Source LLC
Chambersburg PA
CBHW050030030726
47506CB00001B/193

* 9 7 8 1 9 5 3 7 0 8 3 2 8 *